D0661669

# Praise for Ava Miles

**NORA ROBERTS LAND**
*Selected as one of the Best Books of 2013 alongside Nora Roberts' DARK WITCH and Julia Quinn's SUM OF ALL KISSES.*
*USA Today Contributor, Becky Lower, Happily Ever After*

*"...finding love like in the pages of a Nora Roberts story." Publishers Weekly WW Ladies Book Club*

**FRENCH ROAST**
*"An entertaining ride...{and) a full-bodied romance." Readers' Favorite*

**THE GRAND OPENING**
*"The latest book in the Dare Valley series is a continuation of love, family, and romance." Mary J. Gramlich*

**THE HOLIDAY SERENADE**
*"This story is all romance, steam, and humor with a touch of the holiday spirit..." The Book Nympho*

**THE TOWN SQUARE**
*"Ms. Miles' words melted into each page until the world receded around me..." Tome Tender*

**THE PARK OF SUNSET DREAMS**
*"Magically transporting...a heartwarming tale that will stick with you long after you've finished reading." Tome Tender*

**COUNTRY HEAVEN**
*"If ever there was a contemporary romance that rated a 10 on a scale of 1 to 5 for me, this one is it!" The Romance Reviews*

*Also by Ava Miles*

The Dare Valley Series:
NORA ROBERTS LAND
FRENCH ROAST
THE GRAND OPENING
THE HOLIDAY SERENADE
THE TOWN SQUARE
THE PARK OF SUNSET DREAMS

DARING DECLARATIONS:
An Anthology including THE HOLIDAY SERENADE AND THE
TOWN SQUARE

The Dare River Series:
COUNTRY HEAVEN
COUNTRY HEAVEN SONG BOOK
COUNTRY HEAVEN COOKBOOK
THE CHOCOLATE GARDEN

# NORA ROBERTS Land

# AVA MILES

HUDSON BRANCH

Copyright June 2013, Ava Miles. All rights reserved. No part of this book may be reproduced or transmitted in any form by any means—graphic, electronic or mechanical—without permission in writing from the author, except by a reviewer who may quote brief passages in a review.

ISBN: 1940565132
ISBN-13: 978-1-940565-13-2

HUDSON BRANCH

*To the two women whose support helped make this book possible:*

*The incomparable Nora Roberts, for being okay with me using her name for this book—and for her stories of happily ever after or Nora Roberts Land as I call it, which always lifts my spirit, but more importantly helped me pass many tense nights in dangerous places when I was trying to save the world in my own humble way.*

*My beautiful sister, Michelle, for letting me tell this story, which germinated from her life—proving truth is stranger than fiction—but happy endings always win out if we are brave enough to seek them.*

*And to my divine entourage, who continues to show me the way to my bliss every day.*

# Acknowledgments

There are a myriad of people who have helped me build a ladder to my dreams:

My former agent, Jennifer Schober, who left the business recently for personal reasons, but who loved this book right away like I did and supported me in seeking its highest potential. I miss you.

Mary Blayney and her willingness to be outfitted with angel wings by providing her generous assistance in seeking Nora Roberts' blessing for this book and being a trusted, dear friend.

Laura Reeth, Nora's phenomenal publicist, who also helped with my request and many others, and has been a total joy to become friends with.

The incredible members of Team Ava, including my publicity helpers, Joan Schulhafer, Debby Tobias, and Alissa Di Giacomo of Joan Shulhafer Publishing and Media Consulting; Elizabeth Bemis and Sienna Condy of Bemis Promotions for my website; my editor, Angela Polidoro; the Killion Group for the cover art; my copy editor, Helen Hester-Ossa; Gregory Stewart for my publicity photos, the amazing Dare Valley map, and a million other things; Dr. Tabitha King and Janet Geary for being research consultants; and lastly, my amazing Indie guru, Meredith Bond.

Diane Gaston, the first writer I met on this journey, who assisted in nailing a few rungs in place on my ladder and is always willing to share her tools and skills when I need help, especially on this book.

Evie Owens, who helped me see a new direction for this story and always makes me laugh.

My Inn Boonsboro retreat gals who make our annual trek to Nora's inn one of the highlights of my year.

Inspiring writing teachers from my sixth grade teacher, Jackie Mason, to college professors Dave Jauss and Michael Kleine—and many others unnamed, including a whole bunch of women in Romance Writers of America and Washington Romance Writers, who share their insights so generously.

Dan Baumstark, Kerrith McKechnie, Christine Spence, Julia Turner, Abhaya Schlesinger, Zahra Yousefi, Karen Dobson, Francis Ramirez, and other helpers for supporting me in magnificent ways.

My cousin, Terry Miles, for being my family newspaper source and for sharing new stories about our great-great grandfather, the founder, who reportedly won the first paper in a poker game when The Plains were the Wild West.

Jai Singh and Thuy-Doan Le for creating space for me to be my true self, and always finding the laughter in the divine or mundane.

My always supportive family, who have cried over my characters' pain and laughed at their antics, confirming I was on the right track in touching people's hearts while entertaining with a tale.

My TF, for things known and yet unknown. I love you.

And lastly, to all of you who are reading this book. Thank you. I wish you all your own Nora Roberts Land—in whatever way is best for you.

# Prologue

*Fairy tales, like shoes, come in all shapes and sizes. Frogs turn into princes. Princes assist ladies into glass slippers.*

*And now I'm back to shoes again. Shoes are comforting, right? They haven't let me down, run around on me, or destroyed my dreams of happily ever after.*

*My husband never transformed into a handsome prince. He stayed quite firmly in the reptile family, a chameleon, perhaps? And I'm pretty sure that if I had ever lost a shoe—even if it were priceless, like a limited edition Manolo Blahnik—he wouldn't have lifted a finger to find it. Why didn't I see that he was never going to be my prince?*

*Modern fairy tales only exist in romance novels crafted by writers like Nora Roberts. For years, her words carried me to an enchanted place where love conquered all. And I bought into it—hook, line, and sinker. Now I need to set aside love and all of its false promises. It's a messy business anyway.*

*So, I'll...buy more shoes. No, scratch that—I'll buy...La Perla lingerie.*

*I want to be a superhero now...like Divorcée Woman.*

*She'd know what to do after signing these papers.*

*Maybe an alter ego will help me regain my confidence.*

*After all, I already have plenty of shoes, and they've never helped me much anyway.*

*Diary entry by journalist Meredith Hale on the day of her divorce*

# Chapter 1

Meredith Hale scanned the bookstore window. There it was—the new Nora Roberts book—the cover a bold, powerful landscape of sky and water.

Her superhero alter ego, Divorcée Woman, couldn't override the rash of goosebumps on Meredith's arms or her knotted stomach. Meredith patted the red lace La Perla bustier hidden under her black suit jacket and took one hesitant step closer to the glass, her breath hitching as she scanned Nora's prominent display. She imagined Divorcée Woman telling her to suck it up. It was only a bookstore after all. It wasn't like she had to take a bullet for the president or anything.

She'd gone cold turkey on Nora's books a year ago, when her ex-husband, Rick-the-Dick, threw *Black Hills* at the wall, snarling that her favorite author had given her an unrealistic view of love. "Our marital problems are *her* fault," he said. "She's made you believe in happily ever after—something *any adult knows* is a myth. Grow up." Then he packed his custom-tailored suits and slammed out the door of their swanky Manhattan apartment.

At first she'd thought maybe he was right. But she missed Nora's books. And not reading them hadn't made the whole divorce thing any easier on her. It hadn't made the panic attacks go away.

She wanted her Nora Roberts back, dammit. It was time to reclaim her life.

Unfortunately, just looking at the cover had her hovering on the edge of a panic attack. Her hands grew clammy. She wiped them on her black suit and dug into her matching purse for her cell phone. Her sister would be able to talk her into going into the store. After all, Jill could talk anyone into anything.

"Hey, Mere," Jill greeted, the ever-present sound of her favorite band, Abba, in the background. Jill wanted to live life like a dancing queen.

"Hey," she said, making sure to sound calmer than she was. "How's business at the coffee shop?"

"Well, after a regional dairy salesman tried to talk me into changing my store's name from Don't Soy With Me to Don't Milk Me, I'm about ready to bash my head against the espresso machine. He was so dense. I tried to explain it's a play on words, but he just blinked like one of those dairy cows and went, 'Oh.'"

Meredith's panic slowly eased. Jill and her stories were always a comfort. "Being in New York, I don't run into too many milk salesmen. Does he wear a special outfit?"

"No, thank God. Speaking of milk, did you get my present?"

Ducking closer to the store window so she wouldn't be mowed down by a rush of pedestrians, Meredith said, "You mean the coffee mug with the line, 'You're My Udder One'?"

"Yes. I tried to appease the milk guy by telling him I'd put those mugs out for display, but he wouldn't leave. He even offered to teach me how to milk a cow. I think he was hitting on me."

As Meredith muffled her laughter, a passing banker gave her a disapproving stare. His shoes, belt, and briefcase matched—the Wall Street uniform. "And I thought my love life was pathetic."

"What love life?"

"Funny. Speaking of which, I'm outside a bookstore. I woke up this morning and decided I want to read."

"Oh, honey, I didn't know you were illiterate."

"Hah." She eyed the rush of people heading in and out of the bookstore on 82nd and Broadway.

"Okay, take a deep yoga breath. Jeez, Mere, you sound like Great Aunt Helen when she put down her oxygen to steal a swig of Grandpa's scotch at Christmas."

"Right. Breathe." Was her vision blurring? "I'm taking a step."

"Oh, baby, I wish mom and I were there to see it."

Her sister's wicked humor cut through the fogginess in her head. Meredith wasn't sure she was in her body anymore, but it moved when she walked. Her hand managed to open the door. She walked in on legs wobbling like an untangled yoyo.

"Are you inside yet?"

She squeezed into a book aisle as people cruised by. "Yes."

"Welcome back to the land of the reading."

Was there anything more comforting? "Thank you. I'm standing by the thriller and suspense section. Makes me think of Grandpa. He's convinced there's some sort of conspiracy going on at the university. I'm researching the college drug trade for him on the side. Maybe I should buy him a John Grisham book instead."

"I know! He keeps pumping me for information about the parties I've gone to. I told him people drink too much and puke. End of story."

"Tell that to his infernal journalism gut." Not that she could point fingers. Hale DNA had given her one too.

"I know the fam's grateful you've been helping out with the paper after Dad's heart attack," her sister said, "But Dad's still working too hard. He loves that paper like it's a child—just like Grandpa."

"I know, Jill." Suddenly guilt pressed down on her, its force almost as strong as the panic. She *was* helping, but she wished she could do more. Sometimes being long-distance sucked.

Her sister cleared her throat. "I don't know how to say this, but you need to know. Sorry the timing's not great with the whole one-year-divorce anniversary thing, but..." Her sister's breathing went a little ragged on the line. "The doctor's concerned about dad's progress and wants him to take some time off. Mom hasn't wanted to ask you, but someone needs to help Grandpa. I know he can run circles around us all, but he's in his seventies. Is there any way you can come home to help out for a few months? I'd do it, but I have zero journalistic instincts. Plus, I have Don't Soy with Me to run."

"Come home?" She bumped into a book display, and a whole parade of James Patterson hardcovers slid to the floor. Her lungs seemed to stop at the thought. "I can't breathe...and I really want to." She gulped in air.

"Go to the coffee shop and sit down. Put your head between your knees."

She wobbled over to a chair and caught sight of the romance section. The tightness between her ribs could have competed with a boa constrictor as it killed its victim. She didn't care what people thought. She put her head between her legs when she saw red.

Her phone buzzed in her clenched hand, signaling another call. She ignored it, breathing deeply. When her equilibrium returned, she took deep breaths until she was sure she'd inhaled all the circulated air in Manhattan. She put the phone to her ear again.

"You still there?"

"Yep. You okay?"

Question of the year. "I didn't pass out, but it was close."

"Meredith, your husband cheated on you, and then blamed it on you—and Nora's books. You've been through an emotional wringer. Give yourself a break. I keep telling Jemma that too."

Jill's best friend had just been dumped by her childhood sweetheart. "You're pretty good at giving advice."

"Practice. Jemma's devastated."

"Yeah, I get that." Her eyes burned, and she pinched the bridge of her nose. "I can't stand another night in my apartment. I miss my Tribeca place and eating out in restaurants and visiting gallery openings. I don't miss Rick-the-Dick, but I do miss being part of that jam-packed world."

"You have the Power Couple Blues, Mere. Maybe coming home to help the paper will give you a new perspective. You don't have any family there. Most of your friends changed when you got divorced."

True, she had become intimately familiar with the term "fair weather friend" over the past year. "I miss you guys." But going home? She'd been in New York since starting at Colombia. "Let me grab a coffee."

"I wish I was there to make your favorite. Then I'd give you a ginormous hug and tell you about Paige Lorton snorting whipped cream up her nose and old man Perkins giving her the Heimlich."

Her laughter popped out like the final popcorn kernels in the microwave. "Oh, Jillie, I love you."

"I love you too. You're my big sis. I miss you, Mere."

Holding the phone away from her face for a moment, she walked up to the counter and gave her coffee order—a tall, no foam latte—before shuffling back to her chair. She slumped against the metal back, returning the phone to her ear. "Let me think about coming home."

"Surely Karen knows how hard you've worked after joining her paper. You've been there for a year now. Plus, it's Rick-the-Dick's rival paper. That's gotta be extra bonus points."

Her coffee magically appeared in front of her. She looked up to see a petite barista with flat-ironed hair. "You look like you needed me to bring it over."

Kindness didn't happen often in New York. In her hometown of Dare Valley, Colorado, it happened more times than she could count. "Thank you." A wave of homesickness hit her. "Maybe you're right, Jill. It would be nice to be around people who know me."

"Good! So think about it. Talk to Karen. Now, drink your latte, and then we'll talk you into the romance section. Nora Roberts Land awaits."

A smile tugged at Meredith's lips. "I forgot how mom always used to call Nora's books that. She'd point her finger at dad and say she was taking a few hours to visit Nora Roberts Land, and then she'd seal herself off in the bedroom. Like it was an adult version of Disneyland. Dad never got it."

"Yeah, but at least he didn't blame divorce on Nora's books. Rick-the-Dick's the kind of man who can't take responsibility for his cheating, so he blamed it on you—and fiction. Isn't that the most pathetic thing ever? It's like blaming teen suicide on *Romeo and Juliet*. It's asinine."

"Actually, I think that's been done." She took the last drink of her latte and stood. Tested her balance. "Okay, I'm ready."

"So strut your stuff over to the romance section."

She didn't strut. She stumbled—twice. Thank God there were scads of bookshelves to grab. As she passed the periodicals, she stopped in her tracks, her eyes zeroing in on a picture of her ex and the cocky smile he used to make women fall for him, her included.

"Richard's on the front of *The New York Man*," she rasped, taking in the navy suit and patriotic red tie. "Huh?" Jill asked, probably because Meredith sounded like a smoker on oxygen.

"Rick-the-Dick is on the cover of a magazine," she said, enunciating each word. "It's like a weekly local *GQ*."

"What does it say? Please tell me he's come out as a cross-dresser and is modeling your La Perla lingerie."

After her split with Rick, she'd thrown out all of her cotton underwear, substituting it for La Perla bustiers and matching panties. Cinched in luxurious lingerie, Divorcée Woman was kind of like a superhero, sans the billowing cape and iridescent tights. Sure, it was a bit strange to create an alter ego for yourself, but it was helping her move forward. She could pretend she was a young and hot New Yorker, capable of bringing any man to his knees.

It had been a while since she'd brought a real man to his knees. A long, long while.

Since Rick-the-Dick. The bastard.

She read the headline: "Media Mogul Throws Hat into Political Ring."

"Oh, shit," she said, picking up a copy.

"What?" her sister yelled.

"The rumors were true." She thumbed to the article. "Rick's finally going to do it. He's formed an exploratory committee for the Senate."

"You're kidding. Man, this is the only time I wish I was a New Yorker so I could vote 'no' in the ballot box."

She scanned the article, holding her breath as she checked to see if he'd stuck to their bargain. Her unease grew when she reached the part about their divorce. He hadn't. Isn't that why her pulse had started pounding the second she saw the cover? "He broke our agreement not to talk about the divorce."

"Asshole fink. What does it say?"

"It says…" Her heart rate doubled as she read the print. She was tempted to put her head between her legs, standing up. "He said we had *different* ideas about our life together. He wanted to serve a higher good. Give the public information to…improve their lives. Bullshit. Oh, and now he wants to be a public servant in an elected office. He said I wanted a more traditional family with kids—*the kind you read about in books*—not that he's against that." Pain seared her temple at the betrayal even as she wanted to rip apart the magazine. Her old wounds emerged, raw and fresh.

"Asshole, dickwad…" her sister said.

Jill continued to call him names while Meredith's head spun. She tagged a bookstore worker, who was carrying an armful of books. "When did this come out?"

The young woman stopped and puffed out her chest. "That's an advance copy. We negotiated to receive it a few days earlier than the other outlets since it's such a big story. He's cute, huh? I'd vote for him." She sashayed off without another word.

Meredith turned back to her cell phone. "We *agreed* we wouldn't talk about the divorce. We shook on it."

"When did he ever keep a promise? I'll bet he's super nervous you'll tell the media about his infidelities. Voters don't like cheaters."

Or politicians who paid for sex…But that hadn't stopped him. Nothing did. That's why people called him a mogul. Her phone beeped again. She looked at the display. The familiar number had her breath hitching again. Then her anger dug in.

Rick-the-Dick was calling her. Well, he wasn't the only one who had something to say.

"Jill, it's Richard. I'll call you back."

"Wait—"

She clicked over. "What in the hell do you want?"

"Meredith," he uttered brightly. "I take it I didn't reach you before you heard the news."

"No, you didn't."

"I called your assistant three times this morning. When she finally said she couldn't reach you, I decided to try your cell."

She leaned against a display. The sound of his smooth, charming voice made her knees shake. It was the first time she'd spoken to him in a year. "You bastard. You broke our agreement."

"Well, it couldn't be avoided. Voters want to know. I was as charming as I could be. I praised you to high heavens, but the writer didn't choose to include those quotes."

Clorox couldn't clean the bullshit off that one. "I'll bet."

"So, I'm calling to touch base. I don't think too many reporters will call you now that I've announced I'm forming an exploratory committee, but I'd appreciate it if you'd keep your statements short and sweet. You can say what a great guy I am, and think I'd be a great senator even though we couldn't make it work as man and wife."

The nerve. She saw red for reasons other than a lack of oxygen. "You bastard."

"Now, Meredith..."

"No, you stop right there! You didn't call earlier because you knew I'd object. You're selfish to the last."

A few people browsing raised their eyebrows at her and hustled by.

"Dammit. I hoped you wouldn't be like this. I gave you a generous settlement for Christ's sake."

Money was one of his many tools of manipulation. "It was never about the money. God. I loved you!" She ground her teeth for control. Two could play this game. She had tools of her own. "Were you hoping to buy my silence?"

"Meredith—"

"Shut up. You know what I know, and if you don't leave me alone and out of your...bullshit public servant messages, I can't be held accountable for my actions, just like someone else I know."

"Don't threaten me."

"Don't *manage* me! You don't have any right to tell me what to do, and if you try, I swear I'll make you regret it. Goodbye, Richard."

She hit the off button so hard she broke a nail. Her head buzzed like a swarm of bees had found honey in her hair. She stomped over to the Romance section.

She was not letting him control her anymore.

Her feet rushed forward, and before she knew it, she was holding Nora's newest hardcover in her hands. She caressed the spine. Traced the NR logo. Took deep breaths to calm her pounding heart.

How could she have ever bought into Rick-the-Dick's accusation?

He was full of shit—a whole crock of it.

Their divorce didn't have anything to do with some highfalutin image of romance and marriage. It had ended because she'd been married to a cheating, megalomaniacal asshole.

God, she had to get over this, over him. She was not going to let him ruin the rest of her life.

She pressed the book to her chest. Her racing heart calmed. She could feel a warm embrace from Divorcée Woman.

Nora's books lifted the human spirit, making her readers hope for the best—romance, hot sex, love, independence, family, and good conquering evil. Nora Roberts Land. She wanted to believe in that again.

No, she *needed* to believe in that again.

She walked through the stacks to pick up the other books released since her divorce—especially the ones Nora published under the pen name J.D. Robb. She needed a Roarke fix big-time. Maybe someday she'd find her own version of him.

Her eyes fell on Nora's anthology *Going Home*. It reminded her of Jill asking her to come home and help their family. What was more important than that? If she remembered the story right, that's what Nora's heroine had done in the title story. And in so doing, she'd found Mr. Right.

*So, what would a Nora heroine do right now?*

The question was a whisper in her head. She tapped her fingernail on the book, thinking.

A Nora heroine...would face her greatest fears head-on, without making excuses.

Meredith's mind cleared, and with it, the threads of a brilliant idea emerged. A new purpose.

*I don't know if I'm ready for it,* she thought, *but I'm going to give love another try.* She was going to march back to her office and tell her boss she needed to go home to help her family's newspaper. But while she was there, she'd also be working on an article for *The Daily Herald*—a personal-interest story about a divorced woman returning to her small town to find Mr. Right and a new happily ever after, aka Nora Roberts Land.

Her family could pick up her salary while she worked for them, so budget wouldn't be an issue. Karen knew she brought something special to the paper and would hold her position while she was away. If she didn't, well, Meredith could find another job. The Hale name opened doors, and she'd built her own reputation across town. Plus, she'd write the hell out of this story, however it turned out. Who wouldn't want to read about a scorned woman trying to believe in the power of love again?

She sailed to the checkout. It was time to try something different.

She was going to get over Rick-the-Dick if she had to date every man in Dare Valley to do it.

# Chapter 2

Tanner McBride stopped on the street corner, waiting for the light to change. He reveled in the controlled chaos, the honks from aggressive drivers, and the rumblings of New Yorkers as they pushed their way down the sidewalk in determined strides. It made him almost giddy that he didn't need to worry about being shot at or stared at for being an American.

British accents caught his attention, and he swiveled his head. Pale fingers pointed at a map of the downtown area. An older woman in a floral dress shook her head and stepped into traffic.

Seeing the approaching cab, Tanner lunged forward and hauled her back to the curb. The cab rushed past, blowing his new sports jacket up like dry clothes on a windy clothesline.

The woman patted her bosom. "My goodness, I looked the wrong way."

Tanner's heart sputtered and then returned to its usual cadence. That had been tame in comparison to what he'd faced on a day-to-day basis in Afghanistan.

"We drive on the opposite side of you folks in England. I wouldn't jaywalk."

She squeezed his arm. "Thank you."

He hustled across the street.

Everyone had told him he'd experience a sense of unreality when he returned home, and he might be bored by the lack of conflict and chaos. So far he could see a grain of truth in that. Hopefully New York would be big enough and edgy enough to keep him from going insane. He scanned the street and the rows and rows of postage-stamp eateries and restaurants. At least there was food. Christ, he was going to eat everything in sight for the next six months since food was safe here.

The out-of-the-way restaurant called The Porterhouse seemed an odd location for meeting his new boss, but Richard Sommerville wasn't known for being conventional. Even though everyone thought he was a prick, he was a well-respected newspaper editor. And now he was thinking about running for the Senate.

Working the International Desk for *The Standard* would give him a terrific opportunity to further his career. He'd paid serious dues as an international correspondent. Now, it was time to come home and have a normal life—whatever the hell that meant.

But he planned to find out.

He was good at finding things out.

A bell chimed when he opened the door. Sommerville sat three tables up on the right, chatting on his phone, looking like what his mother would call a Pretty Boy Floyd in some fancy, gray, pin-striped suit Tanner would bet cost more than his plane ticket from Kabul to New York City. The restaurant sported worn red booths, scuffed hardwood tables, and no other customers. The smell of hickory aged steaks made his mouth water. Tanner pulled out a chair, hoping he wouldn't have to wear a suit for this job. A sports jacket, button-down shirt, and creased slacks were about as much dressing up as he could take on a daily basis.

Sommerville lifted a finger to convey he was finishing up his conversation. "Listen, I need to run. You do what I tell you. I don't want any more excuses." He clicked off and laid his phone on the table as delicately as a priest would handle a sacred instrument. "Tanner McBride, it's great to see you. Welcome to The Big Apple."

They shook hands, measuring each other. Sommerville might be a well-respected journalist, but he was too *GQ*. Man used crap in his blond hair that had it swirling in a way some people might call fashionable. It looked fussy to Tanner. The guy probably got manicures too, if his hands were any indication. Yet the gleam in Sommerville's eyes couldn't be missed. Predatory, but in a classy way. Stupid people wouldn't see it.

Tanner wasn't stupid.

A man at the front turned the CLOSED sign over in the window and locked the door. Tanner's radar went up, but he kept his face expressionless. Sommerville wanted privacy. Must be something big. The out-of-the-way venue began to make more sense.

"Let's order, and you can tell me about your last days in Kabul."

He was tired of talking about Kabul, but he indulged his new boss. Journalists who rode desks tended to get off on the war stories of other journalists.

Sommerville nursed his scotch as Tanner gave him the highlights of his recent tour. Lies, blood, and death pretty much summed it up. There were good people there like anywhere else, but if he never saw the place again, he'd be happy. God, he was tired of seeing kids get killed over politics and drugs.

Tanner waited for Sommerville to share the reason for the private meeting. He was halfway finished with his medium rare ribeye steak when Sommerville set aside his drink, finally ready to talk. Tanner reached for his water.

"So, I have a new assignment for you. A big one." He rubbed his hands together, the sound like sandpaper on wood.

"What is it?"

Sommerville's phone beeped, but he ignored it. "First, I've been checking up on you. People are saying you're burned out. Need some time out of the fast lane. So, I'm switching you back to domestic for the time being."

Tanner's jaw clenched. "That's not what we agreed to."

Sommerville waved his hand. "I know, but this is a really juicy assignment." He dug out his wallet and pulled out a picture.

Tanner studied it. The blond woman looked to be in her early thirties and as cool as a cucumber. Her blond hair reminded him of the coif women journalists on CNN preferred. She was attractive—beautiful, if he was being honest—and intelligence and confidence radiated from her direct green gaze.

"Who is she?"

Sommerville laid it on the table like he was a Vegas dealer, the photo facing Tanner.

"She's my ex-wife, and I want you to make her fall in love with you."

Tanner started laughing. He jostled Sommerville with a hand to the shoulder like he would a Marine who'd told a dirty joke to break the tension as they rode through hostile territory. "Christ, that's a good one. Flipping me back to domestic. Right."

Sommerville smiled. It thinned out his full lips.

Tanner's laughter died. "You're serious?"

"I never joke about journalism. If Meredith—that's my ex—writes the article she's pitched to her boss, my reputation will be damaged. I'm not entirely sure she's going to leave me out of it. We had a...disagreement recently. I need someone to handle her. Be the focus of her article, and then crush her premise to bits." He drained his scotch. "I won't let her ruin my run for the Senate."

Tanner spread his hands on the table. "I don't see how this has anything to do with me."

Sommerville raised his drink to a passing waiter for a refill. "Then let me fill you in. I have it on good authority my ex-wife is going to return to her hometown in Dare Valley, Colorado, to write an article about her attempts to find love like a heroine in a Nora Roberts romance novel." He suddenly slapped a paperback on the table. "Ever heard of her?"

Tanner picked up the book, *Montana Sky*. Had Sommerville gone off his rocker? "Sure, my mom reads her. Why?"

"I blamed these books for our divorce. My ex-wife is planning to prove I'm wrong by actually trying to *live* the life of a Roberts' character and showing happy endings do exist."

*Okay*...Tanner signaled the waiter. "Bourbon. Neat."

Sommerville grabbed the book. "Do you have any idea how many people read Nora Roberts?"

Tanner lifted a shoulder. Were they actually talking about romance novels? *This* was his big assignment? His dream job lay in ashes at his feet. Sommerville was certifiable. There was no way he'd work for him now.

"We're talking millions. This article will be read by every woman in America—possibly overseas too. Meredith has to be stopped! I won't let her divulge...less than favorable information about our marriage and what drove her to this ridiculous stunt. She's acting like a hysterical female."

Tanner crossed his arms. "So you think making your ex fall in love with me is going to somehow stop this?"

Sommerville reached for his drink. "Yes. If she falls for you, and then you dump her, she can't write the article. Plus, you can keep tabs on her. Bottom line. I can't let her create an unfavorable impression of me."

Unbelievable. "This doesn't seem like a job for a journalist."

"Bull. It's perfect. Think of her as a target. Plus, it will give you some time to recharge. You'll like Dare Valley. It's a small college town in the Rockies. Meredith's family owns a small paper there. You've probably heard of it."

Then it clicked. "Holy shit. *The Western Independent.*" Every journalist worth their salt knew about the small, independent paper that had been founded by one of journalism's best, Arthur Hale. The blond chick had some pedigree.

"Her grandfather never liked me, never even considered letting me take over. He's a crotchety old bastard. Of course, marrying into the Hale family opened a whole set of doors for me, so it was worth it. It'll help my campaign once we get past this whole exploratory committee process." He crunched ice cubes. "I've arranged through a third party for you to be an adjunct professor in the Hale School of Journalism at Emmits Merriam University this coming semester. They were delighted someone of your reputation would want to teach last minute. It's a small, private, liberal arts school."

Tanner set his bourbon aside. "Wait a minute. You accepted a position at the journalism school *for* me?"

Sommerville drained his drink. "Yes, keep up, McBride."

Tanner stood, shoving his chair back so hard it scraped across the wood floor. "I don't know who the hell you think you are, but you have the wrong man. My lawyer will be contacting you about dissolving our employment agreement. Since your new offer breaks all the conditions we agreed upon, I don't expect you'll fight it."

Sommerville leaned back in his chair. "I won't have to. Sit down, McBride. There's more."

*There had to be,* he thought with dread. Tanner landed hard in the seat as Sommerville slid a file toward him. He opened it and rocked back in his chair. Dirty black and white photos filled his vision. The time stamp indicated they were ten months old. The woman with his brother wasn't his wife. Shock and sadness rolled over Tanner.

"Your brother is expecting a baby, I hear. It's a shame he wasn't more careful about the company he kept when he fell off the wagon last year. Prostitutes have a way of ruining a man's political position, notwithstanding his marriage and his family life."

Tanner closed the file with the flick of a finger. Red hot rage flashed through him. "I don't believe it," he said, but the photos looked real. And David had always been a ladies' man. But a prostitute?

"You can check, but I promise you they're real. You helped raise him, right? After your dad left? Must have been tough for a fourteen-year-old kid. All that responsibility."

"You fucking bastard."

Sommerville chuckled. "As if I haven't heard that before. This is business. It's not personal. I need you to do something you don't want to do, so I found leverage. It's the way of the world."

Tanner had seen people be used in despicable ways, but typically he was the one writing about it...not the victim. His objectivity went through the window. He reached across the table and grabbed Sommerville's blue silk tie.

"I could fucking kill you for this."

Sommerville's mouth curled. "We're not in Kabul, and that tough guy routine won't help your brother. The only way I'll give you the negatives to this photo is if you go to Dare and keep tabs on Meredith, make her fall for you, and stop her story. Let go, McBride."

Tanner gave the tie another yank before releasing it and flexing his hands. Sommerville didn't intimidate easily. It was something to remember.

"I could tell you I don't care about the photos." The lie burned his lips like a blister.

Sommerville rattled his ice cubes. "We both know you do. Call him and ask. I'll wait."

He'd wait all right. Like a spider with a fly. "I need to use your phone. I haven't bought one yet."

He made the call and received the confirmation he no longer really needed. If he lived in a parallel universe, he might have walked away. But he'd made his mother a promise to look after his kid brother. Even though they didn't live together anymore, and David was of age, he couldn't refuse to help him. Especially not now that he'd clawed himself back to AA and was re-building his life. Actually doing something good for a change. Serving in the local government to help his community.

"Okay, so you either set him up or bought these pics from someone. Which was it?" he said when he clicked off.

Sommerville leaned back against the booth. "Does it matter? When people run for public office, they step into the spotlight, just like I'm about to do. Your brother made a mistake. I capitalize on people's mistakes. I won't let anyone capitalize on mine."

"Why me? You could hire any number of better-looking jackasses to stop your ex."

He twirled his drink. "You're the perfect match. You and Meredith both went to Columbia University on swimming scholarships. You can reminisce about being a Columbia Lion. Ra-ra and all that. Plus, you've been in war zones and have racked up a pretty impressive reputation. Meredith will respect you as a journalist."

"I think you're overestimating my influence."

"No, I'm not. I've done very well with the ladies using that script—or something like it." He raised his glass in a mock toast. "More importantly, teaching journalism in Dare is the ideal cover, and it's a move that would make perfect sense for someone of your caliber coming back from overseas. Don't you admire Arthur Hale?"

"Who doesn't?"

"No one knows you were joining my staff, which keeps everything under the radar. As far as Meredith goes, you've got nothing to worry about. You'll never fall for her. She's not your type, and you're too ethical to take pleasure in this situation."

Their waiter approached, but turned around when Tanner pinned him with a look.

Sommerville nudged the picture across the table. "Listen, it won't be that bad. Trust me. Meredith is gorgeous. You'll have some time off. Think of it as a vacation."

Tanner picked up his steak knife, fingering the blade. He wanted to shove it in Sommerville's neck. "You must really hate your ex."

Sommerville veiled his eyes. "She wanted a life out of a romance novel—eternal fidelity, partnership, a family. That's not me." He picked up the paperback. "This stuff put ideas in her head. I'm only protecting my interests."

Tanner dropped the knife. He would have to go along with this lunacy until he found a way out. "Are we done here?"

Sommerville reached into his briefcase for another file. "Here's your ticket to Denver, your rental car information, your new address in Dare, your contact at the journalism department, and a complete account of Meredith's likes and dislikes. Study it and get out there. She's arriving tomorrow."

"When does school start?"

"In two weeks, right after Labor Day."

Tanner stood and reached for the file. He spread his legs in a fighting stance. "If you don't hand over everything you have on my brother when I'm done, I'll destroy you and any chance you have of being in the Senate. It's not a promise. It's a blood vow—like the kind I've seen in Afghanistan."

He turned to leave, his mind already building scenarios of how to escape this deal with the devil before his reputation suffered and he hurt an innocent woman.

"And here I thought we could go back to the original agreement," Sommerville replied in a voice laced with irony and malice.

Tanner's boots pounded the floor.

"I'll want weekly updates," Sommerville called.

He unlocked the door and slammed it behind him.

He'd give that asshole an update.

# Chapter 3

M ermaid!"

Meredith's wince was as much from the nickname as the shriek in which it was delivered. Her sister ran off the family porch, red hair flying behind her like flames.

"Jillie Bean!" She set her purse on the hood of her car and braced herself. Her sister plowed into her, wrapping her arms around her, jumping like a pogo stick all the while.

"Mere, I'm so happy you're back!" Jill leaned away, Hale green eyes sparkling, and then launched herself again. "Oh, you're here, you're here!"

Meredith squeezed hard. Even though her little sister had three inches on her, Jill was acting like a Labrador puppy—albeit dressed in a purple and white polka dot dress. Her heart lifted. Laughter erupted from her, dispelling the knots in her Pepcid-coated stomach.

"You idiot. Get off me."

Jill leaned back and slung an arm around her waist. "Is this the Audi you bought with Rick-the-Dick's money?"

"I leased it. I figured I'd need a car again if I'm going to be living out here for a while. Moves like a dream."

Jill leapt away like a giant fairy, making footprints in the freshly mowed grass. "I can't wait to go for a ride." She bounded back toward Meredith and reached for her shirt. "Now, show me La Perla."

Meredith swatted her hands away. "Stop it!"

Unphased, Jill tugged up her T-shirt. "Oh, a cranberry bustier. Ooh-la-la. My cotton-clad sister goes over to the wild side."

Meredith waved as her parents shuffled down the porch's steps, obviously a little uncomfortable with the strip tease that was unfolding in the front yard. "Shut up! Mom and dad are coming."

Jill blew out a raspberry. "Like Mom wouldn't want to see this. *I see London, I see France, I see Meredith's underpants.*"

"Behave!" Meredith said, socking her in the arm. "I'll show you my new stuff later."

"Promise?"

"Yes."

Her sister ran across the lawn. "Mermaid's here."

"We can see that," Linda Hale confirmed. Her lightly wrinkled face had that weird glow moms get when their kids come home. Her mom's red hair had even more gray-streaks in it than when she'd seen her after her dad's heart attack. "Thank you for coming, honey. It means the world."

"You look wonderful," Jim Hale commented with a wink. Deep grooves cut a trench around her dad's eyes and mouth. "Love the hair. But while I'm thrilled you're here, you didn't have to come relieve me of duty. Jeez. Doesn't anyone listen to me?"

"No," her mother and sister replied.

Her parents embraced her one at a time. She held on, taking in their smells with a fond smile. Mom used lemon verbena lotion. Dad's turpentine odor from his hobby—furniture restoration—never faded.

Seeing the toll her dad's health problems had taken on them, she was glad she'd made her decision to come home for three months. It was the first time she'd looked at her parents and thought they were getting old. The house they had rented in Sedona would provide the needed retreat, and since Sedona was only a day's drive, they could pop back to Dare when they wanted. She'd never met anyone who loved to drive like her parents did.

Her mom hugged her again. "I'm so glad your boss agreed to let you have some time. You don't know what it means."

Meredith caressed her back. "It's okay, Mom. I'm glad I can help."

The anchor usually dragging her heart down to her stomach disappeared. Here, people loved her. Here, she could be her true self with no fear of betrayal. She could laugh and relax. Let down her hair a bit. For way too long, she'd felt like she was wrapped up tight in saran wrap.

Arthur Hale stepped forward from behind her parents. "About time you got here," he muttered, tapping his cane near her foot. "Give your grandpa a kiss." He bussed her cheek, his red hot candy breath making her smile. He squinted down at her, a white shock of hair falling over his brow. "Well, I see you reverted to being a red head again. Good. You never were a blond bombshell."

She squeezed his arm lightly, his weathered skin tough like faded leather. "Thanks, Grandpa. You sure know how to turn a girl's head."

He poked her—a strong jab for a seventy-five year old man. "I turned plenty a girl's head before I met your grandma. So, you're going to be my new protégée, huh? I suppose you'll do."

She narrowed her eyes. "Oh, I'll do all right."

He nudged her with his cane again, peering at her through his glasses. "It's what families do, helping out."

"I know it."

Her heart clutched when her mom wiped away a tear. Oh, God, her mother never cried. When her dad grabbed her hand, she looked frantically at Jill. Her sister was wiping a tear away too. Her insides slithered to the floor. It really *was* bad.

Grandpa stepped closer, candy clicking against his teeth. "I heard your jerk of an ex-husband is thinking about running for the Senate. How are you taking that?" His silent stares could be intimidating. Arthur Hale had a way of sizing people up and looking into their souls.

She dropped her gaze as a flood of rage burst through her. Digging through her purse for her car keys, she averted her eyes. "It's his business, isn't it?"

"Oh Grandpa, give it a rest," Jill interrupted. "You're spoiling her homecoming. Don't make me take your cane, old man."

He growled. "The girl has no respect for her elders." But he ruffled Jill's hair and stepped down. "Fine. I'm glad your boss didn't give you any trouble and that your dad can take some time off. I don't want him to have another heart attack. Hell, he's only fifty-two. He's got my dad's infernal genes."

"He'll go a few more miles, Arthur," Meredith's mother said with a smile. "Yes, we're grateful to your boss. Please tell her thanks again for me, Mere."

She smiled. "Mom, you've said that about a hundred times. I've told her."

"Well, it's so generous of her."

"I'll be...working on a few things for her." She didn't dare say what. If it got out she was planning on trying to find true love Nora Roberts-style and writing about it, everyone would be talking about it in their small town. There was no way she was opening herself up to that scrutiny. Plus, she wasn't sure how the local guys would feel about her article. If she were a guy, it would be a definite turn off.

"Easy for Karen to be generous. She's not paying for it," Arthur huffed. "Girl's charging me highway robbery for her salary."

"I'm worth it."

"We'll see, girlie."

Her mom took her purse. "Honey, I made all your favorites. Fried chicken, mashed potatoes, and corn. Lemon meringue pie for dessert."

Her dad patted his medium-sized girth. "Your mom's giving me a free pass today from my diet. I owe you, Mere. If I have to eat any more fiber, I'll—"

"Oh, put a sock in it, Alan," her mom ordered. "It's for your own good."

"Okay, you two. Can I simply say it's good to be back?" Meredith interjected.

And it was. Her eyes darted to the surrounding mountains. The jagged gray rocks rose up around them like temples. The aspen, alder, and cottonwood trees exploded everywhere with early fall color. Goosebumps broke out across her arms. God, it was beautiful here, and so utterly different from New York. She had a moment of panic. Could she really come back here for three months? She pressed her hands against her bustier. She could have sworn she heard *Yes, you can* in a throaty voice in her head. Well, that was weird.

"Are we going to stand here all day, admiring the view?" Grandpa Hale called. "I'm starving."

As her parents headed for the house, Meredith went to pop the trunk.

Jill tugged her arm away from it. "You're going to be staying with me, Mere. We'll go to my place after dinner."

Stay with Jill? She loved her sister, but... "I don't know..."

Jill shook her head, her chandelier earrings brushing her shoulders. "Don't say no, Mere. You don't want to stay here at mom and dad's house alone, do you?"

"Let's—"

"Grandpa offered too, but we flipped for it."

"Girl cheated." He tapped his cane on the sidewalk. "You don't have to abide by the coin toss, Meredith."

She hadn't banked on her family having everything figured out before her arrival. "I..."

Her sister pulled her toward the house. "It'll be fun."

Fun? What had she gotten herself into?

# Chapter 4

Jill's apartment resembled a shrine to all things funky and strange. Bold colors dominated the space, which reminded her of a Dali painting on crack. Meredith wondered if something had happened in the womb. She sure as hell preferred things a bit more…muted.

"You know, you pretty much made everyone's year, coming back like this." Jill said as she hefted one of Meredith's many suitcases inside. She propped it against a red monkey statue, which, thankfully, did not have real hair like the African mask on the wall.

Meredith brushed some brownie crumbs off an ancient shaggy green loveseat.

"Don't sit on that. The leg is broken. You'd be better off on the couch."

"Okay, but why do you still have it if it's broken?" She pushed aside colorful pillows in red, yellow, and blue and sat on the orange monstrosity.

"I like it. Just because stuff is old, doesn't mean it's not useful."

"Grandpa would agree."

Jill set two microbrews on the well-worn, purple coffee table. "So tell me the truth. I heard your bullshit answer to Grandpa. How are you really handling all this stuff with Rick-the-Dick? Hey, we should call him 'Tricky Dickie' now."

"Please. No Nixon references." Meredith grabbed the beer. "I'm taking action, getting on with my life. I'm fed up with his games, and I told him to leave me out of it or else."

Jill rested the beer against her chest. "Good. That'll make his balls shrivel."

"Exactly." Meredith took a drink. The fragrant beverage hit

her tongue and had her coughing up a lung. "Yuck! What the hell is this stuff?"

"Pumpkin beer. Jemma and I love it." Jill settled back on a rickety purple chair covered in bright lime green scarves.

"Gross. I only like pumpkin pie. Who'd put pumpkin in beer?"

"Someone who got drunk in a pumpkin patch and had an epiphany. Have you become a wine snob in New York?"

A wave of silliness hit her, and she threw a pillow at Jill. "So? You going to disown me, pumpkin girl?"

"No way. I'm too happy you're back, even if it's just for now. Mom's over the moon about becoming a snowbird. You know how much she loves Sedona, and their trip will do them both a world of good. She's got him signed up for all sorts of things—yoga, juice cleanses, you name it. He's complaining, but deep down, I think he's scared too."

Meredith kicked her shoes off. "I could tell. It scares me. They looked...old." Her ribcage tightened, pressing in on her like the pillows on the couch were suffocating her.

"Grandpa's a spry old man. Tough as steel, that one. You better watch out. He's got plans for you."

"I know."

Like him, she'd gone to New York to learn about the newspaper business. He'd intended to come back. She hadn't. Yet, here she was—for a time, anyway.

"Do you have anything stronger?"

"Nope, only beer. So, you mentioned working on an article for Karen, but you were pretty vague. What's up?"

"It's an idea I had in the bookstore when I bought all the Nora Roberts and J.D. Robb books that have been released since my divorce."

"Spill it." Jill bounded over to the couch.

Moment of truth.

"I'm here for a story." And she proceeded to tell her the whole thing.

Jill slapped her beer down on the coffee table and grabbed Meredith by both arms. "That's awesome, Mere! That's like the best idea ever. Nora Roberts Land. I love it!" She jumped up, and flicked on the stereo. "Dancing Queen" blasted out. Jill had always had a flair for the dramatic.

"I'm glad you like it," she shouted. "You're the only one I'm telling."

"Awesome! And Nora." Jill sashayed over to a cluttered bookcase and pulled out a paperback. "Well, she's like the Oprah of the written word." Jill launched herself back onto the couch with *Homeport* in her hand. "It's the coolest idea ever!"

"Well, the will to do it is there. I'm through with letting Rick-the-Dick screw up my life. But the thought of dating guys again turns my stomach into buttermilk." She set her beer aside, wanting an antacid instead.

"You'll do great!" Jill pulled Meredith up from the couch, her eyes shining. "I'll help you. I know most of the single guys in town. Running the coffee shop keeps me plugged in." She hugged her. "Oh, I'm so glad you're doing this. I've hated seeing you so sad. You deserve a wonderful guy, Mere. You deserve a hero from Nora Roberts Land."

Meredith pressed her face into Jill's hair. She still wasn't sure a good guy was out there for her or that she was even ready, but by God, she was going to try. Karen had loved her idea, and she thought their female readership would go crazy for it.

"You can't tell anyone," she whispered, breathing in the smell of Jill's sugar cookie lotion.

Her sister pulled back. "Duh. We don't want to scare anyone away." She let out a whoop. "Oh, Mere, I'm so glad you're back. Plus, if you find Mr. Right here, you might decide to stay forever."

"It may not work out that way, Jill," Meredith said, her insides jittering like the music. She turned it down. "I like New York. I have a good job there."

Jill froze in mid-twirl. "Bullshit. You've been miserable lately. Why go back to a place where you're too embarrassed to hold up your head? And now Rick-the-Dick is probably going to run for the Senate, putting your divorce in the spotlight again. You know what that jerk did to you."

"Better than you."

She'd never told a soul about catching him with a prostitute. She'd told her family he was a cheater, but the whole hooker thing made it much more sordid. Her husband had paid another woman for sex. When she'd asked him why, he'd told her he'd wanted a professional, letting the unspoken accusation hover in the air like a stink bomb.

Jill flew across the room. "You changed for him because you wanted him to love you. Don't you see? The more he liked the fake you, the less you liked yourself. And then what happened?"

She looked away. "He stopped liking the fake me because I did."

Her sister framed her face with her hands. "He was too self-absorbed and too much of an asshole to ever truly like anything or anyone but himself. You know it."

The song changed to "Gimme, Gimme, Gimme A Man After Midnight."

"I know it here." Meredith pointed to her head. "But I can't feel it here yet," she added, putting the finger to her heart.

Jill wrapped her arms around her. "You will, Mere. Believe it."

Thank God for sisters. She blinked back tears. She had a story to do. This was no time for self pity.

"So, do you want to see my new underwear?"

Jill laughed and let her go. "Okay, but I think I'm going to need more beer first." She sailed into the small kitchen.

Meredith had been too embarrassed to tell Jill about it before, but now seemed like a good time. "The underwear goes with my post-divorce alter ego," she called out. "It's a superhero."

Jill popped her beer open. "Do you have a cape?"

Meredith put her finger to her lips and smiled. "Not yet."

*** 

Jill caressed Meredith's La Perla like it was fine china, a sudden feeling of envy shooting through her. She wanted to be the kind of woman who could pull off wearing sexy lingerie.

"I'm going to embroider DW on some of these for you," she informed her now wild-side sis. "Give them a real superhero feel. Divorcée Woman. I love it!"

She still couldn't believe her always-cotton sister had ditched comfort for pure sex appeal. If Meredith couldn't get her confidence back in this stuff...

"The lucky guy—or guys—in this town are going to lose it when they see you in this."

Her sister blushed, actually blushed, so she ragged some

more. It's what sisters did. "They'll last about thirty seconds the first time, but hopefully it will get better after that."

Since that was Jill's limited experience with sex, she could only hope. Maybe when she found her true love, he'd be able to go all night, like Nora Roberts' heroes.

"It's not like I sleep with a lot of guys."

"Right," Jill murmured. "That guy in college, the one when you first moved to New York, and then Rick-the-Dick. We need to find you a real man, honey," she drawled.

"You're incorrigible."

"That's what Grandpa says." She plopped against the headboard, settling in beside Meredith. "So, we need a plan."

"We?"

"Well, I'm going to be your pimp, so to speak."

Meredith jostled her. "Oh yuck. Never call yourself my pimp again."

"You don't think it's funny?"

Meredith nailed her in the head again with a pillow. "Right, I'm a divorced superhero with a pimp sister. What's not to laugh about?"

Jill jumped off the bed and rifled through Meredith's larger suitcase, sorting through the paperbacks. "You've lost your funny bone. So tell me, Divorcée Woman, who's your favorite Nora Roberts hero?"

Meredith crawled over to the edge of the bed. "Man, that's like asking me about my favorite food."

Jill held up a book. "Mine's Roarke. Hands down. That guy is smokin' hot. I could write an ode to his hotness." She threw aside a J.D. Robb paperback. "But we're not going to find a Roarke here."

"Okay, but I'm still going to fantasize about finding him." Meredith picked up *Sea Swept*. "Ah, my first Nora book. Hard to find someone hotter than Cameron Quinn."

"Oh yeah. Badass race car driver returns home when dad dies to take care of an orphan boy. That was a great series. His advertising executive brother, Phillip Quinn, was pretty hot in *Inner Harbor*, but a little urbane for my taste. The guy complained about getting blood out of a cotton blend, remember?"

"Yes, but he was a wine snob like me. We'd be a match made in heaven."

"Haha. Okay, give me two more." Jill leaned against the suitcase. After Meredith's crazy attraction to Rick-the-Dick, she wasn't sure what her sister went for in a man. "Then I'll have something to work with. All of them need to be small-town guys."

Meredith flopped onto her back. "How about Bradley Vane from *Key of Valor*? Owner of a home goods empire who looks hot in a suit, but isn't afraid to get his hands dirty."

"Oh, I love the Key series. It's awesome how the heroines battle evil with their hunky heroes. Keep going."

Pressing her finger to her lips, Meredith gave a secret smile. "It's an oldie but a goodie. How about Alex Stanislaski in *Convincing Alex*? He likes redheads, and I've always loved a rugged detective even though I think having handcuffs in the bedroom would scare the bejesus out of me."

Jill hooted. "Oh, Mere, you're too much. I personally like his brother, Mikhail, better in *Luring a Lady*, but I'm more into the hot-tempered artistic types."

"Your love affair would end when he discovered you painted your coffee table purple."

"So we'd argue about my taste, and then we'd have great make-up sex. I'd paint everything purple for that."

Meredith bashed her with a pillow. They grappled before pushing apart, panting.

Jill reached for another book. "What about the McGregors?"

"Who doesn't love that series? But they're hardly small-town people. They're as rich as Croesus."

"Who?"

"Never mind."

"Now that I think about it, Grandpa kinda reminds me of The McGregor."

Boy, Jill wasn't far off there. He was the patriarch of the Hale family. "Let's hope he doesn't meddle more than usual. So what do you think? What is my hero type?"

Jill crossed her arms like she'd seen her old professors do when stating an academic opinion. "My conclusion is Meredith Hale likes a man who's smart and a little urbane with a healthy streak of badass," she concluded in a stuffy English accent. "Hot. Definitely hot."

"Anyone come to mind?"

"The cop's easy. We have a new deputy sheriff in town. Larry Barlow. Ripped and intense with a big dose of badass. As for the others, I'll make a list. Then we can plot—haha—how you'll meet them and draw them into your La Perla web." She bopped Meredith on the head with a book, enjoying the childish playacting. "Of course, if you flashed them your undies, we wouldn't have to do much to draw them in. Ever thought about streaking through the grocery store in your ittie bitties?"

Meredith rolled over and gave her the stink eye. "Like Mr. Jenkins did a few years ago after his wife died?"

"Well, it did get him more casseroles from our local widows. He's happily married now."

"Great, even streakers find happy endings."

Jill sat on her heels. She didn't like the despair in Meredith's voice. Damn Rick-the-Dick to hell for messing with her sister.

"Wait here a minute. I have something I want to give you."

She raced across the hall to her bedroom, stubbing her toe on a hardcover of *Black Hills*. "Shit, that hurt." Sifting through the necklaces hanging from a nail on the closet door, she untangled the one she wanted and raced back.

"Here," She thrust it out. "I want you to have this."

Meredith rose up to a sitting position, and Jill plopped down next to her.

"It's made of crystals. I bought it from a local artisan in Aspen when I went skiing last winter."

Since Meredith didn't believe in anything supernatural, Jill didn't mention the crystal's power to heal. La Perla was a good start, but Jill thought Meredith could use an extra boost.

Meredith raised it over her neck. "It's beautiful, Jillie."

"Then it's perfect, since you are too."

Her sister's head drooped. "Believe it," Jill said, stroking Mere's hair.

"I know, I know."

She let the less-than-believable litany go. Meredith would get her groove back—just like Stella. "Okay, I need to focus on my pimp duties. Let me do some thinking while you settle in."

"Thanks, Jillie. With your help, I think this might just work. Gosh, I missed you."

"I'm going to find you a wonderful, hot, kick-ass man,

Mermaid. And then you're going to owe me for the rest of your life."

Her sister touched the crystals on the necklace with shaking fingers. "What if I don't find anyone?"

Her hushed whisper wrung Jill's heart out like a dish rag. She gave her a saucy wink. "With me as your pimp, how could you not?"

Meredith's mouth turned up at the corners. "Okay, Sista Pimp, get going."

"Don't try and be a rapper, Mere. It's so not your thing."

When she left the room, Meredith was still laughing.

The weight of Jill's assignment hung on her like that thing an ox carried. What was it? Oh yeah, a yoke. She needed to find her big sister the perfect man. And after what she'd heard today in the coffee shop about the new arrival coming to town, she already had someone in mind.

# Chapter 5

Tanner surveyed his Denver hotel room and threw his keys on the bed. After years of living overseas and being driven around, he was the one at the wheel. Even though it was a rental, his forest green Nissan Xterra had the new car smell. Funny how that lifted his spirits.

He dialed up his sister on his new cell phone.

Peggy answered on the fourth ring. "Hello?"

"Hey, there. It's me. This is my new number."

"Tanner! So you really are staying. I wasn't sure."

He walked over to the window and looked out. It wasn't much of a view, but it was safe. A welcome change. "I can't turn my back on David. Not when he's finally getting his shit together."

"So you're sure this happened before he went to AA?"

"Yes. He told me the whole sordid story."

The parallels between his brother and their father were painful. At least David hadn't left his family. Tanner had to stick by him for that. He rested his head on the cold glass.

"It's a fucking nightmare though."

Peggy's sigh was audible. "I don't like what you have to do to this woman."

His conscience was already having fits over Meredith Hale. He tried to block the phrase "innocent victim" from his mind. He rubbed his tired eyes. Wasn't that why he hadn't been sleeping?

"I don't have a choice."

"I'll keep digging on Sommerville, Tanner. So far, everyone seems to think he's a world-class asshole. He's a big drinker, probably a functioning alcoholic, and a womanizer. But he's spinning it pretty well. He says he found a higher purpose after his divorce. He's been going to church, confessing his sins. It's the standard redemption schtick these politicians pull."

"It's bullshit. Of course, with his money and the spin, he could win."

"Yeah. Their divorce was pretty public. Meredith got herself a fat settlement."

Tanner drew X-O game dashes in the fog that his breath left on the window. "Good for her."

"She's a fighter. Going to Sommerville's rival paper was another nail in the proverbial divorce coffin. She won't fall easily."

He drew an X and snorted. "You questioning my charm?"

"What charm? You're out of practice after all the hell holes you've been in."

"It's like riding a bicycle."

"I thought that was sex. Relationships are harder."

"I've heard that before," he drawled.

Which was why he didn't do them. And he didn't want to think about how long he'd been without sex. His sister was right. Where he'd been working...well, there weren't too many available women. He didn't sleep with people in the same business. Too much pillow talk could kill a good story. And he didn't do prostitutes. Never had. Never would. Even though it obviously ran in the family.

"We need to find an angle, Tanner," his sister reiterated, sounding like the cop she was.

"I'm working on it. Sommerville's careful. He'd have expected the press to dig." He rubbed the window clean and walked over to the mini-fridge to pull out a Dr. Pepper. Man, it was nice to have a constant supply.

"Use a bigger shovel," his sister said.

The sugary syrup and carbonation made his nose twitch. "Plan to."

"I'm so pissed at David."

"I know." And totally understandable. Peg's ex had cheated on her. After kicking him to the curb, she'd decided to raise her seven-year-old son alone. "We'll find something. I have a few journalist friends digging quietly too."

"I need to run. I have to pick Keith up at a birthday party."

Tanner clicked the TV on and settled onto the bed, channel surfing. "Tell him hi. Maybe you can come out and see me in Colorado in a few months. We could do Thanksgiving together."

"That would be nice. We'll get through this, Tanner."

Her support made him squirm. It felt...weird when he was used to doing everything alone. "I know. Bye now," he said, setting aside the phone.

After a moment, he opened the file folder and stared down at Meredith Hale's picture. She'd followed in her family's footsteps by attending Columbia University's school of journalism. On a swimming scholarship no less. As Sommerville had said, it was something she and Tanner had in common. Since he was six years older, their paths hadn't crossed. His research indicated she didn't trade on her Hale name, which he liked. Sommerville clearly hadn't been as scrupulous.

Her articles were strong. Human interest stuff. She had a good voice, a way of humanizing painful and difficult topics while maintaining her objectivity.

The more he learned, the more he liked.

It pissed him off he'd have to break her heart.

# Chapter 6

M eredith dragged her feet as Jill pulled her along Main Street. Her sister was taking her on her first dating expedition, rather like a fishing expedition, but not for anything cold-blooded.

"I don't know if I'm ready for this."

Snapping her fingers in front of Meredith's face, Jill said, "Sure you are, Mermaid. We're taking a male shopping tour for potential Nora Roberts-type heroes. I did some research based on the books in my collection, and I came up with some perfect places for us to look for your dream man."

Meredith smoothed her hands down the navy top and tan skirt they'd picked out for her to wear. "That's pretty logical."

Jill waved a hand. "It's simple. You're back in town. We're reintroducing you. Hell, it's been twelve years since you've lived here. A lot has changed."

As Meredith surveyed Main Street, she could only agree. Dare had more high-end stores with cutesy names than she remembered. Within one block, she spied three new businesses: Posh Ice Day Spa, which had a glowing chartreuse door; Rugged Trail Sporting Goods; and With Sprouts, a trendy-looking vegetarian restaurant. Containers filled with orange, purple, and yellow chrysanthemums lined the sidewalks, and new parking meters took money from sparkling 4x4s and hybrids.

"Town's doing well." She nodded to a college student who smiled as he walked by.

"Yes, lots of new blood beyond the university. Baby boomer retirees have been coming here and opening up small businesses. Dare caters to a healthy ski crowd now that Aspen has become so crazy expensive. It's insane. You can't have an affordable meal there anymore. Ticks me off. But it's been great for the coffee shop."

Meredith patted her sister on the back as they walked past the old-school Barber Shop where their father always got his hair trimmed. She was delighted to see it hadn't been run out of town. "I'm so proud of you, Jill."

"Say no more. I'll mist up."

"So, where to?"

Jill flung up the end of her neon green scarf, letting the wind take it. It streamed behind her, fluttering along in time with her long red hair. "Guess."

Meredith traced the bottom of her bustier for courage. She could do this. "Where?"

Jill pointed across the street. "Smith's Hardware. Old man Smith's turned it over to Wayne. He might just be your Bradley Vane."

Meredith slowed her pace. "But he was a big weenie in school."

Jill dragged her toward the store. "Wasn't there some story about an ugly duckling?"

"She was a woman."

The bell pealed as her sister opened the door. Chemicals and wood competed to make her eyes tear up.

"How about the frog prince? He was a man."

The sound of shuffling boots cut their conversation short. "I'd recognize that red hair anywhere. Meredith, I'd heard you were back. Still hale and hearty, I see."

Wayne's old joke fell flat. How many times had she heard that one growing up?

"Hale and hearty indeed." She grimaced. "Good to see you, Wayne."

He was mostly bald, save for a few dark squiggles he was using as a comb-over. He was two inches shorter than Meredith and probably weighed ten pounds less. She'd crush him in his sleep if she rolled over in bed. The terrifying image made her eye twitch. She elbowed Jill in the stomach as she stepped forward to shake the guy's hand. He hadn't changed a bit. He was still a weenie.

Jillie was going to die.

She pasted a polite smile on her face as she listened to Wayne's story about why he'd taken over the store. His dad's hemorrhoids had gotten too painful. Yuck!

Bradley Vane, her ass.

Fifteen minutes later, she bought a hammer and followed her sister out of the store.

"Where are the nails?" Jill sputtered between giggles. She leaned against the wall and belly laughed.

"I don't need nails. I'm planning on using it on your head!" she said, pulling it from the bag.

"Oh, you should see your face!"

"I could kill you," Meredith muttered without heat. Then she started laughing too, her sister's glee contagious.

"You all right, Jill? That woman isn't threatening you with that hammer, is she?"

Meredith dropped her weapon hand and spun. A hunky officer leaned across the passenger seat of his Eagle County Sheriff's SUV, the window wide open. He had the whole Nora hero look nailed down, that was for sure. She thought of Nate Burke from *Northern Lights*.

"No, Larry." Jill dug her elbow into Meredith's ribs. "She's my sister."

"Larry Barlow. Deputy Sheriff." He tipped his finger to his forehead in some type of a guy greeting. "I heard you were back in town. Welcome."

The hammer felt conspicuous, so she stuffed it back in the bag, paper ruffling. "I'm Meredith."

"Don't take that hammer to your sister this early," he said, his face breaking into a broad grin. "You haven't been here long enough for it to be self defense, but if you need some advice on how to get away with clocking her, let me know."

His sense of humor had an edge, but he wasn't hard on the eyes. "That'd be great, Larry," she replied. At least Jill had picked one winner.

"See you around, Meredith, Jill." He sped off into the slow stream of cars.

Jill made a play for the hammer. "Gimme the weapon."

Yanking it back, Meredith said, "No." She won the tussle and shoved it into her oversized purse. "This is a reminder of what happens to you if you pull that kind of shit again."

Jill bit her lip. "Okay, but I had to do it. First, I needed a good laugh. Second, it was part of my diabolical strategy as your pimp."

She knocked her sister in the arm with her fist. "Stop saying that."

Jill spun around, trailing the scarf like a flamenco dancer. "I figured after seeing Wayne, everyone would look better."

Meredith sidled around a dog tied to a lamppost. "You're right. No one could be worse than Wayne. I won't date men who weigh less than me, Jill. I have my principles."

Jill knelt down to pet the brown and white bulldog, who rolled onto his back, begging for more. "I could probably find a few more weenies to torment you, but with that hammer, I'll think twice. So what did you think of the deputy?"

"Kinda cute," Meredith said with a shrug.

"He's more than cute. You're only torturing me over Wayne. In that uniform, he could cuff me *and* do a full body search."

Meredith's mouth dropped as a man stepped outside and reached for the dog leash wrapped around the lamppost.

"Well, that's nice to know, Jill. Do you prefer the police get-up or dress whites?"

"In your dreams, McConnell," Jill ground out, causing the dog to growl.

"Hi Brian," Meredith said, the wind cooling her hot cheeks. She'd have to remember she couldn't have spicy conversations on the street here like she did in New York. There was no anonymity.

"Hey, Mermaid." He kissed her cheek. "Heard you were home. Good to see you." He tugged the dog's leash when it lurched at an approaching poodle. "No, Mutt."

"You named your dog, Mutt?" Jill asked. "I'm surprised you can handle the responsibility of having a dog."

Meredith fiddled with her coat. Where had that come from? Jill and Brian had been best friends growing up. He'd left town eight years ago, but Meredith had figured they must have stayed in touch. Now that she thought about it, though, Jill hadn't said much when she'd asked about him, just saying he was off in New York. Clearly, there'd been some sort of a falling out.

He shrugged a shoulder that was a hell of a lot more muscular than when Meredith had seen him last. Brian McConnell looked good, from his worn jeans to his white T-shirt. And his thick brown hair still had enough of a curl to make it both casual and sexy.

"So what are you doing now?" Meredith asked, her eyes on Jill, whose body resembled a block of ice.

"He's a meat slave at The Chop House," Jill sneered, tugging on her scarf.

"I'm the sous chef. I actually just got back from New York, too. I'm sorry we never met up while we were both there, but my schedule was insane." Brian thrust the leash into Meredith's hand suddenly. He grabbed her sister's chiffon scarf, untangling it from her neck. "Makes me think of the dance of the seven veils."

"You're a total pig." Jill kicked at his shins.

He danced out of the way, but didn't let go of her scarf, tugging at it playfully. "Then she opens her mouth and makes me think about nooses. Aren't you ever going to be nice to me again?"

She dug her fist into his stomach. "No."

He dropped the scarf like it was a hot plate. "Fine!"

Meredith handed him the dog leash when he turned back, unsure what to say or do. It was like being caught in someone else's couple's counseling session.

"Good to see you, Mere. I need to run before Frisky over there decides to punch me in the nuts. See you 'round." He set off with his lumbering bulldog.

"Carnivore," Jill called.

Brian turned his head and grinned. "Hippie."

When he disappeared around the corner, Meredith grabbed Jill's shoulders. "What the hell was that all about?"

Jill shrugged free. Her hands pressed against her tummy as she took in a few deep breaths. Meredith watched in fascination.

"I am calm. I am at peace. He cannot affect me," she chanted.

"Jill, what's going on?"

"We had a big falling out after high school graduation." Her eyes popped open, revealing despair. "After being friends forever, he *finally* asked me out. I thought he was getting serious. We were both going to school in Denver. I asked him to be my first. He turned me down, and then hooked up with Kelly Kimple. If that's not bad enough, he'd hidden the fact that he'd been accepted into The Culinary Institute of America and planned to attend. He broke my heart. Now he's going to pay."

Jill took off like a missile, and Meredith had to run to catch up to her. "You never told me all this."

"You were off somewhere when it happened," her sister said, flicking a hand in the air as if dismissing the memory. "And I was embarrassed. I leaned on Jemma. She's forgiven Brian. I haven't. It doesn't matter now."

"But you're still pissed. And acting really out of character."

Jill loved everybody, and everybody loved Jill. It was practically a rule of the universe.

"Don't worry. I don't run into him too often. He's only been back for a month."

Meredith pulled her to a halt. "I'm sorry he hurt you."

Jill kicked at the sidewalk, refusing to meet her eyes. "I tried to get over him. I even went as far as getting it on with Freddie Pilpipper, a hot-looking skier who was really pathetic in the sack. I never knew a man could have such great equipment without knowing what to do with it."

What to say? Even though they talked frequently, she was out of practice with the big stuff. "Guys suck."

Jill sputtered out a laugh. "Yes, they do."

"Kinda odd, leaving New York's restaurant scene and coming back to Dare to work at The Chop House."

"Yeah, Jemma and I wondered, but he hasn't said. Besides, I don't care."

"Okay then, let's go and have some cinnamon rolls at Kemstead's Bakery and forget the search for my dream man for a while."

The spontaneous hug rocked her back on her heels. "I'm so glad you're here, Mere."

From the corner of her eye, Meredith caught sight of Mutt lurching out from around the corner. She repressed a frown. Why would a man hover around the corner after a run-in with his former best friend?

Jill squeezed her tighter, and Meredith returned the embrace, the wind rushing over her face.

Who the hell could account for what a man was thinking anyway?

# Chapter 7

Tanner was dreaming up ways to murder Sommerville without being put in jail. Coming out of what his GPS called Sardine Canyon—aptly named—he surveyed Dare Valley. Fall had broken out across the land, and crayon-colored trees made the jagged peaks of the mountains look like they'd caught fire. Knuckles white from veering to avoid some stupid ass deer that had tried to cross the two-lane highway, Tanner read the town's population sign. Only forty thousand people? Holy shit. He couldn't live here. He needed the city, the chaos.

Something plopped on his windshield, leaving a white stain. He grimaced and looked up at eleven o'clock. The eagle's majesty should have given him pause, but he didn't need some damn bird splatting his SUV, although it might be a common occurrence in Eagle County. He cursed at the sky and hit his window washing button.

Nature. What the hell did people see in it? Too much space, too few people, and too many dumb animals waiting to careen into your car or drop a load on your windshield. He liked *National Geographic* just fine, thank you, but its proper place was in a school classroom or on a coffee table.

His phone rang. He plugged in one earbud, keeping watch for other dumb-ass animals that might want to put natural selection to the test.

"Hello."

"So, you're on the way to Dare," Sommerville said. "What do you think so far?"

Tanner cursed under his breath. It had only taken the son of a bitch two days to find his number. "I don't like you keeping tabs on me."

"Don't growl, McBride. I have a personal interest in this story. I told you I wanted updates."

"I'm only just arriving in town. I was going to call." And tell him to go straight to hell. Or so he fantasized.

"That's good to hear. I don't want to have to exert any more undue influence to secure your cooperation. Did you read the file on Meredith?"

He turned right when the smooth voice from his GPS instructed. The road led east of the downtown area. "Yes, it was quite thorough." He'd included everything down to her favorite flowers—yellow roses.

"What's your plan for approaching her?"

Too bad Tanner had a good signal, or he would have happily blamed a dropped call on this Beyond Fucking Egypt—BFE—town. The road rose up the mountain. He passed private driveways among the foothills, and through the blur of trees, he caught sight of a few McMansions.

"I don't know yet. I need to get the lay of the land. See where she hangs out. If I push too hard, she'll be onto me."

"You'll be okay. She won't see this coming. She's pretty trusting. You'll simply be another interested male in a limited meat market."

He slowed when the GPS alerted him to an approaching left turn. He veered onto a gravel road, the crunch under the tires making him slow down. Aspens and assorted conifers crowded together on both sides. The boughs waved in welcome. The narrow road opened up to showcase a killer house.

"Holy shit."

"Are you finally there?"

Was the guy tracking his GPS? Hell, it was why his friends never used it overseas. It made it too easy for the bad guys to target you. He wouldn't put it past Sommerville.

Tanner pulled into the circular driveway and stepped out. The sunlight reflected off the squeaky clean massive windows. The cool air carried a pine scent combined with the smell of the damp loamy soil.

"I'm here."

"I know you're pissed, but I hope the accommodations will soften the edge. What do you think?"

He studied the trendy cabin—if it could even be called that. It reminded him more of the natural architecture of Fallingwater by Frank Lloyd Wright. Gray stone and natural wood converged into a two-story dwelling recessed into the forest. It was secluded and quiet. Tanner instantly disliked it.

"Not my style."

"Well it beats where you've been staying. You'll get used to it."

Did the man ever listen? "Look, I'm here. I'll start working and get back to you."

"I want an update every three days."

"Don't micromanage me, Sommerville."

"All right. Every week."

Tanner popped the trunk. Rustling in the nearby trees made him swivel his head. He stared into the eyes of a frozen deer before it bounded away. Great. They were everywhere.

Maybe he'd buy a gun.

"Give me two weeks before I make my first report. I'll have a lot to do with my new faculty position."

School started next week. He was going to teach. He couldn't fucking believe it. His old professors would laugh themselves blue. He'd been the student who couldn't wait to leave the classroom and do something.

"Fine, but you're not there for school. It's only a cover. You're there to make Meredith fall in love with you and stop her story. Making a move on her quickly is key. I had her in bed in a month. If you give her—or any woman—too much time to think, they drag their feet."

So you drag them off to bed? Tanner pulled out his suitcases and started for the house. This man had no respect for women. Since his dad had shared Sommerville's philosophy before he'd taken off, Tanner had a real aversion to the female-equals-fuck mentality.

"The realtor left the key under the mat," Sommerville told him.

He turned his head at the sound of a barking dog. The animal was just ten feet away from him. It looked like a Labrador and sheltie mix, its coat streaked with gold and brown, its head on the small side. He didn't see a collar, so he shooed it away. He was *not* picking up a stray dog. He'd never been tied down by an animal before, and this detour was not going to rob him of his freedom. Dammit.

"Quit fooling around. Did you hear me?"

"Yes." Did the man have a camera planted somewhere too? He'd have to check.

"Okay, get going then. The sooner you make her fall for you, break her heart, and stop the article—the trifecta—the sooner you resume your life. Are you sure you won't reconsider returning to our former agreement after you're done up there?"

Tanner stabbed the key into the lock and opened the door. "No offense, but that's not going to work."

"Too bad. We could have done great things together."

He hauled the suitcases inside. "I need to unpack. As you said, the sooner this is done, the better."

"Good luck. I'll be in touch. Feel free to call me if you need to brainstorm. Meredith can be complex, but again, if you move quickly, she won't have the time to think things through. Nail her, nail her heart."

Tanner clicked the phone off, resisting the urge to hurl it across the polished hardwood floors. The house's open layout made him feel small. He surveyed his new pad with a scowl. Large wooden beams covered the ceiling. A massive stone chimney merged into a staircase, creating what some architect junkie would have called a nice line or flow or some bullshit. What was wrong with four walls and a roof anyway?

He thought about what Sommerville had said about rushing Meredith. Since their relationship had ended in failure, there was no way he was going to go for the same approach. Plus, he needed time to figure out how to extract himself from this mess.

And he didn't rush women.

He'd find a way to befriend her so he could update Sommerville and keep him off his back.

But first, he needed to check the house for cameras and bugs. He could disable the GPS later.

An hour later, he stomped a row of brand-new listening devices and kicked three small cameras against the stone wall.

"Goal!" He thrust his hands in the air and smiled for the first time in days. His phone chimed moments later. "You rang?" he answered smugly.

"I'm impressed," Sommerville responded.

Tanner picked up the destroyed equipment and dumped it into a trash can.

"We need to set some ground rules," Tanner began. "I don't want you spying on me. No cameras or listening devices. I also don't want you paying anyone here to keep tabs on me. You have me where you want me. You need to trust I'll do the job or you're going to compromise my cover. Meredith graduated from Columbia, so she's smart. It's a small town, and she's a journalist. You don't want her to look into why someone's keeping tabs on me, do you? If this ever gets out, it could ruin both of us."

Silence reigned for a full twenty seconds.

"Fine, but you'd better not pull a fast one. I'll print those pictures of your brother without thinking twice."

"I believe you. That's why I'm here."

"Okay, but don't fuck with me, McBride."

Tanner simply clicked the phone off. He headed to the back to look for the main receptacle, whistling shrilly in the quiet. Taking out the trash had never felt so good.

# Chapter 8

Meredith clutched the door to *The Western Independent* for a moment before pulling it open. The comforting smell of paper and ink hit her immediately. She took a cleansing breath and smiled as people called out greetings.

Her gramps had given her some time to settle into Dare, so today was her first official day.

She was hugged and kissed all the way down to her father's office. He sported new wire-rimmed glasses and was frowning at an article covered in red ink. It was good to see him ten pounds lighter. She hoped it would help his heart. He and her mom were leaving for Sedona the next morning.

"Problems?" she asked from the doorway.

His face broke into a grin. She felt the answering tug on her lips. How many times had she stood in this place, watching him mark up articles?

"Hi there." He stood up to hug her. Unlike his usual perfunctory embraces, he held her for a long moment before stepping back. "Welcome. I still don't know what to say about all this."

"You don't need to say anything, Daddy. Just promise me you'll take it easy."

After tossing and turning all night, she'd given herself a firm talking to. Being home was more than just a family duty. *The Independent* was a haven, a place where she'd grown up and learned the trade. This was her opportunity to give something back.

He took her shoulders. "A word of advice. I know you pretend not to be sensitive, but sometimes Pop Hale is a cranky old man with tough standards."

"I know. You don't have to protect me. I want to be here, Dad." And she realized it was true. Her heart wasn't racing anymore. She could breathe. And she didn't have to channel Divorcée Woman to feel comfortable.

This was her natural skin.

"I'm glad. Give me a call if you have any questions."

"No, Dad. I can ask Gramps anything."

The grooves around his face eased. "Okay, let's go talk to Pop. Just don't let him pressure you into taking over. I know you have a great job in New York, and I don't want you to stay here for my sake. You go where you're happy. Promise me, Mere."

Her eyes burned. "I promise."

He kissed her forehead like he used to when he picked her up from school to take her to the newspaper. She wrapped him in a hug until he cleared his throat and stepped away, and then they walked down the hallway together.

Various news broadcasts were playing in Arthur Hale's office, and stacks of newspapers covered his battered desk. It was chaotic and loud and messy—the complete opposite of her father's quiet sanctuary. Grandpa Hale was rubbing his neck when he caught sight of them, and his chair squeaked as he leaned back in it.

"Well, well, well. Seems my granddaughter does have black ink running through her veins like the rest of us." His wink was pure mischief.

Meredith held up her wrist. "Do you want to cut me for proof?"

He rose and gave her a bear hug. "Ah, that smart mouth. You raised her right, Alan. Can't have any mealy-mouthed women in the Hale family."

The ringing phone went unanswered.

"No, we can't," her dad responded.

"You ready for a permanent name plaque yet?"

"Now, Pop, she's only here to give me a break. Lay off."

"Hmm...We'll see about that. So, are you ready to get to work, missy?" Grandpa popped a red hot in his mouth.

"What do you have in mind?"

He scratched his chin. "Well, since you have a good sense of that East-coast bias we try to guard ourselves against, why don't you draw up some ideas for Sunday's editorial?"

The Sunday editorial was the most coveted spread in the paper. Only her father and grandpa wrote it regularly, with other famous ad-hoc people making an occasional cameo. Like presidential candidates trying to share their vision of the future with Western voters. Or the president himself. Carter had written on Middle East peace. Reagan had written on Russia being the evil empire. Clinton had waxed poetic on the importance of balancing the budget. Bush had shared his thoughts on the war against terrorism.

"You want *me* to write it?" She rocked back on her heels. Boy, Grandpa was certainly dangling the right carrot to make her stay. Her childhood dream had been to write the editorial.

"Isn't that what I just said, girl?" He tapped his ear. "Hell, I'm the one with the hearing aid."

"I'd love to!"

Her dad patted her back. "Good. I need to finish up some stuff before I leave. I'll see you both at dinner tonight."

"Yep," she replied as he left, her gaze drawn to the headlines on her grandfather's desk like a cat to catnip.

Grandpa Hale leaned back against his desk. "Now that your dad's gone, I want to be honest with you. I'm going to do everything in my power to make you want to stay and take over."

His intense gaze had her shuffling her feet. "I don't think I'm going to stay, Grandpa."

His bushy eyebrow winged up. "I know, but perhaps we can start with why you came back."

She looked over his shoulder at a picture of him shaking hands with Harvey Milk in San Francisco three days before the politician's death. Her goosebumps intensified. Her grandpa had done so much with his life. He'd interviewed every important American political actor in his storied career. People questioned her about him in hushed tones in New York City. Sometimes she forgot his achievements. To her, he was just her grandpa. But right now he was looking at her like an interview subject. It made her squirm.

"*Meredith.*"

"Ah...what? You know why."

"Bullshit. This timing is too coincidental. You decide to come home when Sommerville announced he's exploring a bid for the Senate. Are you sure you weren't running away?"

"Ah..." She couldn't tell him about her article. Her cheeks reddened at the mere thought.

"He's a self-important prick, and he was never the right man for you. I know your heart got broken, but it'll mend. Trust an old geezer who lost his sweetheart of fifty-plus years." He glanced down at the picture of Grandma Hale he kept on his desk, brushing his finger along the frame. "It's like relationships. You have to work at it."

"Are you saying you have to work to get over a broken heart?" Of all the things she'd read on the topic, his simple words made sense.

"And it takes time too. We'll help you all we can now that you're back, but we can't fully support you until we know why you're here."

She fingered the button on her blouse. God, she hated evasion.

"You're only making this more interesting to an old newspaperman." He reached over and tipped her chin up. "You know I'll find out if I put my mind to it. Did Sommerville threaten you? I always wondered if his cheating might be the kind that could ruin a man's reputation—especially if that man has political aspirations." He cracked his knuckles. "He didn't fight you much on a settlement. Do you have something on him?"

Meredith licked her lips and walked to the other side of his office, trying to control her panic. If he caught even a whiff of what she knew, he'd print it without hesitation. It would look bad if it appeared in her family paper. She couldn't allow that. If anyone was going to divulge the secret, it was her...and she'd only do it if Rick-the-Dick pushed her into a corner.

To distract him, she picked up *The Daily Herald*, which was lying on the top rack of his antique newspaper holder. "You read this?"

He snorted. "My granddaughter writes in it. Of course I do."

She fingered *The Standard* and held it up. "And this?" Rick-the-Dick would be flattered.

He studied her through his rimless bifocals. "I always read the enemy. It's the—"

"Third rule of journalism. I know all your rules. You're a good teacher."

"Don't think you can distract me." He sat back down in his chair, rubbing his hip. "You're tight-lipped. Fine. I'm going to find out if there's more. I'm damn good at digging."

Her lungs seized. Yes, he was. She didn't need this.

He rocked back and forth, the squeak competing for volume with the news programs on the TV and radio.

"Aren't you ever going to fix that squeaky chair?"

"No, it's a comfort. Reminds me of my age. Like this chair, I'm still working." He picked up a file. "If you change your mind about telling me, you know where to find me. You don't have to deal with Rick-the-Dick alone."

Her mouth dropped open. "How—"

"You Hale women. You think I don't know what you call him?"

She cleared her throat. "I've finished my research on the campus drug trade. There's not much to go on."

He handed her a file. "Well, take a look at this one. Like I told you, more and more college kids are ending up in the ER puking their guts out. A few of my friends' grandkids have been involved. Jill swears it's alcohol poisoning, but..." He popped in another red hot and crunched. "My gut says there's more."

She flipped through his notes, not even bothering to ask how he'd received the tox screens. "Doesn't look like the hospital found anything but marijuana and alcohol."

"Neither of those things usually make kids sick enough to puke like that. Something's not right." He pointed to her. "You need to convince Jill to ask some questions."

"No way."

He huffed.

"Anything else?"

His mouth twisted. "No. Have your ideas for the editorial on my desk tomorrow."

She picked at her button again, wanting to close the loop on his earlier speculation. "Please leave me in peace, Grandpa."

His eyes lifted from the page. "If I believed you were in peace, Mermaid, I would. But you're not. And since you won't tell me why, I'm going to have to dig." He picked up a file. "You're my granddaughter, and if that prick is bothering you, I won't tolerate it. Now, get out of here and let an old man do some work. Kitty has a desk for you."

Meredith left with feet of clay. Her hope of keeping things a secret had soured. Arthur Hale had teased the truth out of mendacious politicians. She didn't stand a chance. Damn. She didn't want to protect Rick, but the information she had on him would keep him from bothering her.

Would her grandpa care? Hell no. The public had a right to know.

She was dead meat.

# Chapter 9

Yºou girls have a good time," their mom called out as Jill and Meredith walked away from the house. "See you in the morning before we take off."

"Okay." They both waved at her, and she hustled inside.

"Man, I'm stuffed." Jill rubbed her belly. "Mom really is glad to have you back. Otherwise, why would she cook a spread like that right before they leave for three months?"

Meredith unlocked her Audi, marveling at the return of her appetite. It was like the switch to her taste buds and stomach had been flicked. She was actually craving food for the first time in forever. And she didn't feel too badly about it—yet.

"I've gotta start swimming again, or I'll be fatter than Aunt Harriet."

Jill snapped her seat belt on. "Right, like you'd ever have a weight problem. Fingernails feeling a bit heavy? Muffin-top cuticles?" She snorted. "You're skinnier than I've ever seen you."

"You can credit the divorce diet. And working out like crazy. Kept me sane."

"Well, those days are a thing of the past. We're going to go home, get dolled up, and head out to Hairy's tonight. Make sure you wear your best La Perla. I have a plan."

An hour later, Meredith followed Jill into Hairy's Pub. The owner had famously misspelled the name on the small business permit. Poor Harry O'Brien had too much Irish pride to admit he'd been drunk, so he called the name ironic. Since he was super hairy, most people agreed.

Harry had given into the new non-smoking ordinance, but he hadn't changed much else. A hardcore Irish band played on the speakers, reminding her of the theme song to *The Departed*. Stains and scuff marks dotted the hardwood floors. Wooden booths ran in rows, while the bar angled in an L shape.

A neon-colored rainbow with a pot of gold at the end flashed in time with a naughty leprechaun. Vintage Guinness beer signs and mirrors lined the wall along with placards of funny Irish sayings like *As you slide down the banister of life, may the splinters never point in the wrong direction*—ouch.

"It's packed," Jill yelled over the music. "I figured we could try some informal speed dating."

Meredith unwound her white scarf so the V-neck of her navy top was visible. "What?"

"This is a legal-only zone. Harry hates students. He'll call the cops over a fake ID, and everyone on campus knows it."

Jill sidled up to the bar and pulled Meredith through a throng of women. The TVs in the corner were playing old football games and ESPN's current programming. Meredith clutched her purse, channeling Divorcée Woman. She could do this. It only took confidence and courage, right?

Right.

"Hey, Mike," Jill called to the bartender.

Meredith remembered him—he had the reputation for being a total ladies' man. So not Duncan Swift from *High Noon*, more's the pity.

"My sister, Meredith, is back in town. We need your best pull. Murphy's."

He flashed her a wicked grin and reached for two glasses. "Let me know if you need a tour, sis."

"I will," she responded, not meaning it. She had no interest in a ladies' man. Been there, done that.

The bartender handed Jill the full glasses with a wink. She set Meredith's beer down while taking a sip from her own. "Okay, let's migrate to the corner. I can scan better from there and run you through your options."

Options? Meredith's lungs collapsed beneath her emerald green and black lace bustier. She couldn't draw a full breath. "I don't know...about this. I'm not big on the bar scene."

"Breathe."

"Trying." No panic attack. No. She took a drink of her beer and wiggled her nose. If she drank, she'd have to breathe, right?

"It'll be great. Trust me." Jill said, turning Meredith toward the room. "Ah, we've already got some attention. Good. You're new meat in town. This is going to be easy." She secured their purses on the hooks under the sideboard. "So, the tall one with the big shoulders in the corner is a fire fighter. Robbie Blaine. Think Gulliver Curry in *Chasing Fire* without the whole forest fire thing. He's single. Hot. Knows how to use his hose."

Meredith choked while taking a sip. Beer went down the wrong pipe, hops and something bitter burning her throat. She hacked like someone with emphysema while Jill pounded her back.

Suddenly strong hands took her shoulders and raised her up. "Okay, breathe now. Slow, easy breaths," came a deep voice from behind her.

When she could finally inhale normally, she looked at the man holding her. He had a round, serious face. Then he gave a slow smile, a dimple winking in his cheek. His glasses reflected her now red face.

"Better?"

"Yes," she rasped.

Jill raised her eyebrow. "Thanks, Dr. Kelly."

"My pleasure. Always happy to make sure no one dies from choking on beer."

"I bet you give a good Heimlich," Jill purred.

His mouth twitched. Meredith tried to step back. His hands tightened on her shoulders before dropping to his sides. "It's a difficult procedure. Important to be well trained." His gaze dropped to Meredith's lips. "Or someone might get hurt."

Whoa there, Nellie. This guy was outright flirting with her.

"Thanks," she replied and winced. Divorcée Woman would have come up with a more seductive response.

"My pleasure. You're new in town." He slid even closer.

"Sort of. I grew up here." Again, lame. She pressed her hand to her bustier, hoping for some inspiration.

He reached for a strand of her hair. "You're a Hale. No mistaking the red hair."

"Yes, Meredith." Help, please.

"Dr. Matt Kelly."

Jill bumped her with her hip, making Meredith want to hiss. She pasted on a smile as his gaze went further south. Man, the guy was totally checking her out.

"Maybe we could meet for a welcome-back-to-town coffee sometime."

His eyes came back up to meet hers. She could see her surprised reaction on the reflection on his glasses. It was unnerving. She lifted a shoulder. Did she want to go out with this guy? He was coming on a little strong for her, but what did she know? Besides, she was supposed to go out with guys. She pressed her hands to her ribcage, feeling the bustier again. Divorcée Woman could handle him. She could show him some interesting ways to use his stethoscope.

"Sure. How about Sunday?"

He flashed an all-perfect-teeth smile. "Great."

Matt took out a business card, making her feel like she was back in New York. Who in Dare gave a card?

"Give me a call, Meredith. We'll set something up." He ran a hand down her arm, ending with a small squeeze. "I'll take you someplace where you won't have to worry about choking. See ya around, Jill."

When he sauntered away, she let out a long breath.

Jill shook her hips, her teal skirt twirling. "Well hello there, tiger. I don't need to worry about you. You're a pro."

Her heart didn't agree. It was pounding like an Olympic runner's. "He made it easy."

Jill chuckled. "That's because he wants to get laid. It's every guy's dream."

"So what kind of doctor is he?"

"OB/GYN."

"Oh yuck."

No way Divorcée Woman would go out with someone who spent all day putting women in stirrups. Nothing hot—or even kinky—about that. Even Nora wouldn't go for that profession in a hero. Doctor, yes, but not a man who made his money looking up a woman's hoo-ha.

Jill bent over laughing, and then popped back up like a puppet. "Oh, that was fun. You should see your face." She wiped her teary eyes. "He's an internist at the hospital."

"I should have brought the hammer."

"Maybe he's your Dr. Brady Tucker from *Unfinished Business*. Okay, let's go find you some more action. Larry Barlow just came in."

She scanned the crowd until she saw Larry's bulky body moving toward the bar.

Meredith smiled when he waved at her. She lifted her hand in response. Divorcée Woman would cruise the room, her eyes heavy-lidded, her mouth pouty. She threw a wiggle into her hips as she followed Jill through the crowd.

Suddenly Larry appeared by her side and pressed a hand on her shoulder. "Jill, you don't mind if I borrow Meredith for a second, do you?" he asked.

When Jill nodded, Larry guided her away. She returned her sister's finger-fluttering wave.

"Look, I wanted to see if you wanted to go out sometime," he said, edging closer, making her feel a little crowded. "I'm sure it's hard to get back out there after your divorce. I can help."

When he pressed his hips against her sand-colored skirt, she got a pretty good idea what he meant by "help." Whoa. "That's kind of you, Larry." God, nice girl genes.

He rubbed his finger along her throat. "When I see something I want, I go for it."

His pushiness was off-putting and then some. Any comparison to a Nora cop hero went up in smoke. "That's good to know."

He leaned down and pressed a kiss to her neck. She tried to move. He wouldn't let go.

"Let's get out of here. I have a hankering to see the Big Apple."

Whatever he meant by that didn't bear contemplating. "Please, let go of me."

His beer breath fanned her face. So, he'd already been drinking.

"There's no need to pretend. I know you want it."

She pushed harder when she couldn't dislodge his grip. She tried to tell herself she was safe in public. His mouth skimmed her neck again.

"When I say, 'let me go,' I mean it, Officer."

He finally let her wrench back, but he kept his meaty hand on her shoulder. "The cool ones always fight the hardest. Makes it all the sweeter. Come on, Meredith. Let's go someplace."

Just then, Jill materialized from the crowd. "Excuse me, Larry," she said, "but my best friend just arrived and wants to see Meredith." Pulling Meredith away, she gave him a bright smile over her shoulder. "We'll catch you later."

Meredith heaved out a breath. "I could have handled it."

Jill pushed through the crowd. "I don't give a damn. He was all over you. You looked scared."

"I was. Thanks for coming to my rescue."

"You're not alone anymore, Mere. Besides, Jemma really does want to see you."

"It's been way too long."

When they reached Jemma, Meredith gave her a big hug. She hadn't seen her since her visit home right after her dad's heart attack. "My God, look at you! I love what you've done with your hair."

Her short black hair was curled close to her head, and with her big, dark eyes, she looked like a modern-day flapper.

"I cut it all off when Pete dumped me."

Meredith nodded. Jill had told her about Pete Collins and Jemma breaking up. They'd been cozy since high school and everyone had thought were headed for marriage.

"I told her she looks hot." Jill put her arm around her.

"She's the best, isn't she, Meredith?" Jemma cried. "I'm so glad you're back. I love your hair too, by the way."

Meredith flicked a red curl. "Back to eau natural."

"Looks good on you."

"Thanks. How've you been?"

"Besides Pete breaking my heart? There's not much else. Got any pointers for getting over worthless men?"

It was depressing to see Jemma so muted over a man. She and Jill were usually two peas in a pod. Loud, energetic, and affable.

"Sorry, no great wisdom. Eat lots of chocolate."

"Already tried. And ice cream. I only gain weight." She slapped her hip.

Jill threw up her hands. "Okay, enough moping. We're here to help Mere get back in the saddle. We need to erase the Larry episode from her mind, so let's troll."

"Jillie, please don't use that word."

Her sister only winked bawdily in response. "Follow me."

Two hours later with Jill and Jemma guiding her through the room as the perfect wingwomen, Meredith had three more numbers. Jill was right about Hairy's being the right place to go to on a Friday night. Her arms felt tenderized from all the flirtatious squeezes she'd received. Divorcée Woman would consider it a badge certifying her hotness.

Robbie the fireman didn't have a card. When he wrote his number on the inside of her wrist, her skin tingled, and she was instantly transported back to college. Who *wrote* on people anymore? He was cute in a hulky way. His offer to take her for a ride in his fire truck was one of the worst attempts at flirtation she'd experienced in a long time. He clearly didn't know their family was close friends with Ernie, the long-time fire chief, who'd given her and Jill rides growing up. She'd agreed anyway.

Bill Kiever was a forest ranger, a bit short for her taste, but as burly as a rugby player. He'd invited her on an easy hike to "get her back in the swing of things." Meredith hoped she'd be safe wandering into the wild with him. His eyes weren't crazy like some serial killer's. Besides, she'd take her cell phone and a can of pepper spray. She could always claim it was for warding off rogue wildlife. Of course, Divorcée Woman would use the chopstick holding up her hair to take him down and her bra straps to tie his hands and feet. Who needs rope when you have La Perla?

And then there was Avery Miller. He owned the new cheese shop in town called *Don't Wedge Me In*. Avery was definitely a metrosexual or whatever the heck the current term was. He was a San Francisco transplant, and he seemed to be a nice guy and a good conversationalist. And he wasn't pushy. He hid his regard for her better than the others. She didn't think he'd try to force his tongue down her throat like Deputy Larry. After all, Divorcée Woman liked slow, come-hither kisses on the first date.

She was on her third beer when she caught sight of a new man coming through the door. After flirting all night with a few different guys, her sexual attraction meter was humming along quite nicely. She was channeling Divorcée Woman without thinking. No touching her bodice or anything.

Her gauge did more than hum as she watched this man's well-muscled body walk across the room to the end of the bar. It gave a *Pa Rum Pa Pum Pum*.

His height made him easy to follow. His dark, thick hair wasn't fussy, and she could tell he wasn't one of those guys who used more hair product than she did. His face had the rugged appearance of someone who lived with constant tension, giving him a hot Alpha look she usually didn't go for. There was an air of danger, a watchfulness about him.

And then he smiled at the female bartender. His granite jaw turned devilish, and she'd swear his eyes twinkled. He didn't laugh with the woman pulling his beer, but he gave her his total focus, like she was the only person he was interested in listening to in the whole world. That intensity made her stop breathing for a moment. Oh, to have a guy's full attention like that. She bet he'd smell good too—all musky, like a man should.

*Pa Rum Pa Pum Pum.* Meredith winced as she realized the lyrics were about the Baby Jesus at Christmas. So not appropriate for lusting after a man in a bar.

What would Divorcée Woman do? She would saunter down the bar, give him the look, and lead him out of the bar. Take him to a hotel room, strip him down slowly, run her hands over his gorgeous body, and use him for hot, screaming sex.

He scanned the bar with focused intensity. Meredith couldn't make out the color of his eyes, but she wanted to know what it was. His jaw sported a five o'clock shadow. Her heart pounded to the beat of the Irish drums blasting over the speakers, and she licked her lips. Wow. Just wow.

"Who are you looking at?" Jill asked and then uttered, "Oh, him."

"I feel like Shane Abbot when she saw Vance Banning for the first time," Meredith muttered.

"Ah, *First Impressions*. I loved that book," Jill hummed.

"You two," Jemma complained.

Meredith continued to study the newcomer. Her eyes fluttered when he turned his back. Muscles rippled under his white shirt as he reached for his Guinness. She catalogued them in her mind—trapezius, latissimus dorsi, rhomboid, and serratus. Oh, God, why did she have a thing for strong back muscles? Oh yeah, because she'd spent her formative years with swimmers. And boy, did male swimmers have good ones.

"I don't know him." Jill craned her neck when a gigantic older guy stepped in their line of vision. "But yummy, yummy. Let's get closer."

Meredith pressed her hands to her ribcage and tried to draw a breath. Her skin was tight. And her nipples were hard. Her chemical reaction to this man was over the top.

Fear suddenly trickled down her back like an ice cube. She hadn't been with a man since Richard. Was she really ready to get involved with someone who had this type of power over her body from across a room? Well maybe...not really...oh hell.

*But it's the power that makes you scream*, that throaty voice said in her head again, the one she'd heard when she arrived. *And when have you ever let yourself do that?*

Even though it was a little weird having the voice in her head, she knew it was her alter ego talking. Funny how the words kinda comforted her.

Jill pushed her toward the bar, Jemma following behind, but before Meredith could make it to the mystery guy, a strong arm wrapped around her shoulders. She looked up into Brian McConnell's smiling face.

"Hi there," she cried, feeling both relieved by the delay and annoyed by it.

"Hey, Mermaid. You out cruising?" He looked back at Jill, who immediately turned her head away, scanning the bar. "Hi, Jem."

"We were getting a drink, dipwad," Jill announced.

He reached for Jill's beer and pried it out of her hand. When he took a sip, he said, "Tastes sweeter than I remember." Jemma looked from one of them to the other, a worried expression on her face.

Inching out from under his arm, Meredith cringed when she saw her sister's feral expression. "Must be the keg. Or maybe you actually brushed your teeth before you came out tonight."

Brian lifted his arm, pretending to sniff. "I think I put on deodorant too. Wanna check?"

He took a step toward Jill, who immediately took a step away from him. The two of them marched backwards three steps like graceful tango dancers before Jill knocked into a couple at the bar. She elbowed Brian hard and stalked over to Meredith and Jemma.

"We need to go, Brian," Meredith said. Time to be the big sister before things got ugly.

"Didn't know I could scare you off, Red," he yelled over the music.

Jill leaned in toward him before Meredith could pull her away. "You don't scare me. You never have, and you never will."

"Okay, you two, that's enough," Jemma cried out. "I'm tired of seeing my friends fight."

Ignoring Jemma, Brian snagged the beer from Jill's hand again. As he raised it to his lips, his eyes were fixed on Jill's face. "That's bullshit, and we both know it. You damn well know why I scare you."

"Brian," Jemma warned.

Jill crossed her arms. "Oh yeah?"

Resting the hand holding the beer on Jill's shoulder, he said, "You're afraid I'll ruin you for other men."

"Brian—" Meredith and Jemma said at the same time.

"Stay out of it," Jill snapped. "Your arrogance is beyond words, McConnell."

Brian took her hand and put the beer back in it. He didn't let go though. Was he looking to get hit?

"Maybe." He lowered his head. "The truth is I was worried you might ruin me for other women."

Meredith's mouth dropped open. Well, that was hot.

Brian kept Jill in place with a hand. "But I was too young and stupid to let that happen."

Jill bit her lip, but didn't step back. "And you're telling me this now because..."

The forced indifference in her voice made Meredith clutch her purse tighter. Oh, Jill.

Brian ran a finger over her cheek with his free hand. "I'm saying it because I'm not so young anymore."

Jill's throat moved. She pulled away from Brian, edging back. "Thank you for clearing that up for me, McConnell, but since we're the same age, I damn well know how old you are. Now stay away from me."

Grabbing Meredith and Jemma's arms, she angled them through the crowd like a snake through grass.

Jemma hugged her when they got to the door. "I'm going to go talk to him, Jill. I'll call you later," she said, and then headed back toward Brian.

Meredith gave the tall guy a final wistful look before they burst out into the cool night air. Well, too bad, but her sister needed her more than she needed a hook-up.

Jill made a beeline for the car. "That man is a total and utter..." She trailed off, put her hands in her hair, and shrieked so loud the couple making out by the door disengaged from each other. "And I'm tired of Jemma trying to make us get along. I'm not forcing her to be Pete's friend."

"Let's go home, Jill."

Jill leaned against her. "Mere, maybe you shouldn't do this article. What if there are no good men out there? What if you only get hurt again?"

Meredith thought about Nora Roberts Land. She had to believe it existed.

"I won't let that happen."

She thought back to the guy who made her body give a Christmas carol *Pa Rum Pa Pum Pum*. It was almost sacrilegious. She didn't know who he was, but she wanted to find out.

Didn't mean she had to do something about it. She could call it research.

So far he was the one man who had made her insides zing like only a Nora Roberts hero could.

# Chapter 10

Meredith thrust away from the wall of the Community Center's pool after doing an underwater turn and resumed her stroke. It was glorious to have the pool to herself, but there was a price to pay—it was six in the morning. She was fifteen minutes into her swim and hitting her stride. Man, she loved freestyle. Her legs kicked powerfully. Her hand broke the surface at the perfect angle, and she stretched it out before making a powerful S through the water, pulling until her arm reached her waist. Her other arm followed suit. She counted—one, two, three—and then took a breath.

She always swam off her frustration, and boy was she frustrated. After having two dates in the last three days, she'd just sent her first email update to Karen. First up had been Matt Kelly, the Mr. Know-It-All Doctor. Man, that guy had a god complex. He had neither asked her any questions nor bothered to listen when she managed to squeeze a word in edgewise. He'd asked to see her again after trying to kiss her. She'd told him she was busy. Permanently.

The hike with Forest Ranger Bill hadn't been awful, just dull as dirt. He'd droned on and on like she was a biology student titillated by nature stories. He'd even pointed out some cat scat. Well, she wasn't a Girl Scout—she only liked the cookies. When he told her he'd love to show her some falls on their second date, she'd declined.

So far, she only had two things to say in her article, and neither was life affirming.

Dating again sucked balls.

And that whole adage about having to kiss a lot of frogs to find your prince? Well, frog legs were more appetizing.

She made another turn and pushed off the wall again. Another body appeared in the water at the end of the pool, visible from the waist down from her underwater perspective. She noted the rippling muscles in the man's abdomen and the dark arrow of chest hair that headed down into tight black swim trunks. As she swam closer, he pushed off the wall and began to swim like someone had fired the starting gun. Powerful freestyle strokes sliced through the water in the lane next to her, and he passed her in a blur, bubbles rippling. She pushed off the wall again and started swimming faster.

His technique was picture-perfect. He surged ahead, all power and speed. She'd bet her morning coffee he was professionally trained.

And then he switched to the butterfly stroke three laps later and confirmed her impression. His body thrust out of the water, his arms spreading out like an eagle, before surging back into it, giving an eel-like kick.

When he switched to breast stroke, a healthy streak of competitiveness kicked in, and she followed suit. She watched him out of her peripheral vision like she had when she was racing at Columbia. She caught the chop from his stroke.

She knew the minute he started racing her. His head angled a fraction before he submerged himself for another lap. Then she did nothing but concentrate on her stroke—and his position.

He was significantly taller, which made him eat up the distance faster. But she weighed less and was slightly more agile on the turns.

Her heart thundered in her chest as she pulled through the bubbles dancing in the water. When she briefly surfaced, she checked the clock. She'd been swimming for nearly an hour. Her legs and arms burned with fatigue. She craved Gatorade.

She sprinted as fast as she could as they turned into the next lap. He stayed with her, inching ahead. She kicked faster, pulling them even. She caught sight of the cross sign at the end of the pool, and she surged and pulled and snapped her legs together like a demented frog. When she reached the front of the pool, she slapped her hands against the wall to stop. Her competitor made the turn and swam on.

She sucked in air when she pulled herself to a standing position, her skin hot against the cold water, her heart pounding. Sweat drops coated her Gatorade bottle. She took small sips, knowing she'd only cough it up.

Her companion thundered toward her in his blue swimming cap and silver reflective goggles before slowing and stopping. When he finally stood in the water, his breath was whooshing in and out. He reached for his green water bottle.

She couldn't help but stare at his body. His arms looked like they'd been chiseled out of stone, and his abs set a new record for washboard. She left her goggles on. Having red marks around her eyes was so not attractive.

He flashed a grin after draining half the bottle. "You give as good as you get. I didn't expect such healthy competition this early in the morning, but you have my deepest thanks."

She grinned right back. "Ditto. I haven't raced like that in years. You know your stuff."

He took a deep breath, and his rib cage lifted, making his muscles ripple like the water around him. Her nipples tightened. God, what a body. Perhaps he was a lost Chippendale dancer or something. Maybe his car had broken down on the way to Vegas, and he needed to stay here until it was fixed.

"You've got a great form there." He tugged his goggles off. Melting brown eyes crinkled as he grinned at her.

God, he looked good wet. Water dripped down his body like raindrops on a windowpane. He made her want to run into the locker room for dollar bills so she could see how many she could stick to his nearly naked body.

She looked down shyly. "Thanks. I try to keep in shape."

"I was talking about your technique."

He was? Oh, Lord. She'd been drooling over his body, and she'd thought he was doing the same. Who was she kidding? She was wearing a white swim cap and blue goggles—she probably looked ridiculous.

His eyes ran down her body. "Of course, that's pretty nice too."

Her face heated despite the droplets of cool water covering her skin.

He stretched his arms overhead, and her mouth instantly went dry. She reached for more Gatorade. Her nipples tightened when he thrust out of the water onto the deck, his back muscles rippling in perfect motion. Oh man, he had the best back—and ass. He pulled off his swim cap and ran a hand through his short brown hair.

She choked on fruity Gatorade when recognition finally clicked in.

"You okay?" he asked, kneeling on the tiles.

The man leaning over her in all his male glory was the guy she'd admired at Hairy's Pub the other night. He might be wet, but she remembered him now. Right down to the *Pa Rum Pa Pum Pum*. And dammit, he looked as good wet as he did dry.

Her body went nuclear, alarms sounding, lights flashing. Alert, alert. Warning, warning.

He extended his hand. "Let me help you out."

Before she could think, he'd gently pulled her up and out of the water with enough strength to set her thighs to quivering. His cold hands had the power to produce fire, she discovered, as heat shot up her arms even as goosebumps broke out across her body. She wanted to die of embarrassment, knowing how ugly those red bumps looked on cold white skin. Add her obvious nipplage, and she looked like a horny swimmer recently released from a female prison. She dashed for her towel before realizing it would look weird if she secured it around her chest.

This was so not the way she wanted to meet this guy! She was supposed to have on La Perla, makeup, and a hot outfit.

"You swim here often?" He approached her in nothing but those skin-tight black trunks. His defined thighs and definite bulge left nothing to the imagination. Oh my.

He towered over her, likely six three, if she had to bet. His mouth lifted on the right side, but he didn't say anything. He put his hands on his trim waist, making her swallow thickly. "Well, do you?"

Water droplets ran down her face from her swim cap. His damn pheromones were fogging up her supposed anti-fog goggles. Must be a manufacturer's defect.

"I'm planning to."

"Good. We can race some more. I think both of us will like it."

*That isn't all I'd like,* Divorcée Woman purred.

*Oh, shut up*, she replied, and then shook her head. Was she really carrying on a conversation with her alter ego?

His wet, jet-black eyelashes framed expressive chocolate eyes. He slung his towel around his neck, making her already burning legs threaten to buckle beneath her. Was this a faint coming on? Perhaps she needed oxygen. Did the gym have a tank somewhere?

Oh, God, she had it bad. Best to bail now. Introduce herself when she was...put together. No guy would want her like this.

"I'm Tanner." He extended his hand. "I'm new in town and a journalist...ah, I'm teaching at Emmits Merriam this quarter." His smile twisted. "I'm still getting used to thinking of myself that way."

He was a journalist?

Her heart twisted. She didn't care how hot he was. After Rick-the-Dick, she'd made a solemn vow to never date another journalist.

Did she have the worst luck or what?

She eyed his hand, afraid of the sparks any contact between them might generate. She took it with hesitation. A strong current shot up her arm.

"Nice to meet you," she muttered before she said something else. Like, "Would you show me your moves, Chippendale? I've got some money in my purse."

Oh, I'm a total idiot. He's a journalist, and this party ain't gonna happen. Ever.

She dropped his hand when her nipples tightened again. "I need to go." She hurried away from the pool, stopping when she skidded on the wet tiles.

The NO RUNNING sign mocked her as she ducked into the woman's locker room.

Was she running? Oh yeah.

She wasn't up for a do-over. No matter how hot he was.

# Chapter 11

Tanner emerged from the gym with wet hair and headed for his SUV. He looked around the parking lot for a slim woman with delicious porcelain skin and wet hair, but he didn't see anyone. She had been quite a surprise. He'd never imagined he'd come across a competitive swimmer like his lap mate in this podunk town. She glided through the water like a gazelle. And damn did she have good form. Both in and out of the water.

If he hadn't seen a lock of red hair slicked against her ear, he might have guessed she was Meredith Hale, but he knew Meredith was a blond.

He wished she had taken off her goggles and swim cap, but he understood. The female swimmers he knew always complained about the outfit's sexlessness.

It hadn't covered up her beaded nipples. He suspected her reaction was from more than cold, but he couldn't be sure. He'd seen the interest in her eyes before her goggles had fogged up. God knows, his trunks had gotten tight looking at her wet skin and tight body.

Then she'd totally frozen him out and run off.

Maybe she was married.

Maybe he needed to focus on what he'd come here to do.

Still, he couldn't stop thinking about her. She had a few freckles scattered across her skin, a mole under her right shoulder blade, and a tight, rounded bottom. He'd wanted to connect the dots when she'd turned to reach for her towel.

He didn't know her name, but he *wanted* to know it. He'd admired some women in and around town, but this woman—well, there was something about her. And her voice. It was like sipping Baileys, creamy, soothing, with a kick at the end. She was feminine but strong, exactly how he liked his women.

Well, he'd see her at the pool again. Perhaps he'd even run into her beforehand.

Too bad he couldn't do anything about it, he decided. He couldn't go out with other women here, not when he was trying to make Meredith Hale fall in love with him or spend time with him or whatever the hell he was going to do to get Sommerville off his fucking back.

With that in mind, he took off to the coffee shop owned by Meredith's sister, Jill, which Sommerville's file had mentioned as a good place to run into his "target." He pulled into a parking space on Main Street. The shop already had a slow but steady stream of patrons. God, he hoped it wasn't some fruit loop place that only carried sprouts and organic shit. If it didn't have fucking whole milk, he was going to be really pissed.

He pushed the door open, his nose twitching at the smell of the pungent dark roast. After a quick scan, part of him was glad none of the patrons was Meredith. He begrudgingly headed to the counter.

Is this what his life came down to? Being attracted to some anonymous swimmer, stalking someone's ex, and craving whole milk?

Richard Sommerville was going to pay.

*** 

Jill manned the cash register with a swing in her step. She tapped her foot to the Harry Connick, Jr., song pouring through the loudspeakers. It wasn't Abba, but Jemma had won the morning music coin toss. She wasn't going to fight it. A bitchy barista made bad coffee.

She called out another order as the door chimed. When she caught sight of the customer, her eyes opened wide, like she'd just downed an espresso shot. It was the guy who Mere had liked at Hairy's Pub. Oh yeah! Sista Pimp could do some matchmaking this morning and make up for what had happened the other night.

When he stepped up to the counter, studying the pastry case, she gave him a big smile. "Hi there. You're new in town, right?"

His eyes lifted from the long line of muffins. "Yes, how'd you guess?"

"When you work in a coffee shop, you tend to know everyone. I'm Jill. What's your name?"

He straightened, giving her a curious look through deep chocolate eyes. Mere sure could pick them. He was easily a decade older than Jill, but she could still appreciate his good looks. He was a total Clooney—he'd aged well and would probably keep doing so. Mere was so going to owe her.

"I'm Tanner."

"Hi Tanner, what can I get you?"

He scanned the chalkboard menu. "Please tell me you have whole milk."

"Of course. It's only called Don't Soy With Me. It's a—"

"Play on words. Got it. How about a grande mocha with an extra shot of chocolate?"

So he had a sweet tooth to match those eyes. "Whipped cream on top?"

"Yes, please."

Oh, a man who said please. After working retail for a while before opening the shop, she knew how rare that was. She called out his order to Jemma. "Here or to go?"

"To go."

"What else?"

"What's the best pastry in your opinion?"

She hummed. "Well, if I were going to splurge...Are you going to splurge, Tanner?"

His mouth twisted into a cute grin. Mere was a goner. "Splurge on...?"

"Calories. I have to watch myself." She pointed to herself. Her size eight looked good on her because she was on the tall side, but she knew she could easily pack on weight if she didn't watch it.

"You women worry too much about that crap. You look fine. And yes, I plan to splurge. How's the éclair?"

"Not my favorite. How do you feel about jelly donuts? This one has fresh huckleberry compote in it."

He fished his wallet out of his back pocket. "Never had huckleberries. Sounds good."

She rang him up, pleased no one was behind him. It meant she could pump him for information. "So what brings you to town?"

"I'm teaching in the journalism department at Emmits Merriam."

It clicked. "Oh, you're Tanner McBride, the international correspondent I've been hearing about."

He cocked his head, his gaze direct. "Are you a journalism student or something?"

She laughed, twirling the tip jar with her hand. "Oh that's funny, but you shouldn't say that too loud. People will get ideas." She held up her wrists. "No black ink in these veins. Much to my family's disappointment. So, Tanner, do you want to come over to my family's house for dinner on Friday night?" she asked, deciding they'd use her parent's house since her mom had a bigger and better stocked kitchen than hers or her grandpa's.

He dipped his head, covering his expression. "I appreciate the invitation, Jill," he said softly, "and forgive me for being direct, but do you always ask new customers over for dinner?"

Her hand cupped her mouth in an effort to repress her laughter. "Heavens no. And don't worry, I'm not coming onto you either." She pointed to herself and sputtered. "You're way too old for me. No offense."

Jemma barked out a laugh from behind her.

Jill nabbed a jelly donut with the tongs and slid it into a paper bag. "I asked because I thought you'd be interested in meeting my family, being a journalist and all." A little prevarication wasn't a bad thing since she was helping her sister. "Have you ever heard of *The Western Independent*? Would you like to meet my grandpa, Arthur Hale?"

He blinked a few times before a grin broke out across his nicely chiseled face. "He's a legend. I'd love to meet him, Jill."

"Great." She wanted to twirl around like a top. "My sister, Meredith, just got back in town. She's a journalist too."

He tugged on the cuffs of his blue dress shirt. "I've heard of her. She worked for *The Standard* and *The Daily Herald*, right?"

"Yes, she did. How did you know?"

"She's a Columbia grad like me. I'm sure I read it in the alumni news."

"You went to Columbia too?" Oh this was too good. Mere was going to be over the moon.

"I sure did." He walked over to pick up his to-go coffee from Jemma, who still had a big smirk on her face. "I'd love to meet everyone. I've admired your grandfather for years. What he's done out here with *The Western Independent* is remarkable. I used to read it online overseas, especially at election time."

"Oh, Grandpa will just love that. Dad had to do some major convincing to put it online. Gramps isn't much on technology."

"What can I bring?"

"Just yourself. How about seven o'clock on Friday?"

"Perfect, and I'll bring a bottle of something. White or red?"

She wanted to float. "Red." She pulled out her lucky Flying Purple People Eater pen and wrote their address on a napkin, along with her cell phone number. "Here. It'll be fun."

Another customer sauntered forward, and Tanner moved aside. "See you then. Thanks for the invite."

When he walked out, she executed a ballerina leap across the length of the pastry case.

"Good work!" Jemma cried.

Jill took her hands and swung them around. "Mere's going to love me."

Could she keep the secret from Meredith for three full days? Sure, she could.

She did the cha, cha, cha, imagining Meredith's happiness.

# Chapter 12

Meredith choked on her red wine when she caught a glimpse of Tanner sitting next to her grandfather in the family room, looking smoking hot in tan slacks and a gray dress shirt.

Jill elbowed her. "Why do you keep doing that? Maybe you should see Dr. Kelly...professionally."

She turned her back on Tanner, fussing with her green low-back top and black pants. "*This* is our mystery dinner guest?" she hissed.

Like Helen of Troy, her sister's beautiful smile could have launched a thousand ships. "Yes, isn't it great? He walked right into the coffee shop. I invited him to dinner straight away. I owed you after making us flee Hairy's because of all the Brian drama the other night."

"Are you two done conferring like defense lawyers?" Grandpa Hale inquired, tapping his cane on the hardwood floor.

When Meredith turned around, her eyes instantly met Tanner's wide chocolate brown ones.

"*You're* Meredith Hale?" His brows snapped together. "But you're the girl from the pool!"

She clutched her wine glass to her chest. "Ah...how can you tell?"

He walked toward her, pointing to her back. "You have a..." His finger dropped. His gaze slid to Jill, who was eagerly—and unabashedly—listening. "I'll tell you some other time."

He studied Meredith with enough intensity that she feared she'd snap the stem of her wine glass. She dimly heard her grandpa ask Jill something over the buzzing in her ears. Sista Pimp faded away with a smirk.

"You have red hair." He sounded incredulous.

She frowned. "What? You don't like redheads?" Oops, that came out wrong.

"On the contrary." He continued staring. "I...couldn't tell the color under your swim cap." When he leaned closer, her whole body tingled like someone had plugged her into an electric outlet.

"What are you doing?" She clutched her wine glass to her bustier. Come on, Divorcée Woman, help me out.

"I wondered about your eyes behind the goggles. They're green."

"Yes." She noted the golden ring around his pupils—caramel coating chocolate. Desperate to break eye contact, she walked around him to kiss her grandpa, who was sitting on the couch. Her legs shook like a newborn calf.

*Chicken*, Divorcée Woman chimed in.

"It's about time you got to me. I know I'm an old man, but I'm still blood."

She pinched his ruddy cheek. "Old, my...eye. You tore my editorial to pieces, old man."

He waggled his bushy brows. "No, I simply restructured it. It reads better now. Don't you think?"

It did, but it galled her to admit it.

"Makes an old man happy to know he still has things to teach you after being in the Big Apple." He patted her arm. "Better watch out for this one, Tanner. She could run circles around you."

Tanner lifted his wine glass in a mock toast. "We'll see."

Jill was perched on the leather footstool in front of their grandfather, her yellow dress dotted with red dragons.

"I'm Tanner McBride by the way. I didn't give you my last name when we met."

If she'd been drinking her wine, she would have choked again. Tanner McBride, the journalist. And he was going to be teaching at Emmits Merriam. She hadn't put two and two together before.

"So, you two have met before?" Jill asked.

"We...sorta swam at the pool at the same time," Meredith said, glaring at Jill. *Don't you dare say anything, Sista Pimp,* she tried to say with the look, *or he'll know I practically had a sensual seizure over him at Hairy's the other night.*

"I've read your work," she continued smoothly when it was clear Jill intended to keep her trap shut. "It's good."

That was modest praise. He was fabulous at capturing political undercurrents and the human dimension of violence. He'd reported from Jerusalem, Beirut, Baghdad, and Kabul. Under other circumstances, she'd have been delighted to meet him. There was plenty of substance to go along with that incredible body.

But there was still one problem.

He was a journalist.

She hadn't told Jill about her vow, thinking she wouldn't run into any problems in Dare. She was related to most of the people who worked on the paper, after all.

Her vow was like not dating a man with your ex's name. It just wasn't done.

"He's damn good," Grandpa Hale commented. "Have to talk you into writing some articles for *The Independent* while you're here."

"It would be an honor, sir. I'd be happy to start now. My fingers have been itching to write up a good story."

"It's a deal then," her grandpa announced, reaching out to shake Tanner's hand.

"Dinner's ready," Jill announced. "I don't have mom's talents, but we won't starve. Plus, Meredith helped. She's much better in the kitchen than I am."

"You should have cooked at my house," Grandpa scolded.

"I ruled that out. You barely have coffee."

"I'm a lonely bachelor now, Tanner. My wife of nearly fifty years passed a few years ago. If you find one like her, snatch her up quick. They're damn rare."

Grandpa put his arm around Meredith, as if implying she was one of the rare ones. She was tempted to dig her elbow into his side.

"Let's head to the dining room," she said quickly.

Gramps positioned Tanner directly across from her. When he winked, she gave him the stink eye. He was probably imagining happy little reporter children running around with black ink in their veins, asking teachers and classmates if the school milk was contaminated. He'd love to have this guy in the family.

She glanced at Jill, who blew her a kiss. Everyone but her seemed happy with the situation.

Okay, that wasn't fair. Rick-the-Dick had been a journalist, and they hadn't liked *him*. Not one bit. Well, they knew bupkis about their dinner guest, so for all they knew, he could be just as bad.

When she glanced over at Tanner, she noticed he was fighting a smile. Oh yeah, he knew exactly what was going on. Amused, was he? Well, haha.

After eating their way through sautéed chicken breasts, garlic mashed potatoes, and asparagus with nacho cheese sauce—so Jill—Meredith rose to help her sister make coffee and serve dessert.

Tanner put a hand on Jill's shoulder. "I'm sure you make better coffee than I do, but please, let me do something. Meredith, would you mind showing me around your mother's kitchen?"

She rose since it would look impolite to decline. When the kitchen door swung shut behind her and Tanner, Meredith turned and put her hands on her hips. "You're awfully helpful."

He shrugged—all tall, muscular man. "It's the least I could do." He filled the coffee pot with water. "Plus, I wanted to be alone with you for a minute, so it seemed like a good plan. Where's the coffee?"

Meredith pulled the container out of the cherry cupboard. "Why?" she asked, but she already knew. Her heart beat in strong smacks against her ribcage.

He didn't measure the coffee. "You're a smart girl, so I'm sure you can figure it out. I'll tell you anyway, though...I was intrigued by the woman I met at the pool."

She crossed her arms over her bustier, appalled she was so turned on by something as pedestrian as a man making coffee. "How did you know it was me when we met in the family room? I've been swimming for most of my life, and even I have trouble recognizing people when they have their clothes on."

His lips twitched. "Interesting way of putting it." He hit the on button.

The sound of percolating water punctuated the silence. When he walked toward her, she stepped back and hit the counter. His smile spread as he moved closer. *Pa Rum Pa Pum Pum* filled her head again. Her gaze slid to his full lips. He had a small scar near his mouth, but it only made him manlier. Her body tightened as she inhaled the scent of his musky cologne mixed with the smell of coffee.

"You have a mole under your right shoulder blade, and that shirt makes it easy to see it." His hushed tone raised the hairs on her arms. "You also have another mole I found incredibly sexy, but I couldn't see it in the family room..." His gaze slid down her body. "Since you have pants on."

Oh. My.

"Of course, the next time we race, I plan to look for it again."

When he met her eyes, she licked her dry lips.

*Jump him*, Divorcée Woman drawled. *You know you want to.*

Oh, shut up. "So we're racing again?" She sounded like a breathy harlot.

He leaned closer and ran his hand down her arm, setting off nuclear nerve endings. "Be a shame not to when we match each other so well stroke for stroke."

Her thigh muscles spasmed. "Are you always this forward?"

"We're only talking about swimming, Meredith," he said, his dress shoes nudging her black ballet flats.

She cocked her head, fighting the urge to flick her hair over her shoulder. "Oh yeah?"

His mouth tipped up. "Well, yes, and your mole. So what's your favorite stroke?"

Her heart thundered so fast in her chest it felt like someone had pressed the pedal to the metal. Were they really flirting over swimming strokes?

*Who cares?* Divorcée Woman interjected. *It's hot.*

"Freestyle," she responded in that same raspy voice, a la Marilyn Monroe.

Tanner hummed. It reverberated through her body.

"Long, even strokes characterized by power and endurance."

She flushed with heat.

He gazed at her mouth as he continued. "I like to warm up with freestyle, but finishing with the butterfly is the only way to go. It's all about build-up. Once you're limber, you need to take your stroke to the next level. Surging and thrusting out of the water with power and coordination, your lungs burning as you race to the finish line."

Was she going to faint? She felt light-headed.

*Faint into him, you idiot!* Divorcée Woman yelled in her head.

"Perhaps we can compare notes the next time we swim."

Meredith dropped her gaze from his face and studied the strong arms filling out his gray dress shirt. She remembered what those muscles looked like dripping wet. Whimpering would be totally inappropriate, but she wanted to. God, the man was as intoxicating as Valrhona bittersweet chocolate.

He put his hands on either side of her, brushing their bodies together in a wildly tempting caress. "Maybe we could go out for breakfast after our next swim."

The idea of going out for breakfast with this man fired up her imagination about other things...like wild sex and a sleep over. She leaned back for breathing room, but there was nowhere to go. He surrounded her. She couldn't smell anything but him, and the counter was biting into her back.

He had her body purring, but that damn wounded part of her was sounding the alarms. Her lack of confidence—courtesy of Rick-the-Dick's hurtful parting words—clanged like a train trolley.

And Tanner was a journalist. Just. Like. Rick.

She pushed him back with a hand to his hard, muscular chest, needing space. She searched for the caramel apple pie Jill had brought home from the coffee shop and raced over to it. Her hands shook as she took out the plates and dessert forks. Deep breaths seemed like a good idea to clear out Tanner's musky smell, but she couldn't seem to take in a full one. Her lungs had deflated like balloons after a disappointing party.

"I can't...have breakfast with you," she rasped, frantically touching her bustier. Even that wasn't doing much to restore her confidence. Damn it.

Tanner's boots scraped across the tile floor. She could feel the heat of his body behind her, and she imagined him gazing at that mole he'd mentioned. She wanted to lean back against him, but was suddenly afraid of how much she wanted him and where it could lead—especially with her family in the next room.

"Why can't you?"

"I don't date journalists. Ever."

He turned her around. She stood stiffly in his hold.

"Neither do I...usually. But I don't want to talk about journalism with you, Meredith."

Her eyelids fluttered. The buzzing in her head grew louder, and she felt overpowered by the force of her attraction to him. She lurched from his hold and knocked a plate to the floor. It shattered over the final roar of the coffee maker. Shards of her mother's silver-edged Lenox china covered the tile and their shoes.

Her nerves snapped right along with the china, and her breath wheezed out like she'd swum a sprint.

He gentled his hold. "Easy there. Don't move. I don't want you to get cut."

"I have shoes on." Anxiety squeezed her rib cage, and she pressed her hands to her chest, trying to suck in air.

He led them away from the mess. "Meredith?"

"Everything okay in there?" Jill called from the other room.

"Yes," Tanner hollered back. "I didn't see Meredith handing me a pie plate, and it shattered. We'll clean it up and be right out with dessert."

His quick lie made her wheeze. It had been so effortless.

Like Richard.

He opened the back door and led her out onto the porch, putting her hands on the rough boards. "Deep breaths, Meredith. In and out." He caressed her back with gentle hands. "Come on. You can do it."

Panting in shallow breaths, she lowered her head. Black dots spread behind her eyes like she was inside a planetarium. A panic attack. She hadn't had one for months. She concentrated on the thought of Rick-the-Dick bald and crying in front of a mirror. The picture always helped turn the tide.

"Shit, don't pass out on me."

Visualization wasn't helping this time. She clawed at her shirt. Her bustier was strangling her. She was too embarrassed to care. The wheezing made her sound like an asthmatic. She fumbled with her bustier's hooks, needing to...get...it...off.

Tanner swatted her hands away gently. He tugged the bustier off and set it aside before hoisting her to a standing position and smoothing her shirt back in place. She almost cried at his attempts to protect her modesty.

"No wonder you can't breathe." He whistled. "That's one serious contraption." Framing her rib cage with his hands, he said, "Inhale from here. Fill your lungs. Come on."

She rested against his strong body, lightheaded. After a few coughs, she managed a shallow inhale.

"Again," he commanded, his hands softly stroking her.

Her next few breaths spread lower, filling her belly. He smoothed her hair back behind her ears with one hand, pushing away her light-headedness. "Good. Keep going."

Full, deep breaths drew in the pine-scented air and the seductive smell of his aftershave. She finally managed to keep breathing constantly and steadily in his soothing arms, and the buzzing in her head lowered to background noise. When she pulled away, she stumbled into a lounge chair. Her head fell back. Her eyes closed. The burn of tears was strong, but she managed to hold them at bay. She was not going to cry, but she wanted to. God, she had thought she was past this crap. And to do it in front of him...

"You going to be all right?" Tanner asked in a gentle voice.

She cracked her eyes open. He knelt near her feet on the cold porch, his brow furrowed in the white light from the half moon.

"You made me have a panic attack," she blurted out.

He didn't say anything for a moment. "Has this happened before?"

She nodded and then looked away, watching the tree branches shiver in the breeze. Her mouth was dry, her throat swollen, her confidence leveled.

"I'm too attracted to you," she whispered. "And you're a journalist. I swore I'd never...date another one." She looked back and gestured with her hands, desperate not to hurt his feelings and yet equally desperate to make him understand. "It scares me." Her honesty almost did her in. "It's not you."

His deep sigh mixed with the night sounds of crickets and rustling leaves. "I'm sorry I came on so strong, Meredith. I couldn't seem to help myself."

His apology helped her regain her footing. "I meant what I said. I won't ever go out with a journalist again." Her voice was flat. "I made a vow."

He stood and held out his hand. "We'll save that topic for another day. Let's go inside. I'm sure everyone is wondering where we went."

Knowing what his touch did to her, she didn't take his hand. Pushing out of the chair took effort. The cool air brushed her hot cheeks, making her realize she needed to find her bustier. Oh, God, he'd helped her take it off.

He picked it up, studying it in the dim light before holding it out. "What's the DW for?"

She took it from him with shaking hands. "Turn around." She fitted it back on. Of all the luck... Of course she was wearing one of the ones Jill had embroidered. It was black with red stitching. She had almost made it to the back door before his hand grazed hers.

"Are you going to tell me?"

She turned. The kitchen light skittered over his face. She was relieved not to see any pity there. She wouldn't have been able to take that.

"No, it's none of your business." She rushed inside.

The broom was in the closet, just like she remembered. He took it from her before she could swish it across the floor.

Her hands trembled as she moved over to the counter to pour out the coffees. She'd hit bottom again. She'd thought divorce was the hardest thing she'd ever done, but now she wondered if trying to rebuild a life wasn't harder. The carafe shook in her hand.

"Put the coffee down before you burn yourself," he said gently from over her shoulder. He walked over to the pie, and sliced it like a pizza, dishing the pieces onto plates like a pro. "Take these. I'll clean up, and Jill can do the coffee."

She turned away from his intent gaze. As she headed for the door, she could hear the sound of broken china scraping against the floor. It might as well have been the broken pieces of her heart.

Who was she kidding? Flirting with a handsome man had given her a panic attack. Was it simply because he was a journalist? She hoped to God it was, because otherwise she was never going to find Mr. Right and write her article.

Going bald or being hit by a falling piano wasn't good enough for Rick-the-Dick. Maybe toothpicks under his perfectly manicured fingernails would do the trick.

She pressed the plates to her chest, hoping for some words of wisdom from her now vociferous alter ego.

But even Divorcée Woman had gone silent.

***

Tanner slid the broken china from the dust pan into the garbage. Christ, when had he become the King of Heel-dom? Crowding a woman to

65

the point of a panic attack? He'd been attracted to her, and he'd stopped thinking.

He kept forgetting she'd gone through a traumatic divorce.

And that she'd been married to Sommerville. If the prick could screw with Tanner—someone who'd interviewed terrorists—what kind of shit had he done to his own wife? Even divorced, he was taking it to her with a sledgehammer.

Her pale, clenched face filled his mind. He hadn't felt that helpless in a long time, listening to her short, choked breaths, and holding that strong, trembling body.

"Are you okay?"

He swiveled.

Jill edged closer. "I take it Meredith had a panic attack."

He set the empty dust pan on the floor and shut the pantry door. "Yes."

She patted him on the arm, and then headed for the coffee pot. "Don't take it too hard. Meredith's been through a lot, and she's doing so much better. It's not easy trying to build a new life." The cups clinked as she lined them up. "She must have had a strong reaction to you, or it wouldn't have happened. Could you grab the cream? Bottom drawer."

What the fuck? She could say something that charged and then ask him for the cream?

When he handed it over, she gave a small smile. "Don't beat yourself up. Her reaction's a good sign, but you're going to have to give her some space."

"Are you usually this forward?"

She reached up for a tray and slid the coffee cups onto it. "Yes. Do you expect me to believe it would take someone that long to make coffee?"

Smart ass. "No."

"I love my sister, Tanner, and want to see her happy. From what I can tell, you're a good guy. But if you hurt her, I'll blast your balls with the steamer on our espresso machine and give you third degree burns."

He could appreciate vicious family loyalty. He'd had some pretty violent fantasies when his sister's ex had cheated on her.

"How do you know I'm a good guy?"

"I did my homework. The Internet is an amazing thing, Tanner. Since you're a published writer, you're pretty accessible. You care about people. What you've seen makes you bleed."

"I'm not a fucking girl."

"I can see that."

"Didn't you research her ex?" he asked.

Her eyes gleamed with fury. "Yes, and I knew he was a self- absorbed, arrogant prick who'd break her heart. He even checked me out when they came home on a rare holiday."

"Didn't you tell her?"

She pulled a can of RediWhip out of the fridge. "No, I was too young. She wouldn't have listened. Sometimes people have to learn the hard way.

Meredith can be her own worst enemy."

Tanner followed her out. Weren't they all?

He'd eat fast and get the hell out of there. He needed to regroup. Suddenly the assignment had become too personal. Meredith Hale didn't deserve what he was supposed to do to her.

It was too bad they hadn't met under other circumstances.

He might have fallen for her.

\*\*\*

Meredith was so still and quiet in the car Jill was afraid she'd turned to stone.

"It's okay, Mere." She took her hand.

"No, it's not. I humiliated myself in front of him—and over a little attraction and flirting."

Jill spotted a deer on the edge of the highway, its wild gaze shining in her headlights. She passed it with relief. "I wouldn't call it a *little* attraction, Mere. Maybe you should give him a chance. Take it slow. Start out as friends."

"Does Tanner strike you as someone who would be friends with a woman?"

"Okay, no, but he felt horrible about what happened. I think he's a good guy, Mere. He knows you've been through a divorce."

"I can't see him at all, Jill. I don't have control of myself when I'm around him. I had a panic attack for Christ's sake."

"Well, huffing and puffing like one of the dragons on my dress might be a bit awkward when you're having sex, but the French do call orgasm 'the little death.'"

Meredith's head rolled toward her. Her mouth pinched like she was fighting a smile. "Well, he already got to second base, so to speak. He helped me take off my bustier so I could breathe."

"Oh, wow. So did he feel you up while you were having a panic attack?"

"No." She burrowed in the seat.

"That's something, right? Rick-the-Dick wouldn't have restrained himself."

Meredith turned up the radio. "I don't want to talk anymore."

Jill stopped her hand. "Mere, I love you, but this is about you being afraid to lose control and get hurt again."

"Are you getting in my head now?"

"Don't be annoyed. I hate that. I'm only saying you should think about taking it slow with Tanner. There's something special about him. I mean, he won Grandpa over right off the bat, and he handled your panic attack like a champ."

"He ran out after dessert."

"Can you blame him? You should have seen his 'I kicked the dog' face when he was putting the broken china in the trash."

"I know, but I can't go out with him. I promised myself I would never date another journalist."

Oh brother, thought Jill. Sacred promises exacted a price. And the Hales could be a stubborn lot. Hadn't she sworn she wouldn't feel anything for Brian when he came home? That she wouldn't even fight with him?

She was batting a zero there.

All she did was think about him and hope she'd run into him. She got a bigger thrill from fighting with him than she'd gotten from her interactions with any of the men she'd dated in his absence. God, she'd missed that son of a bitch.

She pulled into her driveway. "He's not Rick-the-Dick, Mere."

"I know." Her sister left the car and headed into the house with hunched shoulders.

Jill watched a bat streak across the sky. The hardest part of growing up was realizing life was nothing like the way she'd imagined it. It was supposed to be easy to find a nice guy and coast into sharing a life together. Just like in Nora's books.

Was Nora Roberts Land even real?

She wasn't sure anymore.

# Chapter 13

Tanner's phone vibrated on the counter as he shaved. He snarled when he saw Sommerville's number and nicked himself. "Shit."

It was taking some time to become adept at shaving again. To blend in, he'd usually worn a full beard. He was still adjusting to the face he saw each time he looked in the mirror. What he saw right now was blood mixed with shaving cream. He dabbed it with a towel and hit the speakerphone.

"What?"

"Get up on the wrong side of the bed?"

Tanner tossed the towel aside. "Yes, I did. We have a problem. Your ex-wife has vowed to never date a journalist again. She won't go out with me."

"Well, isn't that flattering?"

Tanner growled. What had Meredith ever seen in this asshole? He didn't mention the panic attack. He felt worse about that than Sommerville ever could.

"Look, whatever ideas she might have about this story, she's definitely not ready for a relationship. I don't think this is going to fly."

"You have to move fast. I told you that."

Right, and he'd listened...that was the problem. Everything had been hot and steamy when they were talking about swim strokes. Then he'd crowded her, and she'd had a meltdown.

"Maybe it's only with you." It galled him to say it, but perhaps it would put Sommerville off.

"Then you'll have to find some other way of getting through to her. I want this story stopped, McBride."

He winced at the sting from his aftershave. "Fine, but it's going to take time. I thought you should know." Snapping his wristwatch on, he reached for a blue shirt. "Look, it's the first day of classes. I need to run. I'll call you in a week." He clicked off and jerked on his clothes.

The urge for strong coffee was like a siren's call, so he headed to Don't Soy with Me before hitting campus. Jill chatted effortlessly with the crowd of customers while handling orders and taking money with artless efficiency. He liked her. She was open and honest and a good sister.

Her smile softened when she saw him. "How are you, Tanner?

Recovered yet?"

"Yep, what about Meredith?"

"Working like a fiend at the paper. Grandpa's overjoyed."

"I bet. Venti dark roast and a blueberry muffin to go. It's nice to be back in food nirvana."

"Understandable." Jill called out his order to Jemma. "Mere's supposed to come in before work. Maybe you should hang around."

He handed her a ten-dollar bill. "I'll give her some room. Any advice for my first day of classes?"

She gave him the change and slid his muffin toward him. "Don't teach anything useless. Most of what I learned there was pretty useless." She twisted the large yellow beads around her neck. "And don't be boring."

"Got it. Nothing useless or boring." He grabbed his coffee. Realizing he was nervous, he looked around at all the students in the shop. Teaching was new to him, but he'd prepared as much as possible. But even with a plan, he didn't have a clue what to do.

Another reason Sommerville had to go down.

He pulled up short when he saw Meredith walking across the street, her red hair waving in the wind. Her step faltered when she caught sight of him. His mouth tipped up when she straightened her shoulders, lifted her chin, and strode to the door. Flat out guts. Something to admire.

He sauntered toward her. "Hi there."

She didn't meet his eyes. "Tanner."

"Meredith, look at me."

She slowly turned her head. Her cheeks had flushed to the color of her crimson coat.

"I'm sorry for the other night. Are you okay?"

"Fine." She fiddled with her buttons.

"Don't be embarrassed. Let's forget it ever happened." What a lie.

"I had a panic attack in front of you. You took my bra off! Of course I'm embarrassed!" she whispered.

He nodded toward a table in the corner and walked over, hoping she'd follow.

She tugged at her white scarf. Since her efforts looked like they'd be about as successful as a novice taffy puller's, he put down his coffee and muffin and reached for it. Her gaze flew to his.

"It's okay. I was only going to help."

He unwound the material, his fingers brushing her soft hair. Boy, did he like her natural color better than the blond. She was more approachable as a red head. He kept his actions brisk and efficient so she wouldn't bolt.

"I don't want you to be uncomfortable around me. Let's be friends, okay?"

When he exposed the long slender line of her neck, she swallowed thickly. He stepped back, even though his fingers itched to touch that smooth skin.

"How about a friendly swim tomorrow? We can race each other. Maybe we can make it a morning habit."

"I don't think that's a good idea."

He smirked. "You afraid I'm going to beat you?"

"In your dreams, McBride."

"How about a little wager then?"

Her eyelids lowered to half mast. "What do you have in mind?"

"Since I'm new in town, how about a tour of the hotspots, including *The Western Independent*?"

"Grandpa would give you a tour if you asked."

"Yes, but we're trying to be friends. That can't happen unless we spend time together."

She looked away. "Tanner, I'm not sure."

He almost reached for her. "Meredith," he said quietly.

She studied him. "You may not win."

He couldn't help but smile. "Then you have nothing to worry about."

"You headed to class?"

"Yes, and I feel like a fish out of water. I've never taught before. Jill told me not to be boring."

"There's no worse offense to Jill. You'll do fine. Talk about where you've been. They'll eat that stuff up like it's candy. You're an unusual commodity in the department, Tanner. They'll all want to be you."

"Are you saying I'll have a cult following?" He realized he was flirting with her, but he couldn't stop himself.

"When was the last time you were around college kids?"

He scanned the shop. "Years. Most of the kids I've been around recently had weapons in their hands."

She picked up his coffee and held it out. "Yes, I can imagine. Here you'll be surrounded by green-as-grass wanna-be journalism students from fairly well-adjusted families whose main goal in life is to do what you do—or maybe be an anchorman like Brian Williams."

He reached for his muffin to stop from grinning like an idiot. He liked this side of her, but pushing it was too risky. He needed to find the right balance. If they spent time together as friends, he'd be meeting the spirit of Sommerville's law. Tanner didn't have to tell him they weren't involved. It bought him time. And he wouldn't need to struggle with his own ethics.

"I need to run. How about a swim tomorrow? I'll bring the Gatorade."

She fingered her scarf. "We'll see. Good luck today."

He studied her for a moment longer. As he watched her, the morning sun broke through the windows, turning her hair to molten lava. His skin tightened. Uh-oh.

"Thanks. And Meredith? I will see you tomorrow."

He waved to Jill and Jemma and headed off to class. Class?

Life couldn't be weirder.

# Chapter 14

A month later, Tanner was no closer to getting Meredith to agree to go out with him. While they raced each other at the pool almost every morning and he ran into her at *The Western Independent* when he dropped off an article, she still was resisting hanging out socially.

She was going out with every available man in sight *but* him. She certainly wanted her story. He'd tallied three dates yesterday. Coffee with a tall, nerdy biology professor. Happy hour with a computer expert from the local Internet provider. And dinner with a divorced local lawyer.

He'd sunk to the lowest form of journalism—paparazzi. He was tailing her on her dates, keeping tabs. And feeling a little jealous. Shit.

Jill was helping him by dropping hints of where they'd be when he came by the coffee shop on his daily run. He could tell Jill wanted him and Meredith to hook up. Tonight, she'd mentioned she and Meredith were heading to Hairy's for drinks.

No one knew Meredith's dating spree was part of a story. The town thought she was looking for a rebound man or a sure-fire relationship with a Dare Valley guy. The matronly lady at the grocery's checkout told him everyone thought it was so sweet.

He'd wanted to gag.

Hours later, he walked into the bar, planning on using the only strategy he had left— disrupting Meredith's playbook.

"Hi, Tanner." Jill skipped down the hall from the emerald green bathrooms, wiping her hands on her jeans.

"Hey, Jill. How's it going?"

She rolled those signature Hale green eyes. "Mere's on a tear tonight. I've never seen her this focused. It's like going out with guys is her new-found religion."

"Except for me."

He wondered if Jill knew about the story. He snorted. Oh yeah, she knew. She'd invited him to dinner the first day they met. He chuckled.

"What's so funny?"

"Life."

She rolled her eyes. "Don't say that. It makes you sound old. My *mom* says that."

He scowled. "Any suggestions about Meredith?"

"Give her some space. If you let something go, it comes back to you."

"She's not a bird, Jill."

"Are you making fun of my analogy?"

"Yep. It's something a kid would get wrong."

She twirled her long necklace of orange beads around her finger. "Hah. Okay, professor, I'll take that from you, but only because your command of the English language is better than mine. How are classes going?"

"Better than expected after I took your advice. I threw out my boring syllabus and described real-life journalism to the students. Tomorrow I'm starting a section on cultivating sources and building trust. They're eating it up."

"I've heard people talking. There's nothing better than the real deal." She waved to a few people. "Let's find Meredith. You need to relieve us both from hell."

The invitation was a golden opportunity. He wouldn't have to interrupt her unbidden.

"Why, what's going on?" he asked.

"Ice-pick to head." She tapped her palm to her temple. "You'll see."

Tanner followed Jill over to a corner booth. Meredith looked up in surprise, looking beautiful as usual in a cream-colored V-neck sweater. He moved her purse and nudged her over, pressing his thigh against hers.

Jill made the intros, and Tanner shook hands with the guy, Avery Miller. With a name like that, he'd be lucky to sprout one chest hair. He had a slight build, but he worked out. His hair was slicked up with some gel shit.

"So, Avery, what do you do?" he asked.

Meredith inched away, but the booth was narrow, and there wasn't anywhere to go. She vibrated against his side.

"I own the cheese and gourmet store across the way."

He gave Jill a "you're kidding" look and decided to have some fun. "Wow. Sounds interesting. Are you into the bleu cheese craze or do you prefer the Italian classics like a good buffalo mozzarella?"

Meredith swung her head to look at him. She'd gone for dark eye shadow, which set off her arresting green eyes. Yeah, she was definitely cruising tonight.

He stared back blandly. "Hey, I've traveled!"

"I see you're a man who knows his cheese."

"Yes, I am."

Meredith elbowed him under the table.

"I have eight bleu cheese varieties and only two buffalo. One is the classic large ball. I also sell the small balls."

Muffling a cough to hide her laughter, Jill hid her mouth behind her hand.

"Packed in oil and herbs? Too bad they don't serve the big balls like that. They're tastier that way," Tanner commented, trying to keep a straight face.

Meredith gave him a sharp kick.

"You could always marinate them yourself," Avery suggested, oblivious to the innuendo swirling around them like the Irish flute playing over the loud speakers. Punky hair and no funny bone.

"I'd have to invite a special guest over to help with that."

When Meredith's leg moved in for another kick, he clamped his hand on her thigh. She jolted and muffled a shriek. He grinned, delighted she'd worn a skirt. She might not like it, but there were enough volts between them to run the Dare electricity plant. He hadn't expected it, but there was a very real connection between them. It was time she stopped fighting it.

"I was just telling Meredith she'll have to come over for dinner soon. A new ash-covered cheese just arrived from Naples, and I'm dying to share it. I love introducing people to new cheeses."

Cheese tasting as foreplay? Seriously?

Since Meredith was trying to pry his hand from her thigh, he gave her leg a healthy squeeze. The muscles bunched as she clamped her legs together, framing his hand. It made him wish he could slide it higher. But he couldn't. Not until she admitted to the heat between them.

"Well, Meredith is a woman of complex tastes."

When she raised her gaze, the silent plea in her eyes made him release her thigh. She was attracted to him. He could wait her out.

"I need to get another beer. Jill, why don't you come and tell me what's good?"

"Nice to meet you, Tanner." Avery stood. "Sounds like you're a cheese man too. Please come by my store sometime. It's called Don't Wedge Me In. On Main and Oak."

His grin was as stupid as the name of his store.

"Good to meet you. I'll ask Meredith about the ash cheese. See if she likes it."

He strode over to the bar. People cleared out of his way as if he were wearing a sign that said "Man Needs Beer" in bold, capital letters.

"Wow, that's a record sprint in this crowd. I'll have to tag along with you more often," Jill commented at his side.

Tanner slammed his fist onto the bar. "Ash. Christ!"

"You have to admit that it's pretty funny," Jill said through her laughter. "Loved that smack talk about mozzarella balls. I thought I was going to pee my pants."

Tanner studied the various beer taps, eying the evil-looking badger. He pointed to it when he got the bartender's attention.

"The Cheese Man?" he said, turning back to Jill. "Does the woman have no taste in men?"

Jill slid him a coaster decorated with a hairy leprechaun. Talk about a sight to make the little kids drop the pot of gold and run from the rainbow.

"She's gone out with some hot guys. See that one?" She pointed with a finger behind her other hand. "Burly guy in the black fleece? He's a firefighter. Didn't click. Nice guy, but not real smart. Mere likes smart."

"Like the cheese guy?" Christ, infiltrating a Taliban stronghold for a story was easier than getting Meredith to go out with him.

"Enough with him. It won't go anywhere. She's only going out with him because he's safe—and a little urbane. Mere got *real* flushed when you arrived."

"She's stubborn." His beer had a nice bite to it.

"Oh, yeah. That's a Hale trait. If Grandpa weren't stubborn, he never would have started *The Independent*. Everyone said he would fail. And yet..." She flicked her wrist. "Here it stands."

"Hey, Red, who's your friend?" A younger man said, caging her against the bar.

Tanner sipped his beer, watching Jill's eyes turn to slits.

Tugging Tanner in close, she said, "He's my older lover."

Tanner choked on his beer. She pounded him on the back.

"He's still having trouble dealing with the age difference," she explained in dulcet tones, taking his glass and raising it to her own mouth.

"I'm Tanner," he sputtered, extending his hand.

"Brian McConnell."

The guy didn't take Tanner's hand—he was too busy studying him like he was an escaped prisoner or something.

"No offense, man, but there's no way Jill's with you." Brian turned back to Jill. "He's got at least ten years on you."

Tanner opened his mouth, but shut it slowly when Jill gave him a pleading look.

She caressed Tanner's arm. "I was looking for someone more experienced in life...someone who knew what he wanted." Her smile reminded Tanner of the angry badger.

"You're new in town," Brian said with a clenched jaw.

"Yes, I teach at the university. What about you?"

"I grew up here with Jill. Went to culinary school back east and worked in the Big Apple until I came back a few months ago. I'm the sous chef at The Chop House."

Jill flicked her green dress with white polka dots like she was a little girl without a care in the world. "We used to be best friends until this guy took an asshole pill. It's chronic."

People called out drink orders around them. The Irish music had the patrons tapping their feet, but the silence between the trio was palpable. Tanner didn't know what to do, but he knew he couldn't leave Jill.

"Okay, Red, have it your way." Brian's hand grazed her arm. "See you around." He charged off without a backward glance.

Tanner took his beer from Jill. "I assume you had your reasons for knocking that guy down."

Pushing her red curls behind her ear with a quivering hand, she said, "He deserved it. Long story."

"Okay, but he's not going to gossip about me seeing a younger woman, is he?"

Her gaze scanned the crowd like she was following Brian's progress. "No, he's not a talker. And don't worry about Mere. I'll tell her about our run-in. Thank you."

He handed her his beer. "I never leave a damsel in distress."

She took a drink, studying him over the rim. "Actually, you got major points tonight, Tanner. I won't forget this."

He noticed Brian doing a car bomb at a back table, the Guinness frothing like a chemistry experiment. The man looked as miserable as Jill did. History sucked.

"It's nothing. How about we play a game of darts? I need to forget all of the cheese talk."

She linked arms with him. "Okay, but you have to buy me mozzarella balls if I win. They sound so good."

He snorted, glancing over at Meredith. Jill was right. This guy was history. Her eyes were glazed over with boredom.

"Large or small?"

"*Large*, darling. Always."

He laughed. Suddenly Meredith met his gaze from across the bar. His skin tightened as he took in the full effect of the recessed lighting on her hair. It looked like fire, and he felt himself developing pyromaniac tendencies. Then the Cheese Man reached for her hand, and she looked away.

Tanner followed Jill into the back game room. He tested the weight of the metal dart she placed in his hands and looked over his shoulder.

Maybe he could drill the Cheese Man accidentally and save Meredith from a lifetime of small, squishy balls.

***

Meredith watched Tanner and Jill stroll away like old pals. She turned back toward Avery. God, Tanner was right. The guy really did like cheese way too much. Mozzarella balls, indeed.

And yet here she was—stuck by her own doing. She was forcing it with Avery, and she knew it.

She glanced around the bar, nodding at a few guys she'd gone out with. Her confidence was being bolstered by all the attention. The only problem was the more she went out with other men, the more she wanted to go out with Tanner. She found herself comparing each of her dates unfavorably to him, thinking about how much broader Tanner's shoulders were, how much brighter his smile was. He had a better sense of humor than anyone else, and she loved how his eyes crinkled at the corners out of sheer mischief. It would be so much fun to get into trouble with him...but he was also the kind of guy who would bail you out.

She knew all that, but she had Coward Syndrome. He was still a journalist.

She *had* to get over him so she could find Mr. Right.

Hard to do when he showed up everywhere. The mornings at the swimming pool were sheer torture. She'd had to buy a dual-lined swimsuit so he couldn't see how turned on she got from looking at his wet, nearly naked body. And then there was her social time. Like tonight.

She sat through another story of Avery finding the most incredible stilton cheese in some remote English village.

*Ditch this guy and go find Tanner*, Divorcée Woman chimed in. *You know you want to.*

She picked up her glass, trying to ignore the voice. Lately, when Tanner was around, she could hear it with crystal clarity.

*I'm only telling you what you already know.*

Do not, she fired back, and then realized she was talking to herself. She shifted in her seat.

*I'm not stopping until you do what you want to do. You created me to give you confidence. Running from Tanner is cowardly. You know it. I know it.*

"Meredith, did you hear me?" Avery reached for her hand again.

"No, it's getting a little loud in here," she lied. "What did you say?"

His crooked smile suddenly reminded her of a puddle of melted cheese.

"I asked if you wanted to go somewhere quiet and talk."

No, dear God, please. He was nice, but more talking?

Avery leaned forward. "Let's get out of here."

Oh, she hated this part. "I have some more people I promised to see. And Jill's still here. How about another time?"

His crooked, melting cheese smile faded. "Okay then, I'll see you later."

"I'll come by the shop."

He beamed. "I'll save the ash cheese."

Great. She wondered if it was like eating cigarette ash, except with a good cheddar flavor.

"See you later, Avery." Weaving toward the bar for a stiff drink seemed like a brilliant plan.

"Hey, Meredith," Larry Barlow called out. He was sitting at a stool by the bar, looking good in his worn denim.

Too bad he was a jerk.

"How ya been?"

She kept her distance. "Great. You?"

"Couldn't be better. Wanna drink?"

In what universe? "Nah, can't. I have to find Jill."

"She's playing with that journalist. He's killing her at darts."

Jill losing at darts? That was a first.

"See ya, Larry."

Brian was watching Tanner and Jill from the darkened doorway of the game room. A chorus of groans erupted from the onlookers as Tanner hit the bullseye.

She edged closer to Brian. "What's this I've heard about a blood letting?"

His head whipped around. "I've never seen anyone hit that many bullseyes. Jill's pretty upset." There was a dark expression on his face.

"She hates to lose."

"Yes, I know. There's no way she's banging a guy that would crush her like that."

"What?"

He punched the air. "I knew she was fucking lying to me! Dammit."

Who'd put that thought in his head? Then she remembered the awkward body language between them at the bar. Ah, Jillie.

Brian shook his head. "I'm not watching anymore. She won't walk away."

Meredith grabbed his arm. "It takes a lot for her to walk away."

Even in the darkened light of the bar, his face fell. "I know it, and once she does, there's no getting her back." He gave Jill a final look, the longing on his face painful. "See ya, Mere," he said, and then walked away.

Meredith pressed through the crowd, heading straight for the dart board. Her sister was strung up so tight her back muscles were clenched, like a ballerina poised for a lift.

Tanner met her gaze as Jill hit the dart board on the narrow sliver of twenty points, scant millimeters from the bullseye. Wiping the chalkboard, he wrote her new score, his fingers coated white.

"Let's make this the last game. This old man's got to get up and teach a bunch of kids in the morning." He yawned and stretched his arms overhead.

Meredith's mouth went dry as she watched his muscles shift beneath his plain navy T-shirt. Even though she knew he wasn't the least bit old or tired, his act had her body warming.

*Admit it*, Divorcée Woman drawled. *That man could make you scream.*

Meredith put her arms around Jill. "Hey."

The pursed mouth and stubborn chin looked familiar. Meredith had seen it in the locker room mirror each time she'd lost a swimming competition.

"You wanna go? I'm pretty worn out from earlier."

Jill's eyes narrowed as she tossed the dart in her hand. "That's your own fault. No one thought that was a good idea."

"Ah..." Wow, she hadn't been expecting that response.

"I'm not through," Jill said. "You can go home. I'll get a ride."

Tanner walked toward them. "I really do need to go," he said. "We'll pick this up another time."

He trained his gaze on Meredith, the intensity causing her to take a small step back. He had this special ability of looking at someone like they were the most important thing in the world. She could see why he was such a good journalist. People talked to someone like that. They couldn't help it.

Jill drilled her finger into his chest. "You better mean that. I want to win those damn mozzarella balls."

Meredith raised her brow. She knew her time with Avery had become a joke between them.

He grinned and tapped Jill on the nose. "They're yours for the taking." His gaze slid over to Meredith again, his brown eyes so rich and direct her heart lurched.

"I'll see you both in the morning."

He was referring to their swim, which he always followed up with a morning coffee at Don't Soy With Me. She hated how he had intruded on her routine—and become a part of it.

"And what if I change my time?" she shot back.

*Big mistake*, Divorcée Woman cautioned. *You won't see a big, wet, nearly naked man. It's better than a cup of coffee.*

"I wouldn't bother. I'll change my time too. And beat you pretty bad for the trouble." He winked at Jill. "I don't like people getting between me and my morning coffee."

"I'll keep that in mind," Jill said.

His grin only widened. "See you around, ladies," he drawled and strode through the crowd of well-wishers.

"Let's go." Meredith grabbed Jill's hand. Pulling out her keys, she led her sister across the street toward her car. She heard a muffled honk from behind them and swiveled around. Tanner slowed, waved, and then sped by. Her heart turned over. Man, she had it bad.

When they got in the car, Jill snapped on her seat belt and turned to look at her. "You're a total idiot. That guy is awesome, and he really likes you. And what do you do? You spend most of the night talking with Avery about cheese. Cheese," she shrieked, pulling her hair. "Avery's a nice guy, Mere, but who are you kidding? I've been silent about this for a while, but this story—about you coming back here to date some great small town guy and fall in love...Well, it's horse shit."

Meredith's hands clenched the wheel so hard her knuckles went white. Jill's tone cut through her like a razor.

"At first, I thought you were getting your wings, but some of your choices are...ridiculous! I mean, after these past two weeks, I keep thinking we need to go back to the hardware store so you can give your old chum Smith a second chance. What's a weenie with early male baldness? I can't think of one good reason why he's not on par with some of the others."

Meredith stared through the windshield. "Are you done?"

"No, I'm not. I understand you not wanting to end up with a guy like Rick-the-Dick, but he wasn't a dick because he was a journalist. He was a dick because he was a dick! No other reason. You're afraid to go out with Tanner because you're really attracted to him and you really like him. I mean, the guy even backed off when you needed more time. He's a good one, Mere. What's holding you back?"

She turned in her seat, the belt cutting into her side. "I told you. He's a journalist, Jillie, and I won't do that again."

"And you called me stubborn." Jill flung a strand of hair over her shoulder. "That's a stupid rule, Mere, and you know it."

"I don't care. I'm not dating him!"

"You sound like a child."

Her face heated, and her heart rate doubled. "You're just upset because Tanner beat you, and you're taking it out on me."

"Bullshit! Yeah, it pissed me off, but he was even gracious about *that.*

I was hoping he'd be a heel so I could feel superior somehow, but he wasn't. You're being stupid!"

She slammed her hand on the gearshift. "Don't call me, stupid! You don't know what it's like to have your confidence stripped away like old paint."

"No, I don't know, but I do know that you're still letting that asshole do it."

"I'm going to need to find my own place if we can't get along," Meredith said, knowing it was unfair. They'd gotten along perfectly well until this moment. "I don't want to fight like this." The words made her look away, eyes blurring from tears.

"Fine, run away! But you can't run far. When are you going to understand that? Your problems go where you do."

"Do you have any idea how hard it is to start over? I'm thirty years old and divorced. A failure. It wasn't supposed to be this way," Meredith cried, leaning her head against the seat.

Grabbing her by a shoulder, Jill said, "No, I don't know, but as they say, it is what it is. You're one of the most awesome women I know. You're a great journalist who made it in New York City. And you're a loving and funny woman who's managed to get the entire male population of Dare Valley under the age of sixty hot and bothered in a month. You can do anything you want to do. You always have."

*Time to start believing it*, Divorcée Woman chimed in.

She was quiet for a long moment, and then she said, "Okay. You're right. I was having a pity party."

"A big one." Jill said, letting out a gusty breath. "Forget the pity party. Have a real party! Live a little."

Meredith tapped her fingers against the wheel. "You mean Tanner."

"Yes, I mean Tanner! The man is smokin'. You should hear his students talk. He's super smart, and he tells them stuff that isn't in the textbooks. And he's into you. Any of the women at Hairy's tonight would have killed to get his attention. Didn't you see it?"

Yes, she'd noticed the gazes, the overtures. She'd expected him to give up on her and give someone else a chance. But he hadn't. It was flattering. But deep down, it also made her suspicious.

Why would he keep dogging her when she said she wouldn't go out with him? Was he one of those guys who liked the chase more than the catch? His history of working overseas with no roots suggested that he didn't want a relationship, but what did she really know about him?

*You won't know unless you give him a chance*, Divorcée Woman advised.

You've got to stop talking to me, she fired back, mostly because now she had two people making her feel unreasonable.

*You're nuts if you let a man like that slip through your fingers.*

She turned to look at Jill. "I'm sorry about what I said before. I love living with you. Even with all your crazy decorations."

Jill reached for her, and they hugged like two long-lost pretzels. "I'm sorry too."

"It's okay," Meredith whispered, her face cooling from the blistering onslaught of emotion. "We're okay."

Jill tucked her head into Meredith's neck. "I love you, Mermaid. I'm glad you're home."

"I love you too, and I'm happy I'm here."

They separated and smiled. Jill wiped a tear slipping down her face.

"Since we're having a moment, I think I should tell you something," Meredith murmured, her face breaking into a grin.

"What is it?"

"Brian said something about you banging Tanner. What the hell did you do?"

"I told him Tanner was my older lover." She kicked at her purse. "Damn, I was hoping he'd suffer longer."

"He got pretty upset, watching Tanner beat you." She filled her in on their conversation.

"He's right, Mere," Jill responded flatly. "Once I walk away, that's it. And anyway, he was the one who left me in the first place."

"You should think about forgiving him, Jillie. You used to be best friends."

"It's different now. We're different now. Let's leave it be," she said in a rush, suddenly fascinated with picking lint off her multi-colored print peasant shirt.

"Who's running now, Jill?"

"Bitch," she muttered without heat. "You sound like Jemma. Fine, you've made your point. Do you feel better now?"

Meredith's chuckle carried in the quiet car. "No, but I do feel like a good sister."

"Okay, so we'll both think about not running away. Deal?"

Meredith winced when Jill thrust a hand at her. She took it with dread, icicles spreading around her heart. Could she live up to her end of the bargain?

Even so, she murmured, "Deal," and put the car into gear, taking them home.

# Chapter 15

Two weeks later, Meredith was no closer to going out with Tanner despite his continued hovering. She could all but hear the clock ticking in her head. Had she really thought she could find Mr. Right in Nora Roberts Land in three months? She had until after Thanksgiving to write her article, which only gave her another month.

Meanwhile, she was doing her best to placate Jill. Eating crow—e.g., setting aside a sacred vow—sucked. Her sister was giving her looks that could have turned even the most faithful prophet into a pillar of salt.

Meredith had a real connection with Tanner—she knew it, and heck, even her subconscious knew it. One morning she jolted awake from a dream about him drenched in sweat, shivering in the silence. But wanting him was different than being with him, and a part of her couldn't seem to take that next step. She was dragging her feet big time.

Her boss continued to enjoy her email updates on her dating antics. She was glad that someone was. Karen was still confident Meredith would find Mr. Right—and if it didn't happen, she'd agreed Meredith could write about dating in a small town. She was glad the pressure was off, but a story like that wouldn't prove Rick-the-Dick was wrong about Nora's books, nor would it help her find her happily-ever after.

She shut off her chatty mind so she could enjoy her second coffee outing—see, progress—with Dr. Kevin Planey, an archeology professor specializing in Colorado's Native American artifacts. He was telling her about some cave dwellings an hour away he wanted to show her this weekend. He was interesting, and well, gangly.

Okay, he was no Indiana Jones, but the archeology thing reminded her of Dr. Jake Greystone in Nora's *Birthright*.

The door chimed, signaling a new customer. She choked on her lukewarm tea as her grandfather walked in. He waved, tapped his cane on the floor, and headed to the counter. Jill wasn't working, which was the only reason Meredith had agreed to meet Kevin at Don't Soy With Me. She was afraid of what Sista Pimp might do if she were present.

Jemma greeted him with a bright smile. "Hi, Mr. Hale. What brings you here? Jill's not working, but Meredith's having coffee."

"I'm not here for them. You do sell coffee in this establishment?" he harrumphed. "I'd like a cup."

"What kind?"

"Just coffee."

Jemma pointed to the chalkboard. "We have lots of different kinds of coffee, Mr. Hale. Why don't you see what sounds good?"

Meredith turned back to Kevin and nudged her shoulder toward the counter. "That's my grandfather."

"Ah, the legend himself," Kevin replied as Meredith turned back to watch the train wreck she knew was coming.

"You sell all that crap, and at those prices?" Grandpa harrumphed as he dug out his wallet. "Just give me the one that tastes the most like plain coffee, Jemma." He leaned forward, adjusting his glasses. "Vanilla shot? Who puts that crap in coffee? It goes in a cake, not coffee."

"Yes, Mr. Hale. I'll get you a dark roast." She had his coffee on the counter in thirty seconds flat. When he pulled out a five, she pushed it back. "It's on the house. Really."

He slapped the money down. "Just because I'm old doesn't mean I can't pay for my own coffee. Take my money, girlie, or I'm going to write an article about elderly discrimination in this establishment."

Meredith muffled her chuckle. Arthur Hale was as likely to make a claim of elderly discrimination as she was to announce Rick-the-Dick had "found" himself and confessed his sins like today's *New York Times* had reported.

Jemma crossed her arms. "What if I'd like to treat you for being such a nice man and my best friend's grandpa?"

He coughed to cover his reaction. "You're a sweet girl, Jemma. That Collins boy was an idiot to let you slip away."

A tear slid down her pixie-like face. Poor kid.

"Here, now," Grandpa crooned. "Don't cry, honey. Come give an old man a hug."

She came around the counter, and he enfolded her in his arms, patting her hair. She sniffed and pulled back. "Thanks. Now it's really on the house."

"No. Take my money. Gotta support my granddaughter's business."

"Thanks, Mr. Hale." Jemma kissed his weathered cheek and accepted the bill.

"As I said, a sweet girl. Come over to dinner with Jill soon." He winked, picked up the coffee, and walked away after waving away his change.

When he sat on an overstuffed ottoman and drew out some papers and his faithful red pen, Meredith's first impression was confirmed. He was here for her.

"I think my grandpa wants to talk to me."

"No problem. I figured he was distracting you. I'll call you later about this weekend."

His head darted forward to deliver a kiss, but his long nose smacked into her cheek when she jerked back. Was he nuts? Her grandpa was sitting a few yards away.

"Bye, Meredith." He hurried out of the shop, fumbling with his briefcase.

She took a deep breath, picked up her purse, and walked over to her grandfather, taking the adjoining ottoman. "Hi, Grandpa."

He lifted his gaze, clicked his red pen, and shoved it into his shirt pocket. "Meredith."

She leaned forward, balancing her elbows on her knees.

"Another kid went to the ER last night puking his guts out," he said to her. "Same MO. Booze and marijuana."

"I know you think your famous gut is telling you something, but there's nothing funky in the marijuana. The tox screens don't show anything else. It's alcohol poisoning, and I'm not researching it anymore. There's no story."

He harrumphed and poked his belly. "There's nearly forty years of gut in here."

"Then you look." She flicked the paper he was marking. "Is that my article?" There were only a few red slashes. It would be nice to receive a near-clean copy. He was always changing her articles, and making them better. She didn't like to admit to herself how much she was still learning from him day in, day out.

"No. This is Tanner's op-ed. Nice piece. He has a good voice. Strong style. Knows how to put what he sees on paper."

She couldn't help the jolt of...jealousy? Envy? Her grandfather always praised her, but his opinion mattered to her more than ever, especially since she'd taken over her dad's duties. To be pissy, she crossed her arms and asked, "How's your coffee?"

"About as shitty as the coffee I had in Moscow in 1962 when I interviewed Khrushchev."

Snorting, she reached for it and took a sip. "Tastes pretty good to me."

He pushed his glasses back up his nose. "Well, your tastes are a bit in question at the moment. Who was Big Bird over there?"

She muffled her laughter with a cough.

"Got a cold, girlie?"

"Yes, there's a little tickle in my throat."

"Hah! Don't be a smart ass. You know as well as I do that if you had children with that man, your kids would sprout wings and fly."

"Grandpa!"

"Well, it's true. Hales have better taste than that. Where's yours gone?"

"I don't know what you mean."

"You damn well do." He pushed his papers aside. "You're off gallivanting with every man in town—even ones who resemble birds. I heard Jill mention the Cheese Man."

"Are you listening through keyholes again, Grandpa?"

His brows slammed together. "I told you it was a good way to get information. You telling me to stop being a reporter?"

"I'm not a story."

"No, but you're a real piece of work. People are talking about how you've got the word rebound tattooed on your butt. I hope that's a euphemism."

"Oh, God, Grandpa!"

"People are also saying you're on a Man Bender. I know my granddaughter, and she's not the town slut like Rita Bellins."

"Thanks, Grandpa." Meredith leaned back in the ottoman, her head buzzing from his words. *This* is what people were saying about her?

"I'm wondering if you've lost your mind. Your parents are too concerned about how you feel about the divorce to ask what the hell is going on with you. Your mother is wondering if she should come home." He leaned forward. "Are you going to fall apart?"

She wanted to put her hands in her hair and yell. "No."

"Good, that's what I thought. I think this bender is part of the reason you came home."

"What makes you think that?"

"I have eyes. The only thing I can't reconcile is why you're not going out with Tanner instead of these men who look like birds and are made of cheese. I know how a woman looks at a man when she likes him. That's how you look at Tanner, but he's not even on your list." He patted his shirt pocket and took out his pen. "Makes an old man wonder."

Pressing her hands to her temples, she met his clear blue gaze. "I'm only going out with men. Is that really such a crime?"

"No." He clicked his pen in rapid fashion. "But this...volume is against your character, which means there's some deeper motive. You aren't trying to make that asshole ex-husband of yours jealous so he'll take you back?"

"Good God, no!"

He popped in a red hot from his pocket. "Glad to hear it. I didn't think you were the type to want to be a politician's wife, but then again, I never understood what you saw in him. He didn't beg you to reconcile to shore up his chances with the voters, did he?"

"Holy...no. Even if he had, I wouldn't have done it."

"Well, thank God that you have some sense. I was afraid I'd have to find some old associates in New York who could arrange his demise."

"You're not serious."

"You're my granddaughter. If you were crazy enough to let that rat bastard back into your life, I'd have to take extreme measures."

"You'd never do something like that."

"I'm an old man. I wouldn't live long in jail."

She could only stare at him. Arthur Hale was known for saying some pretty hyperbolic statements in his time, but this...

"You actually mean it."

"No one messes with my granddaughter a second time."

Her throat squeezed painfully. She pressed her hand to it. His words made her feel so loved and protected. Who would have imagined her grandpa turning into The Great Protector? She reached for his hand.

"Well, now that I know that isn't the reason, do you want to tell me why you're on this Man Bender?"

"Stop staying that!"

"Is this about a story?"

"Grandpa!" She looked around to make sure no one was listening, but the other patrons all seemed too preoccupied with their digital devices and coffee to bother.

"It makes the most sense, now that I think of it. You want to tell me more?"

The lie caught in her tight throat for ten seconds. "There is no story." She could say she was sorry later. If he blew her cover, she was toast in this town. And she wouldn't have her ultimate revenge on Rick-the-Dick, or her own Nora Roberts Land.

"Lying to me now, girlie?"

She gulped like she was a ten-year-old who had been caught with her hand in the cookie jar before dinner. "Please don't ask me anymore, Grandpa. I'd explain if I could."

He scratched his cheek. "I won't ask if you swear you won't lie to me."

She nodded.

"Then take some advice from an old man. Life's short. All the stuff you think you have time to do suddenly evaporates like water boiled dry. You're a young woman who's put one life behind her and is trying to start a new one. Don't dick around."

"Grandpa!"

"You think that's a new phrase? It's as old as dirt, just like me. I mean it, Meredith. Don't squander time. You're a beautiful young woman. You need a man who suits you. Someone like Tanner McBride."

His wisdom was sweet, but his dating directives stunk. "I'll go out with whomever I want."

He stood up and reached for his cane, so she joined him. He still towered over her, even though his spine was curved with age. "Fine, be stubborn, but I see how you look at Tanner, Mermaid." He kissed her cheek, his cinnamon candy smell comforting. "You sure didn't look at the Bird Man that way."

She glared at him.

"And I still think you have something on Rick-the-Dick that will blow up his bid for the Senate. Don't think I've forgotten."

He strolled away whistling "Dixie," his cane tapping the floor.

Meredith sank down in the chair. Too bad Don't Soy With Me didn't serve liquor. She could sure use a shot of something, like a Red-headed Slut. Wasn't that what everyone was calling her?

A Man Bender? Jeez, she was going to have to come up with a new plan.

# Chapter 16

A cold October wind howled outside, and branches scratched against the window like someone trying to crawl inside. Considering it was Halloween, Meredith glanced over to make sure there wasn't a ghost or zombie or something out there. Shivering, she looked in the mirror again, wondering what Tanner would think of her Wonder Woman costume.

He'd seemed surprised when she invited him to go to a Halloween party with her. Jill was over the moon about it. And tonight, the rest of the town was going to see her out with him. Maybe if they hung out often enough, she could curb the Man Bender talk.

She almost reached for a Pepcid.

She'd thought about going as J.D. Robb's kick-ass cop, Eve Dallas, going so far as to locate a long black leather jacket online similar to the one Nora wore in her author photo for the series. Who didn't want to be married to Eve's hot hubby Roarke? But the likelihood of someone identifying her costume seemed remote. And she really didn't want to spread fake blood on her jeans like Nora's heroine.

She pivoted in front of the mirror. Going as a superhero seemed the best alternative given her recent internal monologue with Divorcée Woman. After all, Wonder Woman would have worn red La Perla lingerie too.

"I wish you'd let me make you a cape embroidered with DW."

Jill bumped Meredith's hip, smoothing back her own wig. Her sister's Little Bo Peep outfit was over-the-top adorable.

"No way." Meredith turned as the wind blew in a perfect imitation of a train whistle. "We'll freeze, but we'll look good."

"Oh, yeah."

When Jill slapped her butt, Meredith punched her arm.

"I need to go," Jill said, touching up her glossy pink lips in the mirror. "I was hoping to see Tanner, but you can tell him hi for me."

"Are you ever going to stop gloating?"

"No way. You needed to be pushed. You're like a tick that can't be dislodged about some things."

"That's so sweet."

She backed up and blew kisses. "You'd better have fun. Ta-ta."

The wind slapped the door against the wall before Jill closed it.

Meredith broke out in goosebumps.

"Oh, that's hot," she whispered to herself.

*He won't be looking at those bumps, trust me.*

She was too excited and nervous to respond to her alter ego's prodding.

Ten minutes later, Meredith opened the door and Tanner walked in, dressed as a dashing hero straight off a pirate ship.

His mouth curved. "Oh, man. Wonder Woman. Christ, that's sexy."

*Told ya.*

He stepped into Jill's small entryway and shut the door, leaning back against it, all male nonchalance.

She ignored her alter ego and crossed her arms over her chest, suddenly shy as his intense gaze lifted from her red shoes to her dolled-up face. He hadn't looked at her this way in weeks. Her invitation had changed their tacit agreement of just being friends. Her skin felt as tightly stretched as a newly starched shirt.

"You even have the lasso," he said.

She gazed at his costume. He hadn't bothered to button the white, billowy shirt all the way up, and it exposed the middle of his chest. With the black cloth tied around his forehead and the gold earring dangling from his right ear, he looked somewhat sinister.

And hot too. She wanted to fan herself.

*Shiver me timbers,* Divorcée Woman purred.

Are you actually doing pirate talk in my head now? She almost pulled her own hair, but she didn't want to disturb her wig.

"Did you hear me?"

"What?"

"You can use that lasso to tie me up anytime."

Lustful images of her wrestling him to the ground and tying him up swarmed her mind.

*Oh my,* Divorcée Woman squeaked.

"Tanner?" She cleared her throat. "I want to be clear about tonight."

He readjusted the fake antique gun in his leather-studded belt, drawing her eyes to his scandalously tight black pants. She looked at a point over his shoulder, telling herself not to look at his crotch.

*You know you want to.*

"I want to be clear that we're only going to the party together."

He sauntered forward, flicking back the black cloth brushing his shoulder. "Are you sure you want to set parameters this early on in the evening?"

Her breath hitched.

"You're not starting a panic attack, are you?" he asked, his eyes wide.

She almost lied to make him back away. "Not yet, so let's keep it that way."

"If I were a real pirate, I wouldn't be held off. I'd sweep you over my shoulder and carry you to my cabin and ravish you."

God, the fantasy. Her heart pounded in her chest like a jackhammer.

"That kind of talk is off limits tonight."

He raised a brow. "Last time I looked, there was still free speech in this country. You might be able to set the terms on touching, but I can damn well say anything I want."

This frustrated Tanner was new. Her growl nearly escaped, but Wonder Woman wouldn't back down. "Not if you're going with me."

"Then why did you ask me to come?" The light in his eyes dimmed. "You've been getting pressure from Jill, haven't you? Is this your attempt at appeasement?"

His ability to read her made her squirm. "Well, I...no."

He scoffed. "That was believable. So let me get this straight. You invited me to go out with you because I'm probably the only man in town under fifty you haven't already gone out with." He snapped his fingers. "I'm right, aren't I? It's written all over your face."

She fiddled with her wrist bands. "Well, I thought we could go out a little. Regularly. You know. As friends."

He stepped closer, touching the tips of his black knee-high boots to her red ones. A strong musky smell tickled her nose. A pirate wasn't supposed to smell that good. Where was the brine? The salt water? The B.O.?

"I was okay with taking a step back after what happened in your mom's kitchen. I've tried to give you space. But I draw the line at being another one of your whipping boys, who isn't supposed to act like a man."

Her face flamed. "I'm not saying we can't flirt. But I'm...playing the field." So she was a red-headed slut after all, not to mention a coward. Maybe she should have worn a fraidy cat costume.

He chuckled low in his throat, sending her skin into a rash of goosebumps again. "Meredith, have you been practicing that in the mirror? If so, it needs more work, honey. You're not the type of woman who plays the field. Any smart man can see that."

So, he was smart, was he? She could feel her skin develop an angry burn. "Don't tell me what I am."

"Seems I need to make a point."

He yanked her to him, finding her mouth. His lips caressed hers like an electric charge, making them tingle, the power growing stronger the longer the connection went on. And boy, did it go on, taking her on a slow descent into desire's dark well. She moaned in her throat, her fingers digging into his shoulders. When he traced the seam of her mouth, she opened herself to him. Their tongues tangled, electricity racing down her spine and pooling in the center of her thighs. The kiss went deep, wet. Meredith pressed closer, the places their bare skin touched tantalizing. His hands gripped her hips, making her aware of his arousal. She whimpered again, angling her head for a deeper kiss. He tore her hands away and stepped back, panting.

"*That's* what's between us, Meredith."

She pressed her lips together to stop the tingling. "What do you want me to say?"

"Meredith, I'm not going to be part of your endless male parade. I've been straight with you." He looked away suddenly, but she caught his frown. When he turned back, his gaze pinned her in place. "I like you. I like spending time with you. But I want you, and I'm not going to be one of a dozen or so guys you date. If you want to spend time with me, it's on an exclusive basis. We'll take it slow and see where it goes, but I'm not going to agree not to touch. I want us to touch each other as much as we can handle without killing each other."

Her throat squeezed to the size of a straw.

*Come on*, she heard Divorcée Woman lovingly whisper. *You can do it.*

The fear towered over her like a black cloud. She stepped back from it.

"I...can't." Her eyes burned.

He gave a gusty sigh. "I'm sorry to hear that. I think we'd be good together, in bed and out. If you change your mind, let me know."

"Tanner!" She realized she didn't want him to leave. She'd never been so confused in her life.

"Why are you here?" he suddenly demanded.

"What do you mean?"

"Why did you come back to Dare?"

The desire to fidget was as tantalizing as a nicotine fix to a cigarette smoker. "I'm helping my family, remember?"

"Yes, but that's not all, is it?"

She ran through some versions of the truth. "I want to find out if true love still exists. Okay?"

He flinched. "Oh, Meredith."

His hushed tone had her stiffening. "Why are you here? This is about the farthest place from your usual beat."

He looked down at his boots. When he raised his head, his clenched jaw and fiery eyes made her heart pound.

"Let's just say I have to make good on a promise."

"Ah—"

"No, I think that's enough for tonight." He ran his tongue across his teeth like he was in pain. "Besides, you're forgetting you don't date journalists."

Had she? She wasn't sure she'd be able to open herself to him even if he *weren't* a journalist. The way he made her feel terrified her. Cold seeped around her as he opened the front door. She started shaking. "You're right."

"I'm mostly proud of what I am, Meredith. I've worked hard to get to this stage in my life." The wind whipped the black cloth over his shoulder. "I'm not the fucking Cheese Man. Maybe you should remember that."

The door slammed shut behind him. Maybe it was the wind, but her internal temperature had dropped twenty degrees. She struggled over to the orange couch on wobbly legs and unraveled the green afghan. Go out exclusively? He'd lost his mind.

Hadn't he?

A fresh ache spread across the back of her skull. She thought about the way he'd looked when he told her he liked her. Her heart twisted like she'd fallen on a stake. If she'd dressed up as a vampire, it might have been fitting.

*You're an idiot. Who turns down Wonder Woman/Pirate sex?*

What the hell was she supposed to do now?

*** 

Tanner kicked up snow as he walked back to his car with a hard-on he was sure could be seen in outer space. The tight pants he was wearing had to be the worst idea since pet rocks.

Christ, what did she think he was? He wasn't some fucking wimp who would put up with her "playing the field" crap. Especially when she kissed him back like she wanted to devour him. Her hot skin, wet mouth, and tortured moans had almost made him lose control, pulling her onto Jill's hideous orange couch.

He ripped open the car door. Meredith didn't know what the hell she was talking about. If she was playing the field, she'd have slept with at least one of the men she'd been "going out with," and he knew for a fact that she hadn't. Dare had a betting pool on who could talk Meredith Hale into the rebound sack. He'd walked away from the group of locals when they'd asked him how much money he'd like to lay down.

He'd like to lay down all right.

And it wasn't in the betting pool.

More like pressing his face into her red hair as he thrust himself mindlessly into her strong, slim body. With only a Wonder Woman crown on her head.

He had to stop thinking about it. His pants were squeezing him to death.

He slammed the car in gear. He'd lost all objectivity. He kept forgetting why he was here when he was with her. He turned into some horny, jealous boyfriend. Dammit.

Edge back a minute, McBride. He *did* need her to be exclusive if he was going to convince Sommerville he was making headway. He had jack-shit on that asshole and was getting in deeper with his "target" every day.

He hadn't lied to Meredith about one thing, though.

He really did like her. A lot.

Her quiet admission about coming home to find out if love still existed had squeezed his heart.

They were both trying to be as honest as they could. He'd have to think about that.

It was all getting so complicated.

And he had a hard-on in tight pirate pants for Christ's sake. Pirate pants!

He gunned away from the stop sign and fishtailed on the ice. Needing some outlet for his frustration and the anger he felt toward himself, he pressed on the accelerator. No one was on the street. What did it matter if he took out a mailbox? He'd pay for it.

The tires gripped the ice, and he fought to keep the car straight. When he got to the highway, he rolled the window down and let it rip. He barely saw the deer in time and would have hit it if it hadn't made a sharp zigzag off the road. He welcomed the adrenaline rush.

Memories of another night, another highway surfaced, but he clicked them off. The past was past. Only the present was real.

He'd made a stand with Meredith Hale.

He almost hoped she wouldn't cave.

He had a bad feeling the pleasure of being with her wouldn't be worth the pain it would cause them both.

He shifted in his seat. Who was he lying to now?

# Chapter 17

Jill bounced away from the keg, sipping her pumpkin beer. "Monster Mash" played at a steady volume from somewhere behind her. A mummy made of whipped cream topped a buffet table, tempting her. She took a taste with her finger and gagged.

"Shaving cream," a Star Trek officer noted.

"Gack."

She was squeezing through two bloody vampires holding fake rats when an arm on her shoulder made her jump.

Jemma snorted. "Freaked out by the rats?"

"People are sick."

Jemma's Cleopatra wig shifted as she bobbed her head to the music. "They're from Pat's uncle. He's a taxidermist in Idaho."

"Yuck!" Jill reached over to adjust Jemma's wig.

"You should have come as Ol' Mother Hubbard. I'm fine."

She narrowed her eyes. "You're totally lit. Where have you been?"

"The back room. I decided to live a little tonight."

"Jemma," Jill scolded. "You're not into that stuff." Her nose picked up the pungent smell of marijuana and patchouli. "Dammit, Jem."

The heavy touch of black kohl around her friend's over-bright eyes was smudged. "Pete was here with his new girl. Can you believe it? He's already seeing someone. I wanted to die before, but now I feel great."

Jill wrapped her arms around her. "Oh, honey. Where is he? I'll knock him in the nuts with my staff."

"That would be awesome, Jillie. He took one look at me and bolted." She pushed back, weaving in place.

"Better slow down a bit," Jill said, wrapping a steadying arm around her.

Jemma's kiss smeared red lipstick over her cheek. "Don't be upset. You're my best friend."

"Yeah, yeah, yeah," she muttered, worry darkening her enjoyment. Damn Pete. Couldn't he have waited at least a few more months?

Batman entered Lola Parson's family room, making Jill freeze in place. He was a few inches taller than most of the partygoers. And she'd know that mouth anywhere.

"Brian's here, Jem."

"Go outside. I'll keep him occupied. There's no reason for both of us to be miserable." Still unsteady on her feet, Jemma leaned against a beige ottoman, and then sank down into it, closing her eyes. "I'll get to him in a minute."

"I'll watch her, Jill," someone said from behind her.

As a Robin Hood, Ray Pollack wasn't much of a dashing swashbuckler. He was too short and gangly for the tights, and way too nice to fight the nasty Sheriff of Nottingham. Being the college's main marijuana dealer, he didn't need to be strong. He needed to be smart. And he was—she knew that from the chats they had when he came in for his large soy mochas. Top of his class and pre-law. Jill appreciated the irony. Her grandpa had been pumping her for a name, but she wouldn't give it. He was crazy to think anything serious was going on. People partied. People puked. It was a chemical reaction.

"Seems like your stuff already did its magic."

His face fell. "She was upset about Pete. I told her to be sure."

"Whatever. I'm going outside for some air. Glenda, will you keep an eye on her?" she asked a biology student who was dressed as a nurse.

"Sure, Jill," she said, plopping down next to Jemma. "Best let her sleep it off. Poor kid. Pete's an asshole."

"You said it." Jill smoothed the black hair from Jemma's cheek, and then eased her way out onto the back porch.

The wind bit into her legs like a million slivers, but she could stand it for a few minutes. The clean air filled her lungs, dispelling the strong stench from indoors—strong perfumes and aftershaves mixed with beer and various types of smoke, both legal and illegal.

She jumped when a black form materialized next to her, his cape rippling. His amused smile made her want to bean him with her makeshift staff. He just had to follow her out.

Brian pointed to his chest, bending low so their frozen breath mingled in the air. "I'm—"

"Butthole," she interrupted, depriving him of the famous line.

He rested his hand on his waist, his cape snapping in the wind. "Try another B word."

"Butt blister."

His smile deepened. "That's two words."

His familiar scent and those mischievous blue eyes had her shivering from more than cold. She snapped her fingers. "Bastard."

His mask emphasized his frown. "I don't think Little Bo Peep should talk that way."

She tried to walk around him, but he kept blocking her.

"I don't think Batman should harass Little Bo Peep."

"Batman's only trying to protect her from the big bad wolf. I think I saw one inside."

"That's a werewolf, you dumbass."

He touched her white-ribbed bodice. "Aren't you freezing?"

"Now that you mention it."

He swung off his cape like a bullfighter, wrapping it around her before she could stop him.

"Shame to cover up that costume, though," he said. "I think it's even hotter than a French maid's outfit."

"Wear one often, do you?" Her smile was all teeth.

He rubbed his hands up and down her arms, making her shiver even harder. "Yes, and I always keep my feather duster with me. You never know when it might come in handy."

She pulled away. Damn him for not losing his sense of humor out East. She'd always loved their banter, and the way he never seemed to be at a loss for a comeback.

"I need to go back inside." Her black heel caught in the crack between the deck boards.

His hands steadied her. "You ran out here in that scanty outfit to escape me, and now you're running back in? This has to stop, Jill."

She thrust her staff in his direction. He didn't budge.

"You need to leave me alone."

His eyes met hers dead center. "I've tried. I can't, Jill. Your little lie about McBride pushed my buttons. It forced me to accept the truth."

"That's your problem," she said, but a hitch in her voice betrayed her.

He spanned her waist, his thumbs tangling in the front laces of her outfit. "You wouldn't be this upset if it wasn't your problem too. Can't you forgive me, Jill? Jemma has."

"Fine, you're forgiven," she said even though she didn't mean it. "Now let me go."

He pressed his forehead to hers suddenly, resting the rubber mask against her skin. "I can't let you go, Jill." His sigh caressed her cheek. "Take off my mask."

She tried to kick him, but he slid a hard, muscled thigh between her legs, right above the garter that held up her stockings. Her thighs clenched together around him, and she was afraid her head would fall back in surrender. Her skin was both burning hot and cold, like winter exposure.

"Let me go."

"Take off my mask."

Even cold and aroused, she knew his unmasking was metaphorical too.

"Dammit, Jill, take off my mask."

"No!"

His mouth curled. "Fine, if that's how you want it."

He slammed his lips against hers, mask and all. The impact rocked her back on her heels. He followed, his hands fisting around her waist. Her mouth opened. His tongue swept inside. The feel of it had her body screaming, her muscles clenching hard in response. She dropped her staff and gripped his head.

After so many years of wanting him, her body was screaming *Yes, God, yes.*

He changed the angle of their kiss, deepening it, his cold leather gloves settling on her even colder butt. He thrust his hips forward, making her stomach seize. She wanted him. Now. Was about to make the biggest mistake of her life.

His breath fanned out in short puffs, matching hers. "Let's get out of here."

A scream broke through her aroused reverie. Brian lifted his head as shouting erupted in the house behind them, and both of them turned to look inside. People were running everywhere, yelling at the top of their lungs.

"Something's wrong. We should get inside."

He pushed her toward the door.

All traces of the party had evaporated. Women were crying, mascara running down their cheeks. The few men who weren't wearing masks had the shocked, rubbernecking look people get near a fatal car crash. A few people were kneeling down over something. Jill edged closer, but then stopped in her tracks when she caught sight of a sandaled foot lying lax on the worn green carpet.

"Oh my God," she whispered as the shock hit, and a tremor ran through her body.

She looked higher and saw that some guy was shaking Jemma, who was lying supine on the floor, Ray beside her.

"Jem!" she screamed.

"Christ!" Brian pushed through the crowd. He knelt by Jemma and pressed two fingers to her neck, looking for a pulse. He thrust the guy away with a hard shove and tugged off his mask. Turning her head, he started CPR.

"I don't know what happened," Ray cried, wringing his dark green costume. "She stopped breathing."

Jill edged closer. She watched Brian count in between breaths, his cupped hands making compressions on her chest.

"Call an ambulance, Jillie," he yelled and then lowered his mouth to Jemma's again.

She fell back, hitting people. Oh, God. Where was her purse? "I need a cell phone! Now" she shrieked.

"Here!" a girl cried out to her right, thrusting something at her.

Jill dimly realized she was dressed as Barbie before opening it and dialing in three scary numbers with a shaking finger.

"Man, the cops are going to show up. I'm outta here," one of the vampires said. "Ray, you'd better take off too."

His gaze met hers before he stumbled off, a few of the other guests following him. Cowards, she wanted to yell.

When dispatch picked up, Jill relayed their location, and reported that her friend wasn't breathing. She didn't hear what the lady said next, or if she did, she couldn't process it. Barbie took the phone from her limp hand.

Brian continued CPR. Jill waited for Jemma to push him off and say, *Yuck, McConnell, get that mouth away.* And then laugh with gusto.

But she didn't.

Jill stood frozen, locked in ice.

Brian's red face beaded with sweat. "Dammit, Jill, get over here!"

She tripped as she took a step, off balance, and fell next to her best friend. Tears rolled down her cheeks as she reached for Jemma's hand. It already seemed cold to her. She fingered her wrist for a pulse. This is bad, her mind said, but she couldn't feel that. She couldn't feel anything.

"Bri, she doesn't have a pulse," she gasped.

He took a deep breath as he pumped his hands on Jemma's chest. "She will. Dammit, Jem! Come on. Come back to us."

Then he pressed his mouth to hers again, trying to breathe life into her.

His emotional reaction triggered Jill's. "Jemma, please!" she cried, sobbing now, her hands tearing at her hair.

"I think she's gone," someone commented.

Brian started pumping again—one, two, three. "Shut the fuck up! She's going to be fine." He lowered his mouth to hers again.

Putting a trembling hand on his arm," Jill said, "Bri."

He shot up, his blue eyes red-rimmed, wild. "No! She's not dying on me."

Jill's heart exploded, the fragments burying deep into her bones, pain radiating everywhere.

Brian didn't give up. Not until the paramedics arrived, pulled him off, and pronounced Jemma dead.

She walked over to him, feeling like she wasn't in her own body, but in some glass room where she could see everything but not be touched by it. Brian was panting, watching with glassy eyes as they laid a blanket over Jemma, covering her beautiful face. Jill wrapped her arms around him, pressed her face into his chest, and fell to pieces. His hands fisted by his sides, and she rubbed at the tension in his back, wanting to comfort, seeking his comfort. Then his arms squeezed her in a vice, and he buried his sweaty head in her neck, making her sob all the harder.

# Chapter 18

Meredith set the morning paper aside when she heard the muffled rap on the door. She darted forward, her slippers sliding on the hardwood floor. She hoped Jill wouldn't wake up.

She looked through the peephole and saw Tanner holding two cups of coffee. Even though she wasn't dressed, she cinched her blue terrycloth robe closed and opened the door. If anyone expected her to look presentable, they weren't her friend.

"I heard what happened. I brought you guys coffee."

After what had happened between them the night before, she thought about telling him to get lost, but she didn't want that. God, she hurt—it felt like she'd been beaten by a bat everywhere.

"Come in," she said in a soft voice, "but please be quiet. Jillie's finally asleep."

She took the coffee, and stepped back to let him in. He removed his outerwear, displaying jeans and a black fleece—a far cry from the pirate outfit. When he followed her into the kitchen, she gestured to a worn chair.

He laid his hands on the table and pinned her with that intense gaze of his. "I had a bad feeling this morning that you didn't show up at the pool because of what happened between us last night. So I swam off my mad and headed to Don't Soy with Me. Margie told me what happened. It's a tragedy. How's Jill?"

She wanted to hold his hand, so she gripped the coffee cup instead. "She's devastated," she said after a moment, "and she's afraid it's her fault. She left her to go outside. Brian had arrived." She rubbed her neck, remembering how Jill's streaming tears had mixed with her black mascara. "He followed. They had another row. When they heard the commotion, they went back inside."

She took a sip of the coffee—it didn't do much to soothe her throat, but at least it was warm. "Brian started CPR. Jill said he didn't stop until the paramedics dragged him off."

"That's tough."

"Yes. Yes, it is." She couldn't stop thinking that her grandpa might have been onto something about the kids getting sick from booze and pot. Oh, God.

"Any idea what happened?"

She pushed the other coffee toward him without answering. She didn't want to say anything yet. "Drink it. Jill won't once it's been cold."

"How are you holding up?" Tanner asked, taking her hand.

Her fingers jerked, but he didn't let go. "Umm...I don't know. Jemma was always around growing up. She, Jill, Brian, and Pete were the four musketeers." When he squeezed her hand, she looked down at the grooves in the farm table. "It's a damn waste," she whispered, fighting tears. "She was so young."

He pulled her out of her chair. Her bones felt like plastic from fatigue, shock, and grief, and when he enfolded her in his arms, holding her tight against his chest, she rested her head on his shoulder.

"Yes, she was," he whispered.

The burn of tears alarmed her, but she was too tired to do more than rub her face into his fleece.

His hands rubbed her back without demand. "Shh...You should rest too. You're about ready to fall over."

Meredith pulled back and wiped away a stray tear.

Nudging her hand away, he traced a finger down her cheek. "You look beautiful. Probably an odd thing to say right now, but it's true."

No, it was dear. She realized she couldn't move away from the heat he radiated. It was as warm and comforting as sunshine drenching a window seat on a winter's day.

"Why are you here?" she made herself ask, her heart hopeful but still guarded.

He sighed. "I don't have a good explanation. I only know I couldn't stay away."

Oh God. "This is getting complicated."

He rubbed his hands up her arms, and then let go. "Let's leave that for now. So, do you know what happened?" he asked again.

She sat back down and gripped her coffee in both hands. His touch felt too good. She realized it was nice to lean on someone. She'd been the strong one last night when Brian dropped off Jill, who was shaking and wrapped in a black cape and a police blanket.

"Jill didn't see it, but others said Jemma started to shake violently. Then she stopped and went limp." But she hadn't puked like the kids who'd been hospitalized, so what did that mean? She shook herself. "Brian couldn't find a pulse. She wasn't breathing."

"Was she using?"

Meredith pushed her hair behind her ear. "Just alcohol and pot. Pete—her childhood sweetheart—showed up with a new girl. Jemma was devastated, and she acted out."

"That wouldn't kill her."

"No, it shouldn't have."

"Who's handling the case?"

"Are you asking as a journalist?"

He held up his hands, palms up. "I have a journalist's curiosity."

Right. She needed to remember that. "Larry Barlow, the deputy sheriff, and the coroner, a family friend. We'll have to wait for the autopsy. Grandpa checked to make sure it's being expedited."

Grandpa had called her an hour or two ago after coming by late last night to check on Jill. He was heartbroken, but his gut was quivering too. They'd have to wait and see what the autopsy report said.

His fingers drummed the side of the cup. "Her family will want to know why."

"Yes. My parents are flying back for the memorial service."

"I should go. You need to rest."

The realization that she didn't want him to leave made her hand clench around the coffee. Not good. Still, she followed him to the door. He stuffed his boots on and wiped up the snow-melt on the floor.

When he opened the door, their gazes locked. "I'll call you later to check on you guys."

"Don't you need my number?"

The wind ruffled his thick hair as he started down the sidewalk. "Don't insult me, Mermaid," he said over his shoulder. "I'm a journalist." He jogged to his car, making footprints in the snow.

She shut the door and leaned her forehead against it. A warmth cupped her heart.

*He called you, Mermaid,* Divorcée Woman practically sang. *How sweet.*

Yes, it was.

# Chapter 19

Nearly a thousand people attended Jemma's funeral, a mix of college students and Dare residents. The college had offered the use of the basketball arena. Meredith winced at the squeaks from people's shoes meeting the treated wood floor. Somehow, it ruined the sacredness of the ceremony more than the hydrogen stadium lights.

People cried all around her on the cold metal bleachers. Everyone was still in shock over the autopsy report. Jemma had died from a heart murmur. Meredith couldn't believe it. Her grandpa had thrown the report on the floor and stormed out of his office, leaving her to pick it up with shaking hands.

She'd died of natural causes. Her grandpa had been wrong after all—there was no story here.

Why didn't it hurt any less?

She shifted on the bleachers as more students told stories about Jemma from the lily-decorated podium. Even the Anderson family braved the stage, their faces splotchy, wiping away tears. Meredith reached for a Kleenex when Jill adjusted the microphone and told a story of them as kids. She'd chosen one that also showcased Brian and Pete—a nice touch, Meredith thought.

"She was fearless," Jill finished, looking unfamiliar in a black dress with none of her usual colorful accessories. "And so full of life. I'll miss you." She stumbled coming down the dais, and both Pete and Brian jumped from their chairs to help. It broke Meredith's heart. The bond between them might be frayed, but it wasn't gone.

Jill darted back and pressed her face into their mother's neck, crying softly.

Meredith studied Brian for a moment. She hadn't seen him at all over the past few days. No one seemed to know where he'd gone. His face looked green under the fluorescent lights.

Her eyes flitted past the middle section of the crowd and met Tanner's gaze. Her mouth turned up slightly in a poor attempt at a smile. He tilted his head to the side like he was studying her. God, he looked handsome in a simple white shirt and black blazer. They stared at each other until her neck developed a crick. She rubbed it and looked away, her heart pounding in her ears.

The pallbearers carried Jemma's coffin out of the arena, their college bodies hunched over from grief. The Hales shuffled out.

Jill scanned the crowd. "Brian!" she called out, and took off at a run.

Grandpa Hale nudged Meredith. "Best go after her. She'll need you."

Nodding, she kissed his cheek and followed her sister. Brian was heading for the rear exit like his tail was on fire, but Jill increased her speed. So did Meredith. She wasn't sure if she should follow, but she couldn't bear for them to have another fight. Not now.

Jill made it to the side door and pushed the heavy frame open. "Brian! Dammit. Stop!"

He finally turned to face her.

Jill slowed. She was breathing hard. "I've been...calling you...for five days. Why haven't you...called me back?"

His face held a tinge of yellow, and even from this distance, his eyes looked puffy and bloodshot. "I wanted to be left alone." He unbuttoned his navy blazer and rested his hands on his hips. "Why are you suddenly so eager to call me anyway? Fucking-A, Jill."

She marched forward and drilled her finger into his chest. "Don't you dare 'fucking-A' me! I was worried about you."

He scoffed.

Meredith edged a bit closer.

"Just leave me the fuck alone."

"No," she said shoving her hands against his chest.

He grabbed them.

Meredith strode forward. "Stop it. Both of you."

They turned to face her, and Brian dropped Jill's hands. "You keep her away from me, Meredith. I can't take it right now. Neither can Pete."

Jill flinched. "Like he fucking cares. He dumped her."

"He cares! He's suffering just like the rest of us. But I'm not going to argue with you. I just can't...not right now, Red."

Brian jogged off. Jill's shoulders slumped.

"Come here, Jillie Bean," Meredith said, pulling her in for a hug.

Jill clung to her like a monkey. "It's never going to be all right again!" she sobbed.

Meredith gripped her sister harder, knowing how shitty it was to tell anyone time healed all wounds. Blah, blah, blah. She'd hated it when people told her that after her divorce.

"Everything okay?" she heard Tanner ask from behind them. She swiveled a bit to look at him, releasing Jill. He had his hands on his hips, his gaze understanding. "Come on. Let's get the two of you a cup of tea. Then we'll go to the gravesite."

Jill bit her lip. "I don't want to go. I don't want to see them put her in the ground."

"I know you don't," Tanner said, gently resting a hand on her shoulder, "but she's not there anymore. You remember that." He pulled her against his chest. "You go for her family. And because you're still here."

He rubbed her back like she was a little child, and she started crying again. How many people had cried in his arms during a war? He seemed to know exactly what to do, what to say.

Meredith's heart tingled, like it had gone numb and was coming alive again. It...hurt. Seeing him comfort her sister like that had her defenses cracking like a hand through a window. He seemed like someone she could trust. She gripped her charcoal bustier under her black dress.

*You can trust him, Meredith.*

She lowered her trembling hands, realizing her alter ego was right.

Tanner eased back. "You ready now?"

He held out his hand, which Jill took. When he extended his other hand to Meredith, her eyes burned. She grabbed it, his strong hold a comfort as they walked down the cold, quiet hall.

He left them at the gravesite and blended into the crowd. Jill stood tall with the wind whipping through her hair, her face now devoid of tears. Meredith brushed at the wetness trailing down her own face and blamed the wind.

When everyone returned to their cars, she walked over to Tanner's SUV. He rolled the window down.

"I wanted to thank you," she said. "For helping Jill." She looked away when his direct gaze only heightened her awkwardness and vulnerability. "You're...really good with people. I can see why you're such a good journalist."

He was rubbing the bridge of his nose when she met his eyes again. "I lost my best friend in high school. A car accident. I was in the passenger's seat. The car hit the driver's side." He touched the small scar near his mouth.

Goosebumps rippled across her skin. "I'm sorry."

"You should get back to your car. You're shivering. Where are your gloves?"

"I left them in the car."

He pulled his own off with quick efficiency. "Take mine." He reached for her hand and slid one on. Her heart pumped hard and fast in her chest. They were too big, but she didn't stop him. When he'd finished putting the other on, she could barely swallow over the lump in her throat. Could you be aroused and moved at the same time?

"Our car's just over there."

"Take them. You can give them back to me later. Now, get going." He squeezed her hand before releasing it.

She hurried back to the car. Her grandpa raised a brow as she got into the backseat. Jill pressed close to her, crying, and she wrapped an arm around her.

Even though she no longer needed them, she didn't take off Tanner's gloves. Musky aftershave and that special man scent enveloped her. When the car inched forward, she pressed one of the gloves to her nose and inhaled, thinking of Tanner's face when he'd told her about his best friend.

# Chapter 20

Dare Valley banded together like most small towns in crisis. Tanner was oddly touched by the black armbands some of his students wore. People seemed more eager to offer a friendly smile or a longer hug.

Don't Soy with Me was quieter—it was as though Jemma's departure had taken the joy out of the coffee shop. The espresso machine's roar had never seemed louder than it had these last few days.

His morning coffee didn't taste the same anymore.

He knew it never would.

Some people left their mark in inexplicable ways.

His students fell into a slump. Some of them had known Jemma. Others had only known her as the bright barista at Don't Soy with Me. Young deaths made people think about their own mortality in a new way. He'd heard a few people discuss getting a physical or an EKG even though the odds of them having a heart murmur were low.

It was still fucking hard to believe, but he knew how many surprises the body could dish out. He'd seen bodies that had withered in famine and ones that had been blown apart by suicide bombers. And he'd seen bodies overcome all odds. Villagers who'd walked hundreds of miles in snow fleeing the Taliban without shoes, their feet swollen and oozing blood. Amputee soldiers run marathons on prosthetic legs.

Life always held surprises.

But sometimes it fucking hurt.

The people of Dare were hurting.

Oddly enough, it had two effects on people. It could open up closed hearts, like Meredith's. And it could close hearts tighter than a turtle in its shell, like Brian's.

He was of two minds about the change in Meredith. He liked her way too much for comfort, but it killed him that they were heading exactly where Sommerville had hoped.

Only Tanner wasn't pretending.

His new plan was to gain Meredith's trust enough for her to tell him about the article. Then he would somehow persuade her not to do it.

It was something.

Meanwhile, he and Peggy continued to look into Sommerville. He'd covered his tracks well. They hadn't found anything but vague allusions to him "liking the ladies." He had to have known people would be gunning for him.

Smart enemies sucked. He'd take the dumb variety any day.

He wound his way to Don't Soy with Me after class, wanting to offer Jill some support. When he entered the shop, the air fragrant with hazelnut and steamed milk, she looked up at him from behind the register.

Walking forward, he tilted his head, studying her. She was pale and her eyes were swollen and red, but she managed a full, sad smile, and was somehow more beautiful for the effort. The black sweater she wore didn't seem right, but he knew she was in mourning.

"This isn't your usual time."

He shrugged. "I heard you were working tonight. Thought I'd see how you were holding up."

"Well, I'm standing." She spread her hands, silver bracelets clanging together. "I needed to come back to work. Can't let the business fail. Jemma would have hated that. How about a decaf?"

"What do you recommend?"

"Ladies' choice."

She shook her head when he dug out his wallet. "No, it's on the house today."

"Why?"

"For small kindnesses."

He put the money away as she brewed his coffee. When she presented it with flourish, he bowed at the waist.

"Kenya's finest."

He traced the rim. "I've always liked Kenyan coffee, so you chose well. I'll see you around, Jill."

"Tanner?"

"Yes?"

"Mere told me about your friend...in high school."

No one was behind him so he set his coffee down.

"How do you get over it?" She put a hand to the vulnerable line of her neck.

He tilted his head back and studied the neon green ceiling before meeting her gaze. "It takes a long time, and it never fully goes away." Hadn't he thought about it when he was speeding on Halloween? "Try not to beat yourself up. Things just happen." He rubbed the scar near his mouth. "I still don't know why. Try to stop asking why. It helps."

"Thanks."

"Take care of yourself, Jill."

"You too, Tanner."

He didn't speed on the drive home. Shane wouldn't have approved. He'd been speeding that fateful day in his new car. He'd barreled through a stop sign, dare-deviling his way across the highway. How they could have missed that pick-up truck was something he'd wonder for the rest of his life.

His driveway was quiet as a cemetery when he left the car. He was halfway to the door when he heard the unmistakable sound of branches snapping underfoot and leaves rustling. He froze, instantly alert.

It was too dark to see, so he strode to the porch, straining to hear. Perhaps it was that lone dog he kept seeing around his house. He refused to feed it, because then it would stay.

And Tanner wasn't staying in Dare.

"Professor McBride?" a male voice called out from his left.

He narrowed his eyes in the darkness. More branches broke, leaves crunching as the man approached him. When he stepped on the driveway, the gravel ground under his feet with a sound like marbles rubbing together.

"Who is it?" He edged behind one of the beams on the porch. He didn't expect problems, but he'd learned to be cautious.

The man came closer, his gait discernable in the darkness. "It's Ray Pollack."

A student? "Long way to come for a conference, son."

"Yes, sir. I'm sorry, but I couldn't approach you in public."

Tanner's muscles tightened. There was danger in that statement. He could almost smell the cold sweat on the kid.

"Why not?"

Ray cleared his throat. "Because I know how Jemma died."

"That's old news. She had a heart murmur."

The face lifted, stark white under the crescent moon emerging from behind a cloud. "No, sir. That's not the cause."

Adrenaline spiked. "Then what was?"

"I think I killed her."

# Chapter 21

"Why don't you tell me about it while I make us some coffee?" Tanner said after he'd convinced the kid to come inside.

Ray shifted on his feet like a rabbit ready to run, his boots squeaking on the floor.

"You're safe here." He set the coffee to brew. "Let's sit down."

"I need you to promise you'll treat me like a confidential source."

Tanner folded his arms across his chest. So the kid *had* listened in class. "Sit down, Ray." When he complied, Tanner continued. "You know how this works. You need to give me something first."

"You don't understand. These are really bad dudes." Ray's breath grew choppy. "And I can't go to jail. I just can't."

"Ray, listen to me. You need to calm down."

When the coffee maker coughed its last breath, he stood, poured a cup for each of them, and sat down again. Of all the things he'd imagined happening in Dare, this wasn't one of them.

"Talk to me, son."

The kid's hands shook when he gripped the cup. He winced when he took a sip—the coffee must have scalded him—but he kept drinking it. Tanner waited him out, studying the dark circles under his blood-shot hazel eyes. Ray's skin had a light gray pallor to it, and his face was a bit hollower around the cheekbones than normal. His clothes—a brown sweater and jeans—looked like they'd been slept in. He'd missed a few classes since Jemma's death.

"I'm the college's main supplier of marijuana."

Tanner couldn't have been more surprised. He hated to stereotype, but Ray was not drug dealer material. He was an A student with a round face, big eyes, and a weak chin.

"How'd you get into this?"

"I...ah...had trouble paying for some major car repairs my first semester. One of the guys in the garage took me aside and asked if I wanted to make some quick money. It seemed harmless."

*Always did,* Tanner thought.

He coughed and took another sip. "I mean, it's *marijuana*—not heroin or cocaine or meth. And the money is good. I'm pre-law, so I'm saving for law school."

The steam off Tanner's coffee trailed into the air like smoke, but he didn't touch it. The cup was a prop of normality. The human race always drank when they discussed important stuff, be it coffee, tea, or alcohol. He'd seen it in every country he'd ever visited—perhaps drinking somehow made every conversation seem more civilized.

"How does this relate to Jemma?"

"She smoked some of the marijuana I sold at the party."

Tanner studied Ray. He'd been lied to by the best of them, but he'd grown good at reading body language. Tanner wanted to sigh. The kid believed what he was saying. It was time to push a little harder.

"Okay, so why don't you tell me how smoking marijuana ended up killing her?"

Worrying his bottom lip with his teeth, Ray reached for his cup again. "Have I given you enough to be your source?"

"Yes, you have. Now tell me the rest."

"I think my supplier's been adding something into the stash. It's not like the old stuff. People are asking for more hash a hell of a lot faster than usual. They're not waiting for the weekend any more to get high. And some people have gotten sick at parties. Puking, passing out. Some have even gone to the ER. I told my guy about it, but he grabbed me by my shirt and told me to keep my mouth shut. I was like, what the fuck? Scared the shit out of me."

"Keep going."

"I kept hoping nothing was wrong. I didn't want anything to be wrong. I even asked my dealer again, and he flipped. Like bat-shit-crazy flipped. He told me it was just binge drinking that was getting people sick, and I believed him. Until Jemma. Now I'm convinced that they're lacing it."

Tanner leaned forward. If that was the case, the autopsy report should have found drugs in her system. But there hadn't been a word about any illegal substances in the newspaper article he'd read.

"What about Jemma's heart murmur?"

"I don't know, but I think someone's covering something up. That's why you have to find out what really happened." He tapped his fingers on the table like a cigarette smoker on day four of quitting. "I think someone on the police force is involved."

"That's quite a claim."

"Well, why else would they say Jemma only died from a heart murmur? Wouldn't the autopsy have picked up the pot in her system?"

"Yes, it should have."

"Plus, they didn't really interview anyone. I've asked around. That Deputy Barlow showed up after they called for the ambulance. Someone must have ratted me out, and nobody's talked to me. I've been freaking out for days, waiting."

"You have a point." The more the kid talked, the more his gut twitched.

"And there were drugs left at the party. I couldn't find everything before I left, but the police didn't raise any fuss."

Odd. "I see," he said to encourage him to continue.

"I want you to find out what's going on." His eyes teared up. "I can't stand it! I never would have sold this stuff if I knew it would hurt anyone. But they aren't going to let me out now. I'm fucking scared, man."

Tanner wanted to sigh. Nothing was free, and this kid was finally realizing it. God, he was tired of seeing people fuck up their lives. Actions had consequences. Why didn't anyone understand that?

"Do you believe me?" Ray wiped his nose with his sleeve.

"Yes, I believe you didn't want her to get hurt."

"So, you'll figure out what's going on? I have some drugs I can give you later."

Tanner steepled his hands. "Okay. Tell me about your supplier. How do you get the drugs?"

"You promise not to involve me if I tell you?"

"You're already involved, but for now, this is off the record. I'll only name you if you agree."

The kid's eyes bugged out. "What do you mean? I don't want anyone to know! They'll hurt me. I'm not going to keep selling after this. I'm out."

Tanner desperately wanted to reach for his coffee, but he kept still and thought things through. "Well, if we do figure out what happened, and you want the people who did this to pay, you might need to go on the record to have them arrested. Testify in court. I'm not an expert, but a good lawyer could ask for immunity or a reduced charge."

Ray covered his face with his hands. "That would ruin my chance at law school. Fucking A."

Maybe he was feeling the wings of being a teacher, but he put a hand on Ray's arm. "It's good that you feel bad, son. What's happened is fucking awful. Yes, this may ruin your chances at law school, but taking a stand and accepting responsibility for your actions may prevent you from hurting anyone else or ruining the rest of your life. Jemma doesn't have that chance."

Ray's lip trembled, but after a moment he nodded. "I never thought anyone would get hurt," he whispered. "I just wanted to make some extra money for school."

Tanner took his arm away. "Well, it sucks you have to learn this way, but coming forward is a good start."

"So you think you can get them?"

"I'll look into it. I owe it to Jemma—and to you." He tilted his head to the side. "Now, tell me everything else you know."

\*\*\*

Tanner sipped his scotch and studied his notepad. He had a good outline going of the first time Ray had noticed some additional "symptoms" from the marijuana. He had the name of the kid's supplier, Kenny Hopkins, a mechanic at Dare Auto Care. The guy sounded like a serious bruiser. The kid didn't know much more beyond that. Nor did he have a clue which official might be working with Kenny.

After fishing the article on Jemma's death in *The Independent* out of the recycling bin, Tanner had confirmed that it only mentioned her heart murmur and alcohol. The source? The autopsy report. He scribbled the word marijuana on the paper, circling it. Hadn't Meredith told him that Jemma had smoked pot that night? Ray had his gut twisting in the wind. The facts didn't add up. That's where his job started.

His cell rang. Great. Sommerville. "Yes?"

"About time you picked up. Ducking my calls wasn't part of our deal."

"It's been a little busy. A young woman died unexpectedly. She was a friend of the Hales," he added to get the guy off his back.

"I heard. Tragic. She was a pretty girl in the flower of her youth."

Flower of her youth? Is that the kind of hyperbolic bullshit that appealed to Meredith?

"Still, I've wanted greater progress with Meredith. Your time is almost up."

"I told you we had a date the other night." He wasn't about to admit they'd reached another impasse.

"One date after two months? That's not going to do it, McBride. I told you to move fast."

He slapped the couch. "Dammit, I moved on her like a john on a hooker. She had a panic attack. What the fuck did you expect me to do? I had to back off."

"You're supposed to get results. I don't fucking care how you do it! You're delaying, and I don't like it. You aren't going to find a way out of this, McBride. I have you locked up tight. And just to prove I won't hesitate, I'm going to show you what I can do."

Tanner unzipped his fleece, raging hot. Did blood actually boil? "What do you mean?"

A menacing chuckle echoed on the line. "You'll see. Don't fuck with me, McBride. You'd better get Meredith to stop dating other men and start dating you. I want that article stopped!"

Tanner surged off the couch and paced like a panther. "How the fuck do you know what she's up to? I told you not to watch her."

"I'm not watching her directly. Jill keeps me well informed. She can't say enough about her big sister's search for true love."

"What the fuck are you talking about?"

"I'm talking about Jill's Facebook page. She's written dozens of amusing snippets about Meredith's hunt for Mr. Right. As far as I can tell, she's dubbed you the Lost Chippendale."

"Jesus!" A Facebook FUBAR.

"She says Meredith is resisting you pretty hard and going out with everyone else in town but you. She thinks Mere's making a mistake, but a fact's a fact."

The window was cold when Tanner pressed his forehead to it. What a goddamn mess.

"Meredith's only resisting me so hard because she's afraid of where it will go. She's into me." His breath fogged the window. "This groundwork is critical. And I've been very supportive of her and Jill through Jemma's death. It'll pay off soon."

*Christ, was he really saying these things? It was true, it was all true, but he wasn't doing it for this prick.*

"Well, it better. But you'll know soon that I don't make idle threats. Let's call this a little incentive to work harder."

"Fuck you."

"I've studied you enough to know that you're looking for a way out. There isn't one. You need to do your job."

Tanner heard the guy gulp something, probably booze. His gaze tracked to the legal pad on the couch. A light bulb went off.

"She'll be spending lots of time with me starting this week. I promise you."

"Well, bad boys still need lessons. Don't make me give you another."

The phone disconnected.

Tanner kicked the leather ottoman with his boot. "Fuck."

Sommerville was on a tear. Tanner had little doubt there would be some form of payment now. He could only wait and see.

He needed to call Peggy to talk through autopsy cover-ups. And warn her to watch her back. Sommerville had better not go after his sister.

Picking up the legal pad, he scanned his tightly printed outline.

Suddenly he knew exactly how to make Meredith go out with him, and he wouldn't even need to toss his ethics to the wind to arrange it.

# Chapter 22

When Meredith left the locker room, Tanner was leaning against the concrete block wall outside of it, looking oh-so-delicious in a black fleece and worn denim. She was growing to like their swims way too much.

"I need you to go on a drive with me. There's something we should talk about."

She shifted her gym bag, surprised by his serious tone. "Okay."

Stepping forward, he took the strap from her. "Let me carry it. We can take my car."

He held the door open for her like usual, but something was up.

His clenched jaw made her stomach hurt. She hoped it wasn't anything about Jill. She'd been both inconsolable and enraged all week long. Jemma's death had put a hole in her heart, and Brian's continued silence was aggravating—and worrying—her. Meredith didn't know how to help Jill except to visit the coffee shop more often and watch chick flicks with her until she finally fell asleep on the couch.

As soon as they got into the car Tanner turned the heat on, obviously noticing that she was cold. "Do you have any suggestions for a quiet, private place where we won't be overheard?"

The wind blew hard against the car. She rubbed her arms, her heart beating faster. "How about my grandpa's house?"

She didn't ask why he didn't take her to his place. In some ways, she was glad. She wasn't sure she wanted to see where he lived. It was too...personal. Not to mention tempting.

"It'll be okay, Meredith." He put the car in gear.

*He looks hot when he's all serious.*

Meredith didn't even bother to comment. In a scary way, she was becoming used to the sultry voice in her head.

Tanner drove silently, following her directions. She wrung her hands instead of biting her nails, her mind awash with possibilities. When they arrived, she went around back, unearthing the key from the birdhouse by the deck. The house carried the faint whiff of coffee when she stepped inside. Her grandpa had left about an hour ago, she knew. He was always at work early.

"Do you want some coffee?" She surveyed the dirty dishes in the sink and the crumbs on the counter.

"Sure." He shut the door and took her coat, hanging it on the fleur-de-lis coat rack.

She couldn't help noticing how handsome he looked with his big shoulders, thick hair, and brown, melting eyes. The house was suddenly too quiet. She reached for the coffee.

"I had a visitor at my house the other night. I can't tell you who. I promised him anonymity."

She dropped the coffee can on the counter, her hands going lax in relief. A story? He'd brought her here for a story?

*Looking for something more personal, dearie?*

Grabbing the container again, she let out a breath. "Okay. What can you tell me?"

"The source thinks Jemma's death didn't play out like the autopsy said."

She dropped the can again. All her grandpa's suspicions shouted in her head. She leaned back against the counter. "Why would your source think that?"

"He supplied the marijuana she smoked. He thinks his supplier's been lacing it. The autopsy should have picked that up. It only mentioned the heart murmur and alcohol, according to *The Independent*."

"Hmm." She'd figured the reporter had stayed silent out of respect for the dead. The paper didn't always include all the details from an autopsy report. "So your source—a known drug dealer—thinks there's a cover up? And you believe him?"

He walked forward, eating up the space between them. "Sit down. I'll make the coffee."

She batted his hands away, guilt making her shake. If her grandpa was right, they might have stopped Jemma from dying. "I'm fine! I can do it." His intense gaze made her look away. She took a shaky breath. "Maybe they didn't release the information to protect her family."

She managed to start the coffee, her mind spinning. He waited for her to sit before turning a chair and straddling it.

"If I didn't believe my source, I wouldn't be telling you any of this. Most drug dealers wouldn't disclose to a journalist that their drugs caused someone's death. Usually they'd let a bogus autopsy fly."

"Wait a minute! We don't know anything was bogus. We only know what the paper said. I know the coroner. He's a family friend."

"Hold the fort a minute and listen." He outlined more of what he knew—and what didn't add up.

Bile rose in her stomach. So, his source had been concerned about clients visiting the ER, so much so that he'd even asked his dealer about it. That jived with her grandpa's hunch. She needed to talk with him about all this before she said anything to Tanner. Even if he hadn't been family, it was still reporter's courtesy. It was her grandpa's story.

The coffee brewed in the background, filling the kitchen with its dark roast scent. "So why did your source come forward? What's his angle?"

Tanner crossed his arms on the top of the chair. "A guilty conscience, I think, and reparation. He was a pawn. He wants the people who laced the drugs to pay for what happened to Jemma."

"We'd have to prove they were laced."

"I know."

She studied his face. She responded to his calm and collected approach, and it made her earlier knee-jerk reaction subside. She could trust this man, and if her grandpa agreed, they could share what they already knew.

"So why are you telling me? A good journalist doesn't want someone else stealing his scoop."

He raised his hands like a white flag. "I need your help. I don't have the same access to things in Dare. You just said you know the coroner. That's the kind of help I need. People will suspect something the minute I start asking questions. Plus, your paper has access to a lot of information. We can start there without tipping anyone off."

He was right. Outsiders were not part of the inner circle. She was a Hale. People considered her one of their own.

Plus, his source was exactly the kind of break her grandpa had been looking for.

"So what do you want to do?"

"Well, first, get me the autopsy report. Then, we have to create a cover for our investigation. Otherwise people are going to wonder why we're spending so much time together. There will be a lot of man hours on this. We'll need to be alone more often."

All the ideas racing around in her head stilled. Her heart bounced against her chest like a kid playing jacks with a rubber ball. She knew where he was going with this. Her mouth went dry.

"We're going to have to pretend we're going out."

What? The coffee machine coughed and sputtered, so she pushed back from the table to pour them a cup. When she extended his, the rim dipped.

He covered her hand. "Don't burn your fingers."

His touch instantly raised goosebumps across her arm. Damn those stupid pheromones.

"Why can't we simply say we're working on an article?" she asked, knowing the answer.

"If we do, people will want to know what we're working on. We're two high-powered journalists from New York who just arrived in town. It'll look funny."

"I don't—"

"If we tell anyone, it's your grandpa, no one else."

"You're darn right we'll tell my grandpa. I just have one question." She dropped her gaze to his lips before meeting his eyes. "Does this have anything to do with your intentions toward me?"

Those chocolate eyes twinkled. "My intentions? That sounds pretty old school. If you're curious to know, Meredith, my intentions toward you haven't changed."

*Well, hello, Mr. Darcy.*

Meredith pressed her fingers to her navy cashmere bodice with ivory lace cups. "I told you we could go out on Halloween."

He rubbed the scar by his lips. "I remember. I can't stop thinking about that kiss we shared. Have you decided to go out with me exclusively?"

She'd thought about it until she was blue in the face with no resolution. She snorted while her heart beat wildly in her chest. "No."

*Chicken,* Divorcée Woman snarled.

He rocked forward on the chair. "Then we're at an impasse. You're acting pig-headed. Just because I'm a journalist doesn't mean I'm Richard Sommerville."

She sucked in a breath. "Have you been *investigating* me?"

"Because I know who your ex is? Please. Besides, that's what this is all about, isn't it?"

"How do you know?"

"Because his reputation for being a fucking prick extends far and wide." His hands clenched the chair frame. "Okay, let's drop this."

"So you still want me even though you said no to me on Halloween?"

"Are we really having this conversation? You're making me crazy!"

She pointed to herself. "Me? How am *I* making *you* crazy?"

"I want you," he said, his eyes darkening. "I can't stop thinking about you. But I want us to be exclusive. You don't. So until you change your mind, we're only going to pretend to date. Got it?"

A headache spread around her temples. "No. Most guys would be content with being non-exclusive. Heck, they'd be thrilled. Why not you? You're expecting me to do what...surrender?"

His pulse pounded in his neck. "I'm expecting you to give yourself to me without holding anything back. Can you do that?"

Her breath hitched once, twice, three times. "Shit. God. No."

His chair scraped when he thrust out of it. "Oh Christ, don't have a panic attack again."

"I won't." She held out her hands to keep him away. His words had turned her skin to brushfire.

He hovered nearby like some hot paramedic waiting to see if she'd need mouth to mouth.

*Oh, my,* Divorcée Woman drawled.

"Stand up." Tanner said. "Meredith, look at me." A frown-mark appeared between his brows. "I need you to trust me."

"I...want to."

He shook her. "Then do it."

A burning warmth spread out from his hands down to her arms. She moved closer and inhaled the forest musky scent of his soap and shampoo. His gaze dropped to her mouth. She was sure of it.

*Kiss him, you idiot.*

As she was about to lean in, he pushed her away. He walked to the other side of the kitchen, reaching for her red coat. She tried not to look at his jeans when he turned back toward her and handed her coat to her. But she did. He was aroused, the cords of his neck looking more defined than usual. Suddenly, she could barely draw in a full breath.

"You'll get the autopsy?" He reached for the door handle like a prisoner ready to make a break for freedom.

"Of course."

"I'm going to wait outside." The door slammed behind him.

*What are you doing, Meredith Hale?*

Good question. She scrubbed her face with her hands and set about putting things back where they belonged, using the time to let them both regain control.

She couldn't let herself slip again. He was coming too close. Something had to give.

It couldn't be her.

# Chapter 23

Tanner thrust back from the desk in his home office the next morning and gave it a hearty kick. Fuck Sommerville. "Fuck!"

An hour ago, he was heading out the door for his morning swim when his brother gave him a frantic call. Sommerville hadn't lied. He'd shown his intent to hold Tanner's feet to the fire by running a nasty article on some discrepancies in David's voting record. Now David's opponent would have good fodder against him in the upcoming campaign, which would be a tight race. The article had stayed silent on his brother's good work as a councilman, of course.

Shoddy, personalized journalism. Well, nothing could be done now. He would have to pretend he was cozy with Meredith. Hopefully their cover would buy him enough time to bury Sommerville without hurting Meredith. The thought of her drove spikes in his gut.

So why the hell had he told her he wanted her when they were in her grandfather's kitchen?

Because he did.

Desperately.

It was more than being horny. He was old enough to know the difference.

He wanted her. And only her.

God help them both.

Even while he was telling her that she needed to trust him, part of him knew she shouldn't. The man in him wanted her trust—wanted to earn it. It was impossible. He'd hurt her and come off looking like as big a sleaze as her ex if she ever found out why he was really in Dare.

He gripped the chair to stop from throwing it across the room. His situation was impossible and infuriating.

Glancing at the clock, he called Peggy.

"Did you see the article?"

"Yes. David already called. He's going to crack, Tanner. He thinks it's all going to come out and ruin everything. I'm afraid he'll fall off the wagon again."

Knowing Peggy's tense relationship with their brother over his past binges, Tanner knew she was feeling more than she was letting on. Like him. He rubbed the back of his neck. "I hadn't thought of that. I was too mad."

"That's understandable. I want to take Sommerville down with my bare hands."

Her violence quieted his own. "We will, Peggy. We just need to keep digging."

Hearing something from outside, he turned toward the window. Seeing the stray dog again, tail wagging eagerly, only made him feel like a bigger heel. The animal's ribs were more prominent from hunger. Twigs and leaves dotted his mangy coat like he'd been rolling around on the ground. The mutt's golden eyes gleamed with excitement when Tanner approached the window. It gave three short barks and charged the glass.

"Is that a dog?"

"Yes, it's a stray that's been coming around."

"If you feed it, it's yours."

"Yes, I know."

"No collar?"

He knelt by the window, putting his hand against the glass where the dog danced. It licked the place he'd touched. "Nope."

"You always wanted a dog growing up."

She didn't say they hadn't gotten one because there hadn't been enough money to feed it. Jesus, he didn't need to remember crap like that.

"Let me tell you about something else that's come up."

He ran her through what Ray had told him about Jemma and the drugs.

"Well, life over there just keeps getting rosier for you. Sounds like you may have someone obstructing justice, but you'll need more evidence."

The dog continued to dance. "I know. Meredith is getting the autopsy report. It's a start. My source has a sample. I want to get a second test done."

"I can pull some strings. I'll get the drugs from you when I come out for Thanksgiving, and I'll have them tested in our lab. We can confirm whether they're laced."

Tanner sat back on his heels. "Huh?"

"You know, that pesky holiday between Halloween and Christmas when families come together. Keith wants to see you and the mountains. We talked about this, Tanner."

A family holiday? Man, he hadn't had one in...

"Three years ago at Christmas," she supplied.

"You a mind reader now?"

"I know you don't like holidays because of Dad, but you need to start making new memories. Frankly, I do too. Mom is going to New York to be with David and his family."

"I'd love for you to come."

"Try and sound more convincing when I call next time. I need to get going. Criminals to catch, and all that."

He chuckled finally, feeling the tension around his throat ease. It would be fine. They could show Keith how to ski. Have a snowball fight. It would be...nice.

"I love you, Tanner. Gotta go."

"Love you too." He clicked off, lifting his shoulder to shake off the awkwardness.

The dog started barking again, his black eyes gleaming. He nudged the glass with his wet nose, caramel hair fanning out on either side of his face.

Tanner found himself smiling. After a few minutes of fighting with himself, he turned and headed to the kitchen. He would see what he had to feed the dog.

Then they were going to the vet.

In the quiet, he decided it was finally time to accept that he wasn't going overseas again permanently.

Somehow there was peace in the decision—even as he feared his reasons for staying.

# Chapter 24

Meredith knocked on Tanner's front door. She was fidgeting, but couldn't help it. This was his home? In Frank Lloyd Wright style? Somehow she didn't equate wealth with Tanner. He wasn't flashy.

The house wasn't flashy exactly, but its quiet strength and the spare rocks and timbers it was constructed of bespoke power and decadence. Maybe he'd grown tired of living in hovels overseas. Maybe he loved nature.

Maybe she was thinking way the hell too much.

She pounded her frustration out on his mammoth door when he didn't answer.

Things were getting too personal. She was pissed at having to lie to Jill about "dating" Tanner, but she also didn't want to share their suspicions about Jemma. She wasn't going to do that until they had something solid. Grandpa had agreed, but it didn't make her feel any better.

What a fine web of lies she'd managed to weave. She was pond scum.

The door opened. Tanner looked hot and rustic with stubble coating his face. Damn him. She nearly goggled at the cascading wall fountain cut from stone that faced the open door. Recessed lighting from behind the water illuminated the whole thing.

"I brought the autopsy report since you didn't come swimming this morning," she snapped to cover her discomfort. "Where were you?"

She didn't want to admit she'd missed him...and worried about him. He never missed a swim.

When he tried to help her with her coat, she batted him away. "I can do it."

He held up his hands, looking so masculine in a navy sweater and jeans. "What crawled up your ass?"

At his direct approach, she threw her coat aside. "I don't like lying to Jillie about this. That's what." Who cared if it were a half-truth? She

120

wasn't about to say she was mad at him for asking her to give him everything.

His hearty sigh filled the silence. "Yes, lying fucking sucks. Hopefully we won't have to do it for much longer, and this will all be over."

The emotion in his voice stopped her from yanking off her gloves. "What are you so upset about?"

The intensity of his gaze rocked her back on her heels. "I don't like lying to a Hale either." He hung her coat. "I missed our swim because something came up with my family. I should have called."

She pressed her hands to the navy bustier she was wearing under her green sweater, seeking balance. She didn't know what to say. Their conversation made it seem like she had a right to know where he was. Like they were exclusive.

"Is everything all right?"

"No, but it will be. Thanks for bringing the autopsy report. I assume you read it."

She let him change the topic, but it only made her more curious. What was his family like? What had made him the man he was? Scary thoughts.

"Of course, I read it. The suspense was killing me. There's nothing there. It's a paragraph." She dug into her purse and thrust the paper out. "Read it yourself. Then I have some things to share."

He grabbed the report. "Let's have some coffee."

She followed him into the kitchen, trying to ignore what a showstopper it was. Gleaming stainless steel appliances, acres of granite countertops, and copper pots hanging from iron beams over a double stove.

"Grandpa and I are still trying to figure out how to ask for the police report without raising suspicion."

He started the coffee in a shiny, expensive appliance that had to be European.

"You talked to him? Good. Let's wait a bit on the police report until we think this through." He grabbed the autopsy report and started skimming it.

Hopping onto the bar stool in front of the massive gray granite counter, she swung her leg back and forth. "Then I can tell—"

"It mentions alcohol in her system, but nothing else? What the hell?" Tanner tossed the report aside.

"I've thought about this. I think Gene left out any illegal substances to protect her family. They're elders in his church. We can ask him quietly."

"I'm sorry. What are you talking about?"

"Gene Kerris, the coroner. He goes to the same church as Jemma's family."

"Christ! Obstruction of justice for moral purposes?"

"Who said it was obstruction of justice? He would never do that!"

"There's no mention of marijuana or anything laced. How do you know him again? Gene, right?"

Meredith inhaled the dark roast scent of the coffee before taking a drink from the cup he offered her. "He's my dad's best friend. Lives down the street. They're fishing buddies."

"Well, you said he was a family friend."

"Yes. He and his wife have been part of our lives forever. They're probably my favorite of my parent's friends." She smiled, rubbing her thumb against the rim of her coffee cup "Gene's a nut, always cracking jokes. He has the scariest house around Halloween, and he used to freak out all of the kids by saying that he had a real corpse in the basement. Anyone who had the nerve to show up at his door got a whole bag of candy."

He leaned back. "Did you?"

She took a deep breath as his long, lithe form stretched out toward her. "Yes. My dad promised Jill and me Gene was only kidding, but he held our hands as we walked up the steps." It was a good memory. Her dad had helped her face her fears. Where had that brave little girl gone?

"Now, I'm officially in *The Twilight Zone*. We have a Halloween-loving coroner with a sense of humor who left out details about marijuana and maybe more in an official report to protect some people in his church? What century is this?"

She pulled her hair. "You don't get it! This is a small town. Gene's protecting Jemma's family from a church scandal. She was a good kid. People can be narrow-minded sometimes."

His mouth flattened into a grim line. "You're kidding?"

She gave him a cold stare.

"Okay, so you trust him. I get it. Family friend. But you've been gone for a while. Are you sure nothing's happened to him financially? Maybe he wanted to make some cash on the side? Or maybe someone asked him to leave something out of his report."

"There's no way he's involved. I know you want to find a link, but it's not Gene. This isn't the first time that minor family wrongdoings have been left out of the public record. Gene's old school. My grandpa agrees. Now, let me tell you—"

"Have you seen Gene since you've been home?"

His continued interruptions had her tapping her feet. "Sure. Ran into him at Jill's. He said he envied my parents for their trip to Arizona. Gene was supposed to retire this year and begin what he calls Fishing Paradise. But the stock market didn't cooperate, so he's got to cut people open for another year. Said it's good practice for all the fish he's planning to gut."

"So he *does* have financial—"

"Jeez, are you always this suspicious? Tons of people had to delay their retirement because of the stock market."

"I always keep an open mind, like any good reporter."

She pulled on her hair. "Shut it. I have more to tell you."

"Why are you so pissed?"

"Because you keep interrupting me, and I have something to tell you." She took a breath. "Keep in mind that I decided not to tell you this when we were at my grandpa's house because I knew I needed to talk with him first. He's agreed we can share the info with you. He trusts you." She couldn't add that she did too.

The look he gave her could have petrified wood.

"Okay then, so before I came home, Grandpa's famous gut was twitching about an increase in the number of college kids ending up in the ER. The tox screens only showed alcohol and marijuana. He had me do some research on any new developments in the Dare drug trade. Nothing popped. The market is too small for bigger networks to be involved. I told Grandpa it was only binge drinking, which is an increasing problem on college campuses. Like your source's supplier said."

His gaze met hers dead on. Damn his chocolate eyes anyway. She wrung her hands in the silence.

"I understand you wanting to talk with Arthur first. I would have done the same thing. But I'm damn glad *someone* trusts me enough to share information like this."

She crossed her arms. "Then you'll be even more pleased to learn Grandpa wants to discuss everything with all of us together."

His exhale could have sent paper airplanes across the room. "I take it you guys have a file."

"Yes."

"I want to see it. Set up a dinner with your grandpa. I want everyone to put their cards on the table."

"You don't have to sound so bitchy."

"I forgot to take my nice pill today."

She smiled—all teeth. "Fine, then you should know that I already told Grandpa about our cover."

He growled. "Great. Now, what do you know about Barlow? Ray said he was the officer who showed up first at the scene."

The name made her stomach clench. "Well, he's the deputy sheriff of Eagle County, but not a local boy. Only moved to the area sometime this year, I think."

"Not a crime, but worth looking into. Did you go out with him?"

"You really are in a shitty mood."

"Meredith."

Her mind flashed back to Barlow's grip on her arms, the uninvited kiss to her neck. She shivered. "He's...pushy. Not afraid to use force." Telling him Barlow couldn't have been more different than Nora's hero, Alex Stanislaski, didn't seem like an important detail. Tanner wouldn't know what she was talking about anyway.

"Did he hurt you?"

Goosebumps broke out across her arms at the utter flatness of his voice. "No. Let's leave it at that." The sound of a dog barking filtered into the room, and she turned and looked at the back door.

Tanner walked over and opened it. A golden dog with prominent ribs jumped on Tanner, who rubbed his ears.

"Hey, boy. You done playing?"

The dog barked in three short bursts and then raced to a nearby water bowl, slurping heartily.

"I didn't know you had a dog."

"He wore me down. Kept hanging around the house."

She couldn't imagine anything wearing Tanner down. She certainly couldn't.

"What's his name?"

"Hugo." He laughed when the dog raced over. "I wasn't talking to you. Silly dog."

His hand rubbed Hugo's coat in long strokes, making Meredith look away. Part of her wondered how those hands would feel on her skin again.

*Pretty sad when you envy a dog.*

Since Meredith couldn't agree more, she didn't respond. Divorcée Woman was more right than wrong these days. It was annoying as hell.

"Why Hugo? And what kind of dog is he?"

"The vet thinks he's a golden sheltie, which means he's playful and likes to herd. Don't you, boy? And he's named after Victor Hugo, my favorite novelist."

Her heart thudded hard against her chest. Wasn't Hugo's *Les Misérables* her favorite novel? She wasn't voicing that one. No siree. Seeing this sweet side of him was more than she could take. She didn't even want to consider the fact they had yet another thing in common.

"I'll call Grandpa. He should be home tonight. I don't think there's Bingo at church."

"Arthur Hale plays Bingo?"

She drained her coffee. "He says he hears more information there than anywhere else. And it's the only gambling in town. We had a hotel and casino once, but it closed during the Depression. I wish I had seen it at its peak. Dare was *the* destination for the jet set and mobsters back then. Now The Grand Mountain Hotel is just a condemned building up in the canyon."

Tanner reached for his North Face coat. "It almost ruins his image. The towering independent journalist and newspaperman who taps into the heart of the West like no other plays...Bingo."

"It's what makes him good. He likes to be with real people. Not all journalists do." She thought of Rick-the-Dick. He didn't like people. He used them and then cast them aside.

Tanner was different. He liked people. He understood them. No one could feign that interest, that intensity of listening. When he walked toward her and tapped her on the nose, her lashes fluttered.

"I suspect being with real people is a Hale trait." He sauntered out the kitchen, Hugo trailing after him. "Do me a favor though. Try not to act like it's such a chore to be my pretend girlfriend. Otherwise, I'll make you a bumper sticker that says *Real People Play Bingo* and put it on your nice new Audi. Come on. I'll walk you out."

Her lips twitched. "I'll do my best not to gag."

Deep down, she knew being his girlfriend wouldn't be a chore at all—pretend or otherwise.

# Chapter 25

Arthur Hale was as sharp as a tack. Tanner caught the gleam in the man's eyes as he re-read the autopsy report. Seeing the legend work was like watching Brokaw or Woodward. The ground under his feet suddenly felt holier. He didn't question it, simply enjoyed it.

They were gathered together in Arthur's living room, sitting on a well-worn blue couch next to an antique coffee table. Tanner listened as Arthur explained all he knew. Meredith added her two cents, looking beautiful in a red sweater and gray skirt. Then Tanner ran them through what Ray had told him.

Arthur crunched down on a red hot. "Well, between the three of us, we don't have a pot to piss in. I couldn't reach Gene, but I'd bet my grandfather's Winchester he left the drug use out as a kindness, like Meredith said. You'd have to know their congregation, Tanner. Something like this would send the faithful into an apoplexy. We're still a small town. People watch out for each other without being asked. Gene knows that information won't bring her back."

"So, you don't think he could have another motivation? Like making some extra dough since his stock portfolio crashed?"

Arthur tapped his cane—hard. "No, Gene may have to work for a year longer than he wanted, but he'd never make a wrong step. I've known him since he was a kid, playing with my boy."

"Okay." Who could fight against that character reference?

Arthur frowned and looked him in the eyes. "I won't ask if you trust your source about the drugs."

Tanner met his gaze.

"I doubt the police report will say much," Arthur continued. "From what I've heard, it's been treated as a straightforward case. Her alcohol level was well above the legal limit. She died from a heart murmur. Case closed."

Meredith handed Tanner a file. "Grandpa compiled the names of the kids who were admitted to the ER. Have your source confirm he sold marijuana to them. If we triangulate they were his clients—"

"Then we add Jemma to the list and have something that's consistent," Tanner interjected.

"Exactly," Arthur added. "Then maybe your sister, Peggy, will be able to prove the drugs were laced, like your source says. Dare doesn't have any fancy equipment. Gene's tests might have missed it."

"In the meantime, we start with my source's main supplier and follow it up the chain," Tanner said. "Shake the bushes."

Arthur popped in another red hot, rolling it around in his mouth. "So, your source only knows the guy who gives him the drugs at the garage. Kenny Hopkins. We need more. I'm still not clear why Jemma died and no one else. Is it because they threw their guts up?"

Tanner wondered the same. "We've got more questions than answers, but that's always the way a good story starts."

Meredith raised her hand. "Why don't I stop by Gene's house tomorrow night after work? That way we can keep it social."

"Okay," Tanner agreed. "Can you ask him to run another test if he didn't find anything on the first pass? I want a second set of results. Gene tested her... remains. Peggy can test the drugs. It's a different base. But please don't tell Gene about the other test."

Just because they trusted him didn't mean he had to do the same.

Arthur leaned forward. "Fine. Two tests will carry more weight. Better confirmation for the courts if we find anything. Why the hell was a nice girl like Jemma smoking marijuana anyway? Such a damn waste."

Meredith patted his liver-spotted hand. "Pete showed up at the Halloween party with another girl, and Jemma was acting out."

Arthur gripped his cane. "I'll ask for the police report. Even if there's nothing useful in it, it'll tell us who else was on the scene with Gene besides Deputy Barlow. I don't like the fact that no one was seriously interviewed."

"The coroner is in charge of the crime scene according to Colorado law," Meredith told Tanner.

Arthur nodded, and then said, "Mere, ask Gene if any drugs from the party were submitted as evidence."

"Someone might have flushed them," Tanner suggested. "My source said he couldn't find everything he sold that night."

"We'll know more after I talk to Gene."

"How are you going to explain your questions?" Tanner asked.

Meredith tapped her chin. "I'll tell him that Jill's desperate to know more. He has a soft spot for her. She always bribed him with mom's chocolate chip cookies to take her fishing."

"He'll buy that," Arthur replied. "Jill is having a hard time. Details might help."

And then again, details didn't change a damn thing. Jemma would still be dead.

"I'd like to meet your source." Meredith reached for a red hot in the crystal candy bowl on the coffee table.

Tanner shook his head. "No way."

"But we're partners. You brought me—us—in." She looked at Arthur. "We know the local scene. We can ask him things you can't. Grandpa, tell him."

"No, Meredith. I would feel the same way. A good reporter never gives up his source."

Tanner looked up and met the older man's eyes, and a moment of complete understanding and respect passed between them.

"Give me your questions. I'll ask the ones I haven't covered."

Meredith tapped her foot. Tanner was afraid steam would start spewing from her ears.

"He might have to come forward anyway," she said in a persuasive voice.

"He's hoping if we find enough evidence he won't have to."

She snorted. "Right, because he'd go to jail."

Not answering seemed a good approach.

"You don't give an inch."

He stared her down when she put her hands on her hips. "I lost a source when I was young and stupid by trusting another journalist. I won't make the same mistake twice."

"That's to your credit, Tanner."

Arthur uncurled from the sofa, rubbing a hand on his aged back. Tanner would love to have seen the man in his prime, riding a horse through the pyramids like in the photo above the fireplace.

"And you thought Dare was going to be boring," Arthur said.

Tanner picked up his coffee cup when he stood. "I never said boring. Just not the pressure-cooker I'm used to."

Arthur popped in another red hot, crunching. "What's your source doing? Still selling?"

"He said people are freaked out about Jemma and aren't buying much right now. Plus, there's fewer parties with the end of the semester looming. If someone asks, he's going to tell them he's out or forgot to bring his stash. I asked him to keep a low profile."

"Stalling is a good plan. See what else you can find out." Arthur unwrapped another candy, making Tanner wonder if his tongue held a permanent red tinge.

"Will do."

Meredith reached for a piece of Dove from the crystal bowl. Funny, Sommerville hadn't included chocolate as one of her likes in his file.

"We'll have to wait until after Thanksgiving for Peggy to do the drug tests," he added.

Meredith's eyebrows slammed together.

"Problem?"

"I'm only here until Thanksgiving. Uh, maybe I can ask for more time." She wrung her hands and frowned,

Arthur grinned.

Tanner grunted. If she left without finding Mr. Right, there couldn't be a story, right?

"Your grandpa and I can finish this."

She pressed her hands to her ribs. "No, I need to stay here. Finish...everything."

He bit his cheek to stop from frowning. Damn, she wasn't giving up.

Arthur tapped his cane. "I could always look into getting the sample tested by a closer lab."

"No," Tanner declared, his voice gruff. "I want someone I know."

Arthur glanced over to Meredith. "Yes, you can always trust family to be straight with you."

Her chin lifted, and they shared a look Tanner couldn't decipher. Did Arthur suspect Meredith was in town for reasons other than those she'd told him? The man wasn't stupid. Hadn't he heard the wheels turning when she'd realized her time in town was almost up?

"Too bad you can't ship it through the mail," Meredith commented.

Tanner leaned down and straightened the end of the Persian carpet he'd kicked up with his pacing. "It's too risky, and Thanksgiving's only a little over a week away."

Arthur put his arm around Meredith. "In the old days I could have gotten away with mailing drugs or getting on a plane with them."

Meredith kissed his cheek. "Ah, the good old days."

"Oh hush up, girlie." He tugged on her hair. "Now, why don't you run upstairs and get this old man a sweater? The gray one."

"When have you ever cared about the color?"

"Since I started dating again. You might try it. Not the pretend kind."

Suddenly, the black boots on Meredith's feet fascinated her.

Tanner took the red hot Arthur offered him. "I keep telling her it can be more than a cover, but she's stubborn."

Meredith sauntered out of the room. "It's a Hale trait. Besides, I'm not the one being stubborn."

"Stop that muttering," Arthur called as her boots pounded on the stairs. "You." He pointed at Tanner. "Come with me."

His radar went up immediately, but he followed Arthur into his study. Photos covered the wall, telling the remarkable tale of Arthur's career. He forced his gaze away from a picture of Arthur and JFK when Arthur thrust a newspaper into his chest.

"Do you want to tell me why there's a shitty article about your brother in Richard Sommerville's paper today? Seems strange, since he's a local councilman."

Tanner's heart rate doubled. Christ, hadn't he said Arthur was as sharp as a tack?

He made himself shrug nonchalantly. "Everyone knows Sommerville's a prick. This is shoddy, personal journalism. I can't understand why your granddaughter married that asshole."

Arthur adjusted his glasses. "And yet one of Sommerville's best friends recommended you for your teaching position at Emmits Merriam."

Tanner forced every emotion from his face, but the quiver went to his toes. Too damn smart by half. And he'd have to lie to him. Fuck.

"I didn't know he knew Sommerville. Journalism's a small world."

Arthur smacked Tanner's boot with his cane. "I certainly hope so. I don't know you well, McBride. I had you figured out until today. Now, I'm not so sure. I intend to watch you closely." He nodded to the closed door. "Especially since you're cozying up to my granddaughter. Anyone with eyes can see there's nothing pretend about it."

"You should know I only have the highest respect for you and your family."

Arthur grabbed the newspaper. "Doesn't mean you haven't gotten yourself tangled up in something. I don't plan on telling Meredith about this article. At least not unless I have to."

Tanner inclined his head, grateful for the reprieve.

"If you need help, the door's open. Just make sure you don't hurt my granddaughter, because I still believe in vigilante justice."

He sauntered away, adjusting a photo of himself on a horse with a shotgun in his hand. Arthur looked like a teenager in the aged, grainy picture. "Another thing I miss from the old days."

Tanner gestured to the paper Arthur had tossed on his desk. "I understand the feeling, sir."

"I think you do," Arthur said, studying him intently as the antique clock ticked in the silence.

Meredith sauntered into the room without knocking. "Grandpa, I couldn't find your gray sweater, but here's a black one instead. It'll match your gray pants better anyway. Since you're so worried."

He pinched her cheek, and then pulled it over his head. "The other one must be in the laundry. You're right. It does look better. Thanks, honey."

"What were you two doing in here?"

Tanner stayed quiet, his insides still shaking like he had the flu.

Picking up the photo of him and the shotgun, Arthur said, "I was showing this picture to Tanner. Do you remember the story?"

She beamed. "Sure. You and Great-Grandpa Hale tracked some

thieves up Sardine Canyon who'd stolen your horses right off the old ranch. I love that picture. You look so young."

He puffed out his chest. "I was fifteen. I never did tell you the whole story, Mermaid."

"You didn't?"

Tanner leaned against the wall, hoping his best poker face was on.

"We got the horses back and turned two good-for-nothing horse thieves into the sheriff. Their partner didn't make it though."

"What happened?" Meredith asked, her eyes wide with surprise.

"He tried to shoot my dad in the back. I was coming out from behind the rock. Got my gun up in time. Killed him."

Meredith put her hands to her ribs—something Tanner noticed she did a lot.

"Oh, my God. Grandpa!"

He sighed and put the photo down. "Think I'll go to my grave remembering that moment, but it taught me one important lesson." He lifted his hand to her cheek. "I'll do whatever it takes to protect my family."

He wrapped his arms around Meredith, his gaze challenging.

Tanner didn't look away.

# Chapter 26

"Ray," Tanner called out as class broke up two days later. "Could you stay after?"

The boy immediately dropped a book. When he looked up, his red-rimmed eyes gleamed like a cornered rabbit's. Poor kid.

"It's about your last article," Tanner added, putting a leading hand on Ray's back. The muscles bunched under his green shirt. "It wasn't up to your usual standard." He lowered his voice but not enough to make sure they weren't overhead. If they were going to have a cover, people had to believe it. "I figured you might be a bit distracted. A bunch of people have been upset about that young woman dying."

The kid's eyelid twitched. He rubbed it with ink-stained fingers.

"Did you know her?"

Ray choked like he'd inhaled a bug. "Yes."

Tanner led him out. "Let's go to my office. I want to walk you through some of my comments."

The minute the door was shut, the kid lunged at him. "What the fuck are you doing?"

"Creating a believable way for us to talk. You can't come to my house again. Trouble with an assignment was the best I could do."

Ray paced in the small windowless office. "Man, I almost had a heart attack. What the hell were you asking about Jemma for? There were people out there!"

"Because if I said you were getting bad grades without a reason, people would begin to wonder what the hell was going on with you. Everyone knows you're an honor student." He kept his voice low and gentle. "Other students have been upset by Jemma's death too. It was a good excuse. Plus, you won't have to fake that."

He thrust his hand in the air. "No, I won't have to fake that. I'm freaking out here!"

"Settle down. We don't have much time. I need you to get me that sample you mentioned. I'm going to have it tested by someone I trust.

The autopsy report was a dead-end, Ray." He almost winced at the pun. "Can you do that?"

The kid ran his hands over his face. "I have the drugs she took. I'll give you something from that batch and another sample."

"Good. Bring it to class next time. We can have another conference about your homework. Trust me, Ray."

"I do, but you don't know what it's like. I feel like shit! Every day. A few people have wanted to buy from me to help them cruise through exams. I told them I was out right now, but I can't keep that up for long."

"Have you talked to your guy at the garage?"

Ray popped in a stick of gum, chewing hard and fast. "Yes, Kenny called. I told him I needed some time off. I was upset about Jemma. Got backed up at school. People weren't buying as much. He started yelling at me to grow some balls...He wouldn't listen."

Tanner's gut burned.

"Okay, don't visit the garage. Call him. Tell him you understand, and you'll man up."

Sometimes that's all the bad guys needed to hear. Bullies never questioned their power of intimidation. They'd expect Ray to fall like a house of cards. And it would buy them more time.

"Listen, I know it's hard, but you need to keep acting like everything's normal. Keep saying you forgot your stash at home."

Ray popped his gum in loud bursts.

"Look, Thanksgiving is next week. I'll have the drug results shortly after. You said people won't be partying too much before they take off. You're going home, right?"

"I don't know if I can do this, Professor McBride. What if someone else dies?"

Ray's gum-smacking grated on his nerves. "Jemma's death was probably related to her heart murmur."

Part of him hoped Ray was being paranoid about the drugs being laced. He expected shit like this in Afghanistan. He didn't expect it here.

"So, what am I supposed to do until then? Ask people for their medical history? Fuck, man. You've got no idea how this works."

"Ray, you know I've been in a lot of tough situations. You need to follow my advice here."

When the kid looked up, his acne-pocked face crumpled. "I'll try, but it's so hard."

He patted the kid's back before he realized it. "Ray, you've got a real future ahead of you. Your latest article was incredible. You have everything it takes to make an incredible lawyer."

His whole face lit up. "Really?"

"Give me a little more time to look into things. The only alternative is for you to leave school."

Tanner heard voices outside. Tensed. They were taking too long.

"It'll raise questions though. Staying here and acting normal is better. I know it's hard, but you need to keep calm. Now, you need to go. We'll talk after class next time."

"Thanks. It helps knowing you're on my side."

"Thank me by getting through this. Call me if you need to."

The kid programmed Tanner's number into his cell, and then scurried out of the room and down the empty hallway. Walking back to his desk, Tanner was reminded of how much pressure he'd lived under while he was overseas.

It had found him again.

People's lives were on the line. One had already died.

He was tired of it. Maybe he needed to finally consider the worst possibility. Was it time to give up journalism? How could he stand it anymore? Was anywhere safe?

Seeing this kind of death and danger in Dare might finally break him.

He picked up his tattered leather valise. He'd washed blood off it in too many countries to count. He couldn't seem to throw it away and buy a new one. It had become a part of him.

Fingering the hole a stray bullet had left in the leather, he walked out of his office, listening to every sound—a habit he wasn't sure he'd ever shake.

Fuck.

# Chapter 27

Pretending to date Tanner made Meredith believe in karma for the first time in her life.

Being with him was driving her insane. He was always touching her—at the coffee shop, on the street. Tonight they were at Hairy's, being blasted by a Denver-based Irish band appropriately named The Bangers.

Tanner was playing with her hair again. It wasn't a friendly touch either. No siree.

His sneaky hand always reached up to rub her back when they were walking somewhere. He pressed his leg against hers whenever they were sitting close. And who could forget the absentminded kisses on her forehead, cheek, and neck? But he hadn't kissed her on the mouth.

*You want him to kiss you on the mouth again. Admit it.*

The familiar voice made her grind her teeth. Did she need medication? Seriously, was she going crazy? Like Howard Hughes and his milk bottles crazy?

*I won't let up until you do what you really want to do.*

They'd only been undercover for less than a week. What in the hell was she going to do? Explode probably. He had her hotter than a lead coffee cup, and she wasn't cooling down any time soon.

"Something the matter?" Tanner murmured close to her ear as the band announced a break in their set. He wrapped his arm around her, of course, looking ridiculously hot in a simple white shirt and jeans.

Yes, she almost responded. My alter ego has gone rogue and won't stop talking about you.

*Oh, stop bitching.*

"No. Why would it be?"

He tilted his head to the side. "You need to work on lying. You're terrible."

He placed a kiss on her cheek before she saw it coming.

"And stop frowning. You're supposed to be crazy about me."

"Believe me," she replied, thinking of Divorcée Woman. "I am." She pressed her hands to her ribs, visualizing the pink bustier under her powder blue shirt. She had to reassert her control.

*Good luck with that.*

She threw up her hands. "Okay, I give up."

Tanner's breath tickled her ear. "So you're finally ready to have wild, exclusive sex with me?"

Her elbow ploughed into his side. She had to give him credit. He didn't grunt. He had rock hard abs, which she saw every morning at the swimming pool. Damn him. Why couldn't he have a paunch and that wrinkly skin some older men have?

*He's not that old.*

"How much longer do we need to watch Kenny?"

"Until he does something that helps our case."

They were following Ray's supplier since they had bupkis otherwise. Gene had kept quiet in the autopsy about the marijuana to protect Jemma's legacy and her parents, but he hadn't found anything besides marijuana and alcohol in her system.

And the police hadn't recovered any drugs from the scene—or so the report said.

They were all waiting for Thanksgiving to arrive. If Peggy didn't find anything...

Then maybe Tanner's source wasn't reliable. Maybe her grandpa's gut was off.

Maybe she needed to focus on her own problems.

Tanner caressed her palm with his thumb. She broke out in goosebumps. How he fought against his own desire mystified her. If she hadn't seen the evidence of his arousal, she would have thought he played for the other team.

*Oh, please. Now you're just being bitchy.*

*Well, he only touches me in public,* she fired back.

She was beginning to see a pattern. Despite how he acted when they were in public, he didn't want to be alone with her. If they had to be alone to discuss the case, he always invited her grandpa.

He lifted a strand of her hair again, his hot gaze liquefying her insides. "You need to practice your acting skills. You don't make a convincing girlfriend."

"You're enjoying this way too much."

He kissed her neck as slowly as honey sliding down a spoon. "You have no idea."

She kept her eyes glued to Kenny. He was ex-military with a few tattoos on his huge biceps. His pretty blond wife sat next to him drinking a light beer. She'd bet a hundred bucks the wife didn't have a clue her hubby was up to something.

The question was, was it more than marijuana?

The deputy sheriff had written and signed the brief police report, which showed all the investigational prowess of a kindergartner. Had he simply been satisfied with the coroner's report? Or was marijuana such a small deal he hadn't pursued it?

She jumped when Tanner's fingers rubbed her neck. The urge to close her eyes and enjoy it was strong. That third beer hadn't been a good idea. She was relaxing under his touch. Too bad she couldn't make him suffer by responding to his attentions.

*Why the hell not?*

She turned her head and gave him the stink eye. His mouth lifted. He had no remorse.

Why couldn't she make him suffer?

Because she didn't believe in public displays of affection.

*God, you are such a goody two-shoes.*

True. It was sad really. She blamed her mother.

*Why not try being bad for a change?*

If that's how Satan had sounded when he'd told Eve to eat the apple, Meredith could understand how mankind had gone to hell in a hand basket.

What would a Nora heroine do? That's why she was here, right?

She thought of her favorite character. Hot-blooded social worker Anna Spinelli in *Sea Swept* would have tortured her race car driver turned reluctant guardian, Cameron Quinn, until he was eating out of her hand.

Could Meredith do the same?

She decided not to think about her lack of progress on the article. Her boss had granted another week post-Thanksgiving, but that was it. If it didn't work out, she would have to settle for writing a more general piece about dating. Crikey.

She reached for Tanner's beer and drank half. They didn't call it liquid courage for nothing. His eyebrow winged up.

Leaning into him, she slid her hand under the table and rubbed his denim-clad thigh. His whole body bucked forward. She almost laughed out loud. As she trailed her hand down his knee, he kissed her ear.

"You're playing with fire, honey." He closed his mouth over her neck, biting gently.

She lurched in her seat. Unlike her, he didn't hold back the chuckle. It was throaty, and it slid across her skin like warm bath oil. Since he had his arm around her, he had the upper hand, but she was going to change that.

She opened a few buttons on her blue shirt, exposing a flash of her pink lacy cups.

"Meredith."

Sliding her hand to his belly, she rode the ridges of his abdomen to his ribs and then drew her hand slowly back down.

Up and down. Up and down.

His breath hissed out. "You're killing me."

She turned her head. His eyes were dilated, shining hot with lust under the muted lights of the bar.

"Not yet."

A tick appeared in his jaw when her hand slid close to his belt buckle. His jeans had to be tight, poor guy, but she wasn't backing down. She half expected him to stop her, but he surprised her. He pulled her closer, one arm still twined around her shoulder while the other stroked her belly. His fingers slipped under her shirt and played with the hot skin above her jeans. She nearly moaned.

"You kids need to get a room," Jill said, appearing by Meredith's side.

Focusing was difficult, given that her eyes were nearly crossed with desire, but Meredith managed. Looking at Jill's bright smile and equally bright dress in aqua blue, she tried to jerk her hand back from Tanner's chest, but he held her in place.

"There are no nice hotels in Dare," Meredith responded, her voice saucy.

"Well, go somewhere. People are watching, and as much as I want you two together, I *really* don't want to see it. So, scram! I'll even take care of the bill."

Tanner shifted and dug out his wallet. "I can take care of the damn bill."

"See, Mere, now you made him grouchy. Go put a happy face on him."

Meredith kicked at her sister. "Shut up, or I'm going to put all your Abba CDs in the microwave."

"You wouldn't."

"Try me."

Jill pulled at her gold necklace. "Huh, maybe you would. You made a bonfire out of Rick-the-Dick's Yankee baseball cards."

Slapping a large bill on the table, Tanner pulled Meredith up with him. "Rick-the-Dick?"

"That's what we call her ex," Jill informed him.

Great. Always good to show one's true colors. Torching baseball cards and calling your ex bad names.

Tanner leaned in to kiss her ear. "Kenny's leaving. Let's go." He gave her sister a killer wink. "See ya, Jill."

Waving goodbye to Jill, they tugged on their coats and stumbled outside.

The minute they hit the cold air, Tanner wrapped his arms around her. "Give me a sec," he said, nuzzling her neck. "I want to see where he goes."

When he turned her by putting his hands on her ass, she almost forgot this was pretend. Her hips settled closer. His curse warmed her like clothes out of the dryer.

"Cut that out, dammit. I'm trying to see where he's going."

"Then you shouldn't put your hands on my butt."

He let go of her ass and pulled her along the sidewalk, nudging her into an alley. Her back was pressed against the icy cold brick, his body pinning her in place. She craned her neck to see.

"That's Barlow's car," she breathed as Kenny stopped by the driver's side.

"Turn your head to the left. I don't want them to see your face."

She shivered from his touch. The light ended a few feet behind them, casting their shadows on the icy pavement.

Thankfully, he didn't kiss her neck, but the nuzzling didn't dull the increasing, insistent throb in her body. How much longer could she ignore it without going supernova?

"Conversation looks heated. I wish we could get closer."

A rustling sound near a garbage can made Meredith cringe. God, she hoped there weren't rats in this alley. If one ran over her foot, it would be hard not to scream. Better to close her eyes. Unfortunately, that only enhanced her other senses. Tanner's cedar and musk aftershave tickled her nose. His touch was protective and arousing at the same time.

"Kenny is headed back inside. He looks pretty upset." He dragged her further into the alley. "Barlow is speeding off." He stopped touching her and rested his forearms against the brick on either side of her.

She hunched her shoulders as a gale blew a mist of snow off the roof and into her face. "Do you think this is proof of Barlow's involvement?"

"I doubt they were arguing about his last oil change."

Her teeth chattered.

He stared at her, shifting from business to personal in a second. "I didn't give you enough time to put your scarf on." He wiped away the moisture on her cheek with a gentle hand.

He hadn't pulled his gloves on either. The friction of his fingers against her bare skin made her want to purr. He tugged the scarf around her neck twice and played with the ends. When he looked into her eyes, his face shadowed in the darkness, she knew she was in trouble.

His tenderness eroded all the walls she'd erected.

"That's better. We should go now."

He stared at her a moment longer, his gaze dipping to her mouth. She licked her dry lips, willing him to take the decision away from her again and simply kiss her like he had before. When she stayed still, her gaze arrested on his face, he ran his hand down her back, pressing her closer. She jumped when someone slammed the pub's front door, the crack echoing through the alley. Tanner stepped back.

*Coward!*

For once, Meredith agreed.

He took her hand and led her to the car. Though it wasn't unusual for him to open the door for her, the gesture put her more off balance.

How was she supposed to stop from giving into his exclusive-or-else ultimatum when he treated her like this? If she gave in, would she have the story she'd come to Dare to write? Would he be her hero in Nora Roberts Land?

Could she even admit he was The One, given all that it would mean?

Just thinking about it made her experience the first symptoms of a panic attack. She took deep breaths to calm herself. When he rubbed her hand, she leaned against the window, off center.

She *could* fall in love with him...She knew that. Maybe she'd always known it.

"Let's get you warmed up." He turned on the car and cranked up the heat. He checked his phone, which he always kept on silent when they were on a "date." Listening to a message, he pulled out of the parking space with one hand. She jumped again when he swore viciously.

"I need to drop you off," he uttered in the flattest tone she'd ever heard. He punched up the speed.

She gripped her seat belt. "What's the matter?"

"My source is in trouble. I need to go."

He took a hard right turn, and the tires shimmied on the ice.

Her internal temperature dropped twenty degrees. "Let me go with you."

"No, I won't put you at risk. Plus, I need you to get help if I don't come back."

He ran a stop sign, making her heart throttle like the engine. "What are you talking about? Let me go with you."

He screeched to a halt in front of Jill's house. The locks clicked open. "No. Now, get out of the car. We're wasting time. I'll call you later."

When she didn't move, he reached across her and flung the door open. "Please, Meredith."

"Dammit, Tanner!" she exclaimed, seeing his clenched jaw. He wasn't going to back down on this one.

"Be careful. And you damn well better call me. If I don't hear from you in a couple of hours, I'm calling the police."

"Don't bother. I don't think we can trust them now. Get inside and lock the doors."

When she hesitated, he kissed her firmly on the mouth. "Move!"

The minute she slid out the car, he yanked the door shut and sped off.

She walked slowly to the front door. Dammit. Why did he have to be a hero? He was racing after his source to do what? Protect him? The guy was a drug dealer.

Her mind clicked like the locks when she threw the deadbolt.

He *was* a hero. A no-frills, rough-and-tumble hero...just like in Nora's books. Who else would work as an embedded journalist in Afghanistan and Iraq? Not some milquetoast person, that's for sure. She hadn't really seen it until now.

She sat down on the couch, shaking, not bothering to take her coat off.

Fully realizing that the time ticked by slower in a crisis, she looked at the phone anyway, and then pulled Jill's afghan over her for her long vigil.

She cared what happened to him. What a time to admit it. She prayed she'd be able to tell him.

After tonight, she didn't plan on being anything but exclusive with him—even if it meant learning how to give someone everything she was again.

# Chapter 28

Ray's car was gone, and all the lights were off in his apartment. He tried Ray's cell again, cursing himself. He should have followed Barlow. His gut had told him the heated argument between Kenny and Barlow had something to do with Ray, but he hadn't pursued it. Hindsight was a bitch.

He listened to the voicemail again. "Professor McBride, I'm sorry to call, but you said I could if I was in trouble. And fuck, man, I think I am." He spoke so fast he didn't take a breath. "I just left the garage after talking to Kenny. I didn't want to meet him, but he told me that if I didn't, he'd come to my place. He kept pushing and pushing me about my numbers, so I told him I couldn't do it anymore."

The kid panted on the line. "He got all quiet like. Freaked me out. Then he asked for the drugs back, especially the ones from the party. I told him I didn't have them. He shoved me against the wall and got all crazy, yelling that I'd better bring them. I'm scared, man. I told him I flushed them, but I don't think he believes me. He told me I'd better keep my mouth shut. When I got home from class, my room was a mess. Someone had been in here! My whole stash is gone besides the stuff I gave you." He sniffed. "I'm freaking out, man. Call me!"

Tanner hit the off button and rubbed the bridge of his nose. Jesus. This was bad. Here he was back in the U.S. with a security situation, and he wasn't even sure he could call the police.

He pulled into a parking place in front of Ray's, praying the kid would come back. Over an hour later his phone rang. He jumped a foot. It was Ray's number, he realized, his heart stopping. Thank God. He clicked on.

"Stay out of our way," the muffled voice said. "This is your only warning."

Tanner threw the phone aside when it went dead. Pounding the steering wheel wasn't enough of an outlet for his rage. He got out of the car and pounded the hood until he cracked his skin. Fuck. Shit. Damn.

When he got back in the car, he called Meredith. "I didn't find him," he said gruffly. "I'm heading home."

"Do you think he's all right?"

"Let's hope so." He knew he was lying. He couldn't bear to tell her about the warning call now. He'd failed to protect another source. A fucking twenty-year-old kid. He'd tell her tomorrow.

He didn't want to, but he couldn't risk her safety.

"Why don't you come over here? I'll make you some coffee."

Her invitation made him grip the steering wheel. "No thanks," he managed to say over the roaring in his ears. "I need to get some sleep." The lie flowed smoothly off his lips. "I'll see you at the pool tomorrow."

He clicked off before she could say more. When he drove past the road to her house, he turned the corner. The front light was still on.

Part of him wanted to make sure she was safe. The other part wanted to accept her invitation. He could give a flying fuck about coffee. He wanted to wrap his arms around her. He wanted to take comfort in her.

He parked the car and sat in the silence for a moment, fighting the urge to go in. When the house finally went dark, he pulled away. He could not allow himself to need her.

He was only going to lose her in the long run anyway. No reason to add to his growing list of sins. She deserved better.

She deserved someone who hadn't been sent to crush her to pieces by her ex-husband.

Someone who could protect a scared college kid.

Someone other than him.

# Chapter 29

Meredith arrived at the pool at their usual time only to find Tanner already slicing through the water like he was chasing Olympic gold.

He didn't pause when she jumped in after pulling on her swim cap and goggles. He made his turn and kicked off, water frothing at his ankles.

Her stomach quivered. Did he know anything more about his source? She pushed off the wall and searched for the peace swimming always brought her. She didn't race him today. Challenging him didn't seem like a good idea. He was fighting his own demons. Well, so was she.

Somehow, he'd snuck under her armor.

She liked him.

She respected him.

She wanted him.

And she was so scared of everything he churned up in her.

Her hands cupped the water, her legs frog-kicking. She hated to see him hurting, and she knew beyond a doubt he was hurting this morning.

She wanted to comfort him.

She turned at the wall and pushed off. An hour later, she swam down the lane and saw Tanner's body from the waist down. So, he was finally stopping. And without a cool down. She halted when she reached him, surfacing too. Pulling off her goggles, she studied his tense face. He stretched his hamstrings, breathing hard, his muscles corded with tension.

"Any word?"

His dripping jaw ticked. "No."

She took a deep breath to calm her heart rate. "Let's get some coffee." Then she'd tell him about her decision.

After pulling herself out of the pool, she held out a hand to him. He didn't take it.

"I don't want to take you down."

The words seemed to hold greater meaning. She headed to the locker room with them reverberating in her mind. She showered quickly and dressed in the blue sweater and gray skirt she'd brought, not putting it past him to leave. He didn't want company right now.

When she emerged from the locker room, he was waiting for her in his standard black fleece, jeans, and boots, fingering his phone. "I got a warning last night," he said without looking up at her. "From my source's phone. Someone told me to back off. I don't think we should go for coffee."

"But I decided..." Her hands clutched her bag, and she inhaled jaggedly. "We'll be quick, and then we can talk at your house." She moved toward the exit.

He grabbed her arm. "Didn't you hear me? It's too dangerous for us to be together right now."

Shrugging free, she decided to joke. "You don't break up with a girl—even if it's pretend—when her hair's wet."

His quick steps behind her eased at least one knot in her stomach. He opened the door for her and followed her out, scanning the parking lot. When they reached their cars, he drilled her with those intense dark eyes.

"We need to talk about this, Meredith."

"I know. Coffee first."

Opening her car door, she turned the key with a shaking hand. He was not getting rid of her. She didn't care about the warning. They were in this together.

*Congratulations, you've finally admitted you don't want to stop seeing him.*

She hit the gas, cranked up the radio, and didn't respond. When she arrived in the downtown area, she parked and waited for Tanner. He approached her like a boxer preparing for a fight, and she took his hand.

He immediately froze. "What are you doing?"

She gripped it when he tried to shrug free. "Holding your hand."

The wind ruffled his hair. "Why? You never do that."

"Because that's what people going steady do."

"We're pretending."

Without answering, she tugged him after her. He followed since he was too nice to dislocate her shoulder. Don't Soy with Me was quiet for a Monday. Seconds after they walked in, Jill raced across the room, tears running down her face.

Meredith dropped Tanner's hand. "What's the matter?"

Her sister practically leapt into her arms. "Larry Barlow was just here. There was an accident." She pulled back and sniffed. "Another college student. He lost control of his car in Sardine Canyon and went over the side. Died on impact."

Tanner swore under his breath.

Jill wrung her hands, her black fingernails glittering in the morning light. "I knew him."

The hair on Meredith's arms stood up straight. Tanner closed his eyes, the skin stretching tight over his cheekbones. His pain radiated out like a homing beacon.

"That's horrible," she managed to say over her dry throat. "His poor family. Is he from here?"

"No, he's from the Northwest. Tanner, I think he was a student of yours. He told me how much he liked your class when he came in for coffee."

His whole body jerked as if pulled by a string. "What was his name?"

Meredith could tell that he already had the answer—and how much it cost him to ask.

"Ray Pollack. He was into some stuff, but he was a good kid. Smart. You know? I just can't believe it!" She pressed her hands to her face. "We haven't had this much tragedy since those winter campers were killed in the avalanche in Killer Pass four years ago. Remember, Mere?"

"I've heard about Killer Pass. Thought about hiking it," Tanner commented with utter detachment. "I need to go. I forgot to let the dog out this morning. You'll have to have your coffee without me, Meredith. See you later, Jill." He turned and strode out, his back rigid.

Still holding onto Meredith, Jill said, "He seems upset. I didn't know he had a dog."

"Yes," she replied in a tight voice. "Get me our regulars. I'll take it to him."

Jill waved off the new barista. "I'll make them. Mere, I still can't believe it. I mean, some people say bad things happen in threes. What could be next?"

"I don't know, Jill."

She was suddenly afraid they were going to find out. She felt like she'd landed in one of Nora's suspense novels, the darker, edgier kind in which the bad guys killed people.

# Chapter 30

Hugo bounded away, barking his displeasure as wood splinters sliced through the air.

"I told you to stay back!" Tanner yelled. "Why didn't you listen?"

He knew his anger wasn't directed at the dog. He cracked the axe through the wood with enough force to make his shoulder throb. His arm was going to regret this venting later, but he needed to pound something.

Ray was dead—exactly as he'd feared.

And it was no accident.

It was all his fault.

Hugo barked again, then took off. Tanner wiped his brow as Meredith's Audi pulled into the driveway. Christ, why couldn't she just leave him alone? He didn't want to see anyone right now. He wasn't in control of himself. He picked up the axe and swung, shredding bark and wood.

"We didn't finish our conversation." She said as she followed the icy flagstone path leading to his chopping block.

"Yes, we did," he snarled, anchoring the next log. "Now, go away."

She clenched her arms more tightly to her body when the wind blew. "Ray was your source, wasn't he?"

He swung the axe. "I don't want to talk about it."

She stepped closer. "Well, I do! Since he's dead, we have a problem."

"We have more than a problem!" He embedded the axe in the log. "We have a murder. That changes the whole situation. I told you about the warning last night. Do you think it was a coincidence Barlow stopped by to tell Jill what happened? It was another warning. There's no way he's not involved. We saw him arguing with Ray's supplier just a few hours before the kid's death. So, you're out of it! We're done!" Snatching his fleece up, he jogged to the house.

"What the hell are you talking about?" She grabbed his arm. "I'm in this as much as you are. That kid didn't deserve to die. And neither did Jemma. We have to take these people down."

He picked her up under her shoulders, carrying her effortlessly to her car. "No, I'm taking them down. You need to forget everything we've talked about and stay away from me. Your grandfather, too."

She kicked him in the shin. He winced. When she raised her knee to his crotch, he dropped her and darted back. "Hey!"

"No, you 'hey!' Don't pull this crap. I am not letting you do this alone, dammit! Jemma was Jill's best friend. You still need our help."

Why couldn't she understand? His breath puffed out in the cold air. "It's not worth endangering your lives."

"I'll keep investigating with or without you, Tanner. So will Grandpa."

Her green eyes held his. He ran his hands through his hair so he wouldn't grab her and simply devour her. Didn't she understand what she was doing to him? First vulnerable and then fierce. How was he supposed to fight against that?

She took off her gloves, shoving them into her pocket. He wasn't sure what she was doing since it was freeze-your-ass cold outside until she took his hands in hers.

"You have blisters. Let's go inside. I'll take care of them for you."

He pressed their joined hands to her ribs. "Meredith, you know if you come inside, we've moved past the pretend stage, right?" Maybe he could intimidate her. He wanted her more than he'd ever wanted anything, but he needed her to stay away from him. "Are you sure this is what you want?"

Her heartbeat increased against his palm, but her gaze stayed fixed on his. The breeze caressed her red hair like he longed to do. He'd heard people talk about having a lump in their throat when they looked at someone. He'd thought it bullshit until now.

"I'm in this all the way now. Exactly like you wanted me to be."

As the wind rushed over the ridge, blowing through the pines, an unusual warmth caressed his heart. He wasn't alone anymore. He was so goddamned tired of doing everything alone. He bit his lip. What was he thinking?

He gave into the irrepressible desire to trace the delicate skin of her face, its shape familiar, beautiful. Maybe he was tired, but he couldn't push her away. He didn't want to, he admitted to himself, regardless of how much it complicated things. He'd simply have to find a way to protect her. From the people that had killed Ray. And from himself and her ex.

"Then God help us both."

# Chapter 31

She stayed close as Tanner led her into the kitchen, really wishing he would kiss her. God, she wanted him to kiss her.

He released her hand. "I killed that kid, Meredith."

Her wish faded. He needed comfort and reassurance now. "No, you didn't. You know that deep down, but it's hard to feel it."

He dropped himself onto a bar stool. "There's a first aid kit in the pantry."

She retrieved it, and he lowered his hand into hers, palm up, when she returned.

"I didn't think they'd go this far. I mean we're in small-town USA, not fucking Kabul where no one thinks twice about shooting some punk dealer kid over heroin."

She could tell his mind was replaying all the nightmares he'd seen, so she tried bringing him back. "Despite everything, you liked Ray, didn't you?"

"Dammit, yes. He was just a good kid out to make a quick buck. He would have made a hell of a lawyer." He told her how Ray had gotten into selling drugs in the first place. "When he told me, I couldn't believe it. I know stereotypes don't always jive, but he was an A student, for Christ's sake."

She cleaned a burst blister. "I'm sorry, Tanner."

He described Ray's voicemail. She didn't know what to say, so she covered the raw skin with a Band-Aid. Silence filled the kitchen.

He tipped her chin up. "They know about me now. That puts you at risk. Do you understand that?"

"Yes." Her gut slithered with unease. "But we're in this together. Besides, there's safety in numbers. And I'm a Hale, remember?" she tried to joke. "They won't do in a Hale. The paper's too strong here."

He sighed, and looked down. After a moment he said, "I should have protected him."

"How?" She cleaned the cracked skin on his knuckles.

"I don't know, but dammit, I should have done something. Made him leave town maybe."

"Before the end of the semester?" She arched her brow. "That would have generated more speculation. Plus, they might have shut down their operation. You did what you thought was best, Tanner. You had no way of knowing what would happen."

She finished with more Band-Aids and lifted his hands to her lips, kissing each owie. "There. All better now."

"Thanks." He touched his finger to her cheek. "It helps to have you..." He trailed off and looked away, his jaw working. When he turned back, his eyes were gleaming. "You aren't going to have a panic attack if I tell you I desperately want to kiss you, are you?"

Her mouth went dry. "Ah...no."

"Good. Then, come here."

He framed her face with his hands. "What's between us has nothing to do with Ray or anything else, okay? I need you to know that."

Her heart quaked, shifting the landscape of her feelings for him. "Okay."

He lowered his mouth, kissing her softly. Sipping. Tasting. Her lips tingled. Somehow she'd expected him to be rougher after seeing his rage outside. His gentleness made her want to give him more.

She pressed closer, her body pressing hot against his. He nibbled her bottom lip, and she lurched forward, tangling her hands in his hair. Her tongue traced the seam of his lips, and he opened to her. A healthy steam of lust blew through her like an overheated boiler. She gripped his neck, changing the angle of the kiss. He lowered his hands to her waist, tasting her.

Deeper and deeper and deeper.

His fingers tickled the waistband of her skirt. Her eyes closed as she let herself feel the pleasure of that first touch. God, it had been so long. She wanted him to touch her, take her, devour her.

When his hands rose to her breasts and cupped them through her sweater, her head fell back. He kissed her neck, his breath hot against her skin. She tipped her head back further to give him better access and ran her hands along his strong shoulders. He stood and walked her backwards a couple of steps until she hit the counter. The sensation of being pressed against his entire body made her tremble. Their mouths met again, tongues dancing and retreating, all playfulness gone. His heart drummed against her hand as she traced his muscular chest.

When he caressed her butt and pulled her closer to his arousal, she lurched. Their kiss grew wilder, and her hands gripped his waist as the world tilted. She wasn't sure how she was standing on her feet anymore.

Something vibrated against her thigh, breaking her concentration. Tanner cursed and stepped back, digging into his pocket.

"Damn phone." He checked the display. "It's my sister. I called her last night about Ray. I need to take this, or she'll worry. Shitty timing." Brushing a thumb down her cheek, he put the phone to his ear and walked away. "Hey, Peg."

She closed her eyes and savored the lingering imprint of his mouth. Her body raged with heat, but there was something more...A deep, urgent tingling told her she was coming back to life after being numb for so long.

What was the saying about someone having the matches to light the fire inside you? Tanner clearly had the right matchbook for her.

And being with him could just be the biggest story of her life. Had she found her own Nora hero like she'd hoped? He certainly had all the qualities.

Her phone chimed. When she saw her grandpa's number, she clicked it on and confirmed his hunch that Ray had been Tanner's source.

When Tanner came back inside, she signed off. "Grandpa wants us to come to the house tonight. He heard about Ray and put two and two together."

"Good, we can run our plan by him."

"Do we have one?"

"Peg had some ideas. So do I. It helped to talk it through with her. I was running on adrenaline. You'd better get off to work. I'll see you tonight."

She fingered her damp hair, sensing a change in him. "I want to stay."

He picked up her purse. "You need to go to work like usual, or you'll raise suspicion. I need to head out too. I'll see you tonight."

She frowned as she walked toward him. His face didn't reveal anything.

Rising on her tiptoes, she decided to test the waters. She kissed his cheek.

He sighed, snuggled her closer, and pressed his mouth to hers. The kiss held the same tenderness he'd shown earlier. Inside her, it was like someone had blown a thousand bubbles, making her float. When he tugged on her lip and drew away, she leaned against him.

"I have your coffee in my car."

"I already had my jolt for the day. Get going. I only have so much willpower."

Heck, yeah. "See you tonight."

She was halfway to the door when he stopped her by saying her name. She turned.

His jaw clenched tightly. "Be careful."

"Count on it."

The reminder burst some of the bubbles, making her aware of her own gravity again.

# Chapter 32

Tanner firmed his shoulders and knocked on Arthur's door, wondering how in the hell he was going to deal with two stubborn, single-minded Hales.

Arthur welcomed him in, one white eyebrow arching at the pastry box in Tanner's hand. "You didn't have to bring anything."

Tanner shrugged. "Cover...I'm concerned about you being involved after what happened with Ray."

"Don't insult me, boy. I've lived a hell of a long time. If you think this is the first time I've been in hot water over a story, you'd be dead wrong."

"What are you two crossing swords over?" Meredith stepped into the entryway just as Tanner set the box on the table by the door. She had on the same blue sweater and gray skirt, and just seeing her made him want to cross the room and kiss her senseless.

"He was underestimating an old man," her grandfather explained.

Tanner growled as he took off his coat. Why didn't they understand he wanted to protect them? Was it a Hale family trait? "I didn't mean any disrespect."

Tapping his cane like a judge's gavel, Arthur picked up the white box. "Then, I'll hear no more about this, or I'll ask you to leave. Meredith and I can conduct our own investigation."

He followed them into the kitchen. "Smart of you to get here early so you two could present a united front," he said to Meredith.

She stopped him with a hand and leaned up to kiss his cheek. "I don't want you changing your mind. We're in this together now."

He liked this affectionate side of her. Of course, he desperately wanted more than a kiss, but his conscience continued to give him fits. He felt like he was being stretched in a dozen different directions.

"Best not argue, son. It's two to one."

Tanner rubbed the scar by his mouth. "Fine, but you have to promise to take precautions. These people are dangerous."

Pouring two single malts into crystal highballs, Arthur said, "What? Do we have the word 'stupid' tattooed on our heads?" He handed one of the glasses to Tanner, who resisted the urge to toss it back in one shot.

"I'm going to shut up now."

Arthur extended his glass for a cheer. The crystal chimed when their glasses met. "Good. Dinner's ready, so let's eat."

Tanner doubted he'd taste the food, but he followed them into the dining room.

"So, let's talk about what you're planning." Arthur folded a blue napkin in his lap.

Someone had lit white candles in silver holders. It was a strange setting to concoct a plan for taking down murderers, but when didn't the Hales surprise him? Arthur passed around a plate of steaks, a bowl of salad, and a platter of mashed potatoes, and everyone served themselves.

"I got my oil changed today." He took the bread basket from Meredith. "At Dare Auto Care."

"That was ballsy," Arthur said, cutting off a piece of steak.

Meredith looked up at him, her eyes wide. "Are you nuts?"

He patted her hand. "No. I wanted them to know I won't back down. I stared that fucker—sorry—asshole Kenny down."

"So you went there for a pissing contest?"

His glance told her what he thought about her accusation. "I wanted to case it out. See if there was anything unusual there."

"Was there?" Arthur asked.

"Nothing obvious. I'm going to plant some listening devices later. See what we can pick up from Kenny. It's the place to start since we know he's involved. He won't expect it after I showed up in plain sight today." He flung his hand out, his impatience surging. "We need a lead. Or we need to pressure them into doing something stupid."

Meredith set her fork down slowly. "You're planning on breaking and entering his garage? Are you crazy?"

"Honey, you're repeating yourself. I've done this before."

"Of course, he has, Meredith. He's an ambitious reporter. Do you think he's the only one?"

She choked on a bite of salad. "Grandpa, are you saying you've done it too?"

His wicked grin lifted the wrinkled grooves around his mouth. "Of course, girlie. Sometimes you have to get your hands dirty."

"I can't believe this."

"We can't all write for the Style section."

"Funny."

Tanner looked down at his plate. Christ, Arthur could get anyone's goat up.

"Seems like it's time for you to get your hands dirty, Mermaid. Tanner will need a lookout. I think you should go with him."

His head shot up. "Absolutely not."

"You said they won't expect it," Arthur reasoned. "Besides, there's an even better reason for you to go there tonight."

Tanner stilled. "What?"

Arthur chewed his steak and held up a finger. The man had a flair for the dramatic. "They took Ray's car there around closing time—or so a source told me. Seems strange since it's totaled, don't you think? Usually cars in that condition go straight to the junkyard once the police release them."

Tanner wouldn't even ask for his source. "Who released it?"

"Our deputy sheriff. That confirms your thinking about Barlow, but it doesn't prove anything. It's another thread to pull as we build our case. When does your sister arrive?"

"Wednesday night."

They'd argued about her and Keith's plans to visit for Thanksgiving. Peggy didn't care about his concerns for their safety. She assured him they would be fine. Besides, she needed to pick the drugs up for testing. No one knew she was a cop, so there was no need to worry. They'd be careful. Like the Hales, Peggy was stubborn.

Arthur made a humming noise when he tasted the mashed potatoes. "I found out something else. Kenny and Barlow went to college together. University of Colorado."

"How'd you find that out?" Meredith broke her bread roll in half.

"I have my ways. They've held jobs in two places over the past seven years. Started in Boulder after school. Met up again in Loveland three years later. And now they're here in Dare. Oh, and Kenny received a dishonorable discharge in Afghanistan. I'm waiting on the file."

"Why would they keep going to smaller towns?" Meredith asked.

Tanner gave up eating. "Perhaps they wanted to keep a low profile. A small town is a good place to operate, especially if you have a corrupt cop in the mix."

"Or maybe their operations fell apart in the other towns." Meredith pushed her food around her plate. "Do I even want to know where you got your listening devices?"

Tanner shook his head. "I don't like the idea of you coming."

"You don't have a choice," she said in a flat voice. "I'll only follow you."

He cursed under his breath.

Arthur chuckled. "Good to see your spirit back, girl. You always were a firecracker, but I was afraid your time in New York might have sucked it out of you. Does anyone want coffee with dessert?"

Tanner declined. He would be jittery enough doing a B&E with Meredith along for the ride.

"Trying to think of a way out, son?" Arthur pushed back from his chair.

In response, Tanner just folded his hands and glared.

"You're stuck with us. Bring your plate to the kitchen. Everyone works in this house."

Tanner picked up the gold-edged china. "Aren't you worried something could happen to your granddaughter?"

"You'll protect her."

"Don't talk about me like I'm not here," Meredith said. "I can take care of myself."

"Glad you remembered that." Arthur bent to kiss her cheek.

"She's not wearing black," Tanner observed even though he knew it was a lame excuse. "You need to wear black for recon."

"You can swing by my place. Let me change."

"Do you have an answer for everything?"

"Yes. Isn't it maddening?"

Arthur put his arm around Meredith. "Come slice the pastry, dear."

Tanner followed them into the kitchen. He'd never had a partner before, he realized.

It was overrated.

# Chapter 33

Nerves and excitement had Meredith's feet bouncing in Tanner's SUV as they drove to Dare Auto Care. And, well, a healthy dose of fear, if she were being completely honest. She and Tanner kept glancing over their shoulders to make sure they weren't being followed. He'd been driving around for a while. So far they were in the clear.

Now she *really* felt like she was in a Nora suspense book. She needed to channel Jack Burdett, the security expert adept at breaking and entering in *The Three Fates*. What did it matter if he was the hero and not the heroine?

"You should go home," Tanner snarled. "I don't need you here."

His insistence only made her dig in deeper. "Stop being mad. You know we're right. Besides, this is a small town. People look twice at a guy who's walking alone in the cold after dark. I'm good cover. And thank God the snow stopped, because otherwise they'd really think we're nuts. Now a walk seems romantic."

Even in the dim light from the console, Meredith could see his clenched jaw. His eyes were predatory as they scanned the street. She wanted to shiver. Part of her still couldn't believe they were on their way to break into Dare Auto Care. She reminded herself two kids were dead.

"I'll park the car a few blocks over. Keep your cap on. Your red hair shines like fire." He shot a glance at her. "And you need to do whatever I say if something happens. I want your promise."

Suppressing the desire to gulp, she lifted her chin. "Why are you in charge?"

"Because I've been in hot spots, and you haven't." He took her gloved hand, squeezing it. "I don't want anything to happen to you."

She stared at his thumb rubbing circles on the leather. Her body crackled with lust like wrapping paper being opened. "Okay, but not if what you tell me is stupid."

"I don't do stupid."

"How are you planning on getting inside?"

"You'll see."

She didn't like surprises, but since she'd pushed him, she let his cryptic answer slide. This outing was about trust.

After parking the car under a low-hanging tree near Washington

Elementary, he took her hand. Snow-coated swings rocked gently in the wind, giving her the heebie-jeebies. Their breaths puffed white in the cold air. Oak Street was quiet, and most houses had their lights off. Since it was after midnight, Meredith wasn't surprised.

A dog barked to the right, and her body coiled with tension. Tanner kept right on walking, scanning the street. He brought them through an alley to the back of the garage. Even with the cold, the metallic smell of trash tickled her nose.

"Stay in the shadows," Tanner whispered.

He headed for the door. Thankfully, Kenny's place didn't have any flood lights. Most people didn't in Dare since animals set them off all the time. Besides, Dare didn't have any crime, right?

At the door, Tanner drew out a key and a small hammer from his bulky fleece. Her mouth dropped as he inserted it into the lock and whacked the hammer against it. The dull pinging sound made her want to scream. He opened the door with ease.

*Well hello, Roarke,* Divorcée Woman suddenly intoned in a sultry voice.

Meredith fought the urge to press her hands to her temples. She didn't need a reference to J.D. Robb's famous male hero. *Can't you see we're breaking and entering?* she saucily replied. Unfortunately, she didn't feel much like Roarke's fearless wife, Eve Dallas, right now.

They wiped their boots with the rag he'd brought before walking inside. Tanner dug out a pen light and scanned the garage.

"Fuck," he hissed, when they caught sight of the twisted and dented metal of Ray's totaled car. Tanner craned his neck like he was listening for something, and then walked forward. She followed.

The windows were all shattered except for the one in the back, which was intact, but resembled a spider web. Two wheels were torn, the rubber shredded to bits. The car's body looked like an accordion. She tried not to think of the kid who had died inside it, but she couldn't stop the images. She only knew what Ray had looked like from the photo in the layout for tomorrow's paper. Tanner was right. He hadn't looked like a drug dealer. Just a short, pimply college kid.

"How did you learn to do that?" she whispered.

Tanner walked around the car, running his hand over its ruined frame. "What?"

"Break into a building." She angled closer carefully. There were jugs of various auto care products scattered across the floor.

"I got involved with a bad crowd in my youth. We liked to break into buildings. I didn't like the stealing, but I liked getting into forbidden places and looking around." He focused the light on the tire. "It's come in handy."

She ran her hand over a single, sharp piece of glass protruding from the passenger window. "I still can't believe you've done this as a journalist."

Tanner leaned into the driver's side, sweeping the light around. "Honey, the places I've posted don't have much law and order. Trust me,

I've only done it when there was no other choice."

He rifled through some papers in the glove compartment while she stood there mute. She was learning a hell of a lot about him on this outing. And she wasn't sure how she felt about it.

"Think less of me?" he asked, shining the light near her face.

Raising a hand to ward off the glare, she said, "Ah...I'm not sure."

He snorted. "Well, at least you're honest."

The light faded as he shifted it to the bumper. He squatted down and ran his hands along the dented metal. His sigh filtered out into the quiet, cold garage.

"There's some red paint and scratches on the bumper. Any idea what car Kenny drives?"

"No, why?"

"Because I'm pretty sure someone helped Ray off the road." He produced a Swiss Army knife and a Ziploc bag.

She realized she was really in over her head when he scraped the bumper with the blade. "Are those paint shavings?"

"Yep. More evidence. Match the car with the paint, and you have more than circumstantial evidence. Too bad his car isn't here."

"If Kenny's ride has dents, he won't drive it. Plus, he can fix his own car."

"We'll check with the DMV. Tie up another thread for the authorities."

"We still don't have much."

He unzipped his fleece and drew out his phone. The camera's flash made her blink. He took a few more pictures.

"Tomorrow, I'll see if I can find a second set of tire tracks where they found Ray's car and take some pictures. Those fuckers." He pocketed the phone. "Sorry, but I'm pissed."

She rubbed her arms. "Me too. Besides, I've heard that word before."

A door slammed.

Her head turned sharply, and her whole body locked in place. "Someone's coming."

"Shit," he hissed, scanning the garage with the light.

He grabbed her arm and darted to the next car over, opening the driver's side door. The car's overhead light turned on as he reached down and popped the trunk. He shut the door and dragged her to the back. Lifting the lid, he pushed her toward it. She caught sight of a bag of ice melt, jumper cables, and a blanket.

"Get in."

She hesitated, but when she heard the sound of muffled voices approaching, she threw her leg over, squeezing inside, her spine against the back of the trunk. Tanner plowed into her, arranging his body against hers in spoon fashion before closing the lid. The trunk went dark.

Oh, God, he'd better have a plan to get them out of here! Her heart pounded like a drummer on speed. She knew she was breathing hard, but she couldn't stop.

"Close your eyes," Tanner whispered. "Take deep breaths."

Right. Having a panic attack in a closed trunk with potential killers outside would be a bad idea. Closing her eyes didn't help much since it was dark anyway. She wiggled, the jumper cables pressing into her thigh.

"Be still," he ordered in a whisper.

Another door slammed. The voices grew louder. They were male, Meredith recognized, and they were coming closer.

"When's the car going to the junk yard, Kenny?"

Was that Barlow?

"The truck's taking it out tomorrow before I open. The compactor only works on Tuesdays. We don't want any evidence."

"Shit, this whole thing's a fucking mess. You were supposed to make sure he left town, not run him off the road."

"I told you it was an accident!"

"Well, lucky for you, I was the first to arrive at the scene. I didn't see any evidence, but dammit, Kenny, two bodies is a lot to explain."

Meredith squeezed her eyes shut. Suddenly it occurred to her that she and Tanner might have left something to give them away—a footprint in the grease on the floor. Anything. Her breathing shattered. She bit her lip hard enough to taste blood.

"Let's get the stash and go. We can't keep any drugs here now."

"I'll hide them in my truck until we decide what to do," Kenny responded.

"Things were going great until that stupid girl died."

A hand smacked the trunk, and the sound reverberated through Meredith's bones. All the muscles in her entire body bunched, poising to spring. *Oh, please don't let them find us.* Curled up like shrimp, they were defenseless. Especially if Barlow were armed.

"We need to calm down," Barlow said.

Meredith could almost imagine him trying to convince himself.

"We've covered our tracks. They're both young. Kids do stupid things. No one's going to believe otherwise."

"Yeah, but that reporter could cause problems, Larry. The kid called him when he was in trouble, and he called back. I found his name all over Ray's school crap. He was taking a class from him—investigative journalism. Didn't know the kid was into that stuff. I looked into this guy, and he's some big-shot war correspondent. Not the kind to shut up because someone warns him off with a phone call."

"Fuck! This used to be a sleepy, quiet little town. This could fuck up everything!"

"The reporter showed up today to get his oil changed. Stared me down good. I've seen the type. He won't back down."

"Fuck that!" Barlow replied. "There's no proof. We'll shut down for a while. If McBride's a temporary professor, he'll be leaving in a few weeks when the semester ends. We'll weather this. I don't want to start up again somewhere else. We've got a cozy set-up here, and our new stash is freaking genius."

"But McBride's..." The voice grew too muffled for Meredith to make out the rest of his words. A door slammed. Her body jerked, and her heartbeat sounded like it was being broadcast on loudspeakers. She focused on her breathing, while her ears strained to pick up any noises from outside.

"I think they're gone," Tanner whispered finally, "but we need to wait a while."

"I'm pretty sure it was Kenny and Barlow."

"Yep, and now we know the truth. That asshole tried to drive Ray out of town, and he got the kid so scared he went off the road. Fuck!"

She didn't know what to say to comfort him.

"And they know a hell of a lot about me now. Not a bad thing. He's right. I won't back down. We've got them running scared. That's when people make dumb mistakes."

She thought of Ray. Chasing a kid out of town and accidentally driving him to his death was more than a dumb mistake. It was second degree murder.

The jumper cables were digging into her skin, so she shifted her arm to pull them out. Either that or there'd be a permanent impression of jagged teeth in her thigh.

"Please tell me you have a plan to get us out of here."

"This model has a trunk release. Don't worry. I wouldn't have stuffed us inside otherwise."

She squirmed. Tanner's butt clenched when her hips thrust forward.

"What are you doing?"

"I'm laying on a jumper cable. It's digging into my leg."

"Jesus. Be quick about it."

She became aware of his body heat, and she felt drawn to it in the cold trunk. She shifted, her hand trailing across his body. They were fitted together like two pieces of metal in a modern sculpture.

"I can't reach it."

His arm crossed her body, searching. "Where is it? I'll help if you stop wiggling like a greased pig."

Pig, indeed. "I can't help it!" she hissed, rolling toward him.

"Oh Christ, stop."

"What?"

The sound he made was something between a chuckle and a groan. "You really have no idea what you're doing to me, do you?"

Her body went rigid. The car had felt too small before, but suddenly it was like all of the air had been sucked out. He was aroused.

*Duh.*

She almost pointed out the ludicrousness of the situation to her alter ego, but she stopped herself. Hell, she was getting aroused too. Maybe it was true what they said about adrenaline making you horny. They both should have their heads examined for getting hot in the trunk after almost being discovered by criminals. Still, she could control herself.

Meredith tried to push up, moving an inch.

"Let me do it. Where is it?"

She nearly gulped. "Under my thigh." Her control wavered like smoke.

His breath released like a punctured tire. "This has to be bad karma, but I can't imagine what I did to deserve it. Okay, hold still. I'll get it. Tell me when I'm getting close."

Her body nearly undulated with desire. *Closer. Please.*

He slid his arm behind her, clearly going by feel, tracing her body like she was some topographic map. His hand angled down her hip, making her leg jerk.

"Jesus, Meredith. Hold still."

"I'm trying." How could she be still when his hand was pressing under her thigh? "Higher."

He swore in the dark, and she could feel him pulling on something.

She nearly moaned when his hand cruised her butt. "The metal part shifted, but it won't move."

He muttered something she couldn't hear. "Lift your top leg over mine and roll toward me."

Her eyelids fluttered, and a shot of pure lust tore through her from her toes to the top of her head. While the metal was putting a crater in her thigh, the rest of this situation was downright sinful. She hesitated. "Can't we get out now?"

"Meredith, I have no idea how long it will take them to grab their stuff and clear out. We need to stay here a while longer. Throw your leg over, dammit, and stop wiggling."

She draped her leg over his hip. She almost moaned. God, the pressure of his body felt incredible. Given how tall he was, his legs were angled even more sharply than hers. His deep-throated groan made her wet. She realized her nipples were tight.

At least it was taking her mind off her fear.

He yanked hard, and the metal finally pulled free from her thigh. The immediate relief prompted a reaction. It allowed her body to totally focus on how hard his body felt against hers. She wanted to run her free arm up his side and tangle it in his hair. She thought about pressing her mouth to his neck and tasting his skin.

"Meredith, you can take your leg back."

She didn't want to, but he sounded pained. Her leg shook as she slid it off him. When her thighs met, her insides clenched at the locked heat. She bit her lip, but a shallow moan bubbled out. Get a grip.

"Meredith?" he said in a silky voice. "Are you getting hot back there?"

Had he heard? Oh, God. Locked in the trunk after breaking and entering, aroused beyond belief. Her mother would be so proud.

"N-no." Her voice squeaked as he shifted.

"Dammit, I can't turn over. Christ, I want to touch you. Which is insane. They could be out there."

Her skin tightened. "I know."

She felt his head lift. "Stop breathing on my neck."

"I *need* to breathe."

"Fine. Let's pretend we're somewhere else. Like alone on a life raft in the middle of the Indian Ocean, where our very survival is precarious." He grew silent. "Great, now I sound like a moron. Look, try and fall asleep. Please. I'll wake you when enough time has passed."

Fall asleep? Was he crazy?

"Meredith, please stop wiggling."

"I'm not," she protested, wanting to rustle her legs.

"I can feel every movement of that gorgeous body of yours. Stop moving."

"I'm not!"

"Try and relax then." He took deep breaths, slowly letting them out. His back rose against her breasts as he inhaled. Her nipples clenched again.

"Now, *you're* moving."

The breathing stopped. "This gives a whole new meaning to being in the backseat."

She snorted. "We're in a trunk." She'd never been in the backseat with a man before.

"Stop reminding me. I'm afraid I won't be able to get out."

"Why not?"

"Because I'm so hard, I've likely turned to stone. People will come from all around to buy tickets to see the male with the stone hard-on in the trunk of a Lincoln town car."

Hearing him talk about his hard-on was beyond arousing. It made her feel powerful, and she felt like her La Perla underwear were glowing under her clothes like armor.

She still had it.

Jill had told her, but until this moment, she hadn't believed it. She was still attractive. She could still arouse a man to the point of insanity. She smiled in the darkness.

"I'd buy an all-season pass to see you like that," she responded in a sultry voice.

"You'd better watch that talk. You damn well know where it will lead."

Armed with her La Perla, she felt emboldened. Unafraid. It was time to take back her womanhood. Tanner was just the man to be with when she did.

"I know where it will lead. I want it."

Silence yawned. Her heart pounded. The sheen of her armor dimmed.

"You shouldn't say that to me in a damn trunk when you know I can't do anything about it."

"We won't always be in here." She basked in his body heat, her fantasies running wild.

"Dammit, Meredith. You have the worst timing. Stop talking! I can't take it anymore."

Divorcée Woman wouldn't care. And neither did she.

She shifted even closer and lifted her head. Feeling her way in the dark, she found his neck and pressed an open kiss to the hot skin there.

He jerked, banging something against the frame of the car. "I'm not kidding, Meredith. You have me so hot, I can barely stand it. Chinese water torture sounds less painful right now. Wait until we get out of the goddamn trunk! Christ, I can't believe this."

She inhaled his musky scent before resting her head on the coarse carpeted floor.

When he reached back for her arm and pressed her hand against his chest, she snuggled closer, smiling.

They waited in the darkness for what seemed like hours until Tanner finally released her hand, fumbling around. She heard the trunk pop. The light blinked on, harsh to her eyes. Tanner uncurled like an old man as he got out. When he pulled at the front of his jeans, she fought a smile. She had to be nuts for smiling in a situation like this, but she couldn't help herself.

He helped her out. Every muscle ached, and her left arm was numb from lying on it. She stretched beside him.

He shut the trunk softly. "Stay here, and keep watch. I'm going to plant the bugs."

His feet were as quiet as Cary Grant on that roof in *To Catch A Thief*. He was really much too good at this. She wrapped her arms around her middle, trying not to fidget and jump at every sound.

He returned minutes later and reached for her hand. "Let's go."

They walked back to his car, listening for company, scanning for menacing movements. Energy pulsed through her as they stalked through the dim moonlight. Not even the cold air could dim the liquid lust flowing through her like a golden elixir of sunshine.

He opened her door and helped her inside, patting her thigh before closing the door. When he put on his seatbelt, he held out his phone.

"Call Jill and tell her you won't be coming home tonight. I don't want her to worry."

His concern only confirmed her decision.

She met his dark, melting gaze. "All right."

Tonight, she wasn't thinking about the article or the future. She was going to enjoy being a woman again. And she would have no regrets.

*Finally*, Divorcée Woman sighed. *Enjoy.*

*Oh, I will.*

# Chapter 34

The dog barked when Tanner unlocked the front door, and he ran forward to greet them, his shaggy tail sweeping back and forth like a broom. Tanner rubbed his pointed head.

"Hey, Hugo. Do you need to go out, boy?"

Meredith stepped inside. He hit the lights, and the main floor came to life. The rush of water from the stone falls broke the silence.

"I'll be right back." Tanner squeezed her elbow.

She walked into the house, shrugging out of her black outerwear. Jill couldn't have been more delighted to hear that she wasn't coming home. She rubbed her hands together, feeling both anxious and excited.

The dog shot past her when Tanner came back inside. "Sorry. I need to put in a pet door."

He stepped closer, looking masculine and powerful dressed all in black. Framing her face with his hands, those chocolate brown eyes stared straight into hers. She shivered. There was more there than just lust.

"Are you sure? I know we got as hot as teenagers in the trunk, but we're not teenagers, Meredith."

Her muscles tensed. "Does that mean you don't want me now?"

He wrapped an arm around her hips, pulling her close. "How can you even ask that? This is a big step. I don't want to presume, but I don't think you've been with anyone since your ex. You're not the kind to take sex lightly."

She didn't want to talk about Rick-the-Dick. He was part of the distant past.

"I haven't been with anyone since, but I'm here because I want to be."

He pressed his forehead to hers. "This complicates things between us. I don't want to hurt you, Meredith. You've already had so much to deal with."

Why was he talking like this? A light bulb went on. Because he wasn't staying in Dare. Until the men in the garage had talked about the semester ending, she hadn't really thought how little time they had left. *And I'll be leaving too*, she reminded herself.

She ignored the tightness in her chest. "We're here now. Don't turn me away."

When he raised her chin, his gaze stripped her soul. "I could never do that. Come with me."

He stepped back and held out his hand. She took it, reveling in its warmth.

His bedroom was another architectural masterpiece. Skylights peaked out behind rustic caramel-colored beams, and recessed lighting coated the whole room in a warm glow. A stone fireplace sat opposite the bed's massive rustic log frame. Animal fur rugs covered the hardwood floors.

He kissed her forehead. "I'm going to make a fire. We'll make love in front of it later."

Her head turned to follow his movements.

"I want you in my bed first."

His deep voice made her insides zing. She unzipped her fleece and pulled off her boots, ready to get started. She was not going to feel nervous.

"That's enough from the Clothing Removal Patrol. I want to do the honors."

His humor couldn't produce a laugh in her. She twisted her hands, not knowing what to do.

Twigs sparked and crackled as the fire came to life. He stepped toward her.

"God, you're beautiful." He touched a strand of her hair delicately. "I can't look at a fire now without thinking of this. It's so much better than the blond."

She narrowed her eyes. "How did you know I was blond?"

His fingers released the lock. "I saw a picture." He cleared his throat, looking away. "Let's get you out of these recon clothes."

When he tugged her shirt off, his eyes goggled. "Holy shit," he muttered with reverence—exactly the reaction she'd prayed for. His hands cupped the black-and-white-striped bustier. "Of all the things to wear for our little breaking and entering..."

Her ice-breaker worked. She chuckled. "I figured that the prison theme would be fitting if we ended up in jail."

He fingered the black lace edging. "I wouldn't have let that happen."

"Good to know." She moved closer, hoping the connection would silence her mind. *Will I please him? Will I be enough?*

He touched the swell of her breasts and ran his hands down the front eye clasps of her bustier. "Do you always wear this fancy stuff?"

She wanted to press his hands to her chest. Why did he have to talk so much? "No. It's part of my new...persona."

He rubbed the material. Her nipples tightened. Take it off, she wanted to demand.

"Should I ask why?" He nudged her backwards. Finally! The right direction.

"No."

"Good, I don't want to be distracted." He framed her ribs in his big hands. "Christ, you look like one of those underwear models."

She snorted.

He tipped her chin up again, making her meet his eyes, all dark and smoky with desire. "You calling me a liar?"

She fidgeted. "It's...an overstatement."

His face gentled as he caressed her cheek. "He really did a number on you, didn't he? Meredith, your ex is an idiot and an asshole. He didn't deserve you. And I'm glad he's a prick."

"Why?"

His smile warmed her heart. "Because you're here with me, and you're the most beautiful woman I've ever seen. Now, let me show you."

He lifted her mouth to his, and her heart swelled as he touched her. Yes, this was what she'd been waiting for.

He took his time, sipping at her lips until she grabbed his hair, pulled him closer, and opened her mouth. Then the kiss went crazy. His tongue met hers, lighting all the matches inside her. She tugged on his bottom lip and reached for his fleece, tugging it over his head. He helped her, and when she pulled at his shirt, he jerked that over his head too. The sight of his bare chest made her mouth go dry. She ran her fingers down the arrow of hair on his belly and reached for the zipper of his black pants. If he knew the fantasies she'd had...

"Oh, God, not yet." He set her hands aside. "I lied earlier. I'm not made of stone."

He cupped her breasts, his thumbs rubbing her nipples. Her head fell back. God, his touch made her body hum. She wanted to belt out an *alleluia*. She could still feel this way. When he put his mouth to her neck, she moaned from sheer desperation.

"You have no idea how much I want you." He flicked his tongue against her ear lobe.

"I want you more." She clutched his waist.

He kissed her again, guiding her deeper into the dark longings of her body. The intensity of their connection shocked her. She knew he could take her places she'd never been. The woman inside broke free of the last chains holding her in check. She undid her pants and kicked them free. When she sat back on the bed, she held out her hand. It was time to take back her womanhood and put the past in the past.

"Make love to me, Tanner."

He peeled his pants off, stealing her breath away. The man's body was star quality. He settled between her legs, kissing his way down her neck to her breasts. She fell back, her eyes closing as he took her breast into his mouth through her bustier. Her back arched, her hands tangling in his hair.

"Take it off," she finally demanded.

He leaned back and tugged. "I've gone all thumbs, it seems."

She was past the point of laughing. His hips pressed into her as she propped herself up, and she could feel his hard length against her. He wasn't lying. He did want her. Feminine power coursed through her. She threw the bustier aside and pulled his head to her breast. The touch of his mouth had her body tightening, readying for him.

God, it had been so long since she'd felt anything like this. Hot, steamy, wet, and wanted. She couldn't remember feeling more.

She turned into one long line of electrified sensation. Her body focused on the feel of his warm, wet mouth. When he kissed her belly and tugged off her underwear, she trailed her fingers down to his black briefs. He set her hand aside.

"Not yet," he murmured darkly, kissing her thigh. "I want you as hot as I am."

She thought she couldn't get much hotter, but she was wrong. Before she'd rather dreaded this part, but with him, it was intense. Perfect. His mouth made her legs open wider. His tongue made her hips lift off the bed. He knew exactly where to touch, and how she needed it.

He was a sorcerer who trailed his magic across her body and sent her over the edge. She was panting when she opened her eyes. He kissed her belly.

"I want to be inside you," he rasped.

Her feelings overwhelmed her. She couldn't speak, so she raised her leg and rubbed it against his back, that gorgeous line of muscles that made her insides quake. He riffled in the bedside stand and drew out a condom. She reached to help him.

"I'm doing my best to make this last. If you touch me, that'll be it."

He pressed slowly inside, drawing up her legs. She was tight. He was gentle. Their groans mixed together as the fire crackled. He didn't rush. Simply slid forward until he was firmly embedded, letting her adjust to his size.

"God," he hissed, his breath warm on her face. "Open your eyes, Meredith."

She struggled to surface, the desire raging so hot she was sure she'd turn to ash. His direct and heated gaze held a thousand promises. He would pleasure her, take care of her, protect her. Her heart shifted in her chest, and she cupped his neck, looking deep into his eyes.

"Take me. Now."

His jaw clenched. He drew out and thrust back with long, powerful strokes. She met them with equal force. He watched her face, noting her every expression.

She'd never experienced anything so intimate. When she broke his gaze, he called her name, beckoning her back. He moved deeper, keeping those intense chocolate brown eyes fixed on her face, his lower body calling forth more passion from her than she'd ever imagined.

He kept the rhythm steady until he took her mouth in his. The kiss was deeper, wetter, and hotter than any they'd shared before. It snapped his control. He leaned back and thrust harder, faster. She wrapped her legs around his waist as he drove into her, groaning, sweat coating his back. His arms corded with effort as they rested beside her head.

She pressed against him, needing more, wanting him to fill up every space inside her.

"Now," he cried, shifting his body against her core with a movement so primal her hands clenched his butt to hold him in place.

The pressure was perfect. She surged into him, falling like she was skiing off a mountain. She cried out, locking her legs harder around his waist as everything exploded.

He threw his head back, his whole frame clenching.

Her release raged on and on. Bright spots shone behind her eyes. Her skin burned. Her legs loosened from his waist and fell to the side.

Tanner pressed his face into her neck, his labored breath hot against her skin. Her hands slid off his back. She lay under him stunned, save for the continued pulses where their bodies were joined together. Even passed out against her, he didn't crush her. He cherished her.

Like she mattered.

She'd never imagined she might have this again.

Her heart warmed, beating hard and fast, melting the blocks of ice she'd erected around it. Old hurt, relief, and a whole mix of messy emotions rushed up from her chest to her throat. She bit her lip at the sudden urge to cry.

He pressed a gentle kiss to her neck, his hot breath melting away more ice.

A horrible sound popped out of her mouth. A tear slid down. Then two. She tried to push her emotions away, but she was as vulnerable to them as she was to him.

A sob erupted. Her chest shook.

He stirred. His hair was mussed and slightly sweaty. "Hey." He pushed hair back from her forehead.

Her face flushed with heat. "I'm...sorry. Oh, God. I can't believe...I'm crying. It's just... I never thought..."

"What, honey?" His gentle voice undid her.

"I never thought...I'd have *this* again."

His throat moved as he swallowed. "Well, welcome back."

He pulled her close and held her while she cried out all the fear, relief, and hurt she'd built up about not being wanted, not being fulfilled.

When she sniffed and wiped her tears with the sheet, she took his face in her hands. "Thank you, Tanner."

Those intense eyes didn't blink. "You're a brave woman, Meredith Hale. I'm glad I could see how much."

"I didn't freak you out by crying?"

His mouth twisted. "First time I got back into a convoy after the guy sitting next to me died when we hit an IED was one of the hardest days of my life. The minute I got back to my room, my knees gave out. I could have cried like a baby. It's not the same, but I get it."

She had to bite her lip again when more tears rose up in her eyes—this time from his story. She decided they needed some levity "Breaking and entering and making love again. It's been a record night."

He smiled, eyes crinkling. "I'm going to have to stick you in a trunk more often. If this gets any better, I'm going to have a heart attack."

"So you were..." She gestured with her hands.

Tanner tilted his head to the side. "You didn't think your ex cheating on you meant you weren't good in bed, did you?"

Her breath froze in her chest.

His mouth twisted. "Did he tell you that was the reason?"

"He said...I wasn't as responsive or adventurous as he'd like."

"He's a prick, remember?"

"Right." She smiled. "Prick. Asshole. Dickhead."

"Exactly." He laid his lips on hers, a mere brush, but resplendent with tenderness. "You were perfect. I'll be right back."

He shoved away and stumbled. Her mouth curved. Delight overtook the...whatever that other stuff was. He was walking like a drunk. Well, she felt a little drunk herself. She rubbed her raw throat. He walked back in naked with two water bottles in his hand.

"You read my mind." She twisted the lid, wanting to settle her emotions. When she reached for the bedspread, he stopped her.

"No, I want to look at you."

She gazed at the fire and drank her water, her skin tightening at his regard.

"You're so beautiful."

Her head turned. He drank heartily from the bottle. The action was so masculine that it made her body tingle.

"You're not so bad yourself."

He polished off the water and set it aside. "For a Lost Chippendale?"

The banter helped. "I can't believe Jill put that on her Facebook page."

When he pulled her onto his body, she nearly purred. Taking back her womanhood wasn't a one-time thing. Her mind spun with all the ways she was going to enjoy this gorgeous, wonderful man. Whoa! She really was falling for him. She rested her hands on his ribs.

He smoothed his hand down her back, igniting fire like a trail of lit gunpowder. "What's it going to say tomorrow? 'Lost Chippendale Takes Local Mermaid to Bed'?"

She snorted. "Aren't you funny?"

"Well, I feel pretty good right now," he said, fitting her against his hard angles.

She settled her head on his chest, listening to his heart. "Do you want me to go?" she made herself ask.

Raising her chin, he stared into her eyes. "No. Do you want to go?"

Feathering back a stray lock on his forehead seemed like a good distraction. He was too observant as it was. He didn't need to know how hard it had been for her to ask him that. She leaned forward until her mouth was inches away. "No."

"Good, because I plan on making love to you in front of the fire, if you recall." When he kissed her shoulder, she burrowed closer. "And then I'll have to take you on a tour of my shower. It's about the size of Jill's living room. One of those new rainforest things. A far cry from Afghanistan."

"I'm so glad you're here and not there."

"Me too."

\*\*\*

Ava Miles

Tanner studied how the firelight brought out the orange and gold in Meredith's hair. Her warm body lay supine against his. He wanted her again, but wouldn't wake her now. He'd already made love to her twice.

As he'd told her, there was no turning back now.

He'd struggled with his conscience while he was walking the dog. Should he tell her the truth now? Perhaps it was rationalization, but he'd convinced himself to wait. Their...connection was too fragile. Her tears after they'd made love had shown him just how vulnerable she was. How could he ruin that trust so soon? Besides, he'd reasoned, he needed her help if he was going to solve Ray's murder. If he told her about his involvement with Sommerville, she wouldn't want anything to do with him, he suspected, and she'd try to pursue the case alone. He couldn't protect her that way. Plus, he needed to focus on proving Jemma's death wasn't an accident.

But they were all lies.

He simply didn't want to lose her. She mattered to him too goddamned much.

She thought she'd taken one step closer to writing her article tonight. Sommerville planned to blow her dreams to bits.

He had to find a way to stop him.

The thought stuck in his gut like a dagger. He'd have to tell her the truth and hope she'd forgive him. He wanted to keep her in his life. He gave up the fight, rolling her onto her back and sliding inside her.

She stretched in his arms and came awake slowly, rustling her legs against his. When he was pressed to the hilt, the liquid friction perfect, she opened her eyes.

"What is it?" she murmured in concern as she studied him.

He lowered his mouth until it hovered near her lips. "I need you," he whispered. "Again," he added, not sure if the qualifier was to comfort him or her.

When she wrapped her arms and legs around him, he let his body shut down his mind, and sought blissful oblivion in her arms.

# Chapter 35

Jill handed a customer her change and grinned when Meredith and Tanner came through the door. Actually, it was cute, seeing Tanner hold the door open for her radiant sister all dressed in black.

Someone had gotten laid last night.

At last!

Man, if that didn't lift her mood from depressed to sad. She did an Irish jig in place and pointed to the clock. "Somebody's running a bit behind." She didn't say three hours. "Are you sure you don't want decaf since it's so late?"

Tanner fought a smile.

Glaring at her sister, Meredith said, "Is this how you treat all your customers?"

"No, you're special. So was it like Dru hooking up with Seth for the first time in *Chesapeake Blue*?"

"Jeez, Jill. Will you lay off?"

Jill batted her eyelashes. "Beats gloating. Tanner, that's girl code. Literary reference."

"Nothing I've read. I'm afraid to ask."

"Smart man. You want your regular or something different? An energy boost, perhaps?"

"Shut up, Jill." Meredith's cheeks were scarlet.

Tanner stepped forward. "I'll have my regular. Meredith?"

When she gave her preference, Jill called out the order and pushed back Tanner's money.

"Not this morning. It's my way of saying thank you."

"This is the second time you've tried to give me coffee on the house. You'll be out of business at this rate."

"Not unless you plan on doing other things worthy of gratitude."

Meredith reached over and punched her in the arm. "Leave him alone. You're acting like a kid."

"No, I'm enjoying myself. Since I'm not going to gloat—yet—I am going to bask in this moment. You look good, Mere."

Tanner ran his hand down her back. "Yes, she does."

Pressing her hands to her cheeks, Jill said, "Oh, could he be any hotter? It's so sad our torrid love affair never got off the ground."

He chuckled. "You were too good for me."

Meredith turned to him. "And I'm not?"

He leaned down and kissed her lightly on the mouth. "You're probably too good for me too."

Jill wanted to sigh. Things were looking serious. She rubbed her hands together. "So, Tanner, what are you doing for Thanksgiving?"

"My sister and nephew are coming to stay with me."

"Oh, how nice. I can't wait to meet them. Is she a good cook?"

"Ah...passable."

Meredith shot her a glance. In response, Jill made a silly face.

"Well, I was thinking how nice it would be for you all to come to our house. Mom and Dad are driving back up, and she's a great cook."

Meredith's glare could have turned her to stone.

"That's kind of you, Jill, but I think you're making Meredith uncomfortable." He leaned over the counter and tapped her nose. "Stop meddling."

When her sister fidgeted, Jill knew she had her.

"Tanner, we'd love to have you and your family over," Mere said with a bright smile.

Handing her sister her latte, he pressed his coffee to his chest. "You don't have to do this, Meredith."

"I know, but come anyway."

The air crackled with more than pure lust. It held tenderness. There was magic all around.

Nora Roberts Land was here at last!

Jill started humming as a familiar silver SUV streaked by. "Double espresso. Stat. And take the cash register, Benny," she called out to her new lip-pierced barista.

Meredith's face tightened. "What is it?"

"Brian. I'll be right back." She grabbed his coffee, which she'd prepared in anticipation of seeing him, and headed outside without a coat or gloves.

Halfway down the block, she felt like a sissy. It was colder than a witch's tit. She picked up her pace and headed to the restaurant. He couldn't hide from her there. She was done with his crap.

The front door was locked, so she went around back. Mud and salt coated his SUV. He'd probably been off-roading like some Neanderthal jackass. She pounded on the steel door to the kitchen. After a good minute of dancing in place to keep warm, it popped open.

"What do you want?" he asked.

Even though his face looked like it hadn't seen a razor in days, her heart still beat faster. God, it only made him appear more rugged—even wearing an unbuttoned white chef's jacket and black pants.

She thrust out the coffee and darted into the industrial-looking kitchen. "Thought you might need a pick-me-up."

"Thanks, but I have my own beans."

She put her hands on her hips and stared him down. "Do you have any idea how pissed off I am?"

He laid the coffee aside and leaned against the metal counter. "In general or at me?"

"What do you think?"

The butcher knife he had started to sharpen was reflecting the fluorescent lights from above. "Pete and I needed some time away. We went to Aspen. Besides, you didn't want to have anything to do with me before this. Hell, you even ducked out of the party when I arrived."

His mention of Pete had steam leaking out of her ears. The sharpening sounded like two swords meeting, stuck in an endless parry and thrust, just like them.

"Stop doing that. I'm trying to talk to you."

"Fine. Get it over with," he said, slapping the knife down. "I have a French onion soup and a mascarpone cheesecake to make this morning."

Since he wasn't going to give in without some inducement, she went below the belt. She crossed the room and framed his face with her hands. His stubble made her fingers tingle. He swallowed thickly and looked away.

"Are you going to be all right?"

His eyes flicked back to hers, the blue as piercing as a cold winter sky. "Are you?"

Some days the pain eclipsed everything she knew, but she'd fumble through somehow. She knew it. "I'm not the one who left."

He ran a hand through his curly brown hair. "I can't stop thinking about her lying on the floor like that. No breath. No pulse. Nothing under my hands. She was gone." He slammed a hand on the counter.

Every muscle in Jill's body locked into place.

"I couldn't fucking bring her back! Thank God Pete doesn't blame me, but he's devastated. He feels like the world's biggest asshole for letting her go."

"Well, he should. She smoked pot that night because he showed up with his new bitch."

"I don't want to fight with you about Pete. We'll never agree, and I can't take it right now."

She wrapped her arms around him. His fingers bit into her hips in response.

"You tried to bring her back, Bri. She couldn't have asked for more."

"And was that enough? She's still gone." He pushed back and stalked away. "I didn't keep in touch with her much when I left. She was pissed at me for what happened between us, but you know Jem. She still emailed and called around the holidays or my birthday. She was never one to hold a grudge."

He didn't say like her, but the ice in his words froze her heart. He'd called her after he'd left, but had stopped when she'd refused to talk to him.

"She chose you over me, Jill. I get it. Doesn't mean it didn't fucking hurt."

Jill traced her fingers over an open cookbook, the words blurring. She'd never thought about him being hurt. She'd been too angry.

"I was here. She was here. It was more about logistics, Brian."

He threw out a hand. "Don't try and be nice. You know it was more than that. And when I came back, there was always this thing between us. Because of you and me, we never hung out together. Then it all went to shit when Pete broke things off with her." Turning away, he ruffled through some invoices. "I'll always regret we grew apart."

"There was nothing you could have done that night. She had a heart condition."

"Yes, I know. I keep telling myself that. It hasn't sunk in yet. This whole thing is a fucking nightmare."

Because she was feeling weepy, she took a moment to answer. "Yes, it is." She stopped directly in front of him and met his blood-shot eyes, ready to share the revelation she'd had while he was gone. "Jemma wouldn't have wanted us to be at odds."

His jaw hardened. "Is that all?"

Her chest contracted like a boulder had fallen on her, robbing her of breath. "That's all." She couldn't give him more.

"That's not enough." He grabbed her shoulders. "Can you forget how it was? On Halloween?"

She removed his hands. "I managed to forget before, when you left. I can forget again." God, what a bunch of lies she was spewing. She'd never been able to forget.

When she tried to move toward the door, he blocked her path. "Why can't we just start over? Why, dammit?"

"Because you refused to be my first, and then you went out with Kelly Kimple. And you didn't once mention applying for the Culinary Institute of America even though we were best friends."

He pinched the bridge of his nose. "I'm sorry. Can you forgive me?"

She'd spent years hurting and clearly all the pain wasn't gone. "I'm not sure."

"Why?"

Her broken heart crumbled. "Because you're not in it forever." She lifted her eyes and let him see everything—all the love, longing, and hurt she saw in the mirror when she cried alone. "And I am."

His face flinched. She darted around him and ran outside. She didn't stop until her lungs burned. Putting her hands on her knees, frozen to the core, she let herself cry. God, why couldn't she stop loving him?

She mopped up the tears and headed back to her shop. She made herself catalogue her blessings—a wonderful business, a great family, her health.

Why wasn't it enough?

# Chapter 36

The students in Tanner's class couldn't focus, so he let them leave early. He didn't know how to help them. He'd have to ask a college counselor how to talk to them about Ray's death.

They'd better get used to it if they were going into journalism. People died all the time. Someone had to report it. Funny, no one had driven that home at Columbia University. Real-world lessons sucked.

His phone vibrated in his pocket as he walked into his office. He wanted to smash it against the concrete wall when he saw Sommerville's number.

"Yes?"

"I wanted to see if you've made any progress now that I've shown my seriousness."

There was no way Tanner was going to tell Sommerville that he and Meredith had made love. "Didn't you get my texts? We're exclusive."

The amused chuckle made his hand clench. "I want more proof."

"Like what?" Tanner ground his teeth. "Would a picture of us in my house suffice?"

"That would be a nice start."

"Good. Now I don't mean to be rude, but I need to go."

"She's getting to you, isn't she?"

His toe smarted when he kicked the desk. "I don't know what you're talking about."

"Yes, you do."

"I don't become emotionally involved on assignment—ever."

"Hmm...I see. Has she been to bed with you yet?"

He tensed in the chair, forcing all emotion from his voice. "No."

"Well, when she does, it's the green light. She never goes to bed if she's not in love. Hell, there was only one guy before me. Her inexperience wasn't exactly welcome, but it did have its advantages. Pygmalion, you know."

His muscles locked as he forced himself to calm down. "I'll keep that in mind." It was time to change the conversation before he lost his composure. He didn't want to think about Meredith with her ex. "She took you to the cleaners, didn't she? Whatever does she have on you, Rick?"

"You think you're fucking smart, don't you, McBride? Well, I have you by the balls. I can destroy your brother. And I can destroy you and Meredith too. I think I'll arrange a nice long massage today to celebrate."

"You'll get your picture. Fuck off!" Tanner tossed the phone aside. "Shit." He paced the small space, feeling claustrophobic.

He hated the idea of sending the guy a picture. Christ, he was getting in deeper every minute. Now that they'd had sex, his lies weighed on him heavier. He'd have to tell her. And soon.

He ran over the conversation again. Sommerville was playing with him like a lion with an antelope trapped under his paw.

He picked up the phone. "Peg, I need you to call the private detective you hired in New York." His fist punched the air. "Check out the massage place Sommerville goes to today."

When he hung up, he gripped the desk. God, they needed a break.

He picked up his bag, his feet suddenly more grounded. Sommerville was going to pay.

For what he'd done to him.

And for what he'd done to Meredith.

# Chapter 37

Tanner insisted on picking Meredith up from the office. He wasn't taking any chances with her, he'd told her. How nice.

Hugo greeted them when they arrived at Tanner's house, barking up a storm.

"How'd you get out?" She rubbed Hugo behind his ears.

Tanner opened the front door, motioning for her to go in before him. "I put in a dog door today."

She wrapped her arms around him as he shut out the cold. "Someone was busy."

"I didn't want to keep you waiting again," he whispered in her ear, nuzzling her neck.

"I have the police and coroner's report on Ray's death," she said, still holding him. "Plus, the report on Kenny's dishonorable discharge. Grandpa handed them to me as I left the office today."

"He's a busy guy, your grandpa. Peggy was too. Guess who drives a 2009 F150 in Royal Red?"

Her hands tightened in his hair. "Please tell me his name starts with K."

"And if I do?" His mouth cruised down her neck.

"I'd say you're going to get lucky."

He pulled her flush against his body. "Words every guy loves to hear."

She pushed back from him, his black fleece soft under her palms. "But I want to read the reports first." It seemed immature, but she was bouncing in place like a kid who was excited to visit the arcade.

"You want to work now?" He kissed her ear.

She firmed her resolve. "Yes, I'll be too tired later. Once I'm in bed, I don't like to be interrupted."

"I'll keep that in mind. Do you want some wine? A little dinner while we read what the great Arthur Hale sent along?"

"That works."

After polishing off a couple of pretty decent omelets, they settled down on the couch—her feet on his lap—and he read the reports out loud to her.

While the information twisted her stomach, his soothing voice smoothed out the dark edges. They were in this together. They were a team. It felt...well, it felt right.

He threw the report aside when he finished. "How convenient for them to say Ray had alcohol in his system when he skidded off the road. Fuckers had to ruin his reputation."

Meredith ran a hand down his arm. "Gene said his tox screen was under the legal limit."

"Why couldn't he have left that out like he did with Jemma? Ray was a good kid."

"This doesn't say he wasn't. Like everyone else, Gene's looking to give people answers to a senseless car accident."

"I still don't like the way he works. Why does he get to decide what people know? Besides, it's against the law. Why doesn't that bother you?"

He was in a fighting mood, and she didn't want to fan the flames. "It does bother me. Read Kenny's file."

He complied, Hugo's ears perking up at the sound of his deep voice. "Hah," he said when he reached the end. "I've seen enough of these reports to read between the lines. They suspected Kenny was smuggling drugs out of Afghanistan, but couldn't prove it. Add in insubordination to a superior officer and some drunk and disorderlies, and he's history. He's a disgrace to the uniform, but his commanding officer's too much of a gentleman to say it."

She rubbed his denim-clad thigh with her bare feet. "Another thread. If he was doing drugs there—"

"Makes sense that he'd do them here. Stick with what you know. Smart to choose pot. It's not opium, which makes it a lower priority for law enforcement, and by lacing it, he's ensuring steadier sales."

"But Gene didn't find anything in Jemma's tox screen besides marijuana and alcohol. We're still missing something."

"All the more reason for Peg to run another test on the drugs. See if her lab finds that missing element."

"What happens if they don't?"

"Don't borrow trouble." He tugged her onto his lap with one hand. "I have a request. I want to take a picture of us."

Her head darted back. "Why?"

"So I can put it on my phone's home screen." He held it up. "Say cheese."

She turned and smiled as he clicked the photo, her stomach suddenly queasy. Pictures signified they were a couple. She was delighted... and a little afraid. They hadn't talked about their future plans, and she wasn't sure they were ready for that conversation.

"It's just a picture, Meredith," he muttered, giving her a squeeze. "The bug I planted at the garage is working, by the way. I did some listening earlier. Kenny's planning on taking a long vacation, and they're shutting down operations like they said. He didn't say where he was keeping his truck. And I didn't find another set of tires where Ray went off the road."

"Tanner—"

"Kenny and Barlow were right. We don't have dick unless I figure out where his car is hidden."

"Don't you dare look! They already know you're onto them. Let Peggy test the paint shavings from Ray's car."

She rubbed his rock-hard shoulders, trying to settle down herself. "We have Ray's statement and the drugs. His phone call to you and the warning after they killed him. Plus there's everything we heard in the garage and the paint shavings. Let Peggy test them. Please! We've got to pray it's enough to have the authorities take this seriously—even if there's nothing weird about the drugs."

"We still don't have enough. Do you really think they'd investigate a deputy sheriff on a whim? They need more. As for what we heard in the garage, we were there illegally. It's our word against theirs. And we never actually saw them. We can't connect the drugs to them without Ray. The threatening phone call came from Ray's phone, not theirs. And I can't prove anyone fucking called me except Ray! Even a shitty lawyer could pick that apart without breaking a sweat."

"I'll circle back to Gene. Gently see if he thinks he might have missed something."

He pulled her closer. "Peg will have some ideas too. She's more objective than I am. I'm worried about getting her involved though. She's bringing my nephew with her. I know she can handle herself, but Keith's just a kid."

She wrapped her arms around his neck. "We'll keep them safe. It'll be okay, Tanner."

He pulled back and stared into her eyes. "Do you really believe that or are you just blowing smoke up my ass?"

"I believe it'll be okay if we stick together. They're closing things down, hoping everything will blow over. They don't want more action now." She studied his dark frown. "This isn't Afghanistan, Tanner."

"And yet, two kids are dead."

His head fell back against the sofa. She traced the stubble on his jaw, the texture prickling her fingers.

"I should shave."

"I'll do it," she volunteered, ready to take his mind off his worry and guilt. When he lifted his head, she smiled to lighten the mood. "Unless you don't trust me with a razor to your throat."

He snorted and lifted her into his arms, heading for the stairs. Hugo stirred from his place by the fire and barked, racing after them.

"I thought for sure you'd protest." His brown eyes gleamed.

She wiggled her ankles playfully as warmth spread across her body, heading right for her heart. "I've decided to enjoy it." He was the first man to carry her, but she stayed silent about that.

"Glad you aren't stubborn about everything." He shut the bedroom door on Hugo.

He carried her into the massive master bathroom and set her on the counter. Opening the cabinet, he sifted through toiletries. "You're lucky I went back to a razor and shaving cream when I returned from Afghanistan.

I had a beard overseas. It made it easier to blend in."

She let her feet dangle. "Oh yeah?"

He set the can and razor by her hip and leaned in, caging her. "Let's make this interesting."

"O-kay."

He tugged her red shirt off. "I don't mind you being my barber as long as you're only wearing your hot lingerie." The black lace ruffled against her skin when he feathered it with his fingers. He traced the DW stitched in the corner near her left ribcage.

"Are you ever going to tell me what it stands for?"

She unzipped his fleece, not taking her eyes from him. God, was there anything hotter than watching someone while you undressed them?

"It's for Divorcée Woman." She decided a little truth couldn't hurt. "I bought a ton of La Perla lingerie with my alimony. It's top-of-the-line." She tugged at his belt. "Part of gaining my confidence back."

He raised her hands to his lips. "He didn't deserve you."

"I know. Now kiss me."

When their lips met, neither of them rushed. He kissed the corners of her mouth before increasing the pressure, sweeping his tongue in her mouth. She ran her hands inside his white shirt, tracing the muscles of his back. She moaned when he framed her breasts.

"I think the shave will have to wait," he murmured.

"You're not the one getting beard burn." Reaching for the can, she shook it and slapped his hand away. "It won't take long."

The can coughed out shaving cream into her palm, and her fingers spread it lightly across his face and jaw. His eyes sparkled, but he kept his hands at his sides. When she ran the razor down his face, it was a slow caress, an achingly gentle slide across his smooth skin.

"You're driving me crazy, Meredith."

She angled the razor against his neck, anticipation electrifying her nerve endings. "I know." She scraped her way across his face, washing the razor off with warm water after a few strokes.

"You have a pretty square jaw." She dragged the razor down a centimeter at a time.

"Beats a rectangular one."

He stared at her with such a hunger she had to lock her hand to stop the trembling.

"You want to hurry up?"

The razor removed the last of the shaving cream. "I need a washcloth."

She wet the one he handed her, and then massaged his face with it. His hands tucked under her knees and drew her to him, his arousal pressing against her core.

"Okay, that's enough."

He pulled her forward on the counter. Their hands streaked over each other, finding weak spots designed to inflame passion and need. Their remaining clothes fell away. He undid her bustier more easily this time and sucked on her breasts until her head hit the mirror.

God, it was incredible. No nerves. No undue concern about her body or her performance. She succumbed to straight, unadulterated pleasure. Urging him closer, she ran a hand down the front of his body to his hard length. His groan echoed off the walls when she traced it with her grip.

He balanced her on the counter's edge, spreading her legs wide. She covered him with the condom he handed her. His breath hissed out as she took her time, smirking. He put an end to her teasing when he traced her opening with his fingers, easing one of them inside. Her hips bucked. His thumb rubbed hard against the spot that made her squirm, unrelenting. She climaxed in one hard jolt, the heat shooting through her like a Roman candle through a dark night.

He took her mouth with a greed that ignited her desire again instantly, and she struggled to hold on.

"Again," he called, his breath hot on her lips.

She twined her legs around him. "Inside me! Now."

He thrust into her core in one deep movement, muscles locked against her.

"Oh, God," she moaned. "Don't stop. Don't ever stop."

He pulled out and thrust again, fitting their hips more tightly together. She steadied herself on the counter and pushed back, meeting him stroke for stroke. When he grabbed her and pushed her to the adjoining wall, she clenched her legs around him. He picked up the pace, thrusting hard and fast. White heat swept up her body again and exploded in one fiery pulse. Her head fell to his shoulder as he came too, groaning into her neck.

The sex was getting better and better between them. Hell, she was feeling better and better, like she was discovering new aspects of herself with him. She kissed his sweaty, clean-shaven neck, gratitude welling—for him, for them, for this.

He pinned her into the wall, and she loved the weight and warmth of his hard body against her. She could see them in the mirror. God, he had a great backside. And her legs were wrapped around his waist. Her face was flushed, her hair mussed. The gleam in her eyes couldn't be mistaken for anything but boneless satisfaction. She wasn't embarrassed. She liked what she saw.

"Am I crushing you?"

She looked away from her reflection when he raised his head from her shoulder. "No."

"I love making love to you."

Her heart tripped as if over broken sidewalk. "I was...just thinking the same thing."

He kissed her lightly. "Were you?"

"Yes." She trailed a hand down his shoulder.

"I didn't expect you, Meredith Hale." He traced her cheek, his expression tender, making her heart pound harder.

"I didn't expect you either."

And wasn't that the truth? She'd come home hoping to find a Nora Roberts hero, but she hadn't really believed she would. Hell, she hadn't really been ready to take the plunge if she was being honest with herself. Why else had she dated so many no-goes? She hadn't emailed Karen an update about Tanner because she wasn't quite sure what to say. Did she want to put it in black ink that he was The One? She didn't think this was rebound, but she'd been wrong before. She'd married Rick-the-Dick, hadn't she?

Better to wait until they'd uncovered the conspiracy and sent the bad guys to jail. Then, she'd see what she wanted, what he wanted. She fidgeted, her thoughts swirling. Her life in New York felt very far away, but she would be returning in a little over a week. Tanner knew she was leaving, but hadn't mentioned it. Did that mean anything?

"I've fallen for you, you know," he said, tracing her cheek.

There was something off about his voice. Boneless muscles switched to rock-hard tension.

"You're pretty special to me too," she managed to say—scared to say more.

He let out a breath and lowered her to the floor. "That's enough honesty for now. I'm not sure we can take any more." He kissed her again. "But the time is coming. Let's shower."

When he turned the water on and reached for her hand, she joined him, her heart pounding from anything but desire. The hot steam swirled around her, cloaking her from him. She angled against the corner, needing space.

What had he meant by that? She was suddenly afraid to find out.

# Chapter 38

Tanner waved to Meredith as she reached the entrance to *The Western Independent* the next morning. Her smile made him feel like slime.

Memories of their early lovemaking, swim, and coffee faded. He reached for his phone and searched for the photo he'd taken of them last night.

She looked beautiful and...confused. He looked just about as uncomfortable. Hopefully, Sommerville would be satisfied. Giving state secrets might have been easier.

He sent the picture and drove to the university for his nine o'clock class.

As he pulled into the parking lot, his phone rang. "Satisfied?" he answered.

"A quiet night at home by the fire. How lovely. When are you seeing each other again?"

"I'm having Thanksgiving with her family."

"Good. Send another picture. Be nice to see if her parents redecorated."

Give the bastard an inch... "I have class. If there's nothing else..."

The chuckle was dark. "Honestly, I wasn't sure you could pull it off. At first I was content with the idea of you breaking up with her and stopping the article that way, but now I'm starting to rethink things. If she finds out you're working for me, she'll hate your guts."

Fear slid down Tanner's spine like ice. "When I break things off and stop her from doing the article, I've done my job. She doesn't have to know about our deal." Even though he planned to tell her, he wanted to be the one to explain the situation. God only knows what Sommerville would say.

"Hmm... I'm not sure now. I'm feeling a bit jealous."

Bullshit. Sommerville was like an Afghani war lord. Only territorial when someone wanted something he'd neglected or thrown away.

"You don't want to piss her off. She could say some nasty things to the press and hurt your political chances."

"True. I'll have to think about my options."

"Stop threatening me, Sommerville. You're only making me want to destroy you."

"You think I don't already know you want it so bad you can taste it?

Tanner, you should hire a better PI. I spotted him when I arrived for the massage. I could recommend someone to you."

"You're a fuck."

"Thank you. Don't have me followed, or I'll rip your brother's life open publicly and ruin your reputation. How would it look for an acclaimed journalist to succumb to blackmail? No source in his right mind would trust you again."

He pounded on the steering wheel, his control snapping. Sommerville was right. Slamming his eyes shut, he counted to ten. Losing it with Sommerville only gratified Sommerville. Fuck it. Today, he didn't care.

"Did your masseuse suck your cock?"

"Did Meredith suck yours?"

Tanner clicked off and threw the phone aside. How dare he talk about her like that?

He exited the car and slammed the door. A few people looked over at him in the parking lot, so he flashed a fake smile and lifted his hand. Stupid of him to goad Sommerville.

Striding across campus, he imagined all the things he wanted to do to Richard Sommerville, all the while praying he didn't have the chance to tell Meredith the truth before Tanner did.

Sommerville was right. She would never forgive him.

# Chapter 39

Meredith hoped she wouldn't have to attend another funeral for a long time. The gymnasium was packed again, giving her the saddest sense of déjà vu. Ray's friends talked about his dreams of being a lawyer, joking through tears about how much he loved legal dramas. There wasn't a whisper of his extracurricular activities.

As they left, Tanner introduced her to a group of his students, clutching her hand while they talked. He did what he did best—listened. Offered a word of comfort. Patted them on the back. They clearly adored him.

He ignored the speed limit as he drove them to Jill's. "Sorry I can't hang around long. I want to make sure everything's ready for Peg and Keith."

"No worries. I have something to show you anyway." She unlocked the door, her nose twitching from Jill's sage incense. Shaking her head, she headed for the kitchen. "Want some coffee?"

He pulled her against his chest, looking beyond handsome in gray slacks and a navy blazer over a white dress shirt. "How about a kiss first? I couldn't give you a proper one in front of Jill this morning."

His mouth tantalized her, but didn't plunge them into the reckless desire of the night before. His tenderness always surprised her. She wasn't used to it, but she liked it a lot.

After releasing her mouth, he held her against him and stroked her hair.

She snuggled closer. "Are you okay?"

His sigh was heartfelt. "I will be. It was hard seeing that photo of him, knowing I'd never see him again. He wasn't a hero, but he tried to do the right thing. I want people to know that. In some ways, it takes more courage."

"You're a good man."

His body tensed. "Why don't you make coffee? I'll need some to keep up with Keith."

She knew withdrawal, but couldn't figure out why he'd reacted that way. Was he one of those good guys who didn't like compliments?

"I'm going to talk to Peggy about hiring someone here to watch Kenny." He followed her into the kitchen. "Someone who can move around and report directly to her. Maybe find out where he's stowed his truck and the drugs."

"He's driving a blue 2010 Ford Ranger now." She selected an Abba coffee cup for him just to be saucy and a plain blue pottery mug for herself.

"And you know this how?"

"Ah, Grandpa heard it at Bingo."

Tanner sputtered out a laugh. "*Bingo*? Again?"

"I told you it's the best place for information in Dare. Hell, he could tell you who has hemorrhoids on any given day."

"Thanks so much for that image."

"Let me say it one more time since I know you're a man of action. I don't want you taking any more risks beyond us gathering intel."

"Fine. You're right. It goes against my nature, but between you and Peg, I'm pretty much hearing the same tune." When she handed him the Abba cup, he raised a brow. "Speaking of tunes, how'd I score this one?"

She laughed. "Because Jill called you my Man After Midnight this morning after their song." Lifting on her tiptoes, she kissed his cheek.

"I won't be your Man After Midnight until my sister leaves. Don't ask me how unhappy I am about that." His chocolate eyes gleamed as he drank the coffee. "I'll miss being with you."

Her insides warmed. "Well, it's not like we won't see each other, but I know what you mean."

Setting his coffee aside, he reached for her. "Maybe we should make this quality time."

"You said you couldn't," she said, twining her arms around his neck. "Admit it. You want to be able to say you've made love on an orange couch."

"You found me out. Now, shut up and kiss me."

Feathering the hair at the base of his skull, she opened her mouth and tantalized him with deep strokes of her tongue. He'd worked her black blouse open when the doorbell rang. She pulled back.

He groaned. "You're kidding."

"Hold that thought," she said, buttoning up her shirt.

When she opened the door, her stomach burned. A delivery man held three dozen yellow roses in a crystal vase. Her mouth flattened. That son of a bitch! How dare he send her flowers. She signed in a scrawl and slammed the door.

"You okay?" Tanner sauntered closer.

She threw up a hand and turned her back on him. "Give me a second." She ripped open the card.

*Meredith,*

*I heard you were back in Dare. I can't help but think of you on our anniversary. I'm sorry for everything. I thought you should know I miss you. Thanks for your continued support.*

*Love,*

*Richard*

"Oh my God! I can't believe him." Stalking around the living room, she put her hands in her hair and pulled. "That arrogant, pompous..."

Tanner stepped in her path. His jaw ticked. "You want to tell me what's going on?"

"It's not what you think. It's not from an admirer."

He crossed his arms. "I didn't think so given the way you're acting."

She took a deep breath and touched her bustier with her fingertips. Divorcée Woman would know how to explain the situation. She handed him the card. "It's from my ex. Today was our anniversary." She stalked to the window, watching the neighbor kids pelt each other with snowballs. "I can't believe...a whole host of things, including how he knew I was staying with Jill. It reads like a...okay I'll say it—a damn political ad." She kicked a side table. "He's screwing with my head."

"Yes, he is," Tanner growled.

"You don't need to be worried." She put her hand on his arm. "I can't stand him."

Tossing the card aside, he pulled her over to the couch. "But he can still push your buttons."

"Of course, he can. He cheated on me! That's not something you forget."

Tanner veiled his eyes. "You can tell me if it's none of my business, but can I ask you something?"

She sat up straighter. "What?"

"What did you ever see in him?"

Pushing off the couch, she threw up her hands. "I don't have to justify myself to you!"

"I'm not asking you to justify yourself, Meredith. I only want to understand. This thing with Richard changed you."

Her eyes burned suddenly. "You're damn right about that. Being cheated on sucks, okay? But it's even worse to have your judgment called into question."

"That's not what I'm doing," he said softly.

She met his gaze dead on. "Aren't you?" She let out a sound between a laugh and cry. "Well, you aren't the only one. *I* question my own judgment. What happened made me lose confidence in myself. Do you have any idea what that's like?"

"No, I don't."

She strode across the room. "Of course you don't. You know exactly who you are. You always do the right thing. And you can probably always tell the good guys from the bad ones."

"Not always, Meredith. I've made plenty of mistakes."

"Yeah, well this one cost me a hell of a lot. You want to know why I fell for Richard? It's pretty simple. He pursued me with a determination I'd never experienced before. I felt wanted. He's handsome. I was attracted. And he's pretty slick. He always knows how to say the right thing."

"Go on."

She gripped the curtain in her hand, seeking some way to stay grounded. "It took me awhile to realize he didn't always mean it. And eventually, I figured out that my name was probably what he liked most about me. He was angling to become part of the paper. Take it over maybe, merge it with his. I don't know. He didn't realize Gramps would never allow that. That's when things changed. I thought I was a good judge of character."

She heard him walk toward her, but he didn't touch her.

"He's fooled a lot of people. I know that doesn't help, but it's true."

"I just wish I hadn't been one of them," she whispered. "I know you probably think I'm not over him, but that's not true." Lowering her head, her vision blurred. "I haven't stopped blaming myself for being so stupid." A tear plopped on her boots.

"Okay, that's enough." He pulled her against him.

She tried to yank away.

"I'm not letting go. It won't hurt you to lean a little. Blaming yourself is cutting you into pieces. I happen to know Meredith Hale is one hell of a woman. She's insightful, savvy, and sensitive. If your ex cheated on you, he was weak. A mega-prick."

"Yes, he is," she muttered against his chest.

"You should talk to my sister. Peg was married to another police officer. They were happy at first, and then they had Keith. She was on a stakeout when she saw her husband coming out of a house. He was supposed to be hunting with friends. She found out that he'd started cheating on her while she was pregnant and couldn't give it up after Keith was born. He said it wasn't about her."

She leaned back. His scar twisted when his mouth did.

"Peg is one of the best judges of character I know. She makes life and death decisions on the job. But she didn't see him for what he was. She blamed herself just like you're doing."

"Did she get over it?"

"Not at first, especially since she still had to see the bastard because of Keith. But after a while, she realized he didn't want to be a father, so she moved to Kansas when her commander took a new position there, promising her a promotion." Tracing her cheek, his eyes glowed with emotion. "She finally remembered what she was inside." He kissed her forehead and cradled her like she was precious. "You're remembering too."

Was she? She supposed she was. How else could she have moved forward with Tanner? Gone to bed with him? She did feel more confident now. But not perfect.

What the hell was perfect anyway?

She framed his face. "I meant what I said before. You really are a good man."

The muscle jumped in his jaw. "Don't make me out to be something I'm not. I told you I make plenty of mistakes."

Okay, so he wasn't going to listen. She dropped the subject and rested against his chest. The clock ticked. The neighbor kids cheered and yelled war cries, pelting snowballs at each other with an innocence that made Meredith nostalgic. She could never go back to that time, that place. She could only move forward.

She nuzzled Tanner's neck. When she pulled him down for a kiss, he flowed into her, filling up every dark and aching corner. She tried to give back the light he had bestowed on her, hearing him murmur words she couldn't decipher.

He kissed her in short, sweet bites. "I've decided I have a little more time," he muttered between kisses.

His hands smoothed her clenched back muscles, but he held her loosely. She understood that he was letting her decide if she wanted more.

She did.

She tugged on his bottom lip, deepening the kiss. When she drew back, she tightened her arms around him. "Make love to me."

He wove his fingers through her hair and lifted her onto her toes. His chocolate eyes smoldered with more than desire. Their gentleness had her body moving into him with new confidence.

"Orange couch or bed?" he asked with a seductive smile.

"The bed. Definitely the bed." Bringing him there would be another way of making him part of her life.

He undressed her slowly in the dim light from the drawn shades. As his hands drew off her bustier, the buzzing increased in her head, and in her body. She pressed his palms to her breasts and let her head fall back. By now, he knew how to circle her nipples to make her gasp. Pluck at them until she moaned.

And still he moved slowly.

When she tried to undress him, he drew her down to the bed. "No, watch."

She watched him slide his clothes off, the line of electricity intensifying through her body. He took her breath away, so defined and strong. When he was naked, he stretched out over her, arms bracketed on either side of her head.

"Just feel."

Even though his whole body was corded with tension, he touched her with gentleness. Kissed her with tenderness. Caressed her with a reverence she could only think of as cherishing.

When he guided her over the first peak, she arched back, letting the feelings wash over her like sunlight on snow.

She opened her eyes, wanting to look at him, and he brushed a lock of hair back from her forehead. She knew the control he exerted over his own needs wasn't easy.

"Be with me," she whispered, touching his cheek.

He came into her inch by slow inch, resting his forehead against hers. Their union felt like a merging—so right. When the crest came for both of them, their hands found each other and gripped. Waves of pleasure washed over them.

After he left the bed, she fingered the crease in his pillow, realizing they'd journeyed somewhere new together.

She wasn't sure what to think about that.

She turned to her side, rolling around words in her mind.

Nora Roberts Land.

The One.

Pleasure. Trust. Fear.

When he came through the bathroom door, all chatter in her head ceased. He tucked her against his side, stroking her skin softly.

No one said anything. No one needed to.

When he finally picked up his watch, he sighed. "I really do need to go now."

They both dressed. When they came out of her bedroom, he took her hand.

"I'm almost sorry we didn't use the orange couch. Not too many people can say that."

At the front door, a smile shimmered on her lips. "Well, it'll be waiting for you when your company leaves."

"I'll keep that in mind." Reaching into his pocket, he handed her his Swiss army knife. "Don't let Sommerville have the last word. Hack the flowers up and stomp them to bits if it'll make you feel better."

It was still warm from his body. She curled her hand around it. "Okay. Thanks."

He'd given her his gloves—and now his knife. Funny how they warmed her heart in a way flowers never had.

He settled his hands on her waist and gave her a slow, deep kiss. "It'll be all right. You'll see."

His voice tightened at the end of the sentence. Was he trying to convince her or himself? After what they'd shared in her bedroom, she wasn't sure either of them knew where they were going.

They'd have to talk about it soon. Her stomach flipped. How would he feel about her writing an article about him being her hero in Nora Roberts Land? Was she ready to even admit he was The One?

She was pretty damn close.

Her fingers cinched his navy scarf. "Have fun with your family. I'll see you tomorrow."

"Can't wait." He walked away and then angled back, kissing her again before leaving.

The roses made her nose twitch. She fingered her crystal necklace, studying the bouquet. She realized she didn't need to pulverize Rick-the-Dick's flowers. Her anger had floated away. There was a new peace inside her. She felt...solid and centered—nothing like the wobbly mess she'd been in New York.

She took the bouquet to their elderly neighbor's house to brighten her day. How was that for progress?

*****

Tanner reached for his phone only to set it aside again. Damn Sommerville. The flowers had driven his point home. He wouldn't think twice about fucking with Meredith directly and letting her know Tanner was scum. That would stop the article in a heartbeat.

Sommerville didn't miss her. He got off on people's weaknesses.

And now he was preying on Tanner's.

If it wasn't for David, he'd tell Sommerville to go to hell and march right back in and tell Meredith the truth in the hopes that she'd listen and forgive him.

But he couldn't risk David. He'd always looked out for him. That's what big brothers did. Plus, if he'd stayed home instead of going off to college and traveling the world, maybe he could have stopped David from following in their dad's drunken footsteps.

He glanced at the house. He didn't think about his fucked up family life when he was with her. She made him believe something better existed. Made him believe he didn't have to be alone anymore.

He froze, the wind harsh on his face.

He hadn't planned on it, but he was in love with her. All the way.

And she loved him too. He knew it.

His gut settled. He couldn't be sure what Meredith would do, but he had to find out. He'd tell her when Peg left.

Meredith wasn't supposed to be here much longer. Neither was he. He could find a job in New York to be near her, although he was surprised to realize he'd miss Dare. The damn town was growing on him.

When he arrived home, he settled in to wait for his sister and nephew, pulling out all the files on Ray's death.

The sooner he could lock up this case, the sooner they'd be free and clear to start a new life together.

# Chapter 40

Meredith's heart landed with a thud at her feet at the sight of Tanner carrying his nephew on his shoulders.

How could she help but love a man who would let a seven year-old mess with his hair?

"He'll make a good father," Jill commented beside her at the window, watching them walk up the sidewalk.

Her heart warmed until she felt rosy all over. "Hush."

"Look me in the eyes and tell me I'm wrong."

"Why don't you get the door?" she asked, wanting a little time to herself.

"Get it yourself, Mermaid." Jill slapped her butt and sailed off.

She pressed her hands to her face. She finally had to admit it. She was in love with Tanner McBride.

Oh boy!

And they were spending a family holiday together. You didn't get much more Nora Roberts Land than that.

The ground trembled beneath her feet. She'd really found The One. She'd have to tell him—about both her feelings and the article. When Peggy left.

The bell chimed. Meredith headed over to the door with a spring in her step, her green dress dancing with her rhythm.

"Hi, there!" Tanner's nephew piped the moment she opened it.

He had dark hair and chocolate brown eyes just like Tanner. She found herself smiling. "Hi, yourself. Happy Thanksgiving."

"Meredith, this is my sister, Peggy, and my nephew, Keith," Tanner noted with a wink. "Keith won't be eating since he doesn't like turkey, but we brought him anyway."

"I do so like turkey! I don't like veggies. You don't have those, do you?"

"Sorry, kiddo. My mom insisted we have them," she joked.

"Please forgive my son." Peggy extended her hand. Her dark, chin-length hair framed a sweetheart-shaped face. "He wants to stay short all his life."

"Do not, mom," Keith cried, pulling Tanner's hair up straight like he was eyeing it for a haircut.

"Watch the backtalk, please. It's good to meet you, Meredith. And thank you for the invitation. It's so nice not to be cooking today."

"Yeah, thanks," Keith mimicked.

Peg gave him the behave look. "I hope he won't be too rambunctious."

"Not possible," Meredith's grandfather replied, walking forward. "It's nice to have a young gun around. I'm Arthur Hale. Please come inside. Couldn't get lucky with a heat wave for the holiday, could we?"

Tanner made the introductions as Jill and her parents joined them with oh-so-pleased grins. When her dad said he'd hang their coats, Tanner grabbed Meredith's arm and led her away. Oh, he looked so handsome in navy slacks and a white dress shirt.

"Thought I'd kiss you while I have the chance."

When he set his mouth to hers, she forgot anyone else was around. His tongue stroked the seam of her lips, but he didn't take it deeper. He pressed his forehead to hers, his breath warm on her face.

"Happy Thanksgiving."

She wrapped her arms around him, the newness of her emotions coursing through her. "Right back at you."

"Meredith? Can you help me with the potatoes?" her mother called.

Kissing him briefly on the lips, she walked backwards toward the kitchen. "Duty calls."

Her mother gave her a hearty embrace when she approached. "So, it seems like things have been going well for you while we've been gone."

"Ah..."

"Jill's kept me informed." She reached for the beater. "I'm so glad, Meredith."

"Mom...don't get too excited. Okay? We haven't been together for all that long."

And there were things they hadn't talked about yet. Her article. Her departure. His. Their future. Teensy-weensy things like that.

Meredith's mother handed her the butter and cream. "Some things don't take much time to develop into their perfect form. Like mashed potatoes."

Rolling her eyes, she took them.

"Don't make fun of me, missy. Sometimes all you have to do is add the right ingredients and whip. Then voila. You have something magical."

"Oh, Mom...is this 'Cooking Meets Psychology Hour'?"

Her mom slapped her butt gently with a wooden spoon. "You're a smart ass, but I love you. Now whip."

*** 

Thirty minutes later, as the last of the mashed potatoes were being served, Arthur turned to Peggy, who was sitting on his right.

"I imagine you're one heck of a policewoman."

"Yeah! She's caught a lot of bad guys. Pow, pow!" Keith's fingers mimed a gun.

"Thank you." Peggy smiled and pushed her son's hand into his lap. "Behave or I'll make you eat broccoli."

Keith made a gagging sound.

Tanner ruffled his hair. "Don't interrupt people's conversations. If you're good, we'll have another snowball fight."

The boy clapped. "Okay, but you can't hit people in the head."

"I'll try and remember that," Tanner replied seriously.

Meredith's mother gave her a knowing smile. Yes, Tanner has his arm around my chair, she wanted to say. She stuck out her tongue. Her mother put her napkin over her mouth to hide her smile. Her father carved more turkey and passed some to Keith, who was bouncing in his chair like a popcorn kernel.

She never would have imagined Thanksgiving would be like this when she'd arrived in Dare, but she was thrilled.

Tanner and Keith went outside for another snowball fight after convincing Jill to join them. Meredith headed out onto the deck to watch, and Peggy came with her. The setting sun cast an orange glow on the snow-covered hills, and snowballs flew through the air amidst squeals and shouts.

"You have a great family," Peggy remarked. "I especially like your grandfather."

"He's pretty charming. You have a great family too. Your son is wonderful."

"He's a handful, but we do all right. He's all boy. Has been since he uttered his first word. Truck."

"Tanner's obviously over the moon about him." Jill was right. He would make a good father. Not that she was thinking about that.

*Liar, liar, pants on fire*, Divorcée Woman insisted.

Great, instead of her nose growing like Pinocchio, her alter ego was calling her out.

*You know how to stop me.*

Yes, she did, but admitting to a truth that big was too scary. She walked to the edge of the deck and knocked off the icicles.

"They have a strong bond. Keith is thrilled Tanner's back in the country. They used to Skype, but it's not the same."

"Tanner mentioned you're divorced too," Meredith said cautiously.

"Yes, my ex was a dick, and he used it to screw around on me."

"I call my ex Rick-the-Dick."

Peggy's mouth showed a ghost of a smile. "Good one. My ex's name doesn't rhyme with anything."

"Can I ask you..."

"Ask away."

"You seem so..." She gestured with her hands. "Together. Do you ever have bad days?"

Peggy cocked her head exactly like Tanner did, causing Meredith to break out in goosebumps. "Are you kidding? It doesn't say perfect on my badge. Last time I checked, it simply said policewoman. Well, not literally. Look, you're wondering if I doubt myself, right? Sure."

"How did you get your confidence back?"

Her mouth curved into a wicked smile. "I bought a new gun and went to the range every day, pretending the target was my ex. Word got out. I was good. Scary good. People stopped ragging me at work. Silenced all the pity talk." She snapped her finger. "My partner told me something in his sick way that clicked. He said if I can work a job where I risk getting shot or shooting someone, I can probably get over an asshole like Frank. It took a man to drill that wisdom home. My mom only patted my hand and told me what a great person I was."

"I bought a whole bunch of lingerie. It's not a gun..."

"Whatever works." She eyed Meredith's torso. "What kind?"

"La Perla."

Peggy whistled. "Got a nice settlement, huh?"

"I did pretty well."

"Have something on him, do you?"

Meredith looked away, off balance. "No," she lied. "I had a good lawyer." There was no way she was telling a cop what she had on Rick-the-Dick.

"Lucky you," Peggy drawled.

Her face heated. Keith's joyful screams reverberated in her ears when Tanner threw him into the air, Jill pelting them with snowball after snowball. "You're lucky to have him."

Peggy grabbed her arm. "You're lucky to have Tanner. If you're still having trouble trusting yourself, let me ask you something. Did kids like your ex?"

"Not that I recall."

"Kids know. Tanner is Keith's favorite uncle."

"I didn't know Tanner had a brother."

Peggy's face tensed. "Ah...yes. He's the youngest. Keith, put your hat back on."

"Where does he live?"

"Outside New York City," she said. And then she stood up abruptly. "I think I'm going to join the fight."

She stepped off the deck and charged her brother before Meredith could ask her anything else. They struggled, but her scissor-kick took him down. He laughed and shoved snow down her coat.

Meredith wrapped her arms around her middle as she watched them. Peggy had acted a bit weird about their other brother. She wondered why Tanner hadn't mentioned him, but then again, she hadn't asked him much about his past. Perhaps it was time she did.

"Meredith," Tanner called out to her, his nose adorably red. "Get your butt over here and join this war."

Enough serious thoughts. Even though she had a dress on, she decided to enter the fray. She charged him, pelting him with snow.

He glowered. "It's good to see you don't throw like a girl."

Both Hale girls paused for a moment before swooping down on him.

"Traitors," he called as Peggy and Keith joined the fray.

Meredith jumped on Tanner's back. Before she could blink, he dumped her on the ground and leaned over her.

"Say surrender," he singsonged, a lock of hair falling on his forehead.

She met his gaze and smiled sultrily. "I surrender."

And meant it all the way to her healing heart.

He must have remembered their conversation on Halloween, because his eyes gleamed, and he kissed her tenderly. Since they couldn't take it any further, she darted her tongue into his mouth and stuck snow down his neck.

"Hey!" He reared back.

She shoved him and ran for the house, her laughter making puffs in the cold air. As she raced, she looked up and saw her parents watching her from the window. They looked tanned and rested. And still very much in love.

She'd resigned herself to never having what they had, but each time Tanner swept her off her feet, she believed she could have her own Nora Roberts Land.

# Chapter 41

Tanner tucked the sheet around Keith, who wiggled like a worm in the massive king bed. "Night, buddy."

"Don't wanna go to sleep yet," he said, kicking at the covers.

Peggy kissed his cheek. "Too bad. It's way past your bedtime. Be grateful we didn't have Thanksgiving here. I would have made you go to bed even earlier."

"You're so strict, mom."

"Comes with the badge." She tapped him on the nose. "Now kiss Uncle Tanner goodnight."

When Keith wrapped his little arms around him, Tanner ruffled his hair. The kid's adoration was up there with his Pulitzer in terms of lifetime accomplishments. He kissed him on the head. "Love you, kid."

"Love you too. Can Hugo sleep in my room? Please!"

He lifted a brow at Peg.

"Okay, but we're still not getting a dog."

"But Mom!"

The stare she leveled would have stopped an armed robbery.

The kid's frown accentuated the toothpaste in the corner of his mouth. "Okay, sorry. We have to wait until I get older, Uncle Tanner. Jeez."

"We'll send Hugo up, but if I hear talking, he's coming back downstairs."

Tanner winked at Keith before shutting the door halfway and calling the dog. "Want something to drink?" he asked Peg as they jogged down the stairs to the kitchen.

"Coffee." She settled on a stool, watching him brew a pot without making conversation.

"What?" he finally asked.

"I didn't say anything."

"No, but you're thinking something. Give."

She cleared her throat. "You didn't tell me you were in love with her."

He dropped the coffee scoop, spilling grounds on the counter. He swore and grabbed a towel.

"I wasn't sure I should say anything, but this is serious, Tanner."

"Jesus, do you think I don't know it?"

"So you are in love with her?"

He glared. "Is that a capital offense?"

"No, but I want to hear you say it."

"I love her." Even to his ears, his voice turned hoarse.

She threw up her hands. "Then tell her the truth. The longer you wait—"

"Don't you think I know that?" He pounded the coffee lid on.

"Okay, I won't torture you anymore." She tapped the counter with her nails. "Meredith has some dirt on Sommerville."

"Jeez, Peg. How did you find that out?"

"I worked it into the conversation. She denied it, but she's a terrible liar."

"Yes, she is."

Her brow rose at his growl. "It was easier for me to ask."

"She wasn't suspicious?"

The snort had his teeth grinding. "Please, I'm a professional. What do you want to do?"

"I'm telling her when you leave. Okay? Get off my back. It's hard enough worrying about how this might affect David."

"He's an adult now. Any promise you made mom—"

"Doesn't have a statute of limitations." He stared at his toes, reining himself in.

Silence stretched in the kitchen.

She set her coffee aside. "Okay. I'll shut up. Let's go through what we know about the kid's murder again. See if we're missing anything."

Tanner knew enough about police procedure to know this was how Peggy worked. Repetition. Going through the files over and over again until something popped.

When he walked into his room an hour later, he wanted to kick the door closed. Nothing had popped.

He thought about what she'd said about Meredith having something on Sommerville. Was he willing to use Meredith to stop the asshole?

He didn't like anyone else fighting his battles.

Well, he'd tell Meredith about the whole damn thing on Sunday and see what she said. Best lock the doors beforehand or steal her car keys. If she bolted... Well, he'd get her back. He was not losing her.

According to the clock, it was just shy of midnight, but he wasn't tired. He drew out his phone, staring at their picture like a teenager. He cursed and hit her number.

"Tanner?" Meredith answered in a hushed voice, so similar to how she sounded when he woke her in the night to make love. "Is everything all right?"

"Yeah. I wanted to say goodnight. I...wish you were here."

"Me too. I like your family."

"And they liked yours."

Of course, what wasn't to like? Her family was completely different from his. Her parents were clearly crazy about each other. In his home, there had been constant fights and tears. And that was before his drunk of a father had left them.

"Your sister said you have a younger brother in New York City. Where did he spend Thanksgiving?"

His throat squeezed tight. Damn Peg. He was sure she hadn't meant anything by it, but it made him break out in a sweat.

"He lives in the Bronx with his wife and daughter. My mom spent the holiday with them."

He pushed off the bed and paced.

"What does he do?"

"Ah...He's a local councilman."

God, he hoped she wouldn't look David up out of curiosity. The recent article in her ex's paper would be the first Internet hit.

"Wow, a cop, a local politician, and a journalist. That's a pretty impressive group. Your mother must be proud."

"Yes, she is. She practically raised us alone while working two jobs. I don't know how she did it."

They'd never had much, but she'd always done her best. He'd finally made his peace with her after realizing that.

"She sounds like an incredible woman. I hope I get the chance to meet her."

He rubbed his throat, liking her train of thought. It implied they'd have a future. "Me too." Since his gut was churning like a whirlpool with all the unsaid things between them, he changed the subject. "So, since we're celebrating what we're thankful for, why don't you tell me what you're wearing?"

She made a humming sound. "Thanksgiving ended a few minutes ago."

"I'm still celebrating."

"In that case..."

When she told him about her lace and satin undergarments, he settled down and decided acting like a teenager wasn't such a bad thing in some cases—especially when it took your mind off murder and mayhem.

# Chapter 42

Tanner smiled as Keith helped him hold Don't Soy With Me's door open for Peg and Meredith. Never too early to start acting like a gentleman.

"Jill, can I help make coffee?" Keith asked as they approached the counter.

Jill bounded toward them and swept him up in her arms. "Sure you can, if it's okay with your mom."

Peggy bopped Keith on the head with her gloves. "You listen to Miss Hale."

"Okay, Mom."

Jill pulled Keith around the counter. "Looks like we have some customers."

As Meredith unwound her scarf, Tanner stopped her. He trailed his fingers along her neck as he slowly slid the white scarf off. Her green eyes warmed.

"Don't make me arrest the two of you," Peggy murmured. "At least let me get some coffee first."

"Party pooper."

"That's me, Tanner. Let's order."

Keith chattered like a magpie as he helped Jill make their coffees. Meredith tensed next to Tanner when Larry Barlow strolled in. Knowing what he had done made it difficult to manage a poker face. Unfortunately Meredith's sucked, so he nudged her.

"Honey, why don't you grab us a table? I'll bring the coffees over when they're ready."

He thought she was going to argue, but she gave a stiff nod. "Okay."

Peggy put her hands on her hips, taking in the scene. Decked out in a green winter jacket with Eagle County's Sheriff's Department stitched on the front, Peggy would no doubt put two and two together.

"Tanner." Barlow slapped his leather gloves in his hands.

"Barlow."

The asshole lifted a brow when Tanner didn't make introductions. "I don't know you, ma'am, and I know most people in town," he said to Peggy. "I'm Deputy Sheriff Barlow."

She turned, flashing a girly smile. "Hi! I'm Tanner's sister, visiting from out of town."

Peggy's fake feminine side creeped him out. Did she just bat her eyelashes? Dear God, she must be awesome at undercover work.

"Hi there," Keith cried out, standing on the stool Jill had found for him. "What can I get ya?"

Barlow strolled closer. "Aren't you a little young to be working here?"

"It's not against the law, sir," Keith said, shrugging, "so long as she doesn't pay me."

Barlow chuckled. "You're correct, young man. Who are you?"

"I'm Keith. That's my mom." He pointed to Peggy.

The urge to prevent Barlow from talking to Keith was strong. Tanner didn't think Barlow would do anything, but he wanted him to stay away.

This wasn't a social call.

"You wanna ride in my police car?" Barlow rested his hands on his police-issue belt. "I do it for all the new kids."

Peggy gripped Tanner's arm when he took a step forward.

"Nah," Keith responded. "I've been in police cars lots of times."

Tanner's insides cramped like he'd consumed bad milk. "Hey, Keith, why don't you check on our order?"

Barlow straightened and tapped the counter. "You been arrested a lot, son?"

Peggy's laughter trilled out. "Oh, that's too funny. My kid loves cop shows. He's taken a few rides. Honey, Jill looks like she could use your help. Don't fall behind in your duties."

"I'm not, Mom." He turned back to Barlow with a frown. "I haven't gotten in trouble, Officer. I ride in my mom's car sometimes. She's a cop too."

Peggy's fingers clenched Tanner's coat. "Keith, honey. Why don't you take this man's order? I'm sure he doesn't have a long break."

She met Barlow's gaze, and her smile dropped.

He smacked his gloves against his hand. "You're a cop?"

"Yes, out of state. I'm only here for the holiday."

Barlow scanned her body. "You carrying?"

"No." She had her gun locked up in his house.

"You didn't think about checking in with us?"

"As I said, I'm here on vacation. It's nice to be away from the job. You know."

Her appeal to professional camaraderie was worth a try. Maybe Barlow wouldn't feel threatened.

And pigs would fly.

"Well, we don't have much crime here. Do we, Tanner?"

He settled back on the balls of his feet and met Barlow's stare dead-on. "I haven't seen any in the police reports."

Barlow's mouth twisted. "Good to remember. We keep things quiet in Dare."

"That's nice to hear," Peggy noted, her voice like rough gravel now.

"Here's our coffee, mom," Keith called. "I've got the bestest hot chocolate in the world."

Tanner reached for their drinks so he wouldn't deck Barlow.

Peggy pointed across the room. "Go sit by Miss Hale. Good to meet you, Deputy."

"Nice meeting you," Barlow said, stepping closer. "Have a safe trip."

Her eyes turned to slits. "Thanks. We will."

Tanner's insides felt like they'd been tossed in a blender. Barlow hadn't known Peggy was a cop, but he did now. Would he wonder if she was involved? Of course he would.

He kissed Meredith's frown as he sat down next to her, placing a coffee in front of her. "Drink up," he commanded gently.

Her worry radiated like the space heater against the window, the blast impossible to ignore.

Peggy wrapped her hands around her cup. "Gee, that was fun."

"Sure was," Keith cried, bouncing in his seat, totally misreading her sarcasm.

When Meredith blew out a breath, Tanner wrapped an arm around her shoulders. "It'll be all right."

"What will?" Keith piped up, his young eyes scanning the adults like they were a mystery he needed to figure out.

Forcing himself to wink, Tanner said, "Everything."

Meredith and Peggy started to sip their coffees, their gazes flicking out the window to watch Barlow tear out of his parking space.

Keith's smile dimmed. "What's wrong, Uncle Tanner?"

"I'm just glad you're here," He said, pulling the boy onto his lap.

"I don't want to go tomorrow," Keith whined, hugging him.

*It's for the best, kid*, he thought.

"It'll be okay," Peggy assured him.

God, he hoped so. He wouldn't sleep well until his sister and nephew had left town.

# Chapter 43

You sure you have everything?" Tanner asked as Peggy loaded the last action figure into the car.

She patted her chest, where she was hiding the two evidence bags. "I'm good." She turned to Keith, who was holding Tanner's leg with one hand and a dancing Hugo with the other. "Are you, young man?"

He lifted his shoulder in the perfect imitation of a sulk. "If not, we can always come back."

She stared him down. "No. Uncle Tanner will have to pay lots of money to the mailman to send anything you forgot. You don't want that, do you?"

"I don't wanna go!"

Tanner picked him up and hugged him tight. "I'll see you soon. Christmas is only a few weeks away."

He'd decided he liked this whole family holiday thing. He was already thinking about what he'd buy Meredith for Christmas—and how they would spend it together. Fucking scary thoughts for a man who'd never had roots.

This kid pulled back. The wet gleam of tears alarmed him. Oh, don't do it, he wanted to say, it rips my guts out. Instead, he gave him another bear hug. "I love you, Keith."

"I love you too."

"We'll call you when we get home," Peggy assured him.

He set Keith aside. When he turned to Peg, she wrapped her arms around his waist.

"This was nice. I'm glad we met Meredith. Good luck telling her."

He eased back. "What will she do?"

"She'll be hurt, and she'll worry about trusting you. But I think she'll forgive you. It may take time, though. We divorced ladies need a little extra patience."

"Got it. Be careful."

"Always. Keith, let's go."

After more hugs and tears, Keith settled into the backseat. As Peggy drove away, she rolled the window down and waved. He lifted his hand in the sudden silence. Even Hugo folded his paws on the cold ground. The wind rustled the trees, but the sound couldn't compete with Keith's laughter. His shoulders slumped.

Being overseas was almost easier. Since he rarely saw them, it was hard to miss them—at least like this. Was there a hole in his chest? He rubbed it and walked back to the house. Hugo barked.

At least he could see Meredith now. Tell her and stop worrying about it. He picked up his pace.

When he picked up his phone, he frowned. Sommerville had left him a voicemail. He listened to it while picking up the family room. Damn jerk was reminding him to send another picture. Well, screw him.

Time to man up. He'd show her the file on David. Explain the blackmail. It wouldn't be pretty, but it was the right thing to do.

Oh, and he would tell her he loved her.

He rubbed his throat. He'd never told a woman outside his family that. Had never allowed himself to feel that strongly for someone. He'd picked a career where objectivity reigned supreme—and he was damned good at it. Transplanting to different cities had suited his needs just fine for his entire life. Until now.

Until Meredith.

"I love you, Meredith," he practiced and cringed.

Hugo barked.

"I'm not talking to you."

People thought he had a way with words. If they could only see him now...He kicked the couch. He hated feeling this way. Like the floor could turn to quicksand. His feet weren't grounded. He took a breath, trying to be still, calm. It would all turn out okay.

"Right, boy?"

Hugo leapt at his leg.

"Thanks for the vote of confidence."

Meredith picked up on the second ring. "Hi, there. Company gone?"

"Yeah." He cleared his throat. "I was...hoping you could come over."

"I can be there in twenty. Start a fire. Oh, and open some wine. I feel like getting silly drunk."

His mouth dried up. Lust tangled with nerves. "Okay."

"See you soon," she sang.

He set the phone away. Tell her before or after they made love? Being a guy, he wanted the latter, but he knew it wasn't right. Best tell her straight out and let her decide if she wanted to stay. God, he hoped she'd want to stay.

His phone rang again almost instantly. When Peg's photo popped up on the display, he smiled. He looked around for something Keith had left. The little stinker.

"Forget something?"

"No. I need you to stay on the phone with me."

Her voice was off. He pushed Hugo from his lap and sat up straight. "What's the matter?"

"A sheriff's car is following me," she said in a hushed voice. "My gut tells me it's Barlow."

"Jesus, Peg." He shot off the couch. "Where are you? I'll come—"

"No. He's only trying to intimidate me."

"Oh, Christ." The thought of Barlow stalking his sister and nephew turned his guts to raw meat. His boots pounded on the hardwood floors as he strode back and forth.

"He turned his lights on, and he's speeding up."

His pumping heart reverberated in his ears.

"Mom, are you speeding?" he heard Keith ask.

"You can't stop, Peg. We don't know what he might do."

"Dammit, I know that. Gimme me a sec. Keith, I need you to be quiet for a minute. Okay?"

The piercing siren carved a ragged edge in his nerves. This helplessness was like watching families be gunned down in a village where he was reporting. Only worse. This was *his* family.

"How far is the next gas station? I'm about two miles out of town. Just passed the golf course."

Tanner pulled the map up in his head. "There's one about a mile ahead of you."

"Okay. Keith, honey. Mommy needs you to do something really important. I need you to tell the officer you have to go to the bathroom really bad when we get to the gas station."

"But I don't have to—"

"I know, honey, but I need you to hold the front of your pants and dance around. It's like you're in a school play."

Tanner put his finger in his other ear so he could hear their conversation over the sirens.

"But why?" Keith asked.

"Because Uncle Tanner thinks this police officer is a bad man. I don't want you to be scared. You know I'll protect you, right?"

"You have your gun?"

"That's right, and I'm really smart. I want you to stay close to me. If I tell you to do something, you do it, just like we talked about. Right?"

"Yes, Mommy," Keith cried, his voice unnaturally high. "He's coming closer, Mommy. I'm scared."

"I know. Tanner, he realizes I'm not going to stop. I want you to get the number for the state police ready, but we won't call them unless there's a need."

"Dammit, just head back to Dare. I'll meet you." He grabbed his keys.

"No! I've got this."

"Peg, let me—"

"No, it's safer this way. Keith and I can make him believe we didn't stop because he had to go potty. Otherwise, he'll know I'm involved in this mess. I'm putting you on speaker now in my pocket so you can hear everything. You'll know if you need to call the police. I love you."

"I love you too," he said hoarsely.

"Okay, Keith, when mommy stops the car, you and I are going to run inside. You remember what I said about pretending you need to go potty."

"Mommy, I'm scared," Keith cried.

"I know, but I won't let anything happen to you. See, lots of people are getting gas. It's going to be okay. I'm turning into the parking lot now, Tanner."

He heard the siren stop and a door slam.

"Come on, sweetheart."

"Hey! Wait."

"Sorry, Deputy. My son needs to use the bathroom real bad."

"Why didn't you stop?"

"Have you ever had a kid who needs to go potty?"

"Mommy, I need to go," Keith whined.

"He's going to have an accident if we don't hurry. Besides, I wasn't speeding. What were you pulling me over for?"

"You were speeding a little," Barlow announced.

"I don't speed. If you want to write me a ticket, fine, but I need to get my son to the bathroom right now."

Tanner heard a door chime and some overhead music.

"Almost there, honey," Peg encouraged. Another door creaked. "Tanner, we're in the bathroom. Come here for a sec, Keith, and let Mommy hold you."

Tanner rubbed the bridge of his nose when Keith started crying. So close. Oh, Christ.

"There's my brave little boy. We're safe now. It's all right."

"Mommy, I'm scared."

"I'm right here, and I would never let anything happen to you."

Tanner didn't say anything as she continued to comfort her son. He fell back on the sofa exhausted, his body made of lead. His mind played images of what could have happened in vivid Technicolor.

"Okay, now. We need to go back to the car."

"I don't want to! I want Uncle Tanner."

Tanner's heart tore.

"We can't do that," Peg answered. "We need to go home. Trust me, everything's going to be okay. You trust me, right?"

He heard Keith blow his nose.

"Now, am I the toughest cop in the world or what? Don't I make bad guys go to jail all the time?"

"Uh-huh." He sniffed.

"Then take my hand."

"I wet my pants, mommy," Keith cried.

"That's great acting! You're the best actor in the world."

He gave a sob. "I am?"

"Absolutely. Isn't he Tanner?"

He cleared his Sahara-desert-dry throat. "You're the best, buddy. I was so impressed."

And terrified. Bone-chillingly terrified. His scalp tingled like someone had held a gun to his head.

"Okay, we'll change your pants in the car. Don't worry. I'm here."

"You have your gun?"

"Right here."

"I love you, Mommy."

"Oh, I love you too. Big hug." She made a squeezing noise and gave him an audible smacker. "Let's go."

The door jingled.

"See, the bad man's gone now. Hear that, Tanner? Everything's fine."

Tanner fell back against the cushions. Right, fine.

"Who's the best cop in the world?"

"You are," Keith responded, but without his usual enthusiasm.

The car door slammed.

"Tanner? Are you still there?"

"Yes." He bounced to the couch's edge.

"I think everything's okay now. Barlow was trying to make a point. We'll leave here in a little while. I'll call with updates."

"Peggy—"

"Don't say it. It's not your fault. We're going to get these guys, Tanner. You have my word. No one messes with my family."

"You stole my line," he managed.

"Watch yourself. I'll be in touch. Tell Uncle Tanner goodbye, Keith."

"Bye, Uncle Tanner. I...I miss you."

His eyes burned. He rubbed them fiercely. "I miss you too. Take care of your mom," he said, realizing how often people had told him the same thing when he was growing up. "I love you guys."

"Love you too."

He set the phone aside, feeling beaten and bruised. How dare they go after a woman and child? Fuckers. Cowards. He kicked the couch and resumed his pacing. He wanted to tear the front door off with his bare hands.

They probably suspected Peggy was helping him since they knew she was a cop. Thank God, she'd put the samples in her bra, thinking it was a good hiding place. If Barlow had tried to search her car while she was in the gas station, he wouldn't have found them.

Hugo darted to the front door, barking. Meredith had arrived. He wished he could send her away, but he didn't have the strength.

He needed her. God, so much.

But Barlow's pursuit of Peg and Keith had changed everything. She wasn't safe. She'd been dead wrong about there being safety in numbers or about certain people being off limits. If a cop and kid weren't safe, a Hale wasn't either.

He'd have to make her see she couldn't keep helping him. He had to make it clear to Barlow she wasn't involved anymore.

But how? He'd told her a dozen times how worried he was about having her help. Each time, she'd informed him she'd pursue the story with or without him. Arthur wouldn't give an inch either. He'd have to think on that.

First, he was going to hold her tight. His plan to tell her about the blackmail would have to wait. He couldn't handle it now. He needed to calm the hell down. When he told her the truth, he needed his full faculties. Otherwise, he'd screw up the best thing that had ever happened to him.

# Chapter 44

Meredith checked her hair in the rear-view mirror before dashing for the house. Joy propelled her up the stairs. She was finally going to tell him she loved him and about the article. God, she was nervous, but she was giddy with relief too. He was her Nora man, and it was time for him to know it.

When he opened the door, she careened into his chest and wrapped her arms around him. "How's that for a welcome?"

His arms clamped around her, but he didn't respond. His silence and the tension in his muscles burst the happy bubble inside her. She tried to ease back, but he gripped her in place.

"What's the matter?"

"I'll tell you in a sec. Just let me hold you."

Alarm spiked as she stroked his back.

"Barlow followed Peg out of town. She called me. I had to stay on the line and do nothing while he threatened my family!"

He clutched her tighter and told her the whole story. By the end, her body was shaking. Going after a cop was one thing. But a little boy? She wondered what Barlow would have done if Peg hadn't eluded him the way she did. Would he have run them off the road like Kenny had done to Ray?

"Don't think about it," she whispered to him as much as herself.

He pushed back. "How can I not? My God, that's my sister and nephew. Those bastards went after them, and all I could do was stay on the phone."

His anger made her shake harder. "Peg handled it. She's smart and tough."

"She's still my sister!" he fired back. He held up a hand. "Sorry. I'm not mad at you. I'm angry that I put them in danger. I never should have let them come here. What was I thinking?"

She stepped closer until they were just inches apart. The tension in his body was contagious. Her muscles bunched when she met his fierce eyes. "You couldn't have known this would happen."

"They must have guessed she was helping when Keith told Barlow she was a cop. But dammit, I never saw this coming."

"So now he's threatened another police officer. It means they're scared. They're going to slip up. Peg will have the test results soon, and we'll know more."

He stalked away. "No, we won't. *I'll* keep looking into it, but I don't want you and your grandfather to be involved anymore."

Her stomach quivered. "I know you're upset, so I'll cut you a break, but there's no way I'm backing out now. This only firms my resolve. I know Gramps will agree."

Hugo started barking and whining.

"Listen to me! You're both out. I don't want them to come after you."

The thrust of his chin told her he was digging in his heels. Well, so could she.

"Come here." She extended her hand. This might not be the best time to declare her true feelings and tell him about the article, but she could still show him how strong their connection was.

Those gleaming dark chocolate eyes narrowed. "Why?"

"I want to kiss you."

His sigh was long suffering. "This conversation isn't over, Meredith."

"I know." She curled her hand around his neck, pulling him closer. "We'll talk later."

"I never took you for the type to solve an argument with sex."

Her ex had constantly. She bristled at the accusation. Took a minute to study him. He wanted her to be upset. Then, she'd walk away. She'd relent.

"I only want to be with you right now. I promise we'll discuss it later."

He didn't look away, searching her face for something.

"Be with me," she whispered, standing on her tiptoes. She brushed her lips against his.

He yanked her to him. When he ravaged her mouth, she opened to him. Anger and anxiety traveled across his lips. She gave back comfort and calm.

His mouth left hers and fitted against her neck. "Oh, God, Meredith."

She held him as the fight left him. "It's okay. I'm here."

Love overwhelmed her. Seeing him like this hurt her heart. She brought his face down to hers, their eyes locked together. She kissed him lightly on the corners of his mouth before tracing the seam of his lips with her tongue. His eyes didn't close. Neither did hers. He opened his mouth and tangled his tongue with hers. Long, slow strokes to match the rhythm of her hands running up and down his corded back.

When she broke the kiss, he cupped her face. "I need you," he said in a guttural voice.

She took his hand and led him upstairs, knowing what it cost him to say it. When she closed the door, she lifted his shirt and tossed it aside. Tracing his chest, she nudged him back to the bed.

"Let me take care of you."

She undressed while he watched, his chocolate eyes burning black now. Kneeling at his feet, she reached for his belt. Together they took off his pants and boxers. She ran her hands down his calves and pulled off his socks, the soles of his feet warm to her touch.

Tracing her way up his legs, she met his gaze and kissed his arousal. His body jerked in response. When she took him in her mouth, he groaned and threaded his hands in her hair, letting her pleasure him.

"Okay, that's enough," he growled finally and tugged her up. "I want to come inside you."

He pressed his open mouth to her neck and bit gently. She fell on top of him, and he pulled her up higher so that his lips caressed her breast. He sucked softly and then with increasing pressure. Her toes curled as he shifted to the other breast. She cried out with pleasure.

He adjusted her legs so that she was straddling him. His hand slid down and pressed against her core. Her spine arched when he slipped his finger inside her.

Her hands tangled with his. "Come into me," she whispered.

When he reached for the condom, she rolled it down his hard length. Pulling her hips forward, he let her take him into her slowly. He kept his gaze on her as he pressed into her core. His neck muscles clenched with control as she moved, her hands on his chest. He held her at the waist, his fingers digging in as she increased her speed, her hips rising and falling.

She drew out their passion. His hips lurched, communicating his need. When he pressed his thumb where their bodies joined and rubbed, she threw her head back and cried out. The climax washed over her like a thundering waterfall, taking her down into new depths. He froze underneath her, enhancing her pleasure.

When she curled forward, he flipped her onto her back. "My turn."

His thrusts drove her back to the headboard, making her hold on. His hands gripped hers on the frame as he surged into her hard. Her body revved up again, every tissue sensitized. As he plunged deeper, she locked her legs around him. When she exploded again, he thrust madly and came with a shout.

She surfaced, realizing they were still holding hands on the headboard. The sight made her heart shimmer like sunlight on a river. Love shot through her, and she turned and kissed his head.

"Sorry," he muttered. "I'm squishing you."

"No, it's fine." She unlocked her shaking legs from his waist.

He kissed her cheek and then pulled back to stare into her eyes, looking at her with emotion so raw it closed her throat. When he settled his mouth to hers in a light brush, she smoothed back a lock of hair from his sweaty forehead.

"Be right back." He eased off her and walked to the bathroom.

She heard his phone vibrate while he was gone. Worried it might be Peggy, she dashed over to his pants and pulled it from the pocket. When she read the display, everything went dark for a moment. She saw stars. Shook her head. Blinked. Narrowed her eyes.

It couldn't be.

Why was Richard's number on Tanner's display? Why was he texting him?

She heard a flush from the bathroom. Her heart pounded hard against her tight ribs. She hit the display and gasped.

*How was Thanksgiving at the Hale homestead? I want an update.*

Her brain turned into scrambled eggs. She fell to her knees, naked, gripping her thighs.

Tanner walked back in and froze. "Did Peg call?" He darted across the room and grabbed the phone clutched in her hand.

"Did she?"

She couldn't answer.

He stilled when he looked at the display.

She uncurled from the floor like she had arthritis. She staggered once before straightening.

"Meredith," Tanner said urgently.

The newfound Meredith found the courage to stand before him. "Why is my ex texting you?"

But she knew. Fear and hurt descended like fog, crippling her sight. Oh, God.

"I can explain," he said in a tight voice.

"You're working for him, aren't you?" She shivered. How had it gotten so cold in here? She reached for her clothes and began pulling them on, suddenly excruciatingly aware of her nakedness.

"Yes. I was going to tell you, but then the thing happened with Peg."

She stared at him, her heart thundering, waiting for an explanation.

"The thing with Peg," he repeated. His face flinched.

He turned away, clutching the phone. The silence was deafening. He finally spun around. Planted his feet. His throat rippled like a snake, and his breath shuddered out.

"Richard found out what you were doing. He sent me here to stop you from doing the article about Nora what's her name. He wasn't sure what else you were going to write about him, but he wasn't about to let you ruin his political chances."

She gasped. "It's not true." The crown of her head tightened like an approaching migraine.

"It is." The scar around his mouth twisted. "My job was to make you fall for me and then dump you so you'd have nothing to write."

His words beat into her like a hammer striking bone. Questions pinged around in her splitting head. How could Richard have found out? And how could Tanner be working for him?

"This doesn't make any sense." Her voice broke. She gripped her hands, willing herself not to cry. She was sick to death of crying in front of the men she loved.

He turned away, looking across the room. "Richard wanted to make you stop, suffer. I was the tool."

Her heart bled, fresh and hot, from this new wound. She believed that. Easily. No amount of suffering would please Richard, especially since she had the means to destroy him. He was a predator. He always struck last, and he always killed his prey. How had she forgotten that?

But Tanner wasn't Richard. He was a good man. She'd seen it.

But you thought that about Richard too, a dark voice inside her said.

She grabbed a sheet to cover herself. "But why you? I believe what you've said about Richard, but how could you do this? To me."

His face contorted. He walked stiffly to the closet and pulled out a robe. "It was the condition for my dream job. After being overseas in stinking villages for the past few years, I was willing to do anything."

Hope retreated. Her guts burned with pain like someone had driven a stake into them. That sounded like Richard. Staring at his clenched back, she shook her head.

"I don't believe it!"

He cinched the robe like a garrote and stalked over to her, punching his phone with hard taps. "I've sent updates." Pushing the phone into her face, she saw the photo of them by the fire.

The yawning pain grew inside her. The picture filled her vision like her tears. They looked so happy. She clenched her eyes shut and pressed her hands to her chest, searching for confidence.

It wasn't there.

"It's not possible."

"It is." He grabbed her arms with enough force to make her eyes pop and jerked her to her feet. "I told you. You don't know me! You made me into something I wasn't."

"No!"

"You were attracted to me. I used that and played on your vulnerabilities."

"Bullshit," she said, to him as much as to herself.

He punched his chest. "This is what I am! A cold-blooded journalist who'll do whatever it takes to snag a fabulous job." He stalked over to the window.

His thundering voice raised the hairs on her arms. She crossed them to keep from falling apart. "I know you care about me," she cried, rising and walking over to him.

His mouth curled when he looked back. "Why do you think I kept pursuing you? No guy would put up with the kind of rejection you dished out."

Her earlier doubts about why he hadn't given up rose like rotted wood. She curled over in pain. He made a move toward her but stopped himself. The ticking in his jaw gave her the courage for one last try. She straightened and cupped his face with shaking hands, his stubble making her skin feel raw.

"This isn't you, Tanner. I know it isn't."

He shoved her hands away. "Yes, it is." He stalked over to the door. Threw it open. It vibrated on its hinges. "Since I've done my job and killed your story, there's no reason for you to get in my way about this Ray thing. I'm out of here after I nail the bad guys, write up the story, and finish classes. Our paths don't have to cross again."

Tears slipped down her cheeks.

"It wasn't personal."

The echoes of past pain awoke in her body like ghosts. She couldn't have been deceived like this again. She was stronger now. She was Divorcée Woman. "Why are you saying this?"

"Why won't you believe me? Listen! I don't know what you have on your ex, but you had to be stopped. I was the perfect man to do it. I was new to his paper, you and I had things like Columbia and swimming in common, and you didn't know me. Do you want me to get my file on you? You love dark chocolate."

"Stop it." She made a fist, wanting to slug him.

"Your favorite color is—"

"Shut up!" She put her hands over her ears.

"Do you need more proof?" He flicked his hand to the door. "You should get out. We're done here."

The slap of his voice made her put one foot in front of the other. At the doorway, she turned to him one last time. His eyes looked like obsidian. How had she ever compared them to melted chocolate? His sneer snapped her control.

"You son of a bitch!" His chest was as solid as concrete when she shoved her hands against it. "I fell in love with you."

She charged out of the bedroom and ran down the stairs to the front door. After fumbling to start her car, she started crying as Hugo raced after her, his barks punctuating the silence of the driveway. The left section of her chest felt like someone had cut her open and drew out her insides.

Coming back here had changed nothing. All it had done was give her another broken heart.

*But the old Meredith couldn't have faced him down and asked him why*, Divorcée Woman finally said.

Meredith pressed her lips together to keep herself from screaming at her alter ego like some crazy person. Divorcée Woman had let her down.

Worse, she'd let herself down—again.

She yanked up her red shirt to tear off her bustier, only to realize she'd forgotten to put it back on. Tanner could take that memento and shove it up his lying ass.

Wearing La Perla hadn't changed anything either. The whole idea of Divorcée Woman seemed so stupid now. She'd been crazy to have conversations with her alter ego.

Had she been so desperate for confidence after the divorce that she'd lost her mind?

With that thought came a more menacing realization, one she knew would keep her awake at night.

How could she have thought he was different?

\*\*\*

Tanner gripped the door to keep from following Meredith. His stomach seized. He ran to the bathroom and vomited. Spent, he laid his head on the floor. He hadn't gotten sick for a while. Not since the massacre in that village in Swat Valley.

Oh, God, what had he done?

He pushed himself upright and wiped his face with a towel. Studied himself in the mirror. He threw the cloth at his reflection and stalked out.

He had done what he needed to do. If this horrible scene had saved her life, it was worth it.

When she'd asked him about Sommerville's text, he'd braced himself to tell her the truth, ready to make things right. But then he'd thought about Peg, and something inside of him had clicked. He'd realized how easy it would be to use the story of his association with Sommerville to make her walk away.

Meredith wasn't the type to give up without thinking that all was lost.

He wouldn't risk her life. He'd protect her at all costs.

The sacrifice burned his skin like a funeral pyre. He'd done difficult things before, but right now, reporting on Bosnian war crimes seemed like a piece of cake compared to lying to the woman he loved. Nobility was overrated, and it hurt like hell.

He could explain his real motivations to her later. He wasn't sure she'd forgive him for the things he'd said, but when this was safely behind them, he'd ask her to just the same. Have Peg talk to her if need be. The faster he pulled the evidence together and got Kenny and Barlow in jail, the faster he could resolve things with Meredith.

He wove in place, his throat burning with bile.

When he walked out of the bathroom, he saw her black bustier lying on the floor. The symbol of her newfound confidence seemed flimsy now. He traced the initials DW. Christ, he'd needed to hit her with words like a sledge hammer to make her walk away.

He prayed it would be enough.

His gamble to keep her safe needed to pay off.

Then he was going to find a way to undo what he'd done.

Convincing her he really loved her might be the toughest assignment he'd ever had.

# Chapter 45

Abba's seductive melody had never sounded more welcoming to Meredith as she opened the door to Jill's house. Her tears picked up, and her numb fingers dropped her purse.

"Mere? Is that you?" Jill called. "I wasn't expecting you back until morning."

She traced the wall to stay upright as she staggered into the family room. Sandalwood incense trailed toward the ceiling like a slithering coil. Jill snapped her book shut and jumped up.

"Why do you still have your coat on? What happened? Tanner?"

Meredith nodded, sobs pushing up her throat. Jill's bear hug gave her permission to let go. Her body shook, her face hot and wet with tears. When she couldn't breathe, she angled back and wiped away the wetness on Jill's shoulder.

"I'm sorry. I'm soaking you."

"It's okay. Just cry it out."

She did. A long time later, when she finally felt emptied and hollowed out, she pulled away from Jill and fumbled over to the coffee table for a Kleenex. Her head buzzed. She fell back against the couch, feeling completely spent.

Jill curled up next to her and grabbed her hand. "What happened?"

Meredith rested her head against her sister's shoulder, sniffing and dabbing her running nose with a tissue. "Oh, God, Jillie."

Jill caressed her hair. Her eyes burned. She swiped at them, coming away with mascara.

"I don't know...how it happened. Tanner's...working for Richard...and he was supposed to make me fall in love with him so I couldn't write the article about Nora Roberts Land."

Jill took her by the shoulders. "*What?*"

"Someone told Richard about the article. Probably an inside source. That's how he knew to deliver the flowers here. And Tanner wanted to get a job with him...so he agreed to sabotage me by making me fall in love with him." She started crying again. "Oh, God, why am I so stupid?"

"Wait, I'm not following. Why would Richard want Tanner to make you fall in love with him?"

The weight in her chest could have crushed stone. "Richard doesn't want me to write the article. He's afraid I'll use what I have on him to ruin his political chances."

"You have something juicy? Why didn't you tell me?"

"I was embarrassed. Plus, it's my only leverage." She sniffed. "I told him I'd use it if he didn't leave me alone."

"Shit, like he'd be good with that. I'm surprised he didn't break into your apartment all Trickie-Dickie style."

She let out a shaky laugh. "He knows I'm not that stupid. But I am. I'm the stupidest girl in the world."

"That's enough. What do you have?"

"Photos of him with a high-priced call girl when he went to a journalism convention in Vegas. I had him followed. They're... grisly. He was careful, but—"

"You're a journalist."

She slapped her forehead. "Still stupid though."

"Stop talking like that."

"No, you should have seen Tanner. I even told him I loved him. He told me to get out. Oh, Jillie, he said horrible things. I...can't breathe."

Jill pushed her back into the couch and raised her arms above her head. "Meredith, you are not having a panic attack. People who are sobbing can't breathe." She said it so matter-of-factly Meredith nodded.

She concentrated on the rise and fall of her chest. Soon, she lowered her tingling arms, the needle-like sensation pricking her skin. "Better."

Jill's eyes gleamed with unshed tears as she reached for Meredith's hand. "Okay, so keep talking. Tanner is working for Richard."

"I still can't believe he did this."

Her sister's hand tightened around hers. "It might have started out that way, but he loves you, Meredith. I know he does."

"He said he talked women onto their backs all the time. I don't know who he is."

Her mouth dropped open. "I don't believe it, Mere. Tanner wouldn't have brought his sister and nephew here to spend Thanksgiving with us unless he loved you."

She sank back into the couch, remembering their snowball fight and how happy they'd looked in the picture at the table. Could Jill be right?

"No." A fresh batch of tears washed down her face. "Peggy was only here to get the drugs and the paint sample." She started crying again, sinking forward.

"What are you talking about? What drugs?" Jill asked, nudging her shoulder so she'd meet her eyes.

"For the case." Her stomach hurt so bad. "Oh, God, it's true. He didn't love me. He wanted the job with Richard. He only used the case as an excuse to bring me closer, to make me fall for him."

Jill grabbed her shoulders. "What in the world are you talking about?"

"I can't think straight!" Meredith sobbed out, rubbing her throbbing temples.

"What's this about drugs and paint samples?"

The pounding in her head increased. "It's...an article we're working on. That's it." Please, Jill, leave this alone, she almost begged.

Jill put her hands on her hips. "No, it's not."

She rubbed the back of her neck. Abba drilled into her skull, which felt like it was on the verge of exploding.

"Why would Tanner have his cop sister take drugs..." Her whole face crumbled. "This is about Jemma, isn't it? At first I thought about Grandpa asking me about drugs and parties, but when they said she had a heart murmur..." Tears filled her eyes.

"Jill."

"Oh, God!" she said, pressing her hands to her cheeks. "Grandpa was right all along. Something was wrong with the drugs."

"Jill, let me—"

"And Ray was the dealer. He didn't have a car accident, did he?"

Meredith's throat squeezed to a centimeter at the pain in Jill's voice.

"Dammit, don't keep this from me! Jemma was my best friend! Losing her cut a hole in me." She put her hand to her heart. "You have to tell me. Please!"

"Jill, I can't."

"How *dare* you keep this from me?" She grabbed her stomach.

"Jill, it's not—"

"Don't lie to me!"

"It's not safe to tell you any of this." Meredith thought of what had happened with Peggy and Keith. "I promise I'll tell you everything once this is over."

"No, you'll fucking tell me now."

Her sister rarely used the f-bomb. "I have to talk to Grandpa."

"Oh, God, he kept this from me too?"

"Jill, he didn't mean—"

"If you don't tell me, you're not my sister anymore."

Meredith sucked in a breath. "You don't mean that."

Lifting her chin, eyes gleaming from tears, Jill said, "I do."

The utter flatness in her voice made Meredith clench her arms protectively around herself. To lose Tanner had been horrible enough, but Jill? She couldn't lose her sister.

"Okay, but you have to keep this quiet."

She proceeded to tell her everything they knew. Jill curled forward like a roly poly bug as she spoke.

"We're going to get them," Meredith said, trying to offer her sister some comfort. "I promise."

Silence yawned between them. Jill finally sat up and wiped her nose with her sleeve. Her shaking hand grasped a photo—in it, she and Jemma were wrapped around each other at high school graduation, huge smiles on their faces. "How could you have kept this from me? You know what she meant to me!"

"I'm sorry."

Jill stood up and walked into the kitchen without a backwards glance.

Meredith followed, the distance between them growing.

"I want you to stay at Mom and Dad's or Grandpa's place for a while," she uttered in a stranger's voice.

"Jill!"

"I need some time." She swiped a hand under her nose. "You lied about my best friend's death. I can forgive a lot of things, but that..."

Meredith took a step forward. The floor squeaked beneath her feet. "Jill, please."

Her sister turned her back to her, reaching for a glass of water. "I mean it, Meredith. Please. I'm going to bawl my eyes out in a minute. I want to be alone."

She wasn't the only one. Sobs clawed at Meredith's throat, but she forced herself to spin around and walk out of the kitchen. She packed quickly, listening for Jill's footsteps. Surely she'd change her mind.

She didn't.

Jill was still in the kitchen when she returned. "I'm so sorry, Jillie." Had she completely destroyed their relationship? "I love you," she whispered.

Jill's back muscles clenched, but she didn't turn around.

Meredith cried softly and left. The bitter wind touched her face as her feet moved like leaden pegs, one in front of the other.

She was alone again.

She had been betrayed by Tanner, and now she was her sister's betrayer.

How could she ever recover?

She walked to her car with no answers, and broke a nail while trying to open the door. When she collapsed into the driver's seat, the sobs started.

*You're stronger than this,* Divorcée Woman said sternly.

Meredith pulled on her hair. Great, she was still hearing voices. Perhaps she should simply check herself into a mental institution. At least they'd keep her medicated.

God, what was she going to do?

She put the car in gear and headed to her parent's house. She needed some time alone, a place to hide where she could cry as loud as she had to. She'd call her grandpa in the morning. He'd be able to think about all of this more clearly. Hell, he could deal with Asshole Tanner.

She wanted to be angry, but she couldn't muster the energy. Her tears had smothered the flames.

Perhaps there was something wrong with her. How else could she explain why the men she loved didn't love her back?

As she drove across town, she asked the darkest question of all.

Was Meredith Hale simply unlovable?

# Chapter 46

His mind racing too much for sleep, Tanner opened his eyes and stared at the dying fire. Peggy and Keith had made it safely home, thank God.

He tried to focus on the one thing that had gone right tonight.

Hugo stirred on the floor beside him, his ears twitching.

After stripping the bed upstairs, he'd cocooned himself in the den. Her scent—their scent—permeated his bedroom. Even down here, he caught a whiff of her, something floral and fresh and all Meredith. He rubbed his chest. Guilt, fear, and hurt clamped down on his heart like forceps.

Hugo jerked up and looked at him, his ears alert.

"What's the matter, boy? You missing her too?"

He raced off. Tanner had no idea what Hugo's bathroom schedule was like at this time of night. Thank God for the doggie door.

Hugo suddenly started barking in loud, nonstop bursts. Tanner leaned up on the couch. Was it an animal? When the barking turned staccato, he tugged on his slippers and walked to the door.

When he opened it, he saw a dark shape running across the yard, Hugo racing behind it.

"Hey!" He sprinted after them, ice and gravel crunching beneath his feet. Smart, McBride. Chasing some guy in the dark. Still, he was too amped up to stop.

He raced down the drive but quickly realized the intruder had too much of a head start. Tanner would be lucky to catch him.

Who was it? Kenny or Barlow?

He pumped his arms as he raced through the blackness. The guy must have driven here and parked at the end of the driveway.

As he neared the sound of Hugo's barking, he made out a car in the distance. And a male body sliding across the hood.

"Stop!"

Hugo uttered a bone-chilling whine, and then his barking ceased. Tanner's heart squeezed over the pounding.

"Hugo!"

He could make out the intruder's black clothes and stocking cap as the guy jumped into the driver's side of the car, the overhead light popping on. Tanner couldn't see his face, but he could see Hugo's body on the ground, unmoving.

The door slammed, plunging the man back into darkness, and the car shot off, spewing gravel. He squinted, but couldn't make out the plates. The intruder hadn't turned on his lights. Tanner picked up his pace, his lungs burning from the below-zero air.

"Hugo!"

The whine assured him Hugo was alive. He skidded to a halt beside the dog and gathered him up in his arms.

"There's a good boy," he crooned between choppy breaths, encouraged when Hugo licked him under the chin. "You'd better not be hurt."

Running to the house, he kicked the door closed, flicked the overhead light on, and laid Hugo on the dining room table. Tanner ran his hands along his soft fur. The swelling in his ribs confirmed the bastard had kicked him. Hugo struggled in his hold and tried to stand, woofing three times.

"Yeah, yeah, yeah. You're trying to convince me you're okay." He slid into a chair, his legs giving out, and rubbed Hugo under the ears. "Well, I'm not. They can come after me, but not my dog. You're a brave boy, aren't you?"

When he tried to stand again, Tanner let him down. "Okay, you win, but you're getting a treat."

He started toward the kitchen and stopped, realizing his dog hadn't followed. Hugo barked and nudged at the front door.

"You want to go out?"

The second he opened it, the dog trotted outside. Tanner went back to the kitchen for a flashlight, and then followed him. The dog's gait was slow and stiff as Tanner watched him walk over to his car. Hugo limped around to the driver's side and barked once. Shining the flashlight in that direction, Tanner caught sight of a red Swiss army knife lying a few inches under the car's body.

"Fuckers were trying to cut my brake line," he whispered, sitting back on his heels. He'd bet money on it.

He headed back inside for a Ziploc bag to pocket the evidence. Maybe they'd catch a break with a fingerprint.

Finding out that his sister was a cop must have made them more reckless and desperate. Hell, they must have cased the house enough to know he had a dog, and they'd decided to pull this stunt anyway.

He'd send the knife to Peg in the morning. Both of the men had prints on file—Barlow because he was a cop, and Kenny because he was former military. Now they just had to sit tight and hope for a match.

After nudging Hugo back, he deftly drew the knife into the bag. The cold, hard ground dug into his vertebrae when he slid under the car. The flashlight showed that his brake line hadn't been cut.

Hugo had stopped it from happening.

He slid out and hugged Hugo to his chest. "You're a good dog."

He'd been targeted before, but never in the good old U. S. of A. He wanted peace. He wanted to believe in happily ever after—just like

Meredith, he realized.

But instead of backing down, the criminals just kept raising the stakes. First his sister and then him.

Who was next?

"Meredith," he breathed out.

Shit, they could be going for her car too. He had to check. He'd done his best to make sure she was out of this whole mess, but that didn't mean the bad guys knew that. He'd planned to spread the news of their breakup far and wide the next morning.

Fuck.

Running inside to get dressed, he then grabbed his phone and bundled Hugo into the car.

He wasn't letting anyone harm Meredith.

# Chapter 47

Jill curled up on the couch and watched *Clueless*, a box of tissues her only companion. The comfort movie wasn't doing much to remove the horrible pain in her chest, but it had erased the intolerable quiet in the house after Meredith's departure.

God, how could her sister have kept something like this from her? Didn't Meredith know how hard she was taking Jemma's death? Now she wasn't sure she could live with herself. She could have stopped it. She should have listened to her grandpa. She shoulda...

She didn't know. More tears welled. She brushed them aside.

When a pounding sounded on the door, she dashed off the couch. Part of her hoped it was Meredith—or Grandpa.

Checking the peephole, she saw neither. It was only Asshole Tanner.

She flung open the door. "What do *you* want?"

"Where's Meredith?"

His commanding voice raised her hackles. "What the hell do you care? You broke her heart."

He placed his hands on his hips and stepped closer, menacing in the outdoor light. "This is serious, Jill. Where's her car?"

"What do you care?" Tired of asshole men in general, she grabbed the door's edge. "Get out of here." She let the door fly.

He caught it. "Dammit, Jill. Where the fuck is Meredith?"

His tone froze her insides, just like when she'd learned that her dad had been rushed to the hospital after a heart attack.

"We, ah,...had a fight. I told her to stay at Mom and Dad's or Grandpa's." The cold turned her bare feet to ice. "Barlow and Kenny don't have her, do they?" She gripped his fleece.

"What did she tell you, dammit?"

Her lip curled. "Everything."

"Christ! Call her. Put her on speaker." He stepped inside and slammed the door behind him.

Running into the den, she found her phone, and hit Mere's number. When it went to voicemail, a blanket of worry rolled over Jill like a hurricane cloud.

Tanner's body seemed poised to leap or hurl something.

"When she's upset, she doesn't answer. Had it off for five days after the divorce," she blabbed. "Scared us to death."

"Call your grandfather's landline." Tanner paced like a caged panther in the Denver Zoo.

Grandpa Hale picked up on the second ring. "Jillie? Why are you calling so late? What's wrong?"

"Grandpa," she said, the mere sound of his voice reassuring.

"Arthur, it's Tanner. Is Meredith with you?"

"No. Heavens, what's going on?"

"Long story. I'll let Jill explain. Is your car in the garage?"

"Yes. Tanner, what's going on?"

"Is it locked?"

"No, Dare's a safe town. Now, tell me what's going on."

"All right, keep watch on it until I get there. Either Barlow or Kenny visited my house and tried to cut my brake line."

His story made Jill tremble. My God, how could this be happening?

"I'm going to your son's place and see if Meredith's there. Check her car. Then, I'll come check yours."

"I can take care of myself," he growled. "Jillie, why isn't she with you?"

She swiped her runny nose with her sleeve. "Gramps, we had a big fight. I know about Jemma and Ray, and I'm so scared."

Tanner put a calming hand on her arm. "Nothing's going to happen, Jill."

"Absolutely right," Arthur muttered and clicked off.

Jill dialed her parent's landline, each ring of the phone drilling into her skull.

"What?" Meredith answered finally, her tone hostile. "You throw me out and then call me?"

"Meredith," Tanner immediately said. "Where's your car?"

"Tanner?" Her voice cracked.

"Your car? Is it in the garage?"

"Yes. Why? What's happened?"

"Someone tried to cut my brake line. I'm coming over."

There was a long moment of silence. "They wouldn't know I'm here." Her voice couldn't be chillier.

"I don't care. You don't have to see me. I'm not taking any chances."

"I don't think—"

"Too bad." He snapped the phone shut. His eyes closed for a moment.

Jill rubbed her arms, her mind spinning. "Can you tell me how you're this upset after crushing her to pieces?"

He pinned her with a stare that could have wilted flowers and stalked over to the door. His cold-reddened hand yanked it open. When he stepped into the harsh porch light, his face turned menacing again. "Just because I broke her heart doesn't mean I want her dead."

Jill followed, cocking a hip. Unbelievable. "Just because you don't want her dead doesn't mean you're not a dick."

She slammed the door in his face.

"Lock the door, Jill."

She snapped the deadbolt in place and listened as the sound of his quick steps faded. A dog barked. His car door slammed. She leaned her head against the frame, her imagination running rampant with images of her sister and grandpa ending up like Jemma and Ray.

Dead.

# Chapter 48

There were no other cars on her parents' street since everyone had two-door garages and hated scraping snow off in the morning. Tanner's gaze flicked to his rear view mirror, checking for a tail, but there wasn't one. He let out a deep breath he hadn't been aware he was holding. Meredith's dark shape moved away from the lamp-lit window as he turned into the driveway. Thank God, she'd parked inside. The garage door puttered up slowly.

"Hugo. Be good."

He ducked under the slowly moving door. His nose twitched at the lingering smell of turpentine.

Meredith's head popped out as she cracked open the door to the house. "I told you—"

The sight of her pale, tear-ravaged face twisted him up like junkyard iron works. "Get inside," he ordered, hitting the garage door button to close it behind him.

She slammed the door hard enough to knock the yellow level off the garage wall.

All for the best, he told himself. If she talked to him, she might see what a raging lunatic he was about her, just like Jill had. It seemed more important than ever to keep her safe now that Barlow and Kenny had upped the stakes. If they went after him, would they go after her?

Jesus, he hoped not. Men usually had a harder time killing women. He realized how sick it was that he knew something like that.

He took some deep breaths, and returned his focus to the task at hand. He slid under her car, his back against the concrete floor that could have frozen meat. Pulling out his flashlight, he checked the body. Nothing. He closed his eyes under the tight, dark space.

"Thank you," he whispered.

He rolled out, thinking through the cluster fuck he had on his hands. Meredith had told Jill for some reason, widening the circle of people in the know. He shoved off the floor and stalked over to the door leading into the house. Rapping on it cracked more skin. His knuckles were bleeding.

Meredith popped her head out again. "What? Now you want to talk?"

His jaw ticked. "Tell Jill not to tell anyone."

"I already did, you son of a bitch!" She slammed the door in his face.

He stared at the white frame, counting to ten. Jesus, he wanted to rip it open, shake her, and then ravish her on the floor until the images of her car going over a cliff were erased.

When the garage door clicked open, he spun around and grabbed the closest weapon. A hammer. The door cruised up, revealing Arthur Hale's clenched face.

"You planning on beaning me, son? Didn't know I'd pissed you off, too." After stepping inside, he pressed the button on the garage door opener he had in his hand.

The door sputtered down again.

Tanner put his hands on his hips. Arthur walked toward him, his hair in swirls on his head, his cardigan sweater buttoned up wrong.

"Did you find anything wrong with Meredith's car?"

Setting aside the hammer, Tanner rubbed his neck. "No. Jesus, Arthur. You shouldn't have come. I was planning on checking your car next."

"You think you're the only one who can see a cut brake line? Hell, the hardest part was getting back up again. Damn old body."

Tanner rolled his tongue around his teeth, seething at the chance the older man had taken.

"Jill told me what happened between you and Meredith," Arthur informed him in his take-no-prisoner's voice.

"You would be better off chastising Meredith for telling Jill about this whole clusterfuck."

"Don't growl at me, boy. Not when you've messed things up so dandily."

The door cracked open. "Grandpa?"

"Get your stuff, Meredith. You're coming to my house."

"I don't—"

"You are *not* staying alone, and this old body would rather sleep in its own bed."

"What about Jill?"

The tears shining in her eyes made his knees lock in place. She was completely ignoring him. Would she ever look at him again? The slice was direct. He could feel himself bleeding out.

"Jill is going to spend the night with a friend until we figure this out."

"Peggy should have the lab results back tomorrow," Tanner said. "She's putting a rush on them."

Arthur smacked his cane on the concrete. "Well, I'm calling the Attorney General tomorrow! This has gone on for long enough. We need to bring in the law before anyone else gets hurt."

Tanner shifted on his feet. "We won't have much to give them until Peg gets the results."

Arthur glared at him. "I don't care. I'm not endangering my granddaughters. We need to trust the law to do their job now. We have enough threads. Let them pull them. This is beyond a reporter's purview, even for a hot-shot like you."

The menace in Arthur's voice made Tanner look away.

"Grandpa's right," Meredith finally said, her voice hoarse. "This just isn't worth it anymore."

When she closed the door, Tanner rolled his shoulders, wanting to follow her inside. Hold her. Touch her. Comfort her.

He should tell her everything right now. He couldn't bear to see her this way, knowing that he was the cause for her pain. He stepped toward the door. Arthur thrust out his cane like a bar on a train track.

"You leave her alone!" he ground out.

He came to his senses. "I will for now." He hit the garage door button, the cracking and rolling sound pounding in time with his tension headache. "But ask yourself this, Arthur. Why would Richard Sommerville print a nasty article about my brother if I was willingly working for him?"

As he strode off, he waited for Arthur to stop him, but he didn't.

Let the law come. Then he'd tell Meredith the truth.

And pray it was enough to get her back.

\*\*\*

Meredith watched Tanner's car careen out of the driveway. The cold windowpane cooled her flushed face. She'd gone from pale to heated when she'd seen him in the garage. Her heart had burned in her chest with the added accelerant of his presence.

"Meredith?" her grandpa called.

She walked into his open arms. They closed around her with a familiarity and gentleness she could always count on.

"Oh, Grandpa," she cried, feeling the tears start again.

"You go ahead and cry, my little mermaid. You deserve it. Then we'll go home."

Where was her home exactly? She didn't know anymore.

"I'm sorry, Grandpa."

"There's nothing to be sorry about. We can talk about everything later. All's not lost."

She hoped he was right, but he was likely an old man giving his granddaughter false hope.

From her point of view, she'd lost everything.

# Chapter 49

I notified the Attorney General," her grandpa announced from the doorway of her office. "Anderson doesn't think we have much evidence without the results from Peggy's lab, but he agrees that it's unusual for two young people to die suddenly in such a short timeframe. He wasn't happy we were using Tanner's sister to run the tests, but he understood. And he also appreciates why we're turning this over to the state now."

She dropped her pen. So the law would come in and, she hoped, tie up all the loose ends. She would leave. Tanner would too. And she'd try to put her life back together...again.

"It's for the best."

"Yes." He set down the file he was carrying and popped in a red hot. "You beat me out the door this morning. I thought we were going to stick together."

"I had to get to work. Besides, I can take care of myself."

"I'm not disputing that, but it makes an old man worry less. My blood pressure." He patted his heart.

"You're healthy as a horse." Still, the guilt added another layer to the bedrock of her emotions, and it didn't sit comfortably.

"Fine," he said, "but don't go anywhere unless it's with close family and friends. Anderson said he'd send someone tomorrow from Denver. He couldn't pull anyone today. I told him that was fine since Peggy should be getting the results to us shortly. Maybe we'll have more to give him by the time he gets here. I want these bastards in a cage."

"God, I do too." Of course, she wanted Tanner to have a cell next to them—with her ex as his roommate.

"Do you want to update Tanner or should I?"

She pressed her fingers to her left temple where a headache throbbed. "You call him."

"That's not my Mermaid talking." He made a basket with his candy wrapper.

"I don't want to talk about it, gramps. Please."

She pressed her hand to her chest out of reflex and winced. She'd intentionally chosen not to wear La Perla or anything else today. Her gray bulky sweater was sufficient camouflage. It was her protest against her alter ego's impotence.

She jumped when her grandpa patted her head like he'd always done when she was a kid.

"Didn't mean to startle you. I have something you might want to look at." He pressed a file into her hand and shuffled to the door.

When she opened it, her brow furrowed, worsening her headache. "An article from Richard's paper?" She checked the date. It wasn't today's edition.

"Check out the focus of the article."

She read the introduction and immediately found flaws with its lead. Talk about slanted. "David McBride?" Her stomach did a flip-flop.

"Tanner's brother." He let his bombshell hover in the air.

Her palms grew damp. "What? Why?"

"Exactly." He popped another candy in his mouth. "Reporter's questions. Why would Rick-the-Dick print a nasty article about Tanner's brother when Tanner was working for him?"

She pressed her palms to her head. "I don't understand."

"Find out," he said and left.

After she read the article three times, she lowered her aching head, more confused than she'd been last night. Why would Rick-the-Dick write this about Tanner's brother? Moreover, why would Tanner keep working for him?

Who the hell was Tanner McBride?

She had a sinking feeling he was hiding something else.

# Chapter 50

Clicking through her emails a few hours later, Meredith paused when she saw one from Gene. She hit the link.

*Meredith, I ran another drug test on Jemma's blood after we talked and found something. Can you come by the lab today?*

Meredith sat up in her chair. Talk about great news! They could hand the Attorney General's people more evidence. Leave it to Gene to follow through.

She grabbed her coat and went to find her grandpa. She sure as hell wasn't contacting Tanner. Her grandpa wasn't in his office, and after asking around, she discovered he was interviewing a city council member until noon. She wrote a note and put it on his desk in case he finished early. She didn't want to worry him.

Since it was only a few blocks away, she settled for a New York power walk down Main Street to the Justice Center, which housed the police department, the sheriff's office, the coroner's office, and the local courts. She had new evidence to collect.

They were going to take these bastards down.

***

Gene's lab had a sterile antiseptic smell that tickled her nose. The stainless steel counters gleamed. Her gaze tracked to the small doors in the far wall, and she shuddered. No need to think about the bodies inside.

"Gene?" She pocketed her gloves in her purse.

Goosebumps broke out across her arms as she surveyed his tools. Scalpel. Saw. Oh, no need to look anymore. She struggled to find something else to focus on. His Halloween cardboard cutout skeleton in the corner didn't help. If Jill had been there, she'd have found something to joke about.

The thought of Jill only made her want to cry. She missed her sister and didn't know how to make things right between them.

When the back door opened, she turned with a smile. "Hey, Gene."

The man was wearing a sheriff's uniform. Her lungs seized. Her body locked.

"Barlow," she breathed out.

Her mind screamed, *Run*. She spun around.

Knocked into a table. Charged around it.

She reached for the door, ready to sail out and slam it in Barlow's face.

Strong arms grabbed her shoulders from behind, making her sockets scream. "Don't struggle. It'll only make it worse." Rough hands dug into her skin when she tried to wrench free.

"Where's Gene?" Oh, God, please don't let him be hurt too.

"He's on vacation today since the weather's so nice. The IT department has his email password. All I had to do was say he was under investigation. They gave it up instantly."

She exhaled sharply, relieved Gene was okay. She didn't know what Barlow had planned, but it was clear he and Kenny had reached a whole new level of desperation. Hadn't last night proved that?

Tanner was right. Desperate people did stupid things.

She didn't want to end up like Ray. She wouldn't.

"You're hurting me," she whined, hoping he'd lower his guard, giving her the chance she needed. The door was only a few yards away.

His grip loosened. "Behave. Then I won't have to."

"Okay." Her voice quivered.

He dropped his hands. She swung her purse in an arc, smacking him in the neck.

She raced to the door.

She was nearly there when Barlow clamped his hands around her chest. He squeezed her like a python. She saw stars. "I can't...breathe."

"Stop fighting me! Kenny picked up Jill. We'll kill her if you try to escape. Do you understand?"

Her legs turned to rubber. "You have Jill?" she choked out. "Oh, God...I want...to see her."

"Not part of the plan. Now, I'm going to let go. Remember, I'll call Kenny if you make a break again. Nod if you understand."

She nodded.

"Now, I need your phone."

Barlow spun her around and yanked her purse away. He riffled through it, his mouth curving when he produced the sleek silver device. He scrolled through it.

"These are incredible inventions. You don't even have to call someone to communicate anymore." His fingers punched the small screen.

"What are you doing?" she asked, panting.

"You'll see." Barlow slid her phone into his pocket. "Now, we're going to drive. If you do anything, Jill dies. In an accident, of course."

Her ribs tightened, the first warning of a panic attack. She steeled herself. She couldn't let that happen. Not now. "Where are we going?"

Barlow took her arm, his hands sweaty. "Shut up. Don't make a wrong move as we leave."

His car was out back. She studied him as he drove east, taking them out of town. His lips were pressed tightly together, and his eyes looked mean. Maintaining control took effort, but she managed to do it. She needed to.

"How could you do this?" she said after awhile.

"God! Why do people always want to know? Look. We didn't plan any of this. What happened to Jemma was shit luck." He tapped the steering wheel in jerky movements. "If she hadn't died, we wouldn't be here. Fucking heart murmur!"

"And Ray?"

"Damn kid got nosy. Grew a conscience. It was his fault he went off the road. We just wanted him to leave town."

The *tap, tap, tap* of his fingers continued as he drove, the sound hitting her like a hammer. How could they not see they were to blame? Anger grew into rage. "What could be worth this?"

He snarled at her. "Money! You wouldn't get that, would you? Driving your brand-new Audi after a stint in the big city. Do you have any idea how much money we're getting from the pot Kenny's buddy sends us from Afghanistan? It's laced with some strain of opium. I don't understand the chemical crap, but it's untraceable in most drug tests. Our sales were up thirty percent!"

No wonder Gene hadn't found anything. Her stomach quivered. "I see."

"You just had to get Gene curious with your questions, didn't you?" His tapping continued to beat in time with her racing heart. "Yesterday, I heard Gene had ordered a more advanced drug test. Kenny and I knew we had to move fast."

"We didn't tell Gene anything!"

"Don't worry. I'll switch the drug tests if he finds anything new."

Thank God he didn't know about Peg's tests. Her hands clenched in her lap. She looked out the window. They were heading into the mountains. Where in the hell he was taking her? Where did they have Jill?

The car swerved when Barlow took the turn too fast. He braked hard, tires screaming. She breathed slowly, suppressing a panic attack.

"What did you do with my phone?"

Barlow gripped the steering wheel and barked out a dark chuckle. "I texted your boyfriend. Told him you'd found something."

She gripped the seatbelt, her lungs burning now. "He won't come." Oh, please let that be true.

"Fuck that! He wants to take us down so bad he can smell it."

Sweat rolled down her back. "He'll think it's odd I texted him."

"No, he won't." Barlow turned onto a mountain trail coated with packed snow. The four-wheel drive chimed when he hit the button. "You didn't spend the night at your parent's house because you're talking. Of course, your asshole boyfriend had to come save the day. Kenny was going to cut your brake line too."

Ice slid down her legs. "He's a regular Boy Scout," she agreed in a daze, the sunlight harsh on her eyes.

"Well, you got a reprieve. But today's another day."

The car bounced as it hit the ruts, snow crunching under the tires. Two gleaming snowmobiles caught her eye. Barlow pulled to the end of the road.

"Tanner will come. It's obvious to everyone in town he's nuts about you. Now get out. And remember what I said about Jill."

She opened the car door, scanning the area. Where is she?

He marched forward. "It's time for us to take a little ride."

"Where are we going?" Ice-cold dread squeezed her throat.

He pointed. She glanced across the sparkling expanse of the snowy basin at the menacing rock wall that was locally dubbed "The Great Wall." The towering shadow of Thorn's Peak pierced the ocean blue sky. She shivered when the wind thundered in from the west, shaking the pines like they were fragile Christmas ornaments.

Her gut bubbled with fear. "But that's Killer Pass. Only idiots go up there this time of year."

"But Tanner's an extreme risk taker. He's mentioned wanting to go. We've had some sunny weather, making it the perfect outing for an adventuresome couple like you two. It's an excellent day for snowmobiling, don't you think?"

"But it's an avalanche basin."

His mouth formed a maniacal grin "Yes, it is." He lifted his phone in her direction. "Now, say cheese."

She froze, rooted to the spot. She prayed Tanner wouldn't come.

Barlow planned to kill them.

# Chapter 51

Tanner tossed the yellow envelope into the passenger seat and waved goodbye to Hugo. Peggy would test the Swiss army knife for prints as soon as she received it in the mail tomorrow. Maybe it would give them their first piece of direct evidence.

He didn't care if Arthur was calling in the cavalry. If he could hand them someone's fingerprints, he would. That would be more damaging than a lab test. No question.

Tanner thrust his homemade coffee in the cup holder. It sloshed out, making him curse. His routine was shot. No morning swim or coffee. He tried not to think about how much it had hurt not to have Meredith in his bed this morning. It wasn't just his routine, he realized.

It had become his life.

Nothing he could do to change the situation until he solved the case and told her the truth.

Tanner's phone buzzed with a text as he drove down his driveway. He hit the display and swerved when he saw it was from Meredith.

*Found something. Evidence at Killer Pass. Headed there now. Don't tell Peggy yet.*

Damn her. Even after last night she wasn't backing down. He threw the phone aside. His gut quivered. What could she have found this morning? The place where Kenny had hidden his car and the drugs?

Dammit, he'd told her to stay out of it! What was it going to take? Wasn't pulverizing her heart into dust enough?

He scanned the glen of trees, thinking. Why tell him? Okay, maybe she wanted to prove that she wasn't giving up on the case. Even as pissed off as she was, who else would she tell? Her grandpa? He couldn't climb Killer Pass.

Still, the allusion to Peggy bothered him.

Was it a trap?

He started counting to ten to calm down, but got as far as four before he slammed his fist on the steering wheel.

"Fuck!"

He took the curve too fast, sliding, fighting for control of the vehicle. Locking his hands around the wheel, he headed there to meet her.

It didn't matter if it was legit or a trap.

It involved Meredith.

He didn't have a choice.

\*\*\*

Kenny was leaning against Barlow's car when he arrived at Killer Pass. Tanner scanned the space as he left his vehicle. The snowmobile caught his eyes. He didn't see Meredith anywhere. His guts oozed out of his body.

"I had a feeling Meredith wasn't feeling up for a hike today. Where is she?"

He caught the phone Kenny tossed him. Meredith's picture shone on the display. She was squinting in a sea of snow. She looked scared.

"And yet you came. Must be love," Kenny drawled sarcastically. "Turn around. Hands on the car. Feet spread."

"I bet you say that to all the girls."

The punch Kenny delivered to his guts made him grit his teeth.

"Give me your phone."

When he handed it over, Kenny shoved him forward. "Okay, let's go." Kenny pointed to the snowmobile. "You take the back. If you try anything, I'll shoot you. And she'll die."

His words burned like a brand. Tanner kept his breaths slow and deep, trying to maintain his focus. If he could get to her, he could save her. He had to believe that.

"You will anyway, right? Me too. Isn't that the plan?"

"Shut up."

Tanner straddled the seat behind Kenny. He hadn't killed before, but now he understood how a man could be driven to murder. He'd do anything to protect Meredith—and himself.

Snow misted his face as they cut through the trail, the engine revving. Tanner looked up at the sun, its rays hot on his black fleece. The snow was wet and dense under the snowmobile. He knew that Killer Pass had a reputation for avalanches. He'd learned a fair bit about avalanches in Afghanistan, where mountains towered above many of the villages he'd visited. Moderate weather alone wouldn't do the trick.

He had a bad feeling the criminals were planning on helping Mother Nature craft another accident.

He wasn't going to let that happen.

In the distance, he spotted Meredith's red coat and another dark form—his gut told him it was Barlow.

His breath caught in his throat as he peered across the acres of snow. He'd seen his share of avalanche basins, but this one took the cake. The Great Wall curved like a comma. The rock face was pocked with holes, small havens for birds or bats, and a few larger openings dotted the harder-to-reach areas.

The tree line stopped where the rock started. Thorn's Peak towered boldly to the left of the wall, its rugged landscape somehow both terrifying and beautiful. It pierced the sky before angling out at a forty-degree angle. Completely free of trees, it flowed into Killer Pass in smooth, silky lines. A humpback-shaped ridge dotted with pines and conifers hunkered down next to the pass.

He scanned the area for possible escape routes. There weren't any obvious options. Kenny and Barlow had chosen well. This would be another accident with little to no evidence, and given their access to law enforcement resources, they could write the report the way they wanted.

The snowmobile thundered closer, exhaust strong in his nostrils. His muscles locked when he saw Barlow next to Meredith, his Glock trained on her.

When they shuddered to a stop, he swung off, loosening up his body. He had to be ready to make his move.

Meredith took a step, sinking into the snow, her pale face clenched. "You shouldn't have come!"

He tore off his glasses so she could see his eyes. He had to tell her. "Everything I told you was a lie. I—"

Kenny punched him in the kidney. He sunk to his knees.

"Shut the hell up."

"Stop it!" Meredith screamed.

Her fear cut through him like razor blades. "It's okay. I'm all right." He rose to his feet. He'd be pissing blood if they somehow survived. He turned to Barlow. "Well, what a surprise."

"No?" Barlow sneered. "I knew you'd come."

"You had Meredith. There was no other choice." His gaze slipped to hers briefly. She shook her head back and forth in horror.

"We figured that would cinch it. You've been a busy boy, working this case like you're in fucking Iraq or something."

Since Meredith was here, he decided to give them an out. "My sister has a report on the drugs you gave Jemma. Ray was right. You did lace them."

Barlow walked forward, snow crunching. "You may have the drugs, but the dealer's dead. Such an unfortunate accident. Besides, poor Jemma had a bad heart, just like Gene said. We couldn't believe our luck when he left her marijuana use out of the report. Thank God for small towns."

"You fucking bastards," Tanner growled.

Barlow's smile turned up at the corners. "Ah, you're going to hurt my feelings. Like I said, if that dumb girl hadn't died, we wouldn't be here."

"She was just a kid," Meredith cried.

"Shut up!" Kenny said, drawing his gun.

Tanner forced himself not to move. "Meredith."

She turned to look at him. He met her gaze and felt the connection all the way to his toes. Her throat moved before she nodded once.

Time to gamble. He chose his words carefully. "Peg knows about both of you. This morning, I sent her the Swiss army knife one of you dropped under my car. I'm betting they'll be able to find a partial print."

"Bullshit!" Kenny tucked his gun in his belt and charged Tanner. They fell to the ground, and he rained hits and kicks on Tanner, who pounded back with clenched fists.

"That's enough!" Barlow yelled. "Kenny, fucking pull yourself together. Didn't you wear gloves last night?"

Tanner didn't give him time to think past the adrenaline. "Look, Peg's police force is working this case with us. We gave them paint shavings from Kenny's truck after breaking into your garage. Arthur Hale called in the Attorney General this morning. It's over."

"I knew I should have killed that bitch," Barlow said, his mouth twisting into a sneer.

Tanner's rage skyrocketed, but he managed to control it. "Don't add double murder to your list. Leave. You'll have a head start on the authorities."

The veins in Kenny's already bruising face throbbed like worms. "Fuck that! We're not backing down." His yell echoed against the Great Wall, raising the hairs on Tanner's neck.

"Tanner!" Meredith cried out, biting her lip. "They have Jill."

His heart rate doubled. He reached deep, studied a smirking Barlow, and went with his gut. "No, he doesn't."

Wagging his gun, Barlow said, "You're only making me want to shoot you more, McBride. And that would leave evidence."

Tanner's breath stopped. So this was it. *It was never like you imagined.* Well, he wouldn't go down easy. He stepped forward.

A shot ripped out, and snow and ice exploded like confetti near Tanner's feet. He came to a stop, his heart pounding, every muscle in his body strained.

"Step back." Barlow walked backward toward the snowmobile, his gun trained on Tanner. "We set charges on Thorn's Peak this morning. In fifteen minutes, that mountain is going to blow."

Kenny kept his gun trained on Meredith as he headed for the other snowmobile.

"That charge will leave evidence, Barlow."

The deputy sneered. "You think we'd be stupid enough to use dynamite or C4? Kenny bought a special binary compound that doesn't leave a signature. Learned about it in the military."

"The Attorney General's people will find something."

"Like you said, we'll be long gone by then. Unfortunately for you, only Kenny and I will have time to reach higher ground before the charges blow. Have fun."

As the criminals sped off on their snowmobiles, Tanner raced over to Meredith, who stood frozen in place. Her wide eyes followed the vehicles' speedy progress toward the ridge.

He grabbed her shoulders. "Look at me! You know this area. Where can we go?"

She didn't move. He'd seen victims paralyzed by shock before, so he knew what was wrong. He dragged her along with him. Heading to the tree line seemed to be their only option.

Another shot kicked up snow in his face. He glanced up. Barlow was going to play with him all right.

Meredith suddenly came alive, gripping his arm. "Wait!" She pointed to the wall. "See that cave? We used to climb up to it in high school."

She started running, and he followed. He forced himself not to look up the wall's towering expanse.

"Can you climb?" She felt for the first toe hold, her red and cracked hands gripping gray, curved stone.

"Yes." Adrenaline rose in him like a tsunami. "We don't have a choice."

# Chapter 52

Jill slammed the cash register door closed. Everyone in the coffee shop grew quiet.

"Something wrong?" Margie asked.

"Just having an off day," Jill replied for the thousandth time that morning.

Did everyone have to ask her what had crawled up her ass? Too bad she wasn't about to share. At this rate, she was set to explode. She was mad at Mere and Gramps—and afraid. She'd checked her rear view mirror a hundred times on her short drive to work.

She still couldn't wrap her mind around any of it.

After tossing and turning all night, some compassion had finally filtered in. Meredith was hurting over Asshole Tanner. It hadn't been nice to kick her out.

After struggling to make a soy mocha—usually so easy—she kicked the counter. She didn't like being at odds with Meredith or Gramps. Gramps was so stubborn. When she'd called him to tell him she was upset, he'd told her to get over it. Why in the hell would he tell her about a dangerous story? He'd never done it before. He wasn't about to start now.

She fingered the amethyst pendant on the necklace Jemma's mom had given her, which her friend had worn all the time, struggling not to cry.

Her hands worked better once she decided to make Meredith's favorite latte. She poured her grandpa a plain ol' coffee. Once she was finished, she headed out after letting Margie know. The sun warmed her face, and she felt an answering warmth inside—this was the right decision—but then someone pulled up alongside her, and her mouth pinched like she'd tasted spoiled whipped cream in the shaker.

"Hi," Brian said.

She scanned his body from the blue fleece to his denim-clad legs, wondering if he ever had an ugly day. "Lost your way? The Chop House is south, not north."

"I know that. I want to walk with you."

"Oh, so now you want to chat, huh?"

Damn, this was the last thing she needed. But even though she was pissed at him, she still wanted to lather herself like body butter against that long, hard frame.

He tore off his sunglasses. His direct gaze punched her solar plexus. "Please."

"What? I didn't hear that," she said, just to be bitchy.

"Puh-lease," he ground out. "Jesus, how many times are you going to make me say it?"

"As many as I can," she drawled.

He followed her into *The Western Independent*. People waved as she walked down the hall, Brian right behind her. When she reached Meredith's office, she skidded to a halt.

Her grandpa was pounding his cane against her sister's chair. "Damn girl!"

"What's going on?" she demanded, her voice horse.

"I can't reach Meredith." Gramps said, shoving his cane aside. "She left a note about meeting Gene, but he's on vacation today. I just called."

Jill rushed over and set the coffees on the desk, sloshing them. "Do you think she's in trouble?"

He pulled her against him. "Yes," he said. "Let me think for a moment."

"Will someone please tell me what's going on?" Brian demanded from behind her.

She turned in a blur, meeting his concerned gaze with her own. "I'll tell you later."

Her grandpa picked up the phone and dialed something. "Hello, this is Arthur Hale. I was wondering if Deputy Barlow is available." He reached for her hand. "He's on patrol, you say?" His breath rushed out. "I have a credible tip Deputy Barlow and my granddaughter, Meredith Hale, are in danger." He listened for a moment, his chapped lips clenched in a tight line. "Okay, thank you."

The phone fell when he missed the receiver. "They're starting a search." He nudged it into the cradle. "I'm not taking any chances. Barlow didn't respond when they called him, and they're using his phone to find him."

"Why didn't you tell them the truth?" Jill demanded.

"We don't know what's going on, but my gut is burning. Better to be safe than sorry. If I'm wrong, I'll blame it on early dementia."

"Why not just tell them Barlow's dirty?"

"They'll work harder to find their own."

Brian rubbed her back, silent and tense. He didn't know what was going on, but he was offering her support nonetheless.

"I'll call Tanner." Jill dialed. The jagged glass in her belly cut deeper the more times the phone rang. "It's going straight to voicemail."

"We'll keep trying. I'll get the Attorney General's people up here too. The main thing is to find Meredith."

The phone rang again. Jill jumped as her grandpa lunged for it, knocking over a pen holder. Ballpoints rained across the floor.

"Yes?" He clutched the receiver. "Barlow's in Killer Pass? Thank you."

"That's nuts. Why would they be there?" Brian asked from behind her.

All the energy drained out of her feet. "Avalanche conditions."

Her grandpa slammed his hand on the desk. "We'll have the sheriff get a rescue team out. If they're planning another accidental murder, we'll nail them in the act. They are not taking my granddaughter. Let's go."

Jill handed him his cane and followed him out, forcing aside her feelings of shock and horror. When Brian brushed her side, she took his hand in hers, needing the connection.

"Stay with me," she said.

He tightened his grip, his face stark white. "I'm not going anywhere."

# Chapter 53

The endless expanse of rock trailed up to a cloudless blue sky. The opening she remembered was somewhere in the middle. They could do it. There was no other choice.

Meredith eyed her watch, now fitted over her coat sleeve. "We have eleven minutes." Her fingers curled around cold stone as she eyed the indentations from past climbers. "Since I've climbed it before, I'll go first."

She fitted her body against the rock and started up the rock face, fighting the urge to rush, trying not to think about her lack of equipment. The impending explosion. God, she'd never seen an avalanche, but she'd heard one before. Deafening barely described it. She shuddered and took a deep breath. Clearing her mind, she reached for the holds she'd used years ago.

When she looked down, she saw the top of Tanner's dark head and his swollen hands gripping the rock. A shot pockmarked the wall to her right. She cried out, her fingers clenching for support. Barlow hadn't been kidding about playing with them.

"Fucker's got a long-range rifle," Tanner called out. "Relax. He's just trying to break our concentration. He doesn't want our bodies to be riddled with bullets. Ruins the whole 'accident' thing."

Relax. Yeah, right. She fitted her toe into another crevasse and reached up for another hold. Her nerves sizzled like an electrically charged fence as she kept climbing, slowly but surely. She bypassed a mossy patch and reached for another ledge. Another shot plowed into the wall a few yards away. Her toe slid, and her foot dangled. She looked down. Oh, God, it was a really far fall. Her head swam. She dug her shoe into a groove.

"You okay?"

She panted for a moment before reaching for the next hold. "If that was Kenny, his ex-military training sucks."

"Remember, they don't want to actually hit us."

No, they just want us to slip and fall. "So he could accidentally shoot us?"

"Try not to think about it."

The idea put a block of ice in her stomach. She glanced at her watch. Six minutes. Holding her panic at bay was the hardest thing she'd ever done, but she lifted her hand for the next edge and kept climbing. How much farther? When she looked down, she saw blood on Tanner's bare hands. She forced herself to look past him, all the way to the ground. Calculated the distance.

Her fingers burned, red and raw, and her joints felt like splintered wood within her cracked skin. Her muscles wept as she continued to climb. The next shot didn't affect her at all—her concentration was absolute.

"We're close." *So close.*

The sound of shoes scattering against rock jolted her concentration. She looked down and gasped when she saw Tanner's leg dangling. He managed to find a hold, and then leaned his forehead against the wall.

"You okay?"

"Peachy. How much longer till it blows?"

She glanced at her watch. The seconds were ticking down in time with her pounding heart. "Not much. Keep climbing."

Another shot near her head pinged a pebble into her chest. She grabbed for the next edge.

Come on, dammit.

A rumbling kaboom made her freeze. The sound spread across the landscape, echoing across the rock. The reverberation shook the wall, and she had to fight for purchase.

*Don't look at what's coming. Don't look.*

"Come on!" She reached frantically for the next hold. When she pushed herself up with her feet and reached again, she finally saw the opening. It was only a few feet away.

"We're here!" The rumble of snow thundering down the mountain echoed in her ears. She forced herself to keep climbing, her muscles burning with effort. When she reached the small cave, she dragged herself up and in, sweat burning her eyes. She crab-crawled on her elbows until she could turn around.

"Oh, God," she chanted, her brain screaming at the crashing and thundering outside. "Tanner!" She leaned over the cave's mouth, balancing her weight.

The roar of snow thundering down Killer Pass pounded in her eardrums. The blinding mushroom spread fast, blotting out the sun. Trees turned cartwheels amidst rock and debris in the sea of white.

"Meredith! Get inside!" He yelled at her from below as a wall of snow fell on him.

She plastered herself to the floor of the cave and leaned out. He was still a few feet away, dangling by one hand.

"Hold on!" She wiggled out farther and curled against the rock face, snow misting her face.

"Get back, dammit!" His hand found the rock and slipped. Searching, his fingers clenched around the jagged edge, and he pulled himself up, the muscles in his neck cording. He groaned as his hand gripped the mouth of the hole. She reached for his fleece and pulled until her shoulder sockets screamed.

A shot hit the wall near Tanner. Pop. Then another. Pop. He lifted his chest up and over, balancing on the edge with his hips. Then a third shot ripped through his shoulder with a thud, the impact knocking him forward. He plowed into her, crying out.

"Tanner!" she screamed, her eyes widening at the sight of the gaping hole in his jacket.

She dragged him into the cave by inches. His weight had her muscles straining like rubber bands, but she kept at it, even as another bullet plowed past her. She leaned back on her haunches and tugged with all her might, moving him out of range of Kenny and Barlow's shots.

The pounding from the avalanche continued. Trees broke like sticks, and chunks of snow and ice catapulted across the basin. The snow level rose in front of them, and Meredith experienced a moment of pure terror when it looked like they'd be sealed in. God, they needed air.

She pulled Tanner's dripping head onto her lap and pressed her hands on his wound to staunch the bleeding.

He opened his eyes, which were clenched in pain. "I'm sorry," he mouthed over deafening noise. "I love you," she read on his lips.

She feathered back his hair, her heart settling into place even though the world outside was coming to an end. "I love you too," she mouthed back.

# Chapter 54

Tanner came to on his stomach, a throbbing pain in his shoulder. The utter silence after the explosion made his head swim. Wet, penetrating cold flooded his system. He groaned.

"Oh, thank God!" Meredith cried. "You're awake, you're awake, you're awake."

Her voice bordered on hysterical. When he tried to roll over, Meredith's gentle hands helped turn him. She pressed a bloody cloth to his shoulder.

"You passed out. I was trying to stop the bleeding." She sniffed and wiped his wet face. "Thank God, you're awake. I didn't know what to do when you passed out."

Since her voice was still shaking, he peeled his eyes open. His whole body felt like it had gone through a meat grinder.

He realized she'd put her scarf under his head. "Where's your coat?" She was shaking, her teeth chattering.

"I hung it out of the hole with a stick. I know Grandpa will figure everything out. He has to."

When he heard her sniff again, he put his hand on her thigh, eager to channel comforting energy. "He'll come. He threatened to come after me if I hurt you. Trust me. No one messes with Arthur Hale's granddaughter."

The effort to converse tapped him out, but he knew she needed the reassurance. Hell, he needed it too. He was bleeding out in a cave. "I take it we can't just walk out of here onto a bed of snow?" he said.

She swiped a hand under her runny nose. "Not unless you like walking through demolition land. The snow curved against the wall like a crescent. The drop's still too steep. Plus, you can't move. You've lost a lot of blood."

"It's not bad," he lied. "I want you to go for help."

"No! I'm not leaving you."

"Meredith—"

"I'm not!" A tear slid down her ruddy cheek. "Please don't ask me to do that."

Pain radiated down his shoulders to his fingers. His breath hissed out. "I'm sorry," he whispered, realizing that she still didn't know why he'd hurt her. His throat tightened. "It's not what you think."

Those bright green eyes grew wetter, putting his heart and his shoulder in a dead heat in the race for most painful. Her palm touched his cheek, and she gently caressed his stubble. "Don't waste your energy. Tell me when we get out of here."

She kissed his forehead and rested her face against his for a moment. He squeezed his eyes shut. God, he'd missed her.

A motor puttered in the distance. He strained to hear. "Help?"

She stopped the pressure, laid him down carefully, and crawled over to the edge to look out.

His wound pulsed and throbbed in vicious beats, blood flowing freely. He pressed his hand to it.

"Oh, God."

He leaned up, his stomach sinking. "What?"

"No." She tunneled back to him on her knees. "It's Barlow and Kenny. They're coming back for us. They've got climbing equipment on the back of their snowmobiles."

Tanner cursed and tried to sit up. "Fuck, we're sitting ducks in here." He wove, seeing stars.

"Lie down! You've lost too much blood."

He grabbed her arm. "No, I won't lose you. Get out of here. Now."

"No!"

"Leave me. I'll be dead anyway if no one comes."

Her eyes could start a fire. "Don't say that!"

"I can give you a chance. I'll jump and go in the opposite direction." Something. He would not let her die.

Tanner felt for the wall and leaned against it. The pain in his shoulder made it hard to concentrate. "Let's go, dammit!"

"No!" She angled herself between him and the opening. "I'm not letting you sacrifice yourself for me. We stay together. We're a team. Remember?" A sob rushed out, and she pressed her hand to her mouth to contain it.

He broke. He lifted his good hand to her. "Come here."

She crawled forward to join him. He touched her cheek, looking deep into those scared green eyes. "Let me do this," he uttered softly, shutting out the pain.

Her face crumpled, and she swayed into him. He curled his arm around her, drawing her close.

"It's the only way," he whispered. He nudged her face up and fitted their cold lips together.

Love overwhelmed him.

"I *want* to do it."

When he pressed his forehead to hers, her breath shuddered out over his lips, and her small frame shook. He wanted so badly to protect her.

She pushed back and crawled to the cave's mouth. "I don't want to lose you either." When she turned, he saw a new determination in her out-thrust chin.

"Meredith!" he cried, terror's deep claws piercing his insides.

She leaned out of the opening, preparing to jump, and he dragged himself after her, moving as fast as he could. There was no way she was going out alone. Halfway there, he picked up another sound—one he knew all too well from being embedded with the military.

"Wait! It's a chopper."

A shot pierced the wall near Meredith's head, and a rock pinged down, skidding across the floor.

"Come back here! We'll wait them out. Help's on the way."

She crawled back to him and cupped his face in her hands. "All right. We'll both wait. Together."

He leaned his head against the cold rock and tucked her close. He took her bleeding, freezing hand in his nearly numb one, careful of the blisters from the climb. God, now more than ever, he needed this connection with her.

"No martyrs."

"No martyrs," she agreed.

They had too much to live for.

# Chapter 55

Dare's Rescue Patrol sure earned their money today," Meredith said, trying to joke so that she wouldn't cry. Her eyes tracked to the back of the hospital, where Tanner was being operated on. She took a warming sip of coffee.

"He's going to be all right, Mere." Jill gently took her sister's bandaged hand. "I'm so sorry we fought. I would never have forgiven myself if anything had happened to you."

Meredith set the coffee aside and hugged her sister. "Me neither. I'm so sorry I didn't tell you the truth. The whole truth."

"We'll deal. But I'll kick your ass if you ever do it again—or scare me like this."

They rocked each other. Jill hadn't left Meredith's side since she'd arrived at the hospital. Meredith was relieved. She had her sister back.

Her grandpa walked back into the waiting room, his cane tapping the antiseptically clean beige floor. "That was Anderson. State police have Barlow and Kenny in custody. They picked them up at a gas station off the interstate. Barlow spilled everything in return for a plea bargain. He said Kenny ran Ray off the road. Brought the drugs in through a contact at Peterson Air Force Base in Colorado Springs. Apparently Kenny knows an Afghani chemist who can lace marijuana with opium, making it untraceable. When hasn't the drug trade been inventive? He told them where to find Kenny's car. They're taking the two of them to Denver until a full investigation is completed."

"Good. Tell Anderson they can interview me whenever they want."

Her gramps nodded.

"I hope they become someone's prison bitches after what they did to Jemma and Ray," Jill ground out.

Brian's jaw ticked. "I hope they burn in hell." He hadn't left Jill's side since leaving her grandfather's office.

Meredith took a long drink of coffee. She and Tanner could have been killed. She wasn't sure she would ever come to grips with that. Her shivering intensified. "I'll need to drink gallons of this stuff to get warm again."

"Here." Brian peeled off his fleece, handing it to her.

Meredith tugged it on gratefully. Her grandpa took his spot on the flower-print couch, and she leaned her head on his shoulder.

"Your mom and dad are driving up as we speak. It just about gave your dad another heart attack, hearing what happened." He popped in a red hot, crunching. "Peggy and Keith are already on their way. That woman can take bad news. Didn't seem to break a sweat." He cleared his throat like he was fighting emotion. "She's pissed Tanner didn't call her before heading to Killer Pass."

He'd walked into a trap because of her. He'd told her he'd lied the other night about his motivations for working with Sommerville. She believed him. No one could fake emotion like that. He would tell her the truth when he was out of danger. Please God, let him be okay. There was no way he didn't love her. He'd been willing to sacrifice his life to save hers.

She fingered her grandpa's wool jacket. "I don't think we would have made it out alive if you hadn't figured things out so quickly." She'd never forget the sound of the snowmobiles coming back for them.

"Mind like a steel trap." He tapped his forehead.

Jill pressed against her. "I'm so glad you're okay."

"Me too."

The doors swung open, and she lifted her head, eyes wide. The sight of the doctor's bloody scrubs made her clench Jill's hand.

"He lost a lot of blood, but he's going to be fine. He won't be able to use his shoulder for a while, and he'll need rehab, but there shouldn't be any long-term effects."

Emotions welled up inside her like a geyser. She curled forward as the first sobs erupted.

"You go ahead and cry, Mermaid." Her grandpa stroked her back. "You're entitled."

*\*\**

Tanner surfaced through the fog to a beeping noise and something that sounded like a pressure cooker. He cracked his eyes open, awash in numbness. His mouth was dry. Drugs, he realized. His hand was taped with an IV. The whiteness of the hospital gown wasn't as pure as the sea of snow beneath him when they pulled him out of the cave on a medical lift, the rescue team working the ropes to make sure he didn't hit the rock face. God, what a day.

Someone shifted at his side. "Tanner?" Meredith rested her hands on the bed's handrails.

"Barely," he whispered. "Need...water."

She shook her head. "I'll get a nurse."

The force of his fatigue made his eyes flutter. "My desk. There are...files. David...Sommerville."

He didn't ask about Barlow and Kenny. All that mattered was making things right.

"I'll find them," he heard her say down a long tunnel before everything went dark.

*\*\**

When Tanner woke again, Arthur was leaning over him.

"You going to live?"

His face itched, he needed a shave, and he still felt like shit, but the sleep had helped. "Looks like."

"That's a good thing. Peg just took Keith to my house to get some sleep. Jill's going to look after him so your sister can come back."

Tanner reached for the styrofoam cup next to his bed. Bliss didn't describe what it felt like to coat his cottony mouth with water. "Been upgraded to liquids. Where's Meredith?"

Arthur tapped the handrails. "Your sister explained what happened with Sommerville, and Meredith found the file you told her about."

The machine monitoring Tanner's pulse blipped as his heart rate increased. So she knew everything now. "I don't remember that."

Arthur drew out a red hot. "You told her about it when you came to after surgery."

"Is she upset?" He struggled to sit up, wincing at the bruises. Would his kidneys ever function normally again?

"She understands now." He leaned back, crossing his ankles. "She's not happy, but she understands why you lied. She was married to that asshole, after all. She knows he's ruthless."

He sank deeper into the pillows and looked toward the door. "Thank God. Where is she?"

Arthur grinned. "She went to see that asshole about some blackmail."

# Chapter 56

Meredith knocked on the elaborately carved entrance to Richard's new townhouse. If she had survived Killer Pass, she could certainly handle this.

When her ex-husband opened the door, his surprise couldn't have been more evident. Then he veiled it with a crooked smile.

"Meredith, my dear," he drawled like she was from the society set. "What a delightful surprise."

She stepped inside and let him take her coat. "You always say that when it's not."

"I assume this isn't a social call, then." His eyes fired, but he extended his arm grandly. "How about we talk in the study?"

Meredith ignored him and walked forward like she owned the place, praying it was down the single hallway like it would be in most houses. She turned and cocked a hip. "Are you coming?"

Her impertinence wiped the fake, toothy smile off his face. She headed down the hall, smiling when she found the study. He followed her inside silently.

He immediately took the massive chair behind his even larger desk. *Hello, Napoleon,* she heard Divorcée Woman intone.

Nice to have you back, she responded.

*Nice to be back.*

His tastes had always run a little ornate. She'd put up with it, not wanting to upset the apple cart. When she didn't kick herself for that, her sense of inner peace expanded.

"What are you grinning at?" he hissed.

"Just realizing I truly am in another place—and it's a good one. You should be glad. I envisioned beaning you with a candlestick after what you did."

On the airplane trip across the country she'd decided against recounting his sins and raging at him. His back would only go up, and she wouldn't get what she came for.

"Colonel Mustard in the library with a candlestick," he said in his best British imitation of a *Clue* character.

His wicked sense of humor had been what first drew her to him. In addition to his good looks. Add in his dogged pursuit, and she'd fallen fast—too fast, she now realized. Well, all in the past now.

She slid a file toward him. "We have some horse trading to do. You get the dirt I have on you for the dirt you have on Tanner's brother."

"I see." He opened the file. After flipping through the photos, he looked up at her. "Impressive. I wasn't sure how much you had. You never would show me everything."

"I'm not stupid. And I'm a damn good investigative journalist. You forgot that."

"Obviously." He shoved out of the chair. "I thought you were my wife. Didn't expect you to spy on me."

This time, his attempt at guilting her didn't make her stomach long for a Rolaid. The firelight danced upon his pretty face, the blond highlights in his hair.

She felt absolutely no regret over losing him.

In fact, she felt like she'd been saved from a life-sentence of misery.

Peace uncurled within her like a precious flower, softening her heart. She let it expand with gratitude. The sensation heralded new beginnings— and a final release of the past.

She sat back in her chair. God, she felt wonderful. Wonderful enough to set aside her anger over what this man had done to Tanner. It was time to devote all her energy toward the good things in her life—exactly as she'd decided in the bookstore all those months ago.

Richard strode over to the bar. She followed. "You get the negatives on you, and I get the negatives on David. It's a simple trade."

He knocked back a scotch, the peat tickling her nose. "What about your article for Karen on Nora fucking Roberts? Are you planning on using it to ruin my political career?"

"I know you won't believe this, but I never planned on hurting your career. I only wanted to reclaim something important to me, something our divorce had stolen. Not everything is about you, Richard."

He scowled. "You threatened me."

"You pushed me."

His sigh rushed out as he poured himself another drink. "Yeah, you never liked that. I wish I hadn't done it."

She looked at him, truly looked at him, and saw him for the first time. He was selfish, vain even. He gorged on power like a three-year-old gorged on Halloween candy. He used people to get what he wanted.

But their relationship had not been barren of moments of kindness, humor, and even love.

Still, it had always come second to his ambition and his needs—for women, for more money, for the ability to screw with people's lives.

"Me too. We could have avoided this whole episode." She fingered a Band-Aid on her hand. "No, I take that back. If this hadn't happened, I never would have met Tanner."

His mouth twisted. "You love him," he accused.

"Yes. It's ironic, don't you think? You're responsible for bringing us together."

His curse didn't bother her in the least. "He won't stick, you know," he said. "He doesn't like to be tied down. The man's never stayed in one place longer than a couple years. He's a loner."

She walked back over to his desk. Smiled. "I know who he is."

He was someone who was willing to give up his life for the woman he loved—a real bona fide hero, straight out of Nora Roberts Land. And he was all hers.

Richard reached for another drink.

"So. Do we have a trade?"

"You don't give me much choice," he said. "My political career is more important than some city councilman. I'm going to do great things for this state. Wait and see. "

"I'm sure you will." He was a politician through and through, always had been, and God knows he had the adultery thing down pat.

He walked to the safe and dialed in the combination. When it beeped, he opened it with flourish.

She pulled the negatives out of her purse and extended them. When he reached out his hand, she pulled back. "No double-double crossing. Because when I say I want to be done with you, I mean it."

His mouth tipped up. "You're tougher than you used to be, Meredith. I don't like it. And I don't like your hair either."

"Well, I do."

He put his hand over his heart while the fire crackled and popped in the stone hearth. "I'm being straight with you here. You always brought out the best in me, Meredith."

"Not always, but it's good to be reminded." She took the negatives he gave her, putting them in her bag.

"You aren't going to check them?"

She studied him. "My gut tells me you're not pulling a fast one. I've learned to trust it."

"You always had good judgment."

*See*, Divorcée Woman called out.

He walked over to the bar again. "How about a drink? For old times' sake?"

"Why not?" she said, setting her bag down.

When he whipped up a dirty martini, a sense of surprise fluttered through her.

"You remembered?"

His face softened. "There's a lot I remember."

She drank the martini slowly as he sipped his scotch. Both of them studied the fire in the silence.

"I need to go."

He nodded and followed her out. When she reached the landing, he helped her with her coat and opened the door. "I'm glad you didn't die in that avalanche, Meredith."

She wouldn't even ask how he already knew about it. He was a journalist, after all.

Her mouth curved. "Me too. Goodbye, Richard. Good luck with the political game."

The door closed. She walked down the stairs, running over their meeting in her mind. She'd known the instant the fight had gone out of him. As soon as he'd realized a compromise was needed, he'd turned reasonable and charming. Some things never changed.

Well, she had gotten what she came for. What Tanner wanted to do now that he was free and clear would be up to him.

She took a deep breath, inhaling exhaust and whispers of food from the restaurant quarter around the block. Her bustier cinched her ribs, and she touched it lightly with her fingers.

It was time to let something else go.

"Goodbye, Divorcée Woman. Thanks for everything."

*Have a good life, Meredith. You deserve it.*

Yes, she darn well did. She headed off in the direction of her favorite lingerie boutique. The first thing she would do was buy cotton underwear— an early Christmas present to herself. With her courage restored, she could return to her old faithful.

Cars streaked by, honking in noisy bursts. Brake lights flickered red when traffic halted. Ah, New York. She was going to miss it, but she was happy to leave it on her own terms. Her future was bright. She knew what she wanted, and by God, she was going to do everything she could do to get it.

Just like one of Nora's characters.

She was going to fly back home to her own Roarke. He did exist in real life.

He existed for her.

# Chapter 57

Ignoring the hospital smell in Tanner's room—pee-yew—Jill looked up from the legal pad she was doodling on, hoping to see Brian coming down the hall for another visit. There was still a certain wariness between them, like they were trying to decide what to do with each other when everything returned to normal. But he'd been coming around—even bringing delicious meals. She'd realized she'd missed him as a friend—even if she were still attracted to him. The other realization had been her need for a new focus. Writing in stream of consciousness on the pad was helping her to see what bubbled up.

Across the room, her grandpa was playing cards with Peggy and Tanner, and her mom and dad had volunteered to make a run for coffee at Don't Soy With Me. The hospital stuff tasted like crap.

Footsteps sounded in the hall. She glanced over to the open door. Brian materialized, looking hot in jeans and a blue fleece.

"Hey," he said to everyone. "How's it going?"

After the pleasantries were exchanged, he sat on the edge of the ugly floral chair where she was sitting. He pointed to her legal pad, his brows knitting together. "What are you doing?"

"Brainstorming. I need a new project."

"You get bored too easily," her grandpa muttered, slapping down his cards. "Just like me. Gin."

"I think you're cheating, old man." Peggy shuffled the cards. "Don't make me frisk you."

"My dear, it would be my pleasure," he responded. "We're going to need a new deputy sheriff here. You should think it over, Peggy. Dare's a nice town. I'll give you and Keith a personal tour when your brother gets back on his feet. Families should be together."

Peggy's mouth twitched. "We'll see."

"How can I stay here when the person I'm staying for left without a word?" Tanner barked.

"Red hot, anyone?" Grandpa Hale interrupted.

"I'll have one." Keith jumped off Tanner's hospital bed, where he sat perched like a parrot. The kid hadn't had a meltdown since he'd arrived, thankfully. Seeing him sob in his mom's arms near Tanner's bedside had pretty much done everyone else in.

Brian sat on the edge of her chair and peeked at her drawing. "So, what's it going to be this time?"

"I don't know," she responded, looking at her hodgepodge of words and symbols. Everything had something to do with food—but on a bigger scale than Don't Soy with Me. She made a humming sound as her intuition finally showed her the way. "Maybe I'll open a restaurant. Something fun and hip."

He rubbed his chin. "Huh. And I'm a chef..."

She trailed her eyes up his chest until she was looking straight into those Bengal tiger blue eyes. "Huh?"

"Are you beating around the bush here?"

"Mwuh-ha-ha-ha!" she uttered in her best villainous laugh because she hadn't consciously realized until this moment she'd been looking for a way to reconnect with Brian. "You've discovered my evil plan."

Her grandpa snorted; Peggy's shoulders shook; and even Oscar-the-Grouch Tanner's lips twitched.

Keith bounded over. "You're funny, Jillie. Don't you think so, Brian?"

"Isn't she just?"

"Keith, come back here. I need you to help Mommy figure out how to beat Mr. Hale."

The kid's sneakers slapped against the hospital floor. "Shuffle harder, Mommy."

Jill set the legal pad aside. "Maybe we should think about joining forces, Brian."

"All right, you two. You were best friends growing up," her grandpa muttered. "Cut the crap and stop farting around. Why don't you make up already?"

"Mommy, Mr. Hale said *fart*," Keith whispered.

Brian held her gaze. "What do you say, Jill? Friends?"

As she looked into those all-too-familiar eyes, she took the first step to making peace with him. "Friends." And maybe more, she thought.

Meredith sauntered through the doorway, looking all New York chic in a black Chanel suit. "What are we talking about in here?"

"Friendship," Brian responded, kissing her cheek. "Welcome back. You look better, Mere."

"I feel better," she declared, throwing back her hair, her eyes darting straight to Tanner.

The heat between them sparked. Jill hoped it wouldn't singe Tanner's medical machines. She leapt from her chair. "Okay, everyone. We're taking a break in the cafeteria. Ice cream on me."

Keith whooped. "Do you want some, Uncle Tanner?"

"Not right now." Tanner said, punching his pillows.

Grandpa Hale wrapped his arms around Meredith. "Everything all taken care of?"

In response, Meredith made a humming noise in her throat.

"Can't wait to hear. Oh, to have been a fly on the wall." Kissing her cheek, Grandpa tapped his way after Keith.

Peggy grabbed her purse. "Meredith, it's good to have you back," she said.

"About damn time," Tanner growled.

"Like most men, he's a bear when he's sick. Ignore him."

"Oh, we'll manage." Meredith set her massive purse onto Tanner's bed.

Brian grabbed Jill by the arm. "Come on. Let's leave them alone."

"Wait! So, how did Rick-the-Dick take it?" she whispered, leaning close to Meredith's ear.

"Surprisingly well. I'll tell you later."

Looking over at Tanner, Jill winked. "Have a good talk, you two."

The standoff had already begun. Tanner sat crossly on his bed while Meredith smiled back at him. The trip to New York had clearly agreed with her.

Catching sight of the new Nora Roberts hardcover sticking out of Meredith's handbag, Jill executed a twirl as she left the room.

Love did conquer all. Just like Nora always said.

Now, she needed to find her own Nora Roberts Land.

She linked her arm with Brian's and hesitantly settled her body closer to his.

# Chapter 58

About time you got back," Tanner barked again when the door closed behind Jill and Brian.

His sour mood couldn't ruin her happiness. She was thrilled to see him again. Even though her family had given her progress reports, his improving health soothed all the worry from her gut. She floated over to him and kissed his cheek. "Someone's grouchy. Shoulder hurting?"

He slanted her a look. "Yeah, but that's not why I'm pissed. Why the hell did you take off and tackle Sommerville by yourself while I was stuck here?"

She folded herself into the chair next to his bed. "I needed to handle things myself."

"I got a text from your ex," he growled. "He said he wishes us well, and there are no hard feelings. What the fuck is that all about?"

Her brows winged up. "Oh really?"

He punched the bed with his good arm, rattling the frame. "Yes, really," he mimicked in a nasty tone, not looking at her.

"He did bring us together."

Tanner snorted. "That's rich. Like that makes what he did okay."

"Mhmm."

"I wanted to handle Sommerville myself."

She cleared her throat until he finally met her eyes. "Well, I had the means, so I did it. Just like a heroine in one of my Nora Roberts novels, which I totally need to tell you about later."

His scowl accentuated his scar.

"After you offered your life for mine, I thought one good turn deserved another."

"I hate that phrase," he snarled. "That's not why I did it."

Her heart warmed. God, she wanted to touch him, but she needed to know one more thing. "I know. Besides, I didn't want this whole blackmail thing to be between us for another moment."

He grew silent, fiddling with his IV.

"Your face is still bruised." The colorful patchwork quilt of pain made her heart beat tightly in her chest.

He ran his hand across his jaw. "Yeah, and I need a shave too."

She folded her arms. "You should have told me about the blackmail."

The monitors droned on in the silence.

"I didn't think I could at first. Then, I thought it would be better to wait until we solved the case." He shook his head. "It all comes down to one damn reason though. No, two." He kicked at the sheet that covered him.

Her pulse stopped. "And those are?"

His chocolate brown eyes gleamed at her. "I didn't want to fucking lose you. Or see you hurt."

Inside she was glowing, but he wasn't getting off that easy. "Quite a gambit. Crushing me to bits in one move, thinking I would come back in the end."

His jaw clenched. "I'm sorry. I hated doing it, but I couldn't think of another way to protect you. After Peg...I couldn't fucking risk you! I was willing to lose you if it meant keeping you safe."

She had to take a moment to clear her throat. His raw emotion triggered her own. How could she have ever thought badly of him?

"You were willing to die to keep me safe." She leaned closer, gripping the hand rails of his bed.

His scowl seemed more menacing under his thick stubble. God, he must have looked like a badass with a full beard.

"I was going to find a way to get out of it! I don't have a fucking death wish, and it's not that I don't trust you." The white straw toppled out of his styrofoam cup when he fiddled with it. "Besides, you're one to talk."

"So, we make a good pair." She rested her chin on her hands. "I went to New York to show you that you can trust me—and that I can handle myself."

His eyes fired. "I know you can."

She snorted.

"I do. It's just that I don't want you to get hurt if I'm around to stop it. Call it the He-man gene, but I have it. Get over it."

Her brows rose even as her heart soared. "You are surly."

He pinned her in place with his gaze. "I was worried you weren't coming back!" He looked away. Swallowed hard. "That you couldn't...forgive me," he whispered.

Her heart pounded in insistent thuds. It took a minute to answer. "I've decided my life is here. I told my grandpa and dad that I want to take over the paper." She finally reached for his hand and threaded their scraped fingers together, careful of the IV. "Tanner."

He met her gaze, his eyes pinched at the corners. God, he was so beautiful.

"I do forgive you. All the way." She smiled softly. "I love you."

His hand squeezed hers in a death grip. "Thank God. I wasn't...I hoped...I love you too. I meant what I said on the mountain. Dammit, I'm not doing this right. These damn drugs."

She scooted closer, wanting to crawl up next to him on the bed. "It's okay."

"No, it's not. I hurt you, and I want to make it better." He snorted.

"Shit, I sound like Keith. I have something for you." When he leaned over to the side table, wincing, she leapt up.

"Let me get that, you macho ape."

It was a pale cream box tied up in a moss green ribbon.

"There's no way you tied this," she commented drolly.

He sputtered out a laugh, holding a rib. "Maybe I have hidden ribbon-tying talents."

"And pigs fly." She undid it slowly, goosebumps dancing across her skin. "You also didn't buy this present yourself, since you've been in the hospital."

"Maybe I ordered it online?"

"Right."

"Oh, shut up and open it. You're driving me crazy."

"Ditto."

"Jill and Peg helped after I told them what I wanted. Then your grandpa threw in a hand. Could have blown me over if I hadn't already been flat on my ass."

When she parted the tissue, she pursed her mouth. A cotton tank in pale pink lay artfully folded, monogrammed with MW.

*MW?*

Jeez, he really was zonked out on drugs. She tucked her tongue in her cheek, wondering if Jill had told him she used to wear cotton. God knows Jill would have zero compunction about talking about her underwear.

He wiggled closer to the rail. "What's the matter? Don't you like it?"

"It's lovely."

"But..."

She rolled her eyes. "Fine. Since we're all Truth or Dare now, I hate to tell you this, but you got my initials wrong."

His scowl made his bruises shift. "Dammit, I told them to put it on top. Keep looking."

When she lifted the tank, her mind went blank.

Her grandmother's ring winked at her. She picked it up, remembering how she used to twist it and make a wish when she was a little girl. Her grandma had told her it was a special ring. It had brought her true love. She'd hoped to inherit it and wear it for her marriage with Richard, but her grandpa hadn't said a word. His disapproval had been clear from the start.

Tears burned her eyes as she clutched the ring to her chest. "My grandpa gave you this?"

Tanner cleared his throat. "It was his way of showing me he wasn't going to kick my ass...and letting me know your family approves of me sticking around and persuading you to marry me."

Her breath rushed out. A bunch of messy emotions jogged up her throat, making her fear she'd do something girly and bawl. She reined it in. She was not going to bawl while her hero asked her to marry him.

"I see," she rasped.

He gestured with his good arm. "I want something different now. I want to settle down with you. Have a few kids like Keith, who'll paper our refrigerator with their drawings." He pointed to a paper card decorated with a lopsided heart and Keith's name in a blue crayon.

"Is that what you're suggesting?" she squeaked out when she could finally speak through her suddenly dry mouth.

She hadn't expected this. No, not at all.

He snapped down the rail separating them. "Yes, and I'm doing a damn poor job of it. Look, I know your divorce wasn't that long ago, but I love you."

The intensity of his expression made a tear slide free.

"I want to marry you. I want kids with you. The whole she-bang." His mouth turned up in a nervous smile as he took a deep breath. "I know you'll need time to start trusting me again, but I want you to know that I'm in this for the long haul. I'm going to extend my teaching position, and if you're okay with it, I want to help out at the paper. Your grandpa has a desk waiting for me."

Oh, her sweet gramps. She fingered the cotton tank, soft as a baby's skin. God, he'd mentioned wanting babies. Her mind skyrocketed with possibilities.

"Why the tank?"

His ears turned a pleasant red. "Well, you said you wore cotton before, so I thought you might consider a new alter ego."

When she lifted her eyes to his, his mouth turned up. "Married Woman."

She pressed her hands to his rough face. "You're too funny. I bought my first cotton underwear since the divorce in New York. While I'll bring the La Perla out every once in a while, I don't need it to show me who I am anymore."

"Who you are is beautiful." He grabbed her hand and raised it to his lips, kissing it like an old-world gentleman. "I love you."

Her whole body relaxed. "I love you, too."

"I won't rush you, I promise. I know you like to take your time."

She thrust the ring toward him. "Some things don't need more time. I thought I was going to lose you, Tanner."

He shuttered out a sigh. "Me too."

When she looked into his eyes, she saw herself. It really was true. You could see yourself in someone else's eyes.

"I don't want to wait."

He pulled her against him with one arm, and she carefully wrapped her arms around him.

"God, I love you," he whispered. "So much."

His kiss gave her the punch, followed by the liquid tide of love, lust, and longing she had only found with him.

He pulled back and slid the ring onto her finger. "I would have followed you to New York."

Oh that wicked gleam in his eyes. It was good to see it again.

"I'm where I belong. I just have one more article to write. Then I'll be done."

He drew her onto the bed beside him. "What's it going to say?"
She traced his lips and settled her body against his.
"I'm going to write about how we found our happily ever after."

# Epilogue

*"Nora Roberts Proven Correct: Happily Ever After Does Exist"*
By Meredith Hale

*If you read Nora Roberts, you are probably thinking, duh, of course Nora's right, but honestly, I went through over a year feeling less than sure. Some people wouldn't make a federal case out of it, but to me this topic was deeply personal. For the past four months, I was on assignment to debunk my ex-husband's assertion that Nora Roberts's novels ruined our marriage and led to our divorce. I dedicated myself to proving happily ever after existed. Trust me, it's harder than it sounds.*

*Let's back up a minute. Like many of you, I love (present tense) Nora's books. There wasn't a paperback or hardcover I hadn't read. I spent hours enthralled by delicious romances with strong, sassy heroines and hot, dependable heroes. They bantered throughout the books while "finding" themselves, being encouraged and challenged by family, and sometimes even catching the bad guys. Regardless of the plot, you knew where you were going.*

*My mother picked up Nora's first book in 1981. She used to tell my father she was heading to Nora Roberts Land when she'd steal away from laundry to read a new release. This land held magic and love.*

*When I came of age, she gave one to me. Like its title, Sea Swept swept me away.*

*With over two hundred books in print—a record in publishing—Nora has influenced an entire generation of women. I'm part of that generation. She's shaped the way I want love, sex, and relationships to work. I've always felt better about life after reading a Nora Roberts book. They made me believe in happily ever after.*

*I believed in it when I said my vows and when my husband and I started our life together. Things didn't work out as I'd expected. He had his faults. I had mine.*

*However, instead of letting bygones be bygones, my ex zinged me with the notion that Nora's books were pure fiction. Love didn't exist in the real world like that, he said. Reading Nora had given me artificial expectations about what a real relationship entailed.*

*We got divorced. I stopped reading Nora (and J.D. Robb too—don't hate me). Worse, I suspected my ex might have been right.*

*A year after I signed the divorce papers, I made a decision. I was not going to pooh-pooh Santa Claus anymore—okay, in this case, Nora Roberts Land. It was time to start believing in happily ever after again. Even more, it was time to find it.*

*I'm a journalist, so I investigate. I journeyed to my small hometown like one of Nora's characters, broken down, but ready to rebuild my life, surrounded by my loving family. I went back to work at our family newspaper in the Rocky Mountains to give my dad some time off after his heart attack, telling no one of my real plans except my sister—because you can trust your sister, right? I made a list of all the available Nora Roberts heroes in our town. These included a firefighter, a forest ranger, a doctor, a college professor. Well, you get the drift.*

*Newly divorced as an early thirtysomething, my quest became a public amusement. The whole town thought I was on a Man Bender. But my heart wasn't in it. Every date was about looking for negatives. Some guys made this super easy by not being particularly nice or by being downright boring.*

*Beyond the fact that my heart wasn't in it, I'd lost my confidence. I felt like a failure and wondered what was wrong with me. Does any of this sound familiar to those of you who've been dumped? I even invented a superhero alter ego named Divorcée Woman to regain my courage. Armored in La Perla's exquisite lingerie every day—bought with my alimony, thank you—I channeled sexiness, confidence, and female power. And you know what? It helped—for a while. So if you need a pick-me-up to help you regain what you've lost, find something. Once you've got your groove back, that crutch can slide away. Mine did.*

*And there was another thing bothering me. I wasn't "supposed" to be dating anymore. I'd gotten married because I thought I was done with that part of my life. But no, I wasn't. Single again, I had to get back out, and it really is a jungle out there. There's a lack of anonymity when you date in a small town. The pitying glances and whispered comments followed me to Dare. There she is, the divorced Hale girl, coming home to get her head screwed back on after falling on her face for some guy in the big city. Of course, there are some who blamed the "big city" for my divorce. I guess everyone needs a reason.*

*Dating as a divorced thirtysomething isn't what I would call fun. When was dating ever fun? There's the initial awkwardness. The "is he or isn't he going to pick up the check?" dilemma. And the whole first kiss nonsense. I preferred to wait and see if it was going to go anywhere, but others suggest getting it out of the way early. You have to go with what's comfortable. But the worst thing, the absolutely worst thing beyond a dull, boring, or downright unattentive date is not being physically attracted to a great guy in front of you. If sexual attraction were the EASY button at Staples, we might all be better off as a civilization.*

*Humans are often drawn to people who aren't particularly good for them.*

*This was a problem I suffered from, or so I thought. I found myself attracted to the last man I would ever want to date. He was hot enough, smart enough, and funny enough, but he was in the same profession as my ex—a rabbit hole I did not want to fall down again—seemed to have zero interest in settling down, and made me pretty much unhinged by a single, intense look. If you're thinking I ran about as fast as the Road Runner, you'd be right.*

*Like a good hero, he kept coming after me. How could I resist my own hot version of J.D. Robb's timeless character, Roarke? Ladies, you know what I'm talking about. It wasn't easy to open up again, but the right one makes it worth it. Like any Nora hero, he made me—the heroine—want to risk everything because the pay-off—love, fun, trust, and happily ever after—was worth it.*

*I'm happy to say we're engaged now. I'm trading in my Divorcée Woman alter ego for Married Woman. And this time, it's going to stick, because he's The One. It really is true what they say. You simply "know" down to your core. So, this is my last editorial for this paper. My guy and I will be permanently working for my family's paper in the Rocky Mountains. Isn't that something out of a Nora Roberts book?*

*After the ups and downs I've been through, there's a lot I learned. First, divorce isn't the end of your life. It feels like it. It's a horrible thing to go through, but it's not the end. It's only another beginning. Second, some men let you down. Some don't. Look at the man in front of you and discern the difference. Third, forgive yourself. You were simply learning some important lessons, and that's okay. Growing is messy. Fourth, when you don't know what to do, plow ahead. You'll run into something. I did. Fifth, opening yourself up to another person after your heart was torched, the ashes scattered to the four winds, is one of the bravest acts you can do. Yet, without love, our lives aren't as radiant as they could be. Mine wasn't. It's cliché, but true. Lastly, with a little help from fate—scratch that, sometimes a big help—we make our own happy endings. But it's a day-by-day process. Never forget that. I don't plan to this time 'round.*

*Happy endings do exist. You can go home, discover who you've really become, and find your match. Not Mr. Right or Prince Charming. I still don't think they exist. If they do, who wants to live with them anyway? I have my faults. He has his. In the grand scheme of things, the world doesn't end when our faults clash because it's cushioned by love and commitment. Oh and a promise—just like my favorite J.D. Robb character, Eve Dallas, said.*

*So, I'm glad Nora was right all along. I can't wait for the day I put her books in the hand of the daughter I hope to have and encourage her to expect her own happily ever after. We're all better off believing in Nora Roberts Land.*

*It's good to be home.*

Dear Reader,

Thank you so much for spending your time in NORA ROBERTS LAND, where dreams come true and love conquers all. As you might expect, I am a big Nora Roberts fan and have been so grateful to have her blessing on using her name in the title and premise. This book actually is even more personal since my sister's ex-husband essentially said the same thing as Rick-the-Dick to her when they were getting a divorce. It's nice to turn that lemon into lemonade. And since I'm originally from a small town, I created Dare Valley to show my love for them.

If you enjoyed the book and want to give your own Nora fan shout-out, I'd love for you to give a review. Your opinion helps other readers want to read my books.

I would also love for you to hear about my upcoming books in the Dare Valley series. Jill and Brian are up next in FRENCH ROAST, and if you want to receive any fun extras or enter our awesome contests, you can sign up for my newsletter at www.avamiles.com and connect with me on Facebook at www.facebook.com/authoravamiles.

Thanks again for making my dreams come true as an author. I look forward to getting to know you along with all of the other characters in Dare Valley. Grandpa says hi, by the way.

Happy reading,

Ava

*The Dare Valley Series continues...*
*Book 2: FRENCH ROAST*
*Jill and Brian's story*

Small-town biz wiz Jill Hale has been in love with her childhood best friend Brian McConnell for as long as she can remember. A falling out led to years of estrangement, but when Brian returns to Dare Valley after trying to make it big as a chef in New York City, Jill's determined to make amends. She's convinced that starting a restaurant together will be the perfect win-win situation, allowing her and Brian to work together *and* play together.

After a series of missteps sliced and diced Brian's career in the Big Apple, he came home to regroup and find himself. He's convinced that reestablishing his connection with Jill, the girl who got away, will put his life back on track. And when she approaches him with her plan for going into business together, he's certain it's the one way he can have it all—his dream job and his dream girl.

Jill and Brian are falling for each other all over again when Brian's ex sashays into town, intent on sabotaging their reunion. Add in a mysterious investor who's determined to get Jill on board with his project, and the bond between the couple is tested to the limit. Will their second chance at love implode, or will they find their own recipe for a happy ending?

# About the Author

*USA Today* Bestselling Author Ava Miles burst onto the contemporary romance scene after receiving Nora Roberts' blessing for her use of Ms. Roberts' name in her debut novel, the #1 National Bestseller NORA ROBERTS LAND, which kicked off her small town series, Dare Valley, and brought praise from reviewers and readers alike. Ava has also released a connected series called Dare River, set outside the country music capital of Nashville.

Far from the first in her family to embrace writing, Ava comes from a long line of journalists. Ever since her great-great-grandfather won ownership of a newspaper in a poker game in 1892, her family has had something to do with telling stories, whether to share news or, in her case, fiction. Her clan is still reporting on local events more than one hundred years later at their family newspaper, much like the Hale family in her Dare Valley series.

Ava is fast becoming a favorite author in light contemporary romance (Tome Tender) and is known for funny, emotional stories about family and empowerment. Ava's background is as diverse as her characters. She's a former chef, worked as a long-time conflict expert rebuilding warzones, and now writes full-time from her own small-town community.

If you'd like more information about Ava and her upcoming books, visit http://www.avamiles.com and connect with her on Facebook, Twitter, and Pinterest.

*If you enjoyed reading this book, please share that with your friends and others by posting a review. Thank you!*

CPSIA information can be obtained at www.ICGtesting.com
Printed in the USA
LVOW10s2236240615

443782LV00013B/209/P